JUSTICE OF METALHAVEN
METAL AND BLOOD
BOOK 4

G J OGDEN

Copyright © 2024 by G J Ogden
All rights reserved.

No part of this book may be reproduced in any form or by any electronic or mechanical means, including information storage and retrieval systems, without written permission from the author, except for the use of brief quotations in a book review.

These novels are entirely works of fiction. The names, characters and incidents portrayed in it are the work of the author's imagination. Any resemblance to actual persons, living or dead, events or localities is entirely coincidental.

Illustration © Phil Dannels
www.phildannelsdesign.com

Editing by S L Ogden
Published by Ogden Media Ltd
www.ogdenmedia.net

1
NEXT STEPS

Finn breathed in a lungful of ice-cold air as the wind gusted past his face, blowing back his hair like he was running headlong into battle, only this time everything was still. All of Metalhaven stretched out beneath him, and from the top of the gene bank close to Reclamation Yard four, he could even see beyond the boundaries of the reclamation sector to the rocket launch towers of Spacehaven and the gleaming gold buildings of the Authority sector. Yet the appearance of tranquilly was an illusion that belied the momentous change that had occurred only forty-eight hours earlier.

With the help of General Riley and the sacrifice of two of his soldiers, Finn's plan to rescue Elara Cage from her trial and spark a revolution had succeeded. Ivan Volkov and Juniper Jones had both escaped, but set against the liberation of Metalhaven, these were minor annoyances that Finn still intended to rectify at the earliest opportunity. For now, he was simply glad that he and Elara were alive, and their dream of freeing Zavetgrad remained alive too.

"Nice night!" said Scraps, who was perched on Finn's shoulder, as usual. "Peaceful."

"A little too peaceful if you ask me," Finn replied.

Scraps frowned his metal eyebrows. "Why-why?"

Finn blew out a sigh and shook his head. "I don't know, it just seems strange that in two days, the Authority hasn't tried to retake the sector, or even send skycars and squads to attack us."

"Golds plotting..." Scraps said, scrunching his little hands into fists and growling.

"That's what I'm afraid of," Finn replied. "I'd almost prefer it if they came at us, all guns blazing. At least then, we'd be done with the agony of waiting."

A squadron of golden prefect skycars moved into Finn's line of sight, and he watched them, eagle-eyed, as the flying attack craft patrolled over Stonehaven's residential district, before skirting the borders of Metalhaven and turning over the Authority sector. There was a crackle of gunfire, followed by a flurry of laser blasts from the rebellion's rooftop gunners, but the flashes of light were merely warning shots. They were a reminder to the Authority that Metalhaven now belonged to the chromes, and that they weren't going to give it up without a fight.

"Finn has meeting!" Scraps said, looking at his wrist as if a watch was strapped around it. "Pen-Pen and General calling soon!"

Finn checked the modified C.O.N.F.I.R.M.E. computer that Chiefy, the robot foreman that Scraps had reprogrammed, had built for him and the other senior Metals, and confirmed that he was running late.

"You're right, we'd best get going," Finn said, jumping

down from his perch on the radio tower that sat atop of the gene bank building and hurrying to the stairwell.

Scraps leapt off his shoulder and sprouted his newly repaired and improved rotors, which allowed his robot buddy to fly faster and higher, while also remaining whisper quiet. The hum of the blades was almost inaudible, like a mosquito buzzing around late at night, and against the background noise of the city, Scraps was all but a ghost.

The little robot reached the stairs first and Finn had to jog to catch up, but when he finally made it back inside the building, it was clear that Scraps was heading in a different direction to where Finn needed to be.

"Hey, where are you going?" Finn called out. Scraps was already on the landing, one flight down from him. "The stairwell to the executive offices and our new headquarters is this way," he added, pointing along the corridor.

"Scraps going to Chiefy," the robot replied. "Check on project!"

"What project?" Finn said, but there was no answer. He moved into the stairwell and peered over the railings, but Scraps was already three floors down. "Hey, what project?" he called out.

"Finn see soon!" Scraps called back, then he was gone.

"Being promoted to general has gone to that robot's head," Finn muttered to himself, but there was nothing left to do, other than resume his journey, alone.

Compared to the rooftop, the inside of the gene bank was stiflingly hot, and Finn started to wish that he wasn't wearing his prosecutor armor. Yet, the situation in Metalhaven remained dangerously unpredictable and he didn't feel comfortable taking it off. Even without the ever-present threat of a sniper round or assassin, he wouldn't have wanted to remove it. It had become like a second skin, as much a part of him as his fists and feet.

"There he is!" Trip said, as Finn walked through the door of what had once been the office suite of the gene bank's Head Administrator, but had since been transformed into the Metal's command and control center.

"Sorry, I'm late, I lost track of time," Finn said, tugging at his collar to let off some steam. "I take it they haven't called yet?"

"We're expecting the transmission any moment now," Trip replied, looking to Briggs, one of the other senior Metals in the sector, to elaborate.

"The uplink is secure, and the transmitter power is optimal," Briggs explained. Xia, the Metalhaven worker and rebel operative who had been beaten so badly by prefects in the past that she could barely mumble more than two words, was operating the console. "The weather over the Davis Strait is good, so the signal should be clean."

Finn moved in front of the console, smiling at Xia as he did so, and the woman acknowledged him with a respectful nod. Even if Xia could smile, Finn doubted that she would have. The screen she sat across from was as wide as she was tall, but the display was blank, save for a blinking icon that looked like Scraps' radar dish.

"Where's Elara?" Trip wondered.

It took Finn a moment to locate the man, then he saw Trip over by a decorative bar in the corner of the palatial office, helping himself to a pint of ale from a keg that he'd requestioned from a local recovery center.

"She'll be here soon," Finn replied, noticing that Trip was

pulling a second pint, though because of the man's appetite for ale, he didn't immediately assume the beverage was meant for him. "She went searching the other floors of this building, trying to find something other than her offender's jumpsuit to wear."

No sooner had Finn finished speaking than Elara breezed through the door, still wearing the chrome-colored jumpsuit that she had been trying to replace.

"Seriously?" Finn said, scowling at her, and she scowled right back. "Given the size of this building and how many people worked here, you couldn't find a single other thing to wear?"

"Oh, I found plenty of clothes stashed in lockers and in the bedroom suites that the executives maintained here," Elara said, nodding to Trip, Briggs, and Xia in turn. "But I'll be damned if I'm going to dress up like a gold, so I just ran this jumpsuit through a laundry processor instead." She shrugged. "It'll have to do for now."

"Well, I like it," Trip said, sauntering over to Elara and offering her his spare pint, which she politely declined. Finn felt offended that he hadn't been offered it first. "It sorta says 'fuck you' to the Authority, you know? It's supposed to label you as a criminal, but instead, you're wearing it as a symbol of resistance."

Elara shrugged again. "If you say so but, honestly, I just didn't fancy wearing a gold-trimmed, white satin pantsuit."

Finn shuddered as the image of Juniper Jones invaded his mind. White, gold-trimmed pantsuits had been the special prefect's go-to choice of fashion during the time she'd masqueraded as Finn's paramour.

"I agree, the jumpsuit suits you," Finn said, happy with

his partner's choice. "It's a shame about your armor, but at least it means you won't be able to sneak up on me quite so easily."

Elara raised her eyebrows. "I never needed my chameleonic armor to sneak up on you before, so you should still watch your back."

Finn shuddered again, though this time it was because a memory of his time in the prosecutor barracks had popped into his head. Elara Cage, in her alter ego as The Shadow, had been a brutal taskmaster, but her training was what had kept him alive.

The communications console that Xia was sitting patiently in front of then began to chime, and everyone quickly gathered behind the operator's chair.

"Haven calling," Xia mumbled through her heavily wired jaw, before punching a button to connect the gene bank in Metalhaven with the Pit, hundreds of miles away across the Davis Strait, deep beneath the barren soil of Disko Island.

Principal Penelope Everhart, or Pen as she preferred to be known, appeared in the middle of the huge display, flanked by General Riley, just off to her right side.

"Good evening, Metalhaven, this is Haven calling," Pen said, with a smile.

"We read you loud and clear, Pen," Trip replied, raising one of his pints in salute to the leader of humanity's only safe refuge from the Authority. "How's the weather over there?"

Pen laughed. "Hot and humid, as always," she replied, before glancing to general Riley, who looked as gruff and surly as Finn expected. "Will has been complaining about the temperature of the Pit ever since he returned from Zavetgrad."

"I'm sure it's hotter than before I left," Riley grumbled. "The principal assures me that she didn't alter the master thermostat but..." Pen raised an eyebrow at the general, daring him to complete the sentence and call her honesty into question, but Riley wisely knew when to shut up. "...but I'll get used it," he grunted instead.

"On more important matters, what new intelligence have you gathered since we last spoke?" Elara asked, not one to waste time with banal conversation. "Is there any sign of a counterattack?"

Pen shook her head. "Nothing that we've been able to decipher, but Will can fill you in on the latest news."

"In light of the security breaches it sustained during Elara's trial, the Authority has tightened up its procedures, which is making it difficult for us to gather intelligence," Riley began. The security breaches he mentioned were all down to Scraps. The robot had hacked a Chief Foreman's logic processor and used it to bypass the Authority's systems. "But thanks to operatives inside Metalhaven, we have been able to monitor some recent prefect redeployments."

"Redeploying from where to where?" Elara asked. Her arms were folded across her chest, and she looked concerned.

"Besides the Authority sector and Spacehaven, every other work sector has been left with a minimal complement of prefects," Riley replied.

"They're protecting the source of the authority, and their ability to reach Nimbus," Finn said, finding the actions of the regents to be logical. "Whoever controls the Authority sector, controls Zavetgrad, so it makes sense that they'd turn their own homeland into a fortress."

"And Spacehaven is their escape plan," Elara added,

agreeing with him. "The regents know that if they lose Zavetgrad, there will be nowhere for them to run, besides up."

"That means they're scared," Briggs cut in. The man laughed. "I never thought I'd see the day when golds trembled at the prospect of another color rising up against them."

"If the other work sectors have been left short-handed, why haven't we seen any more uprisings?" Finn asked. He appreciated Briggs' enthusiasm, but he wasn't about to declare victory before the battle was won.

"We wondered about that too," Riley answered. "So we contacted our Metals in the other sectors and learned that the TV feed from the trial was cut before Finn and Elara faced off against Herald and Inferno. It was only the workers inside Metalhaven that were able to watch the Regent Successor and his cohort have their faces rubbed in the dirt. So far as the other sectors are concerned, Elara was killed, and Finn was never there."

"Fuck!" Trip said, stamping his foot angrily and spilling beer onto his shoes. "That's why the other sectors are so subdued. Even a skeleton force of prefects is enough to keep disheartened workers in line."

"For now..." Riley grunted, channeling his most ominous and threatening tone of voice. "But thanks to our Metals, word is already spreading. Talk of an authority coverup is being whispered in recovery centers from Seedhaven to Volthaven. It's only a matter of time."

Finn nodded but nothing Riley had said was setting his mind at ease, and there was one simple reason why not.

"If time is not on the Authority's side, then why haven't

they attacked?" Finn said. "The longer they wait, the more likely it is that other sectors will learn the truth."

"This is also what is keeping me awake at night," Pen said. Her arms were folded across her chest, and for a moment, it looked like the principal and Elara were reflections of one another, mirrored in the TV screen. "Rest assured we are working around the clock to discover their intentions."

"In the meantime, continue to fortify your positions, and remain alert" Riley added. "An attack could come without warning."

"We're ready," Elara said, though Finn could sense that it was The Shadow asserting control. "We've identified prefect squads holding positions close to the entry points into Metalhaven, but so far none have attempted to break through. We have sharpshooters on the rooftops all around the sector, so they'll get a shock if they do venture too close."

"We're also busy adapting the laser cutters from the reclamation yards to work as weapons, instead of tools," Briggs said. "So far, we've been able to extend their effective range to about a hundred meters, which is enough to bring down a skycar, should any attempt a fly-over."

Finn smiled. The modified cutters were the idea of his ingenious robot pal, Scraps, working in tandem with Chiefy, who had proven adept at building and modifying everything from a laser cutter to the C.O.N.F.I.R.M.E. computers that the leader Metals all wore.

"You can thank Scraps for our new laser cannons," Finn said, taking the opportunity to heap praise on the robot. "Chiefy also managed to design and fabricate a prototype tripod mount out of parts from Yard four, which means we can attach the new laser weapons to vehicles and rooftops. The other foremen are busy making more as we speak."

Riley grunted his approval, but Elara still appeared concerned. This time it wasn't due to her misgivings over the Authority's mysterious lack of retaliatory action.

"Where is Scraps, anyway?" she asked, looking around the room.

"He's in one of the labs a few floors down, working on some mystery project with Chiefy," Finn explained.

"That sounds ominous."

"I tried to ask him what he was doing, but he scarpered like a frightened rat," Finn said. "I think his promotion has gone to his head."

The corners of Riley's mouth turned up as Finn said this. As the man responsible for promoting Scraps, he seemed to be enjoying the fact the robot was getting up to more mischief than usual.

"Since we can't wait for the Authority to reveal their hand, I suggest we proceed with our own preparations," Pen said, bringing the meeting back on track. "While we haven't been able to determine the Authority's next steps, we have learned that Ivan Volkov has been made Mayor of Zavetgrad in his father's absence. That means we at least know our enemy."

The mere mention of Finn's fellow classmate from the prosecutor training academy was enough to sour his mood. "I can't believe that they put that piece of shit in charge, especially after his failure to kill Elara in the trial," he said, shaking his head.

"I don't think it's a promotion or a reward," Riley said, surprising everyone watching, including Pen. "Ivan's father,

Maxim Volkov, has given him the job of clearing up the mess he made, while he and the other Regents hide out in their sub-oceanic villas. That way, they can remain blameless in the eyes of the president, Gideon Alexander Reznikov, who I assure you is watching everything from his palace on Nimbus."

Finn laughed. "What a great father Maxim is. He's hanging his own son out to dry."

"We believe that Juniper Jones is acting as his new personal advisor and bodyguard," Pen added, shocking everyone again, especially Finn.

"I'll bet she's doing more than just advising him, the deceitful fucking slut," Elara snapped.

Her sudden outburst caused a wave of raised eyebrows but not from Finn, who couldn't help but admire and respect Elara's venom for the woman who'd pulled the wool over his eyes. However, it wasn't only Juniper's role in seducing Finn that had gotten Elara's hackles up. Juniper Jones had overseen Elara's interrogation prior to her trial, and while she'd remained tight-lipped about exactly what had happened, it didn't take a genius to work out it was bad.

"Speaking of Juniper Jones, we've managed to discover what her role is within the Authority," Pen continued, after Elara had finished turning the air blue. "She holds the title 'Commissar', and she outranks even the Head Prefects of each sector."

"That would explain how she was able to command the forces of the special prefecture, and why she was at Maxim Volkov's side during Elara's pre-trial ceremony," Finn said.

Elara snorted derisively. "Except the esteemed mayor left

her stranded, so now she's latched onto the younger model, Volkov, instead. What a parasite..."

"We believe it to be more of an ideological role," Pen continued, ignoring Elara's continued vitriol toward the special prefect. "Her job is to root out infidels within the regime and ensure the purity of the gold class."

Finn sighed. The description of Juniper's job made sense of why she had posed as his paramour during prosecutor training. He was exactly the sort of 'unbeliever' that the special prefecture had been established to eradicate.

"So, do we attack Ivan and try to seize the Authority sector, or go after the regents in their underwater sanctuary?" Trip said, neatly encapsulating their dilemma in one sentence.

"We need the regents," Elara said, without hesitation or doubt. "They're not fighters like prefects, or zealots like Juniper Jones. They're just pompous bureaucrats, and with knives held to their throats, they'll do anything to save their own skins. If we can capture the regents, Maxim Volkov in particular, Zavetgrad is ours."

"I agree," General Riley said, with matching determination. "The problem is that no-one has ever managed to break into the sub-oceanic villa complex. Believe me, we've tried."

"Then we try harder," Elara said, undeterred. "There has to be way."

Pen nodded her head in agreement. "We will set our best minds to the task," the principal said. "Until then, sit tight and stay safe."

The members of the war council said their goodbyes and the transmission was cut. Finn rubbed his eyes, which were dry from staring at the bright screen, then Scraps suddenly raced through the door. Thanks to his near-silent rotors, the little robot took everyone by surprise. Hands were clasped around weapons, then pressed to chests in order to ease thumping heartbeats.

"Hi-hi!" Scraps said, waving at Finn. "Oh, Elara-good too!" the robot added, beaming a smile at her. "Come-come. Scraps has something to show!"

"What?" Finn said, but the robot had already spun around in mid-air and zoomed out of the door.

2

LABORATORY SEVEN

By the time Finn had reached the stairwell, Scraps was already on the landing below them, hovering with his hands pressed impatiently to his oil-can hips.

"Hurry-hurry!" Scraps said, a little annoyed at how long it was taking Finn and Elara to catch up.

"We're going as fast as we can, pal," Finn complained, skipping down the stairs two at a time. "Some of us can't fly, you know?"

Scraps dismissed Finn's excuse with a waft of his hand then continued down the stairs, pausing every few flights to make sure that his friends were still following. The robot finally stopped six floors down from the executive office suite where they'd set up their headquarters. Finn checked the sign next to the door and it read, *Laboratory 7 – Experimental*.

"What are we doing here?" Finn wondered, feeling suddenly uneasy. "I don't know what sort of freak experiments the golds got up to in their DNA labs, but I'm very sure I don't want to see them."

"Not here for DNA!" Scraps said. He was either ignoring Finn's concerns or oblivious to them. "Here for metal!"

Scraps raced off again before either Finn or Elara could question him, and Finn saw the robot zip through the entrance to laboratory seven and vanish down a corridor. Finn blew out a sigh and looked at Elara, but she just shrugged.

"Whatever is actually in these labs can't be worse than what we imagine it to be," Elara said.

"I don't know, I can imagine some pretty wild shit," Finn said, unconvinced.

"Let's just see what Scraps is so worked up about, then head back to the HQ," Elara said, taking the lead. Curiosity had gotten the better of her. "And if we find anything bad along the way, we can at least shut it down or destroy it."

Finn sighed again then followed Elara, who had already gone through the stark white doors into lab seven, leaving them swinging back and forth on their sprung hinges. He pushed through, half-expecting to find corpses hanging from the ceiling, like meat in an abattoir, but instead he was confronted by rows and rows of fluid-filled jars of varying sizes. He saw Elara staring into one of the containers and joined her, but the contents of the jar was just an amorphous blob and he had no idea what he was looking at.

"What is this place?" Finn asked. His sense of uneasiness had grown stronger, and his skin felt cold. "And what's in these jars?"

"Embryos," Elara said, and she sounded unsettled too. "Not just human embryos but animals too. This one is a pig."

Finn had seen a pig on his data device, but floating in a huge jar rather than trotting around a field, he barely recognized the animal. At first, he couldn't understand why the authority would try to grow a pig in a jar, then it came to him, and the reason was obvious.

"People used to eat pigs, didn't they?" Finn said, though he couldn't remember exactly which foodstuffs were derived from the animal.

Elara nodded. "The Authority keeps a smallholding on the outskirts of the sector, where they rear these pigs and treat them like pets, at least until they're slaughtered." She tapped the glass with her knuckle, dislodging a bubble, which raced to the surface and burst. "All this, just so the regents could eat bacon again," she added, cynically.

Finn moved to another row of containers; the embryos inside them were recognizably human. At one end of the line, the blobs of organic matter were mere centimeters in size, but the further along the row he walked, the larger and more developed they became, and the more his stomach turned. The final container in the row housed a fully developed baby boy, though the genetic defects were obvious even to a layman like Finn. The proportions of the limbs were wrong, the shape and size of his head distorted, and there were blemishes and marks all over the unborn infant's skin, as if he had been burned or scalded.

"What the fuck were they trying to do here?" Finn said, feeling a swell of remorse for the child that had never had a hope of being born.

"Maybe they wanted to cut out the human element of procreation," Elara said. She was tense and angry, her arms hugged tightly around her body. "Why bother with the trouble of stealing sperm and forcibly impregnating women, when you can just grow the perfect gold in a lab?"

"I've seen enough," Finn said, turning away from the jar and staring at the ground so that he wouldn't accidentally be exposed to the contents of the other containers. "Let's find Scraps and get the hell out of this place."

Finn started walking toward the corridor his robot buddy had vanished down earlier, but Elara didn't move. She was still fixated on the mutated baby, which though long dead, still looked like he was merely sleeping.

"We'll have to free the women in the Birthing Center," Elara said, steel in her voice. "The children from the workhouse too. They're more important even than the other sectors."

"We will," Finn said, forcing himself to look at the infant boy again, realizing it had been cowardly of him to turn away. Elara, as usual, had given him the strength he needed. "As soon as we control the Authority sector, we'll make them our first priority."

"This has to end, Finn," Elara said. She was squeezing herself so tightly Finn worried she might explode from the pressure. "These bastards have to be stopped."

Finn returned to Elara's side and stood as tall as he could manage, despite wanting nothing more than to shrink away and never have to see Laboratory seven ever again.

"We'll make them pay, Elara," Finn said, picturing Maxim Volkov and the other regents on their knees on the steps of the mayor's building in the Authority central square. "We'll drag the regents kicking and screaming in front of the workers of this city, and make them understand the true meaning of justice."

"They don't get a trial, Finn," Elara said. She was looking at him now and her emerald eyes were brighter than laser light. "They made us Prosecutors of Zavetgrad, and for once that title will mean something. We'll be their judge, jury, and executioners."

"Pen won't like that last part," Finn said, reminded of the principal's astonishing capacity for forgiveness.

"She doesn't get to decide," Elara said, coldly. "The ability to be compassionate can be our gift to the generations that come after us."

Scraps suddenly zipped into the laboratory and swiveled in mid-air, like a robotic pirouette, before finally spotting them.

"Hurry-hurry!" Scraps said. To the robot, it was like the jar and their contents didn't exist. "Chiefy and Scraps ready!"

The robot's exuberance seemed out of place in the macabre setting, but Scraps still had a way of lifting Finn's spirits, and he was more than happy to follow his pal out of Laboratory seven. This time Scraps waited for them at the end of each corridor to make sure they didn't wander off into the many glass-fronted offices and smaller labs that adjoined them, but after what he'd already seen, Finn had no desire to explore these spaces. Finally, they reached another large room and Finn hesitated at the door, wary of what he might find inside. The plaque on the wall read, *Workshop 7-Alpha*, though while a workshop sounded less sinister than a laboratory, he still felt a sense of dread while stepping over the threshold. However, instead of petri dishes and fluid-filled bell-jars, Finn was confronted with something that more closely resembled one of the junk piles in reclamation yard four.

"What have you been doing in here?" Finn said, crushing discarded circuit boards and electronic components underfoot. The white floor tiles were barely visible beneath a thin layer of what looked like metal shavings.

"Ta da!" said Chiefy.

The modified foreman stood at the far end of the room, surrounded by workbenches that had been arranged in a square around him. Spread across the surface of the tables were enough tools to equip a full Stonehaven construction team.

"What does 'ta da' mean?" Finn said, kicking junk out of his path so that he could get close enough to see what the robot duo had been working on.

"Ta da!" Chiefy said again, this time stepping aside and pointing to a life-sized mannequin in the center of the robot's workspace.

"It's a skeleton..." Elara said, scowling at the mannequin. "A skeleton wearing armor?"

"Yes-yes!" Scraps said flying in circles around the mannequin so fast it was making Finn dizzy trying to keep up. "Scraps and Chiefy clever!"

"Why are you dressing up skeletons?" Finn said.

He didn't think that anything could unsettle him more than seeing dozens of mutated human embryos in jars, but the life-sized anatomical model looked like an ancient warrior whose flesh had long since rotted away, leaving only its armor behind. He'd read of curses placed on mummies in tombs and worried that Scraps had dug up something supernatural.

"Armor..." Elara said, surprised. Finn scowled at her. Unlike himself, she didn't look the slightest bit perturbed by the skeleton soldier. "They've made me some new armor," Elara elaborated, and suddenly the penny dropped.

"Yes-yes!" Scraps sang. "The Shadow version two!"

Finn laughed and shook his head at the pair in astonishment, but also in admiration at their achievement. Metalhaven had only been freed for forty-eight hours, but Scraps and Chiefy had not allowed a single minute of that time to be used idly.

"This is impressive work," Elara said, dragging one of the workbenches back so that she could enter Chiefy's domain and get a closer look at the mannequin. "Where did you get the materials? A DNA lab isn't exactly the ideal place to fabricate a suit of armor."

"The core components were salvaged from Inferno's prosecutor armor," Chiefy said, managing to make that act of grave robbery sound perfectly innocent. "I sized the panels according to your anatomical scans, which Scraps has stored in his memory banks, and also removed the highland warrior accoutrements, since I didn't believe you would want them."

"Acout-re-whats?" Finn said.

"Accessories," Chiefy replied, smiling at Finn.

"Right..." Finn said, raising an eyebrow at the machine. He still couldn't get used to a smiling foreman.

"Never mind that, I want to know why Scraps has anatomical scans of my body stored in his memory bank," Elara said, though her tone was playful.

"Scraps sized Elara up long ago," the little robot said, giggling. "Scraps clever!"

Finn slid over one of the workbenches and inspected the armor more closely. It was painted black, like Elara's old armor, but the workmanship was arguably even finer, and it looked like it would fit her perfectly.

"It's a shame this won't have the stealth-field generator that my old chameleonic armor had," Elara said, removing a vambrace from the mannequin and placing it on to her forearm, where it slotted into place like a second skin. "Being invisible certainly had its advantages."

Scraps giggled and Finn observed that Chiefy looked decidedly pleased with himself, though neither robot said a word. They just stole glances at one another, as if they shared a guilty secret.

"No way, you didn't manage to replicate that too?" Elara said, narrowing her eyes at the mechanical duo.

"That why took so long-long!" Scraps said, spinning around in mid-air. "Armor easy-peasy. Stealth field hard!"

"This, I have to see," Finn said, plucking the chest piece off the mannequin and offering it up to Elara, but the panel didn't snap into place.

"I'm not wearing my prosecutor base layer," Elara said, explaining the reason for the failed mating. "This offender's jumpsuit doesn't have any magnetic mounting points, and without them there's no way to attach these sections."

"Ah yes, I almost forgot!" Chiefy said, raising a metal finger like an exclamation point. "One moment, please!"

Chiefy began rummaging through what looked like a mound of junk piled up just inside his workspace, while Scraps hovered around the foreman, trying to offer suggestions for where the missing mystery object was. The two robots were like quarreling siblings, and it was a full minute before Chiefy returned, with what looked like an aerosol can in one hand, and a diver's helmet in the other.

"Put this on, please," Chiefy said, hovering the helmet above Elara's head, as if he were a court official trying to crown a new queen.

"Woah, hold on," Elara said, grabbing the helmet. "You

need to tell me what this is for first. It looks like a torture device, and I've had enough of those."

The subtle reference to Elara's ordeals at the hands of Juniper Jones was not lost on Finn, and he resolved to ask her about it when the time was right.

"This is simply to protect your face," Chiefy explained.

"Protect it from what?" Elara said.

"Elara-good no worry!" Scraps said, buzzing around Elara like a tornado. "Trust Chiefy. Chiefy good. Scraps make him so!"

Elara growled a sigh but relented and allowed Chiefy to place the helmet over her head. Scraps laughed and clapped his hands in anticipation of what came next, though Finn could only think of how rare and special it was that the robot had earned Elara's trust. He wasn't even certain that he'd fully regained her confidence.

"Please also wear these gloves," Chiefy said, pressing the garments into Elara's hands, since she couldn't see anything with the helmet on. "Then raise your arms and stand with your feet shoulder width apart."

Elara growled again then pulled on the gloves and adopted the pose that Chiefy had advised. Finn choked down a laugh, and Elara's masked eyes snapped toward him.

"I heard that," Elara said. "This had better not be a trick. I'm not in the mood for jokes."

"No jokes," Chiefy said, taking a single step back. "Now please remain still."

Chiefy aimed the aerosol can at Elara and depressed the nozzle, releasing a cloud of silver-grey mist all over Elara's body, while moving in a circle around her to ensure an even coating. The mist began to spread, and Finn had to step back to avoid the cloud from enveloping him too. Even so, it got into his eyes and mouth and stuck at the back of his throat, making him cough like he'd just smoked a full pack of the Authority's narcotic-laced cigarettes.

"What is that crap?" Finn said, in between hacks. "It smells like burned hair."

"It is a compound that Scraps designed to reproduce the magnetic component of Elara's prosecutor base layer," Chiefy explained, as the aerosol finally gave out with a polite wheeze. "This compound contains billions of Nanomagnetic Amplifiers, which will adhere to Elara's offender jumpsuit."

"I've never heard of nanomagnetic amplifiers before," Elara said, her voice muffled beneath the helmet.

"Scraps invents!" the robot said, proudly. "Sticky magnetics. Like Finn's jumpsuit!"

Suddenly, air purifiers in the lab kicked in and the residual cloud of nanomagnetic smog was sucked into vents at floor and ceiling level. Elara removed her helmet and set it down, before pulling off the gloves, which had become rigid, like they'd gotten wet then frozen solid. Finn moved closer and watched as Elara flexed her arms and legs and twisted her body. The workshop's lights interacted with her modified jumpsuit in a peculiar way, reflecting assorted colors depending on the angle, like a thin layer of oil in a puddle of water.

"Try armor now!" Scraps said, jumping up and down on the chest piece that Finn had set down after the first failed attempt to attach it.

Finn squeezed through the gap in the workbenches and picked up the chest piece before offering it up to Elara. He got within a couple of centimeters of her shimmering jumpsuit before it snapped into place, exactly as his own armor panels did.

"Yes-yes!" Scraps said, throwing his hands up. "It works!"

"Let's get the rest on," Finn said, also feeling the excitement.

With Chiefy's help, it only took another couple of minutes to attach and adjust the remaining sections of armor. When they'd finished, Finn and the robot stood back to admire their work, and Finn had to admit that the set of armor looked even more pristine – and intimidating – than The Shadow's original gear.

"How does it feel?" Finn asked.

Elara flexed and moved again, and the armor moved with her seamlessly, and without the creaks and groans that his own battle-damaged prosecutor armor produced.

"It feels amazing," Elara said, throwing a few punches then snapping a kick at the mannequin that knocked its skeleton head clean off its boney neck. "I'd even say it's better than what I had before."

Chiefy swelled with pride while Scraps did a victory dance on one of the desks, kicking loose components and wires onto the floor as he did so. At the same time, Elara continued to shadow-box, testing the flexibility of her new armor to its limits. It was a dizzying display of dance-like choreography.

"You look *amazing*," Finn said, and suddenly Scraps stopped dancing and turned to him, goggle eyed. Chiefy was also looking at him, mechanical ocular sensors widened, while Elara had stopped practicing and was grinning at him. "What I mean is, it looks great," Finn said, realizing his slip. "The armor..."

Scraps giggled and Finn felt sure that the metal on

Chiefy's face turned a more pinkish shade of steel, but Elara didn't look embarrassed. Then, in the blink of an eye, she vanished, and Finn staggered back, almost falling over the workbench as he did so.

"What the hell?" Finn said, moving toward where he'd last seen Elara, hand outstretched as if he was feeling his way through a dark room. "Elara, where are you?"

Then he saw a shimmering blur in his peripheral vision, and he realized that Elara had activated Scraps' latest invention. He spun around trying to locate her, but he could neither see nor hear his old training master. Suddenly, a knife was pressed to his throat and Elara decloaked to his rear. He grabbed her wrist and stripped the blade before spinning out of the hold and raising a guard. Elara squared off against him as the knife clattered and scraped across the floor between them.

"Nice move," she said, unable to hide the smirk curling the corner of her lips.

"I had a good teacher," Finn said, shrugging.

There was low droning sound then Chiefy's chin dropped to his chest and the robot sank into a slump, his eyes dull.

"What's wrong?" Finn said, turning from Elara to check on the re-programmed foreman. "Is he damaged?"

"Nope-nope!" Scraps said, flying over to a power cord that was coiled by the wall. "Just no juice. Scraps and Chiefy need to recharge."

"How long will that take?" Finn asked, as his robot pal attached the power cable to Chiefy's inlet, before tapping a feed off the foreman to charge his own battery.

"Two hours," Scraps replied, getting himself comfortable on the desk. "We worked hard!"

"Yes, you did," Elara said, stroking the robot's head and causing Scraps to giggle. "Thank you, Scraps. And thank Chiefy too when he's awake."

"Chiefy hears you," Scraps said.

The foreman gave a slow thumbs-up sign, but the rest of its mechanical body remained inactive, giving the robot a creepy, zombie-like presence.

"Then I guess we have a couple of hours to kill," Finn said, suddenly at a loss for what to do next. "The problem is, Metalhaven isn't exactly known for its recreational facilities."

"There is one thing that chromes do well," Elara said. She smiled and shrugged. "So, how about you buy me a beer?"

3

FOUR-FIVE AGAIN

Finn stepped out of the gene bank and onto the streets of Metalhaven, close to Reclamation Yard four. It was past midnight, well after what would have been the curfew time, when all chromes had to be tucked up in bed inside their tenement blocks, and Finn couldn't shake the feeling that he was doing something 'illegal'.

"I keep looking over my shoulder for prefect patrols," Finn said, as he and Elara walked side-by-side under the clear night sky. "I still can't believe we kicked those bastards out of the sector."

Elara smiled. "Somehow, I doubt this is the first time you've been out after curfew. I bet you did it just to spite the Authority. What was that phrase you always used?"

"Because fuck them, that's why," Finn said, laughing. "And you're right, I did have a fondness for breaking the rules, but most of the times I was caught out after curfew were the result of a heavy drinking session."

"Speaking of which…"

Elara pointed to Recovery Center four-five, which was

the bar that Sully, the Autohaven operative who had smuggled Finn and General Riley's squad into Metalhaven, had recently resupplied with ale. Despite the late hour, there were still a dozen or more people on the street, swaying in the icy breeze and spilling their beer onto the sidewalk, while the inside of the recovery center remained packed with drinkers.

"Fancy a pint?" Finn asked.

He offered Elara his arm, planning to escort her to the drinking establishment like she was his partner at a gala ball, but Elara merely snorted at the proposition and slapped him on the back.

"Yes, I do, but you're buying," Elara said, sweeping ahead. "And this isn't a date, by the way. It's just a drink."

"Of course," Finn said, attempting to hide his embarrassment at being left hanging by flexing his arm and pretending that he was merely shaking out some stiffness in his joints. "It's just a drink, nothing funny or unusual about that at all."

Elara laughed but mercifully turned away before Finn's reddening skin became noticeable. Set against the dark and cold of Metalhaven's arctic nighttime, his face glowed like hot coals.

By the time he'd caught up with her, a fight had broken out outside the recovery center, which provided a suitable distraction. The quarrel appeared to be over whose turn it was to buy the next round of beers, and although fists were flying, both combatants were too drunk to do any serious harm to one another.

"Us chromes do love a pint and a fight," Finn said, as the instigator of the brawl landed a wild overhand right that sent a tooth spinning into the snow. A cheer went up from the spectating drinkers and the fight continued.

"My money is on the thin guy with the missing tooth," Elara said.

"You mean the one who just got smacked in the mouth?" Finn replied, wondering why Elara was betting on the smaller and drunker of the two fighters. "He's lucky to still be standing after that last haymaker."

Suddenly, the thin man with the bleeding gums pulled a prefect's nightstick out of his waistband and used it to clobber his opponent across the temple. The bigger man's eyes rolled into the back of his head, and he toppled like a plank, landing heavily in a snowdrift that cushioned his fall.

"I'm glad I didn't take that bet," Finn said, watching the winner revel in his victory by drinking the knocked-out man's pint.

"I could always tell who'd win a bar fight." Elara said, side-eyeing Finn with a smug look on her face. "It was a special talent of mine, one that it seems I haven't lost. It used to win me a lot of drinks chits, back when I was a worker."

The fight had proved enough of a diversion that none of the drinkers had seen them approach, despite their recognizable faces and armor-clad bodies. Finn was able to slip through the door of the recovery center unnoticed but any notion that he and Elara might blend in with the crowd was immediately put to rest when fifty pairs of glazed-looking eyes landed on him.

"Fuckin' ell, it's Redeemer!" one man shouted.

"And The Shadow!" another cried.

"Get the iron bitch a drink!"

"Get her ten!"

"And a dozen for the Hero of Metalhaven!"

The recovery center was filled with a deafening cheer that threatened to blow out the windows like a gust of wind in a storm. Finn and Elara were cajoled inside, hands slapping their backs, pints raised in salute, before being led to a table in the corner of the bar. The current occupants were swiftly evicted, though not without complaint, and Finn and Elara were seated in their place. Within seconds, six fresh pints had been slammed down on the beer-soaked tabletop, along with a half-smoked packet of cigarettes and a box of matches.

"There's nothing like a nice quiet drink to finish off the day," Finn said, sarcastically.

Elara shrugged then picked up a pint and pressed the glass to her lips. Finn watched in amazement as the angle of the glass quickly became horizontal and the contents vanished into her stomach as if she'd poured the entire pint down her front. The glass was slammed down onto the table then Elara belched like a foghorn, which was met with a titanic roar of appreciation from the assembled drinkers.

"Aren't you full of surprises..." Finn said, eyebrows raised.

Elara shrugged again then slid one of the other pints toward Finn. It was a clear challenge, and Finn never let a challenge go unanswered. Grabbing the pint, he sank the contents in one, egged-on by the horde of intoxicated onlookers, then slammed the glass down next to Elara's to another raucous cheer.

"Let's not do that again," Finn said, holding his stomach, which was full of gas. The horrible beer taste was still on his tongue too, but it didn't take long for the alcohol and narcotics in the ale to smooth his frayed edges, and soon he felt relaxed and refreshed.

"I didn't have you down as a lightweight," Elara said, teasing him, while picking up another pint, though this time she only took a couple of polite sips.

"I hope they're not expecting us to drink all of these," Finn said, as four more froth-topped pints were placed onto the table. "We might have to call on Chiefy to carry us back to the gene bank."

Elara laughed then slid a cigarette out of the packet and lit it, shocking Finn again.

"You were always so reserved in the prosecutor barracks," Finn said, as Elara blew smoke past his face. "Who knew you were actually just a beer-swilling, cigarette smoking chrome, like the rest of us?" He laughed. "You're as bad as Owen."

The name of his best friend had escaped his lips without him even thinking, but what surprised him more was that for the first time since Owen's death, he didn't feel a crushing sense of remorse and regret. He figured this might have been due to the alcohol and drugs circulating his bloodstream, but even Metalhaven's strongest ale couldn't dull the grief he still felt.

"You'll have to forgive yourself for Owen at some point," Elara said. She offered Finn the cigarette and he took it. "It doesn't mean you have to forget or try to re-write history, but you can move on."

"Maybe," Finn said, sucking in a lungful of drug-infused smoke. "I don't think I'm quite there yet, though."

Elara nodded and took the cigarette back from Finn, while politely nodding and smiling to some of the other patrons, who were doting on her like she was a celebrity from before the Last War. The drugs were starting to take a hold of Finn's mind, but rather than lift his spirits, he was feeling maudlin and contrite, and he knew he had to ask Elara about her captivity before the not-knowing drove him mad.

"I'm sorry for what you went through, after I left," Finn said, struggling to put his feelings into words. "I can only imagine the hell they put you through."

Elara blew a plume of smoke into the air then tapped her top lip, perhaps considering how much to reveal about her experiences in Authority custody, or whether to say anything at all. However, like Finn, she had a belly full of strong ale, and a head full of mood-altering chemicals, and the combination tended to have the effect of loosening a person's tongue.

"It wasn't much fun," she said, whimsically. "It was a cold, empty cell with a bucket in the corner, and Juniper Jones would come once a day to torment me."

"Torment you how?" Finn asked. He didn't really want to know, but guilt forced him to ask.

"She told me they had you, and that they would cut you up, piece by piece, and feed your liquified remains to me, unless I told them everything I knew about Haven and the Metal operatives in Zavetgrad." Elara shrugged. "But I knew you'd gotten out, because I saw your skycar clear the fence, so when that tactic didn't work, she resorted to beatings and degradations instead. She loved every second of it, but I refused to give her anything."

"Why?" Finn asked.

Elara smiled, darkly. "Because fuck her, that's why…"

Finn laughed. The sudden release of tension was explosive.

"That's my line," he said, narrowing his eyes at Elara. "Well, sort of, anyway."

The sound of glass smashing stole the attention of the crowd, and a fight broke out across the far side of the recovery center.

"Here we go again," Elara said, drawing on the cigarette and blowing a plume of dark smoke into the air, where it mixed with the smog of countless other burned-out sticks.

"Maybe we can slip out back, while they're distracted," Finn said, spotting a side door close to where they were seated.

Elara scouted their possible exit then nodded and slid off her chair, cigarette hanging from her bottom lip.

"Bring your pint," she said, nodding toward one of the dozen glasses on the table. "And one for me too."

With the patrons of the bar still distracted, Elara activated her stealth field and vanished, though Finn could trace her path by the trail of smoke she left behind. Grabbing two fresh pints, he stole after her and the door opened for him, as if by magic. A gust of icy wind blew inside, causing a nearby punter to shiver with cold, but the door was shut, and he and Elara were gone, before the man had turned around to check where the breeze had come from.

"This is more what I had in mind," Finn said, joining Elara in the rear yard of the recovery center. She was visible again and sat on an empty beer keg. Finn pulled up a keg next to her then handed Elara one of the pints, which by some miracle he'd managed not to spill.

"I knew you were trying to get me alone," Elara said, grinning.

"You wish," Finn said. The strong ale had given him courage enough to be himself again, or at least the uninhibited version of himself that didn't act like a fool whenever Elara was close.

"I miss this," Elara said, taking another long toke on the cigarette while staring into the starry sky. "It's the only thing about my old life I do miss. My original life, I mean, before I was The Shadow."

"Scraps told us that this was your old home," Finn said, gesturing in the direction of Reclamation Yard four, out of sight beyond the wall that encircled the rear of the recovery center. "What was it like here?"

Elara shrugged and sipped her pint. "Much the same as it was for you, I'd imagine."

It was an evasive answer but whether wisely or not, Finn felt like pushing Elara for more details, especially about the one aspect of her past he still knew nothing about.

"So, how did you end up on trial?"

Elara shifted uncomfortably on the keg and turned away, using a stack of shipping pallets to remove ash from the half-smoked cigarette. Finn immediately regretted his question and backtracked.

"Hey, I'm sorry, it's none of my business and I shouldn't have asked," he said.

"No, it's okay." Elara drew in a deep breath then stubbed out the cigarette and sat more upright on the keg, as if she were steeling herself to make a confession. "I know everything there is to know about Finn Brasa, so it's only fair you know my story too."

Finn nodded and sipped his pint, finding that his throat was suddenly dryer than a slice of week-old algae bread.

"I wasn't angry at the world, like you were, I was numb to it," Elara began, staring into the distance, her green eyes glassy and sad. "I just did what I was asked to do without complaint, day in, day out. I met my quotas, drank my pints, had some good fights, even willingly donated my eggs so that they can grow more asshole golds."

She laughed bitterly and shook her head, then Finn noticed that she wasn't staring into the distance, but at the faint glow of the Nimbus space citadel in orbit above them.

"What changed?" Finn asked.

Elara shifted uncomfortably again then drank to wet her lips. "What changed is that they reassessed my genetic rating," she continued. "They check every year, as you know, and I'd always been assessed as a three by the same doctor. She was called Clement, though I never knew her first name, and she was one of the better golds."

Finn nodded. At one time in his life, the notion that there were any 'good' golds in Zavetgrad was laughable, but after meeting Pritchard, his valet at the prosecutor barracks, he'd reconsidered that opinion. *Hell, even General Riley, for his many sins, isn't all bad...*

"Then one day I arrived at the gene bank for my annual check-up and Clement was gone," Elara said, snapping Finn's focus back to her. "There was no explanation. I asked where she was and got an electrified nightstick in my ribs for the trouble. Clement's replacement was a disgusting fucking pervert called Doctor Colton, and when I refused to fuck him, it took the bastard all of two minutes to re-rate me from a three to a five."

"A five?" Finn said, wondering why the doctor would upgrade, rather than downgrade her. "Why the hell did he do that?"

Elara took another sip of her drink then looked at Finn

out of the corner of her eye. "Because my actual genetic rating is five, not three. Doctor Clement had been hiding my true rating from the Authority for years, to protect me."

Finn's shoulders slumped and a groan leaked from his mouth, as if he'd been punched in the gut. It suddenly made perfect sense.

"She hid your rating because if the Authority knew you were a five, you'd have been sent to the Birthing Center and forced to act as a surrogate mother, carrying babies to term."

Elara gave him a resigned nod then took another deep breath of the cold night air before continuing.

"Colton called the prefects in to take me away, right then and there, and I flipped," Elara said, anger seeping into her words. "I punched Colton so hard he fell and cracked his head on the tiled floor. He was dead before they managed to drag me away, kicking and screaming, to the detention room in the Prefect Hub. After that, I thought, 'fuck it', I'm not playing by their rules anymore. So, I fought them and fought them until they'd had enough of me and sentenced me to trial. Honestly, it was a relief."

Like all workers in Zavetgrad, Finn had watched Elara's trial and witnessed how the woman from Metalhaven had fought and killed both prosecutors and fellow offenders alike, with the sort of ferocity and pitilessness that was normally associated with a prefect. He had always wondered what had happened to make her so cold and callous, and now he knew.

"I was so angry," Elara said, staring into her empty pint. "I just wanted to hurt people, and I didn't care if they were workers like me or golds. I was going to win that trial no matter what."

Finn laughed, weakly. "Because fuck them, right?"

Elara shrugged and nodded, and Finn found that he understood her completely. In her place, having experienced what she had done, he might have done the same, and had it not been for his guilt-driven determination to save Owen, he could easily have lost himself to rage too.

"I stayed in that dark place for a long time, as The Shadow, and I'd still be there if I hadn't heard about Haven," Elara said. This was another part of the story that Finn didn't know, and he waited impatiently for Elara to continue. "It was a few years ago, and I was in the middle of prosecuting a trial when I found a Metal trying to smuggle an offender out of the city. We fought, but she was no match for me, and I had my knife to her throat, ready to kill her, when she said something that stopped me dead in my tracks."

"What?" Finn asked. His mouth was dry again, but he'd drunk his pint.

"She said, 'I know your mother', and I was so surprised I just froze," Elara replied. "In those moments, she told me about Haven and about Pen, and then she asked me, 'Don't you want to be something more? Don't you want to have hope again?', and I discovered that I did. The rest is history, as they say."

"Who was the Metal?" Finn asked.

Elara's eyes suddenly became hard, and Finn recognized the tell-tale signs of The Shadow asserting dominance in her psyche.

"I never got to find out," Elara said, and the regret was palpable. "Frost, my partner prosecutor for that trial, burst in and shot her, before I could learn more. The bastard never trusted me after that, but it didn't matter. I tracked down another Metal in a later trial and got word to Haven that I wanted to help, but I still had to play my part as prosecutor, so I did what I had to do to survive, in the hope that we could have this day."

Finn took a moment to process what he'd heard, allowing the information to slot into gaps in his mind and complete the picture of Elara Cage that had until that point been unfinished.

"You're going to have to forgive yourself too, you know?" Finn said, throwing Elara's advice back at her. "You're not the same person you were back then."

Elara smiled and squeezed Finn's hand. "What I am is beyond redemption."

Finn laughed. "Hey, that's also my line, you need to find your own."

The joke worked to lighten the mood and Elara sparked up another cigarette, if only to give her anxious hands something to do. She placed the smoke between her lips then lit another and handed it to Finn. The break gave him time to think, and he found that another question had bubbled to the surface of his thoughts.

"What's your full rating?" Finn asked. He now knew she had a genetic rating of five, like him, but he didn't know her worker rating. "I don't think you ever said."

"That's because I didn't," Elara replied, though it was a playful evasion, and Finn simply bided his time, knowing that she'd fess up eventually. "But if you must know, I'm a Double-Five, just like you."

"I *knew* it!" Finn said, beaming a smile at her. "We make the perfect power couple."

Elara laughed then hid behind the cigarette in her hand. "Don't get ahead of yourself."

There was a noise somewhere in the courtyard, and it caused both of them to tense up and listen. They waited, breaths held, until the sound came again, clearer, and closer.

"Someone's here," Finn whispered, standing up. His hand went to his laser cannon, ready to draw it.

Elara also stood up, and the black combat knife that General Riley had given her was already in her hand. Finn was about to ask what they should do when he saw a green dot in the center of Elara's chest, stark against her new prosecutor armor, and his instincts kicked in. Throwing himself at Elara, he tackled her to the ground as a muted gunshot rang out. Ale gushed out from a hole in one of the kegs, then more shots skipped off the ground, but both of them had already slipped into cover, their training overriding the alcohol and narcotics that should have dulled their reactions.

A shape moved through the darkness and Finn darted toward it, catching the barrel of a rifle, and aiming it upward. The suppressed weapon fired, but the rounds sped harmlessly into the starry sky. Then Elara pounced and her combat knife sank into the neck of their attacker, slitting the man's throat as easily as slicing bread. Finn eased the body to the ground and they both got a clear look at the would-be assassin; black visor and black carapace armor with the emblem of the Authority pressed into the metal.

"A special prefect," Elara said. "And he won't be the only one..."

4

THE ASSASSIN

Elara took the dead special prefect's rifle and two spare magazines while Finn drew and activated his laser cannon. The prefect also had a knife held in a sheath that was strapped to his armor and Finn took it to replace the blade he'd lost during his perilous journey to the city.

"It looks like he approached us from rear of the courtyard," Finn said, tucking in behind a stack of beer kegs which they were both using for cover. "Let me check..."

Finn grabbed the dead prefect by the shoulders and lifted the man so that his head was poking around the side of the barrel. A split second later, a high velocity round punched through the man's skull, splattering bone, brains, and blood across the floor.

"I think you were right about the sniper," Finn said, glad he hadn't looked with his own eyes and caught the bullet himself. "He must be somewhere out back of the recovery center."

"Judging from the angle of the bullet, I'd say our sniper is in the abandoned tenement block across the street, probably on an upper floor," Elara said. "Wait here, I'll try to get in a better position."

Elara got ready to move but Finn grabbed her arm. "Woah, you can't go out there. That prefect has us pinned down."

Elara smiled. "You can't shoot what you can't see..." She activated the stealth field in her new armor then vanished before Finn's eyes. Only her shimmering outline, like a heat haze rising off hot asphalt, gave away that she was still there at all. Finn heard her boots scrape across the ground and he felt a breeze brush his face, then Elara was gone, like a gust of wind.

Shuffling to the other side of the stack of barrels, he managed to peek through a gap and spot her footprints in the snow. She was headed toward the outdoor storehouse, which was a fraction taller than the wall surrounding the recovery center's courtyard and would give her a vantage point from which to return fire at the sniper.

Finn waited anxiously and listened, hearing the creak of weather-worn steel sheets as Elara carefully hauled herself onto the roof of the storehouse. Then he heard muted shots and the piercing ping of bullets skipping off metal and echoing into the distance. The roof of the storehouse collapsed, and Finn heard Elara grunt in pain as she tumbled inside. Without thinking, he rushed out to help her, holding his arms up in front of his face and using his vambraces as a shield. There were more muted shots and Finn felt a round punch his chest, but he'd smashed through the door of the storehouse and into cover before the sniper could land a lethal shot.

"Elara are you okay?" Finn said, pressing his hand to his

chest and pulling out the bullet that was lodged into his armor. The round had almost penetrated, and Finn realized how close he'd come to being killed.

"I'm fine," Elara called back, throwing broken boxes off herself. She was angry but appeared unhurt. "The sniper must be using vision enhancement. We had access to the same tech as prosecutors. It's a combination of image intensification and thermal tomography."

Finn nodded, remembering his training at the prosecutor barracks, which hadn't only covered how to use the Authority's advanced weapons and armor, but how they worked too.

"The stealth field bends visible light around your body, but it doesn't fully mask your heat signature," Finn said. "They must have finally got wise to your tactics and made some adjustments to cancel out your chameleonic advantage."

"I don't need a stealth field to sneak up on my enemies," Elara said, still pissed off. "But first we need to get inside that tenement block without catching a bullet."

"We could try to alert the other Metals," Finn suggested, trying to formulate a plan on the fly. "We just need to distract the shooter for a few seconds."

"If we draw anyone to us, they'd just get picked off," Elara said, shaking her head. "We have to handle this ourselves."

Finn tried to think of another approach, but the truth was they were pinned down and at a heavy disadvantage, and the more helpless he felt the angrier he became.

"How the hell did they get inside Metalhaven without being noticed?" Finn growled, venting his frustrations. "We have guards at every entrance and there hasn't been a single skycar over the sector since General Riley and Ensign Thorne left for Haven."

"We can worry about that later, right now we have to get across the street and take out that sniper," Elara said. She'd regained her composure and Finn sensed that this was because she'd come up with a plan.

"What's your idea?" Finn asked.

"Before the roof of this storehouse collapsed, I saw two ale trucks parked on the road out back, one on either side of the street, almost directly opposite one another," Elara said. "There's a row of dumpsters pushed up next to the back gate right where one of those trucks is parked. If we scale the wall, then the truck will give us cover."

"Then all we have to do is run across the street to the other truck, and crawl underneath it to reach the building," Finn added, in tune with Elara's thinking. He huffed a laugh and shook his head. "But how do we do that, without getting shot?"

Elara sifted through the debris of the collapsed roof then dragged a metal tabletop away from the wall. The legs had been snapped off the base, likely the result of a bar fight at some point in the past. Recovery centers went through tables and chairs faster than a Nimbus rocket burned fuel.

"Like I said, if the bastard can't see us, he can't shoot us," Elara said, hoisting the chunky tabletop toward Finn. "You take one end and I'll take the other. Let's see the sniper shoot through this."

Finn looked at the dent in his armor from the high-velocity sniper round and didn't feel especially confident that a recovery center tabletop would provide much more protection, but he also didn't have a better idea.

"Okay, but I hope this thing is tougher than it looks," Finn said, taking the end of the rectangular table and holding it up like a shield. "You ready?"

Elara hoisted her side of the table onto her shoulder then nodded. Finn edged toward the door and spotted the row of dumpsters next to the gate, and he could also just about make out the top of the ale truck's trailer poking above the wall. Reaching it would mean heading directly into the sniper's kill zone. He figured there was a chance the gunman had moved positions, or was in the process of relocating, but it was more likely that their would-be killer was aiming down his scope, waiting for them to wander into his crosshairs.

"On three, we go," Finn said, steeling himself for the sprint.

Elara counted down then they raced into the open. Bullets immediately thudded into the table, but the pitch and tone of the impacts was varied, and Finn realized there was more than one gunman shooting at them. Half-way to the dumpsters and the table was already pitted and chipped but the barrier held, and Finn collided with the gate, heart pounding in his chest. He checked his body armor and saw that the grieves covering his legs were covered in scrapes and dents from where their attackers had tried to shoot out his legs. It was pure luck that he hadn't taken a round in the foot.

"Cover me, while I climb up," Elara said, taking the table and holding it above her like a tortoise shell.

Finn readied his laser and watched Elara climb onto the dumpster. The gunmen all targeted her and shots rang out, giving Finn a chance to lash the building with laser fire, scorching brick, and smashing window frames. He saw shapes move, two or maybe three, then the special prefect's weapons were aimed at him, and he was forced back into cover.

"I'm clear!" Elara called out. "But the table is wrecked, you'll need to find something else."

Finn checked around his feet, but other than trash and snow, there was nothing. He checked the gate, and it was secured only with a padlock, which while hefty enough to deter a potential ale thief, was no match for his laser. A close-range blast melted the metal then he threw open the bolt and pushed on the gate. It creaked open then thudded into the bonnet of the ale truck, providing seamless cover for his escape.

"I wish you'd thought of that before I crawled over a pile of stinking trash," Elara complained, huddled beside the truck, which was taking fire from the windows opposite.

"Sorry," Finn said, smiling and brushing a squashed slab of rotten algae bread off Elara's shoulder. "Sometimes the best plan is not to plan at all, and just see what happens."

"Very inciteful," Elara said, as smashed glass from the truck's cabin windows rained down on her head. "Then maybe you can 'not plan' a way for us to get inside the tenement block."

"Way ahead of you," Finn said. "Just follow my lead, and stay close."

Elara frowned as he holstered his laser then drew the knife he'd taken from the dead prefect and used it to slice open the tarpaulin on the side of the truck's trailer. Climbing inside, he worked his way to the front, drew back the sliding door that led inside the cabin, and dove through it. Bullets started hammering into the vehicle's roof and bonnet, but the truck was parked at a tangent from the building and the shooters couldn't get an angle on him.

"Buckle up!" Finn called back to Elara, who had also pulled herself inside the trailer.

The keys to the truck were still in the ignition and Finn twisted them, forcing the engine to turn over with a labored wheeze and cough until the engine growled into life. Grabbing the wheel, he spun it toward the tenement block then disengaged the parking brake and hovered his foot over the accelerator pedal.

"Hold on!"

Pressing the pedal to the metal, the truck lurched forward then swung around violently, chain-covered tires screeching and slipping on the frozen road, until they gained purchase and the truck accelerated hard and smashed into the wall of the tenement block, punching a hole into it large enough for Finn and Elara to jump through.

"Let's go!" Finn said, helping Elara inside the tenement block, as bullets continued to thump into the roof of the cabin, but the old ale trucks were built like tanks, and Finn knew that it would take a missile to break through. "I saw maybe three more special prefects inside, on floor five or six. We need to hurry. They could already be on their way down."

"They will be, but at least one of them will try to run," Elara said, kicking out what remained of the windshield. "They know they can't beat us in a straight fight but if even one special prefect gets away, we won't be able to even set foot outside the gene bank without risking a bullet."

"That's pretty cowardly," Finn said, jumping down beside Elara and drawing his laser.

"They're not cowards, they're fanatics," Elara said. She

reloaded her stolen rifle and chambered a round. "They came here knowing it was a one-way trip, and they won't stop until either we're dead or they are."

Finn had an idea, and he searched the wall for the main lighting control panel. He knew Metalhaven tenement blocks by heart, since he'd spent most of his life cooped up in one, and quickly located the controls. Lasering the lock, he threw open the door then closed every breaker in the panel, causing the lights in the stairwell to flicker on. The cheap, incandescent bulbs didn't provide much light, but he hoped it was enough.

"I don't think this will help make them any easier to spot," Elara said, curious as to what Finn had planned.

"No, but it makes their image enhancers useless," Finn said, covering the stairwell with his laser. "And without that tech, you can be invisible again."

Elara smiled; the plan had her approval. "We'll still need to draw them out into the open."

Finn shrugged and pointed to himself. "Then it looks like I'm the bait."

Elara activated the stealth field on her armor and became a shimmering blur of movement that whisked up the stairs in front of Finn. He followed but advanced cautiously, aware that the special prefects had preferred the art of stealthy assassination to a straight up fight. On the landing to the second floor, he spotted a shadow dancing across the wall, cast there from the single incandescent bulb that was dangling from the ceiling like a lonely spider. Finn aimed his cannon and watched and waited. Finally, the special prefect sprang out, and though the man's eyes were obscured by the helmet's visor, Finn could still feel them burning into him like a laser.

His ambush foiled, the prefect panic-fired his suppressed sub-machinegun and missed. Finn returned fire, hitting the officer in the shoulder and forcing him back. Rushing up the stairs, Finn continued to lay down fire, harassing the prefect until the man had emptied his weapon's magazine in a desperate attempt to fight Finn off. The prefect went to reload, and Finn saw his chance. He charged at the officer and swung his laser cannon at him like a club. The prefect blocked, using his armored forearms to soak up the energy from the blow, before kicking Finn in the chest and driving him into the wall. A fresh magazine was inserted, and the prefect racked his weapon, but before the officer could pull the trigger, Elara materialized behind the man and drew her black combat knife across his throat. Blood gushed out like ale from a punctured keg and the man gargled and croaked, hands pressed to his neck in a desperate attempt to seal the wound, but Elara had cut too deep.

Gunfire rippled from above them and Elara vanished again without a word, though Finn could hear the sound of her footsteps racing up the stairs. He composed himself and ran after her, lighting up the stairwell with cannon fire and forcing the remaining prefects into a deadly game of cat and mouse, but now the roles had been reversed, and Finn was the pursuer. Eagerness got the better of him, and he was caught in a crossfire on the fourth-floor landing and pinned down. He was about to dive for safety when the firing stopped. Finn looked up and blood splashed across his face. A prefect was draped over the banister railings like a wet towel, throat cut, and Finn could see two more of the Authority zealots running away. A shimmering blur was charging after them.

Finn raced to the fourth floor, legs and lungs burning

from the effort, and kicked down the door, finding Elara locked in combat with the two prefects. She was visible again, but her rifle lay broken on the floor, forcing her to face both officers with only her knife. Finn dropped to one knee and aimed his cannon, but he couldn't get a clear shot and didn't want to risk hitting Elara. The more he watched the fight unfold, the more he realized he didn't need to waste his cannon's energy. Even without her stealth field activated, Elara still moved like a blur.

Elara's knife flashed through the air, parrying strike after strike from the prefects who, despite obvious skill with their blades, were simply no match for The Shadow. Using a combination of her weapon and her dense armor, Elara took everything the zealots could throw at her, without suffering a scratch. Finn couldn't see the prefects' faces beneath their onyx veils, but he could sense their fear and feel their panic. Then Elara's blade struck true, slicing deep wounds into muscles and through arteries, and the officers were cut down like weeds.

Finn was about to go to her when he was alerted by the scuffle of boots inside the stairwell. He pressed his back to the wall beside the door then aimed his cannon inside. A single special prefect remained, taller and more heavily built than the others, and with a scoped rifle in his hand. *The sniper...* Finn fired, and the laser blast hit the marksman square in the chest, knocking the man back, but the shot didn't penetrate, and the prefect was able to recover and escape up the stairs before he could land a second volley.

"There's still one more," Finn called out, as Elara approached, leaving bloody footprints in her wake. "It's the sniper, and his armor is tougher. He might be their leader."

"He's trying to escape," Elara said, pushing through on the landing and picking up a sub-machinegun that she'd forced one of the other prefects to drop. "We can't let him get away, come on!"

Finn ran after Elara, and they chased the sniper up the stairs, but even with their training and fitness, the special prefect was able to keep pace with them and reach the top floor, still with a sizable lead.

"Who is this guy?" Finn said, finding the chase to be as grueling and uncomfortable as any assault course he'd been forced to endure. There was an explosion, controlled and focused, and the door to the roof was blown open.

"That was a grenade," Elara said, pushing on.

Unlike Finn, the chase hadn't impaired her, as if Elara was a robot, untiring and unflinching, but Finn stayed by her side, despite every muscle in his body complaining like a Yard seven foreman.

"But why the roof?" Finn said, struggling to form the words through labored breaths. "He's just trapped himself."

Elara didn't answer and darted thorough the open door, before finally stopping and taking cover behind a HVAC unit that was wheezing more heavily than Finn was.

"Maybe he's trying to escape to another rooftop," Elara suggested. Her chest was rising and falling rapidly, and sweat had beaded on her brow, a welcome sign that she was in fact human after all. "We should split up and come at him from both sides," she added, pointing to water towers on the east and west sides of the roof. "We need to take this one alive. We need to be sure there are no others."

Finn nodded, choosing not to waste his breath on speech, then moved out, tracking Elara out of the corner of his eye.

He could just about make out the prefect on the north edge of the roof, hunkered down and working on something, but the officer had wisely and skillfully positioned his body so that no-one could get a shot at him. Suddenly, there was a pneumatic thud and a grapple sped across the divide from their tenement block to an adjacent building, towing a cable behind it. The harpoon thudded into a water tower and the tether was pulled taut.

"Elara now!" Finn called out.

They burst out of cover and sprang their ambush. The prefect was hit with both laser and bullet, but the officer remained unhurt, like he was wearing prosecutor armor. A grenade was thrown at Elara, and it exploded close enough to blow her back and send her spiraling over the top of a roof light. Finn's instinct was to check on her, but she quickly waved him off.

"I'm fine... stop him!" Elara yelled, trying to untangle herself from a web of climbing ivy and weeds that had infested the rooftop like a cancer.

The assassin attached a motorized ascender to the taut wire and hooked it to his harness, but instead of leaping, the man stopped for a split-second to look Finn in the eyes. Even through the mask, he could tell that the glower was personal. The prefect then turned his back on Finn and activated the ascender device, but Finn was already running, committed to stopping the assassin, no matter what. Finn reached the edge of the rooftop and threw himself at the prefect, hands grasping for the man's harness. Time slowed down, and he hung in the air above a ten-storey sheer drop for what seemed like an eternity, until his fingers slipped around the prefect's webbing, and he clung on like a barnacle on the hull of a Seahaven fishing vessel.

The prefect kicked and thrashed, trying to throw Finn off, but his grip was stronger than iron, and he could not be unseated. Then the two men hit the water tower on the building opposite with the force of a derailed train, and the ascender device was knocked off the wire, sending Finn and the assassin crashing to the ground. His laser was dislodged from its holster and sent spinning into the darkness, but the sniper had recovered with remarkable swiftness and the man was trying to aim his scoped rifle at Finn's head.

Finn charged at the assassin like an enraged bull and drove the man's back into the water tower, before wrestling the weapon out of the officer's hands and clubbing him across the side of the head with its stock. The prefect's visor was smashed, and his helmet toppled to the ground, but still the man fought Finn, like they were two kids quarreling over their favorite toy. Finn managed to knock the rifle to the ground, but the prefect didn't skip a beat and pulled a knife instead. Finn drew a matching blade and was about to attack, when he finally saw the man's face.

It was Captain Viktor Roth, Head Prefect of Metalhaven.

5

METALHAVEN'S JUSTICE

The shock of seeing Captain Viktor Roth again made Finn hesitate, and for a few seconds the two men merely stared at each other, both winded from their earlier struggle. Finn had last seen the Head Prefect of Metalhaven at Elara's trial ceremony, at which the man had executed workers in cold blood before forcing Elara onto the start line. Finn had a long and turbulent history with the tyrannical law enforcer, and that had been only the most recent reason to hate him. Finn and Roth had clashed on many occasions but as a Double-Five rated worker, Finn had always gotten away with his petty acts of insolence. That was until the fight with Soren Driscoll and Corbin Radcliffe that had inadvertently led to the prefect captain receiving the scar that still disfigured the man's face. It was Roth who'd put Finn on trial, and though he'd never downplayed his own part in what had happened, Roth had had a hand in Owen's death too, along with thousands of other workers over the man's long and notorious career.

"What the fuck are you doing here?" Finn said, watching

Roth closely. The man was like a cornered animal, feral and dangerous.

"This is my sector!" Roth barked, as if the question had been a great insult. "And I will take it back."

"This *was* your sector, *captain*," Finn said, angered but not surprised that the prefect still believed he had authority over him. "Now it belongs to the chromes of Metalhaven, and you are not welcome here."

Roth gritted and bared his teeth, and a seething rage was emanating from his every pore, provoked by the mere suggestion that he was no longer the man in charge.

"You think you've won, don't you?" Roth snarled, before laughing cruelly. "Do you really think this little stunt of yours will make any difference? The Authority will never allow you to hold this sector. You'll be forced to give it up, or they'll kill every last one of you, and repopulate the yards from the workhouse. It will be as if you never existed at all."

At one time, Finn might have believed Roth's threat, but not anymore. Together with Elara and the Metals from Haven, he'd proven that the Authority was not as strong as they made themselves out to be. For decades the workers of Zavetgrad had been conditioned through brutal subjugation to believe the Authority was all powerful and unassailable, but that had been a lie.

"Your precious Authority isn't as dominant as you like to believe," Finn said. "Your power was based on fear, but we're not afraid of you anymore." He examined Roth from head to toe, hunkered over like a beast, teeth bared, knife in hand, and laughed. "Look at you now, *captain*..." Finn said, speaking the man's rank with disdain. "Now you're the one who is afraid. Tell me, how does that feel?"

"I'm not afraid of you, worker scum!" Roth bellowed, tightening his hold on his blade, and coiling his muscles, ready to strike. "You're nothing. You're beneath me!"

"We'll see," Finn said. His shock at seeing Roth was gone. Now he saw only opportunity; an opportunity to settle a score and right a wrong. Captain Viktor Roth was on trial, and Finn Brasa was judge, jury, and executioner. "I'm out after curfew, Captain," Finn added, taunting the man. "Aren't you going to arrest me?"

The primal instinct for self-perseveration had driven Captain Viktor Roth to run, and fear had kept the man on the defensive, but now it was pure, blind arrogance that finally compelled him to fight.

Roth charged at Finn and hacked and slashed like a berserker in the grip of a trance-like fury. The man's attacks were fast and hard, but also wild and clumsy, and Finn was able to evade them easily. A swift counterattack sliced a deep cut across the back of Roth's hand and the man cried out pain. The man's fingers sprang open, and Roth's knife clattered across the rooftop and skidded into a vent, where it vanished like a rat into a gutter. Finn could have easily ended it then and there, but he wanted Roth to experience terror in the same way the prefect captain had instilled it into the hearts of Metalhaven's workers. He wanted Roth to suffer, and he wasn't ashamed to admit it.

"I'm surprised you had the guts to come yourself," Finn said, sheathing his knife and stalking the man, who was cradling his hand to his chest as if it were a songbird with a broken wing. "I would have expected you to send others to do your dirty work."

Roth snorted a laugh. "I didn't have a choice," the man

spat, bitterly. "Your old friend Ivan Volkov ordered me to come. That little prick blames me for losing Metalhaven to the rebels, but it was his failure, not mine!"

Finn smiled. It hadn't taken long for the veneer of gold to crack and crumble, revealing the true nature of the man wearing the uniform. Beneath his narcissism and sadistic love of hurting people, Roth was just an insecure, small-minded bully.

"For a gold, you have a surprising lack of understanding of how the Authority works," Finn said, amused by Roth's ignorance. "Your title doesn't mean shit, Viktor. The only golds with any power are the Regents and their aristocratic brats. It must really sting to realize that you mean nothing at all to these people; that you're disposable, like the rest of us."

Roth's temper flared again, and the man attacked, swinging wild punches, which Finn blocked and dodged with ease. Whatever combat training Roth had received, it was rudimentary compared to the rigorous regime that Finn had undergone as an apprentice prosecutor, though this didn't surprise him. The only skills a prefect needed were how to swing a nightstick and how to sucker-punch a man or woman who was too afraid to resist. He let Roth continue to come at him, while countering the man's hopeless efforts with measured punches that chipped away at the prefect's resilience like a tide eroding a coastline, beating it back inch by inch until there was nothing left. Face swollen, teeth broken, and lips split and bleeding, Roth continued to fight until the man had punched himself out and exhaustion forced him to his knees, chest heaving and body shaking. At first, Finn thought that Roth's trembling was the effect of adrenalin, but then he looked into the head prefect's eyes and saw fear.

"Go on then!" Roth wheezed, glaring at Finn hatefully through ballooned eyes. "This is what you've been waiting for, isn't it? So, kill me and take your revenge!"

"I'm surprised you're not dead already, killed by one of the brain bombs the Authority likes to implant into their stooges," Finn said, suddenly realizing that if Roth had been a special prefect, the matter of his death would have been taken out of his control.

"There's no easy way out for me," Roth answered, flatly. The man laughed bitterly, coughing blood. "It was either succeed or die, which is fine by me. So just do what you came here to do, and slit my throat. I don't care anymore."

Finn shook his head. "I'm afraid you don't get off that easily, Captain. You're going to be my prisoner."

Roth laughed again and blood-soaked spittle sprayed from his mouth. "Do you really think I'd tell you all the Authority's dirty little secrets?" Roth shook his head then turned away. "I'm not a traitor like you and Cage. I still have my honor."

"Honor?" Finn had kept an iron grip on his emotions until then but now he felt his composure faltering, and without realizing it, his knife was back in his hand. "You don't know the meaning of the word."

"I'm a believer," Roth said, lifting his chin as if offering his throat for slaughter. "I swore to protect Zavetgrad and the Authority, and I won't break my oath, not for scum like you."

"You swore an oath to murderers and thieves," Finn hissed. "You're loyal only to the mob and that means you have no honor at all."

Finn kicked Roth in the chest and sent the man crashing to his back. Then before Roth's glazed eyes had refocused, he was kneeling over him, the tip of his blade pressed above the man's carotid artery. Roth gritted his teeth and their eyes locked.

"Go on!" Roth roared. "Do it!"

Finn added pressure and the knife cut into Roth's neck but before he could sink the blade deeper and sever the blood vessels that supplied the head prefect's malignant brain, a sound and a flicker of movement stole his attention. Jumping back from Roth, he looked for his laser cannon, but it was out of reach. Instead, he aimed his blood-stained knife into the darkness.

"Who's there?!" Finn demanded. "Show yourself!"

A figure approached from out of the gloom. The intruder was wearing a thick coat over the top of Metalhaven work overalls, but while his hands were up in surrender, his head was covered by the coat's hood and his chin was down so that Finn couldn't get a good look at the man's face. Then the air behind the man shimmered and Elara materialized, pointing a sub machine gun at the stranger's back.

"Who are you?" Finn asked.

The man stepped into the light and threw back his hood, and for a second time that night, Finn was shocked by the appearance of someone he'd never expected to see again.

"Pritchard?" Finn said, staring at his old valet from the prosecutor barracks.

"Hello, sir," Pritchard said, in his smoothly unconcerned manner.

"Another fucking traitor," Roth snarled. The prefect climbed unsteadily to his feet and Elara pointed her submachine gun at the captain instead. "A traitor and false gold!"

"How did you get here?" Finn asked, ignoring Roth's outburst. While Elara had her weapon trained on the captain, the former head prefect was neutered and no threat.

"I got here the same way he did," Pritchard said, nodding in the direction of Roth. "He actually led me to the entrance, though he didn't realize it at the time."

"Keep your fucking mouth shut, valet!" Roth roared. The man started toward Pritchard and Elara squeezed the trigger of her weapon, shooting Roth in the leg. The man roared like a wild beast and dropped to one knee, hissing through cracked and blood-stained teeth.

"The captain and his officers got into Metalhaven through the disused sewer system," Pritchard said, oddly aloof to the pain Roth was suffering, as well as the sheer strangeness of their rooftop reunion. "I'll show you where the entrances and exits are, so that your Metals can block them up."

"Traitor!" Roth hissed again. "You'll hang for this!"

Elara lashed Roth across the face with the butt of her weapon and the man tottered and slumped to one side, barely conscious. She then moved behind the former captain and kept the barrel of the submachine gun aimed at his head.

"They know about your plan to capture the Regents," Pritchard continued. The young valet with the sunny disposition was gone, and instead there was a sadder and older looking Pritchard in front of Finn. "Roth captured several Metals, which I believe is your codeword for Haven operatives?" Finn nodded but didn't interrupt, despite having a hundred questions for the man who was the closest thing he'd had to a friend in the Authority sector. "They're using the Prosecutor Barracks as an interrogation center, and they tortured one of these Metals until he gave up the plan. I couldn't help but overhear." Pritchard looked into the middle distance and Finn could see that his eyes were moist with tears. "I would have given anything not to hear, and for my life to be as it was, but it's too late for that now."

"Don't say another word!" Roth said, and Elara pressed the barrel of her weapon into the nape of the man's neck. "You're a gold, damn you!"

Pritchard looked at Captain Viktor Roth and shook his head. "If being a gold means being like you, then I want nothing more to do with the Authority." He turned from Roth to Finn. "I want to help. I think I can."

"You're a fool!" Roth said, and Elara hooked her finger around the trigger. "You'll never get inside the Regent's sub-oceanic complex. It's impossible, even for me."

"I can do it," Pritchard said, without hesitation or doubt. "I can be quite resourceful."

"Now that, I do remember," Finn laughed.

Finn recalled how Pritchard had always done so much more from him than simply greet him each morning with a smile and a cup of his favorite coffee. Yet the valet's resourcefulness had always been matched by his ignorance of who his Authority masters truly were. Now he knew. Roth had stolen that innocence and naivety for him, and as much as Pritchard was clearly suffering, Finn was glad that the man's eyes were open to the truth.

"Help them and you are a marked man," Roth said, risking more of Elara's wrath, but she held back from striking the captain again. She appeared more interested in Pritchard than the former head prefect. "Help them and you'll never be safe. Every prefect in the city will know your name, and there will be a reward for putting your head on a pike!"

Finn was about to strike Roth himself to shut the man up when Elara finally spoke.

"Why would you betray the Authority?" Elara's question surprised Roth and the man bit his tongue, eager to hear the answer. "You've always known about the trials. You were valet to an apprentice prosecutor, after all, so you understood the Authority's methods. I don't buy it, Pritchard. There has to be more."

The former valet looked at his feet, but it wasn't an attempt to hide a tell that might have proven the man a liar, but to mask his shame. Finn understood guilt and he could see that something was burdening his old valet, something heavy enough to drag down even his seemingly unconquerable high spirits.

"I lost faith," Pritchard said, wiping his eyes. "It wasn't just one Metal that they tortured in the barracks. If it had just been that then maybe I could have rationalized it somehow, but there were more. So many more..."

Pritchard looked at Roth and there was hate in his eyes; it changed the young man's face and his posture, turning the once boyish, hopeful valet into a shattered and hollow shell of his former self.

"They all got what they deserved," Roth hissed, showing no remorse. "I did what I did for Zavetgrad, and for Nimbus!"

"How many more?" It was no longer Elara asking, but The Shadow.

"I lost count," Pritchard answered, the words spoken so

softly they barely reached Finn's ears. "The captain and the Commissar had more and more brought in every day, from every sector. Dozens in the morning, tortured and killed. Dozens in the afternoon. More in the evening. Their screams were never-ending. They would wake me at night and keep me awake till morning. It was…"

"Justified!" Roth cut in. Finn expected Elara to lash out at the man, but she did nothing. She had become glacial, cold. "We had to root out the traitors. The survival of Zavetgrad depended on it!"

"I was taught that the trials were necessary to maintain order, but what he and Commissar Jones did was… unforgivable…" Pritchard continued. "I had no idea the Authority could be so barbaric."

"Then you weren't looking," Elara said, her retort icier than the frozen crystals forming on her armor.

Pritchard nodded, accepting guilt by association. No-one who wore the color gold was blameless, no matter how blinkered they were.

"I took it on faith that the Regents were noble and righteous, and that the prosecutors were an instrument of justice, but I see now how wrong I was." Pritchard sucked in a deep breath then stood as tall as his burdens would permit. "I request sanctuary in Metalhaven…"

"Pritchard, no!" Roth bellowed.

"I ask for no special treatment," the former valet continued, ignoring Roth's protests. "And whether I stay here as your prisoner or you guest, I will tell you everything you need to know to infiltrate the Regent's stronghold."

"*Pritchard!*"

Roth rose and darted toward the valet, but Elara pounced

on the former head prefect like a wolf spider attacking its prey. A sharp blow to the back of Roth's head stunned the man, then Elara cut the prefect's body harness and wrapped it around his neck before steering Roth to the edge of the rooftop, ten storeys above Metalhaven's icy streets. Finn knew what she intended to do. Roth's trial was over. Now all that remained was his sentence.

"You can't do this!" Roth snarled, as Finn tied the captain's harness to the wire that still connected the tenement block to the building opposite. "I am gold! I demand that you release me!"

Finn tightened the harness straps like a noose, causing Roth's eyes to bulge out of their sockets, and the man's tongue to protrude from his mouth with a strangled gargle.

"Then I grant you your wish, Captain," Finn said.

Together, he and Elara pushed Captain Viktor Roth, Head Prefect of Metalhaven, over the edge of the building. The harness constricted around Roth's neck and the man kicked and writhed as he slid down the wire and came to rest between the two tenement buildings. A group of drinkers from the nearby recovery center had gathered on the street, alerted by the gunshots, explosions, and shouts, and they all watched in silence as the butcher and tyrant struggled and fought desperately to free himself, until finally the kicking stopped, and Roth's arms fell limp to his sides.

"Now that's what justice looks like," Elara said, dusting off her hands. "And Viktor Roth is just the first of many."

6

THE DEFECTOR

Briggs and Xia walked into the rebel command headquarters on the top floor of the gene bank, rubbing their eyes and yawning. Finn had asked Scraps to wake the two Metals, who had become brigade commanders in charge of protecting the newly freed Metalhaven. Trip was already there, having been roused earlier and practically dragged to the office by Chiefy, who was now busy repairing Finn's armor. The man was pouring himself a glass of probiotic goop in an effort to mitigate the lingering effects of eight pints of Metalhaven ale. None of the Metals had appreciated being dragged out of bed in the middle of the night, but once they spotted the mysterious new addition to their party, they quickly perked up.

"Who the fuck is he?" Briggs asked, wearing his tiredness-induced irritability on his sleeve.

"His name is Pritchard, he's a defector from the Authority sector," Finn explained, causing the bleary eyes of both Metals to widen. "He used to be my valet. He's here with some vital information."

"How did he get here?" Briggs said. "And what's this I'm hearing about Head Prefect Viktor Roth strung up between two tenements blocks? There's quite a crowd out there, cheering him on, not that I mind. I fucking hated that prick."

"The head prefect entered Metalhaven though the disused sewer system," Pritchard said. He removed a battered looking memory stick from the pocket of his overalls and offered it to Briggs, who eyed it, and the stranger, with suspicion. "This contains a map of all of the entrances into the sector that may still be accessible. I suggest you act quickly to seal them."

Briggs snatched the memory stick out of Pritchard's hand, but kept his eyes fixed on the man, who was still, for all intents and purposes, an enemy in their midst.

"He got here the same way Roth and a squad of special prefects did," Finn explained. The mention of special prefects caused Briggs and the others to look suddenly panicked and alert, so Finn was quick to set their minds at ease. "Don't worry, they're all dead, just like the captain, but Pritchard is right, you need to act fast to seal those entrances, before other Authority agents use them."

Briggs nodded then handed the memory device to Xia, who hurried to one of the computer consoles in the room and set to work alerting the Metals to the potential danger.

"I'll see if I can raise Pen and General Riley," Trip said, shuffling to the primary comms console that was permanently set up just to communicate with Haven. "This is something they'll want to hear."

"I've already sent them a message so they should be calling soon," Finn said.

The blinking signal indicator on the screen then turned to

a solid green and a call tone rang out inside the room, causing Trip to start and spill some probiotic onto his pants.

"Shit, this stuff really stains," Trip said, brushing the thick liquid off his overalls, before dropping heavily into the control chair and accepting the call. Pen and General Riley appeared, projected as life-sized holograms in the middle of the room.

"I see you got the emitters working," Pen said, her ghostly visage looking around the room as if she was physically present. "It's nice to see you all in three dimensions for a change." The principal smiled first at Finn then at Elara, whose eyes she held a fraction longer than his, before Pen turned to Pritchard and her smile fell away. "And who do we have here?"

"This is Pritchard," Finn explained. He realized that he didn't actually know his first name, but his former valet was perceptive enough to fill in the gaps without needing to be asked.

"Charles Pritchard, ma'am," the valet said, bowing in deference to the Principal of the Pit. "I was Mister Brasa's valet during his time in the authority sector as an apprentice prosecutor."

"I see..." Pen said, though it was clear she was none the wiser about Pritchard than she had been when first setting eyes upon the man.

"Pritchard defected from the Authority, and brought us valuable intel on a number of possible routes into Metalhaven that we were unaware of," Finn said, trying not to get bogged down in the details of his valet's arrival, since he'd already been through this once with the Metals. "He got into the sector the same way that a squad of special prefects did, led by Captain Viktor Roth."

General Riley suddenly stepped forward, as if protecting Pen's ghostly apparition from a possible assassination attempt.

"Where is Roth now?" Riley said, fingers wrapped around the grip of his sidearm.

"He's still hanging from the neck, fifty meters up," Elara said, arms folded. "He and his squad are all dead."

"At ease, Will," Pen said, resting a hand on General Riley's shoulder. "I'm sure they have everything under control. Besides, I don't think a holographic bullet can do me any harm."

Riley nodded and released his hold on his weapon, looking slightly foolish for grabbing it in the first place, considering he was hundreds of miles away.

"So, Roth is dead?" Riley grunted.

"Very," Elara replied.

"Good," Riley said, relaxing a little, though a relaxed General Riley was still more rigid than a corpse. "I didn't like him."

Finn glanced at the others in the room, and it seemed that no-one appeared ready to shed a tear for the passing of Metalhaven's tyrannical head prefect. Finn idly wondered if there was anyone at all in the city who cared for the man or who had cared about him, before concluding that he didn't give a shit either way. Roth was dead. Good riddance.

"We've agreed to grant Mister Pritchard asylum in Metalhaven, though he will remain under supervision," Finn said, causing eyebrows to raise on the faces of the holograms and the other Metals who were physically present. "I've been burned before by people claiming to be my friend, so no-one gets a pass."

Pritchard bowed his head. "I understand completely, sir, and I accept the terms of my sanctuary."

"And do you agree with this?" General Riley said, directing the question to Elara.

"I knew Pritchard, and I always considered him one of the better golds, which is why I had him assigned as Finn's valet in the first place," Elara said, and this revelation surprised Pritchard, who had been unaware of her hidden motives. "But Finn is right, he'll have to prove himself first."

Pritchard bowed his head to Elara and did not look offended in the slightest. The man then turned to face Pen, who would ultimately decide his fate, though the principal was not ready to make that decision yet.

"Well, it seems that you've all had an exciting night, though I do wonder if this report could not have waited until the morning?" Pen said. "Unless, Charles has something more to offer that requires our urgent attention?"

"I do, ma'am," Pritchard replied. "I understand that you plan to infiltrate the sub-oceanic villa complex belonging to the Regents. I believe I can help."

Riley stepped forward again. "And just how did you come to this understanding, son?" the general said, somewhat condescendingly.

"I overheard Commissar Jones and Regent Successor Ivan Volkov discussing that this would be your likely next move," Pritchard explained. "Mr. Volkov is using the prosecutor barracks as his base of operations, amongst other things."

Finn frowned at Pritchard. There was something more to his seemingly throwaway comment that Volkov was using the barracks as more than just his HQ, but he didn't want to interrupt the flow of the conversation to find out what, at least not then.

"You are correct, it is our plan to capture the Regents," Pen said, and this admission seemed to annoy Riley, who remained deeply distrustful of Pritchard. "Perhaps you can earn some trust by explaining exactly how you believe you can help?"

"I will require a computer terminal," Pritchard said.

Finn looked for Scraps, who was observing from the sidelines, while Chiefy continued to patch up Finn's and Elara's armor.

"Pal, can you isolate a computer console for Pritchard to use?" Finn asked his robot buddy. "We need to make sure he can't use to it contact the Authority."

"Yes-yes!" Scraps said.

The robot activated his rotor and flew past Pritchard, waving and smiling at the former valet as he did so, before landing in front of an unused computer console. Scraps plugged himself into the machine, bypassing all forms of login security as if they didn't exist, then worked diligently for a few seconds, before stepping away and pointing to the screen.

"Ta-da!" Scraps said, cheerfully. "This 'puter behind firewall. No talky to bad golds!"

"Believe me, I have no desire to reconnect with the Authority," Pritchard said, his demeanor the exact opposite of Scraps' sunny cheerfulness.

The former valet seated himself at the computer then launched a design application and set to work. For a while, it wasn't clear what the man was doing, until a complex and detailed structural diagram of the sub-oceanic complex began to take shape, rendered in three-dimensions on the screen.

"That's a neat trick," said Trip, who had already swapped his probiotic for a pint of ale. "Where did you learn how to do that?"

"I studied at the Authority University," Pritchard said, though he remained distracted and consumed in his work. "After completing my five years of valet service, I was to be employed as an architectural designer. Art was always my first love."

Trip laughed harshly. "Yeah, me too," the former reclamation yard worker scoffed. "Us chromes had plenty of time for painting and sculpture, in between breaking our backs fourteen hours a day in the yards."

It was an unkind comment that was meant to hurt, and while Pritchard reacted in a suitably shamefaced manner, Trip showed no remorse. Finn considered intervening on his former valet's behalf but chose not to. There was no escaping the fact that Pritchard had led a privileged life, and now that he'd toppled from his perch, Finn wasn't about to cushion his fall. If he was to survive outside of the Authority, Pritchard would have to accept it would not be a smooth or easy transition.

"There, this is what the sub-oceanic complex looks like," Pritchard said, hitting the enter key and sending his rendered image into a slow spin.

Finn studied the diagram with interest, while the ghostly forms of Pen and General Riley looked over his shoulder. The complex was much bigger than he'd imagined and was split into ten distinct component parts. There were two structures on the first section, perhaps fifty meters beneath sea level, then a single large structure that spanned the entire mid-level of the complex, and a further ten smaller structures beneath this, anchored to the sea floor.

"The complex is surrounded by a protective ring of surface and subsurface mines," Pritchard said, circling his finger around the image of the complex on the screen. "The only way to reach it safely is from a jetty in a high-security harbor located in Seahaven. There is a single ferry, tethered to the facility's ingress shaft, two hundred meters out to sea. This is the only way into the complex."

Finn spotted the ingress shaft, which sprouted from the upper-level structure that was closest to the shoreline, like a factory chimney. Pritchard had even depicted the harbor and the ferry pier on his diagram. The man had talent, though Finn imagined that this was the first time his former valet's artistic abilities had actually been put to a valuable use.

"The ingress shaft is DNA-coded so that only the Regents can enter or exit," Pritchard continued. "There is a finger scanner that delivers a pin-prick test to take a small blood sample."

"If the door is DNA-coded then how the hell do we get past it?" Riley grunted. He was yet to be impressed by anything Pritchard had done.

"Why don't we hear Charles out first?" Pen said, ever the mediator. "I'm sure we'll all have many questions once he's finished detailing the layout of the villa complex."

"This is a waste of time," Riley said, grunting and grumbling like a rumbling stomach. "Getting inside the villa complex is impossible."

"Go on," Finn said, resting a hand on Pritchard's shoulder as a show of moral support. The man was not used to conflict and the pile-in by Riley and Trip had unsettled him.

"The ingress shaft leads into the servant's quarters, which is the first of the two structures on level one of the complex," Pritchard continued, his voice trembling, like he was giving an important speech to a crowded amphitheater. "This is where the staff live when they are off duty. There is a twelve-hour shift rotation."

"Only twelve hours?" Trip cut in. "Those bastards have it easy."

"I'd rather work the yards than be a whipping boy for one of the Regents," Briggs said.

Elara shot the two Metals a piercing stare, which indicated in no uncertain terms that they should remain quiet, and both former workers glumly folded their arms across their chests in protest.

"The servants' quarters leads into the Office of the Regents, which is where they conduct their daily business and correspond with Nimbus," Pritchard said, grateful for Elara's intervention. "There is an antenna mast that extends from the office structure above the surface of the water."

"I don't care where the Regents swill whiskey and suck up to Gideon Reznikov in his orbital palace, so move on," Riley grunted, still as irascible as Trip and Briggs were. "What's the large structure in the middle?"

"That is called 'Elysium'," Pritchard said, managing to remain calm, despite Riley's brooding holographic stare. Even as a trick of light, the general managed to project an imposing presence. "Elysium makes the cultural quarter in the Authority sector look like a Metalhaven recovery center."

Pritchard glanced apologetically at Briggs, a former recovery center pint-puller. "No offense..."

"Plenty of fucking offense taken, pal," Briggs snorted. "Cheeky bastard..."

Trip chuckled and Finn couldn't help but crack a smile too, and the brief moment of levity helped to lift the fog of gloom that had descended upon the meeting.

"I would actually like to try some Metalhaven ale," Pritchard said, skillfully turning the situation to his advantage, and endearing himself to the rebel leader.

"Here you go then," Trip said, slamming his pint down on the worktop next to Pritchard. "I'll go and pull myself another."

Pritchard scowled at the ale then took a tentative sip. "Quite pleasant..." the man said, though the face he was pulling suggested he'd just drank rancid probiotic goop.

"You were talking about Elysium?" Pen cut in, trying to get things back on track.

"Yes, well, suffice it to say that Elysium is a paradise, of sorts," the former valet continued, after wetting his lips with more ale. Even in limited amounts, its soothing effects were apparent. "It's where the Regents go to amuse themselves with every kind of food, wine, and entertainment you can imagine, and many more that you could not."

"So, it's debauched, you mean," Finn said, reading between the lines.

"Yes," Pritchard replied, his face reddening. "The Regents indulge themselves in every pleasure and every vice, some more than others."

"I think we've heard enough about Elysium," Pen said, and Finn was glad of her intervention. He had no interest in the sordid details of what the Regents got up to in their private orgy pit.

"Below Elysium are the private villas of each Regent," Pritchard said. He pointed to each in turn, starting from the outermost villa pod. "The Regent of Spacehaven and Mayor, Maxim Volkov."

"Our primary target," Elara cut in, just to make it clear that even amongst Regents, there was a hierarchy.

"Then we have the Regent of Volthaven, Victor Kozlov," Pritchard continued, pointing to the next structure on the rendered diagram. "Followed by the Regent of Seedhaven, Theodore Westwood; Autohaven, Vadim Ivanov; Stonehaven, Yuki Tanaka; Makehaven, Amir Khan; Seahaven, Cedric Brathwaite; and finally, the Regent of Metalhaven, Gabriel Montgomery."

"I've had my run-ins with that pompous oaf," Finn said, remembering Montgomery from his own trial. "I wouldn't mind another face-to-face meeting though, just so I can let him know how I really feel."

"Hopefully, you'll get your chance," Riley grunted. The man's holographic eyes fell onto Pritchard. "Assuming this defector can give us more than just a pretty picture of these villas, because without details of their defenses, and a method to get inside, all of this is useless information."

"There are no prefects in the complex, because none are needed," Pritchard said, taking Riley's unsubtle hint. "In addition to the human servants there are housekeeper robots, which are modified foremen, but beyond that, I do not know what else is inside. No-one does."

"What about these servants?" Elara asked. "Perhaps

they're trained as bodyguards, like Ivan's paramour, Sloane Stewart."

"Don't you mean ex-paramour?" Trip said, fresh pint in hand. "That knife throw to the back was something else," he added, raising the glass in salute.

Elara smiled and nodded, acknowledging Trip's appreciation for the fine art of murder. It was perhaps crass to celebrate the demise of another human being, but Finn considered that if there was any moralizing to be done, it would be carried out by their descendants, not them. In that case, Finn didn't mind being the subject of a future generation's judgement, because it would mean that humanity had flourished and remained free.

"The human staff are trained only in how to serve," Pritchard said, unaware of Finn's dark musings. "The Regents personally select their servants from the workhouse at age thirteen. The chosen are then taken to a facility in the Authority sector where they are further evaluated for one year, undergoing intense training and conditioning, guided by the Regents themselves, to ensure they are satisfied. Those who pass are taken to a special section of Elysium, where they are further trained to work as expert servants. From that point on, they never leave."

Briggs snorted and shook his head. "Trained... Groomed more like. The Regents are nothing but filthy fucking perverts if you ask me."

Pritchard smiled nervously but didn't try to deny it, and reading between the lines again, Finn had a pretty good idea what the training involved, and what the duties of these so-called 'expert servants' would likely entail.

"This is all very interesting, but how do we get inside?"

Riley interrupted, impatient to guide Pritchard's report to a useful conclusion. "Without a blood sample from one of the Regents, we can't even breach the main ingress, never mind pass through Elysium and reach their villa pods."

Pritchard reached into the pocket of his overalls and removed a shiny silver box. Finn thought he'd seen something like it before, but he couldn't place where. Then the former valet set the box down on the desk and opened it. There was a hiss of what looked like steam, until Finn realized it was actually a freezing fog, and that the box contained a frozen test-tube phial.

"I hope that's not what I think it is," Elara said, also recognizing the box and the phial it contained from the many like it that were stored in the gene bank building.

"It is a bio-sample, but this particular phial contains blood, not seed," Pritchard said, and Elara breathed a sigh of relief. "To be exact, it is a sample of Ivan Volkov's blood. I stole it before I came here."

"Very resourceful," Finn commented, and Pritchard acknowledged him with a respectful nod. Then Finn asked, "How did you get it?" and the defector's face fell.

"Come on, Pritchard, we need the truth," Elara cut in. "A frozen sample of a regent successor's blood is hardly something you just find lying around."

Pritchard nodded then closed the container to ensure the sample didn't warm up and spoil. He then cleared his throat and adjusted his position on the seat, as if the dense fabric cushion had suddenly turned into a bed of needles.

"After Mister Brasa escaped the city, I was reassigned and required to attend to Ivan Volkov as valet," Pritchard began.

"He thought he might be able to get some useful insights from me, with respect to Mister Brasa."

"And did you dish the dirt?" Finn asked, in an accusing tone.

"I... accommodated him," Pritchard replied, evasively, and Finn released a Riley-esque grunt. He wasn't happy with the answer, but he could hardly blame Pritchard for yielding to the regent's son. "Anyway, after Elara's trial, Mister Volkov was injured and spent some time in the care of medical robots," Pritchard continued, eager to gloss over his transgressions. "They took blood samples to check for infections, and I stole one of them."

"But what good is Ivan's blood?" Elara said, showing signs of losing her normally unflappable cool. "It's Maxim Volkov's DNA we need."

"Now that is something I can answer," Riley said, for once sounding enthused. "Ivan is a clone of Maxim Volkov. The mayor is sterile, and this was the only way he could produce an heir."

"And you've always known this?" Pen asked.

Riley shrugged. "It was the worst-kept secret in Zavetgrad. I didn't think the information useful, until now."

"Then thanks to Pritchard, we have our key," Finn said, feeling suddenly more upbeat about their chances. "Now, all we need to do is sneak inside the private harbor in Seahaven, reach the ingress point, trick the DNA lock to get inside, fight unknown dangers, capture the Regents, and get out again." He shrugged. "That doesn't sound so bad," he lied.

"And get out again..." Elara said, oddly focusing on the last part of the process, rather than the seemingly impossible prior steps. "We talked about getting in, but not about escaping again, and I seem to remember something about a minefield surrounding the complex."

"Getting out is relatively simple," Pritchard said, managing something resembling a smile. It made his old valet look a little more like the young man Finn remembered. "Each villa pod has an escape capsule, which is in effect a miniature submersible. These are programmed to evade the minefield and surface close to the Seahaven shoreline."

"That's where we come in," Trip said. The man had finished the pint he'd pulled only a few minutes earlier. Finn hadn't even seen him take a sip. "We have Metals in Seahaven who can intercept the submersible once it surfaces, and smuggle its precious cargo into this sector."

"Then, when we have those bastards in shackles, pissing in their silk pants, we'll have the leverage we need to topple the Authority and take over the sector," Briggs added.

The mood in the room had suddenly become triumphant. The idea was bereft of detail, and even with a week's planning, would still be the most audacious assault ever attempted against the Authority, but no-one seemed to mind. They had a chance to bring down the regents, and any chance, no matter how slim, was worth the risk.

"I have one question," Pen said. Unlike the others, she had remained on the fence.

"Just one?" Finn laughed. "I have about a million."

"Just one, for now..." Pen clarified. The hologram of the principal then moved in front of Pritchard, who rose from the chair and stood solemnly in front of her. "How exactly do you know all this, Charles?"

Pritchard looked at his feet, either embarrassed or ashamed or both, but Finn could sense that the man was not planning to hold anything back. He had, so far, been true to his word.

"I was one of those children selected at age thirteen to serve a regent," Pritchard said. "I was intended to serve the Regent of Seedhaven, Theodore Westwood, but I did not make the grade during initial training and was rejected."

"Why?" Finn asked. It was a blunt question, but it was also not the time to respect personal boundaries.

"I was not to the Regent's... shall we say, taste..." Pritchard said, the words catching in his throat. "I didn't know what that meant at the time but of course now I do."

"If you ask me, you had a lucky fucking escape, sunshine," Briggs said, echoing the sentiment of everyone in the room.

"But you were never in the workhouse," Finn said, still unsure of the story. "Or were you?"

Pritchard nodded. "I wasn't born gold, but even after the regent's rejection, the Authority considered me gentrified-enough to be transferred to a service role. I passed the basic genetic purity test and so began working for the Authority at age thirteen. I lived and studied in that sector for the next ten years. It was my home, and I was happy."

"Happy and fucking oblivious..." Trip cut in, and Pritchard looked at his feet again.

Finn drew in a deep breath then looked at Elara, who simply nodded. It was all the confirmation he needed, but it wasn't Elara's decision, and it wasn't his either. Everyone turned to the Principal of the Pit.

"Very well, Charles, we will take you at your word," Pen said, and Pritchard met her eyes with a half-smile. "The mission is approved. Now, the hard work of planning begins."

7

THE PLAN

Finn woke suddenly and his head snapped forward like he was traveling in a ground car that had slammed on the brakes. His heart was racing, his muscles were tense, and it took him several seconds to even remember where he was. Owen's face was burned into his mind, though for once he hadn't been dreaming of his friend's brutal murder, but of a happier time when they'd been drinking in a Metalhaven recovery center, winding down after a hard shift. It was a memory he tried to cling on to, but as wakefulness asserted itself, his friend's face fell into the periphery of his mind. Then it was gone.

"You okay?" Elara asked. She was sitting on an identical chair opposite him, legs tucked up beneath her and head resting on the plush fabric cushion. "You were dreaming, I think."

Finn nodded then rubbed his face and neck, which were still sore. "It was Owen again," he said, and Elara looked concerned, so he was quick to dispel the notion he'd had another nightmare. "This dream was okay, though, for a change." He tried to remember more about it but the harder he struggled to resurrect the memory, the faster it slipped away. "How long was I out?"

"A couple of hours maybe," Elara said, sliding her legs off the sofa and stretching like a cat who'd just woken up.

"Did you sleep too?" Finn asked.

"A little, I don't need much rest," Elara said, moving closer and seating herself on the arm of Finn's plush wingchair. "Besides, I have too much on my mind."

Finn nodded then looked around the executive office suite. Trip was asleep by the bar area, an empty pint glass sat on the table next to the stacks of fine spirits and liquors that only the most important golds could afford. The man was snoring softly, head tilted back and mouth slightly open. Xia and Briggs were across the other side of the suite, also sleeping. The two Metals had arranged the quieter and more private corner of the floor into a sleeping area and set up cot beds so that they were always on-hand, should an emergency situation demand they quickly contact the other leaders. Scraps and Chiefy were also close by, but both robots were in standby mode, plugged into power outlets to recharge their diminished battery cells. Scraps was sitting in Chiefy's lap while the larger robot cradled his pal's head in his hand.

"Why does that make me feel jealous?" Finn wondered, torn between appreciating the wholesomeness of the situation, and lamenting the fact that his robot buddy had found another friend.

"You're just worried you might lose him," Elara said. She slid beside Finn and hugged her arm around his body, resting her head on his shoulder, and Finn froze, not wanting to move a muscle in case she drew away. "But you won't. That robot is a survivor, like us."

Elara kissed him on the cheek then stood up, and Finn almost toppled over, though he thought he did a good job of styling out his stumble so that he didn't look like a buffoon. The smirk on Elara's face, however, suggested otherwise.

"I guess we should run through the plan again," Elara said, already looking bright and alert.

"Again?" Finn grumbled, shoulders sagging. "We've been at it for hours, already. I think the sun has come up and set again twice in the time we've been cooped up in this room."

Elara just shot him a withering look and Finn knew that his protest had fallen on unsympathetic ears.

"Fine, let's go through it again." He pushed himself out of the wingchair then walked past Trip and gently kicked the man's feet. Trip started and snuffled like a hog before his eyes peeled open. "We'll need Trip to listen in and sense check everything we're saying."

"I need to do what-now?" Trip said, yawning.

"I need you to listen to our plan and point out if anything sounds crazy," Finn clarified.

Trip snorted a laugh then began to pour himself a pint. Briggs had needed to bring up a second keg to accommodate the man's titanic appetite for ale.

"The whole damned thing sounds crazy, if you ask me," Trip said, skillfully tilting the glass and ensuring that his pint was finished with a perfect, frothy head. "But go ahead and knock yourselves out, I'm listening."

Elara relocated to one of the computer terminals furthest

away from where Briggs and Xia were sleeping, so as not to disturb them. The screen turned on and the glow was dazzling, like looking directly into the sun.

"Okay, phase one..." Elara said, cracking her fingers then resting them on the keyboard. "Getting inside the sub-oceanic complex."

Elara loaded up the program that Charles Pritchard had helped them to create, in order to visualize their plan. The valet was no longer with them and had retired to a room in the gene bank, under guard. Finn had considered the guard unnecessary in light of what Pritchard had already given them, but Elara had reminded him that no-one got a pass. Everyone had to prove their loyalty, especially those who had worn gold.

"The first step is actually getting inside Seahaven, which should be simple thanks to the map of the disused sewer network that Pritchard gave us," Elara began. "Haven thought they already knew of all the tunnels running beneath Zavetgrad, but it looks like we'd only uncovered a fraction of them."

Elara operated the computer and the screen rendered a three-dimensional schematic of the tunnel network that ran from Metalhaven to Seahaven, which adjoined their sector along its eastern edge.

"I've only ever seen Seahaven from the air. I had no idea how different it was to Metalhaven," Finn said, as the computer program began to render an image of the coastal sector in perfect fidelity. The tenement blocks, recovery centers and gene banks were all clustered closely together, in squat buildings that gave Seahaven a characterful, shantytown look. However, it was the rows upon rows of boathouses and repair docks that butted up against the many ports and harbors that made Seahaven unique.

"Metals will be standing by at the exit tunnel, here," Elara said, zooming in on the point where he and Elara would emerge into the sector. "They'll alert us to prefect patrols and run distractions if necessary, drawing any officers away from us."

"It helps that Ivan has redeployed more than half of each sector's prefects to guard Spacehaven and the Authority sector," Finn commented. "That means there will be significantly fewer street patrols."

"True, but the ones that remain will be on high alert, with even itchier trigger fingers than normal," Elara said. "We've also heard from our contact inside Seahaven that foreman robots have been pulled off regular duty and reprogrammed to act as enforcers."

Finn nodded. His sleep deprived brain had forgotten that aspect but now he remembered, and agreed it would be a complication.

"The Authority also got wise to how easily Scraps was able to hack the foremen, and have added a new software firewall to keep him out," Elara continued. "Scraps thinks he can still break through, but he'll have to be close to one of these new robots to try."

"We can't rely on that, which means it's likely we won't reach the secure harbor without meeting some kind of resistance," Finn said.

He glanced across to Trip, worried that the man who was supposed to be sense-checking their plan had fallen asleep again, but he was watching closely, pint of ale in hand. It was already half drunk.

"Are you with us so far?" Finn asked, checking that Trip had been paying attention.

"So far so good," the Metal replied. "But how are you going to get inside the secure harbor without alerting these new enforcer foremen, or the prefects?"

"Scraps may not be able to hack the updated robots, but he can still hide us from the Authority's scanners," Elara said.

She updated the program and a rendered image of the secure harbor appeared on the screen. The area was enclosed by a five-meter electrified fence and contained the guard house, boat house and various sentry posts where the special prefects who guarded the harbor would shelter from the blistering storms that frequently wracked Seahaven's barren coastline.

"We don't know exactly how many special prefects are inside the harbor, but we think it's somewhere between ten and twenty," Finn said. "We can't fight them without raising the alarm, which means that part requires stealth."

"That's all well and good for The Shadow," Trip cut in, pointing to Elara with his pint, "but you don't have any fancy cloaking tech."

"Actually, I do," Finn said.

By way of a demonstration, he activated the stealth field generator that Chiefy had retrofitted into his prosecutor armor and disappeared before Trip's eyes. The man started and took a step back, before looking into his empty pint and wondering if it was the beer clouding his vision. Finn took the empty glass from Trip's hand, refilled it from the keg in the bar area, then returned it to the Metal, all while cloaked. To everyone else, it looked like the glass had been floating through the air, as if carried by a ghost.

"Nice trick," Trip said, as Finn materialized again. "I especially like the part where I get a fresh pint."

"I thought you might," Finn said, smiling.

"What about their night vision gizmos?" Trip asked. Despite his constant beer swilling, the man was fulfilling his function by highlighting potential flaws in their strategy. "That twat Viktor Roth, long may he rot, was still able to see Elara, right?"

"Good question, but we have that covered too," Finn said, turning to Elara to expand upon his answer.

"Scraps analyzed the image-intensifier technology that Roth and the other special prefects had integrated into their visors, and came up with a way to counter it," Elara explained. "Finn and I are both wearing new base layers beneath our armor, which are coated in a material that Chiefy cooked up in the lab. It will hide us from their visors."

"How the hell does that work?" Trip asked.

The man had clearly slept through that part of the briefing and while Finn had not, it still took him a moment to dredge up his little robot's explanation for how the camouflage tech worked.

"I don't know exactly how it works, but Scraps said he developed a metamaterial that scatters the EM frequencies used in the prefect's night vision sensors, and also dissipates heat to minimize the temperature differential between our bodies and the surrounding air," Finn said, rattling off what Chiefy had told him, parrot fashion. "If it works, and I hope to God it works, we should be practically invisible."

"But we still can't use the ferry boat because that would be a dead giveaway," Elara added.

Trip laughed. "Sure, a boat just heading out to sea without a pilot might be a little suspicious." The man gulped down some ale then frowned. "So, if you can't use the ferry, how do you reach the ingress?"

Finn and Elara both also sucked in gulps, though of air rather than ale. This was a part of the plan that neither of them was looking forward too.

"We have to swim," Elara said.

Trip stopped drinking and drew the pint glass away from his mouth, leaving a covering of brown froth on his top lip, like a dirty mustache.

"But the water out there is freezing, you'd never survive," Trip said.

"Thanks for the vote of confidence," Finn said, and his body physically shivered at the prospect of diving into black water in the dead of night.

"The water is thirty-seven Fahrenheit, so yes, it's barely above freezing," Elara said, looking altogether too cool about the prospect of an icy swim. "But so long as we're fast, we'll make it."

Trip shrugged and looked unconvinced. "I've heard stories of Seahaven workers falling into the Davis Strait and dying within minutes. No offense to your plan, but I don't see how it's possible to swim two hundred meters out to the ingress and not be half dead by the time you get there."

"Believe me, I get it, but on this occasion, it was Chiefy who came through for us with a genius idea," Finn said. "We had him pore through the gene bank's archives, looking for anything that might help, and he struck gold with a cryoprotective agent."

Trip scratched his head. "That's a new one on me."

"It was news to us too," Elara said. She worked on the computer and put a product analysis of the cryoprotective agent onto a second screen. "Gene banks don't just source and sort workers' genetic material, they also conduct experimental research on new technologies to help the Authority make its workforce more efficient." She pointed to the chemical analysis of the agent on the screen, which was indecipherable to anyone other than an Authority-sector scientist, or a genius-level robot built from junk parts. "They developed this originally for the Volthaven workers who spend all their time out in solar fields in the most exposed areas of Zavetgrad. It allows them to withstand extremes of cold for extended periods, though don't ask me how."

"We've also got the Seahaven operatives to put together a sort of disaster package, which we can use to warm up once we reach the ingress," Finn added. "It's heated blankets, meds, that sort of thing. Enough to keep us warm and alive."

Trip exhaled and the man's lips vibrated together, producing a resonant sigh that implied he thought the idea was insane.

"Rather you than me, Chief, but I guess it could work," Trip said, shrugging again. It was hardly a vote of confidence, but nor was it an outright rejection.

"Once we're out of the water, thawed and dry again, Scraps will unlock the ingress point, using the DNA key we've built from Ivan Volkov's blood," Elara said, advancing her schematic to the next stage. "Assuming the rumors are true, and Ivan is a clone of his father, this should get us inside."

"That's a big if," Trip said, and Finn was beginning to regret asking the man's opinion. "I hope that gold valet is as trustworthy as you say he is, because this plan stands or falls based on what he's told us."

"I know that, but I do trust him," Finn said, sticking his neck out. "Hell knows I've been wrong in the past, but not about Pritchard. I'm sure of it."

Trip nodded and smiled but Finn could see the doubt behind the man's eyes, and despite what he'd just said, he harbored lingering concerns too. Juniper Jones had made him question his ability to judge a person's character, yet despite these fears, he chose to press on, because without the Regents, they were stuck.

"That's phase one in a nutshell," Elara said, advancing the computer program to the next step. If she had doubts too, she was hiding them well, Finn thought. "Thankfully, phase two will be a lot warmer, and involve less sneaking around."

Finn and Trip gathered around the screen as the computer rendered a detailed external schematic of the sub-oceanic compound, based on Pritchard's recollections of it from his year of training to become a Regent's servant. However, even Finn's former valet didn't know anything about the internal layout of the facility, beyond the purpose of each module, which meant that phase two would require them to make it up as they went along.

"The ingress shaft takes us to an airlock that leads into the servants' quarters, in this module," Elara said, continuing with the run-though of their plan. "Because of Pritchard, we know that the servants have all been there since childhood, so we should expect them to be loyal to the Regents, but that doesn't mean they're our enemy. So, in addition to our normal weapons, we'll take sub-guns loaded with tranq-rounds. If we come across anyone who is flesh and blood, we knock them out, but if they're made of metal, then either Scraps will hack them, or we destroy them."

This part of the plan had been Elara's idea and it had given Finn comfort to know that, despite her ability to be as ruthless and cold-blooded as any prosecutor in Zavetgrad's history, she was not a mindless killer. Despite whom they attended, the servants were innocent and didn't deserve to die.

"From the servant's module we move into the Offices of the Regents, which is the second module on the upper level of the compound," Elara continued. "Given that Zavetgrad is in crisis, we don't expect the Regents to be sitting at their desks like they might otherwise have been, so my guess is that this module will be empty."

Trip raised an eyebrow but didn't make a comment. It wasn't quite wishful thinking to believe that the office module would be abandoned and easy to pass through, but it was certainly erring on the side of optimism.

"Next, we enter *Elysium*..."

Elara let the word hang in the air, adding to the sense of mystique that already surrounded the regent's playground beneath the sea. Having spent time in the Authority sector, Finn had come to understand how golds enjoyed pampering themselves and indulging their every whim. He was prepared for Elysium to be debauched and even shocking, yet he couldn't help but worry about the true depths of the regents' depraved desires.

"We have no idea what we'll find in this cesspit, and since we can't plan for what we don't know, we'll just have to play this part by ear," Elara continued. "It's possible that Maxim Volkov and the other regents will be in Elysium, pampering themselves in the belief that they're safe, but we can't count on that fact."

"That means we may need to break into Volkov's villa pod, and take him by force," Finn added, and Elara nodded.

"Just Volkov, or are you planning to capture all the regents?" Trip asked. His pint was empty, and the man still looked thirsty.

"Volkov is the key," Elara said, without hesitation. "If we can snatch another one or two regents along the way, they'll be a bonus, but we have to take Volkov alive. His son won't surrender the Authority sector if we just threaten to execute Victor Kozlov or Theodore Westwood, because he won't give a shit about them. His father, however, ... that's different."

This part, Finn wasn't so sure about. He'd seen Ivan and Maxim together, and he'd hardly describe their relationship as close and loving, but it was just one of the many gambles they had to make. Elara was right that no other regent would have the same sway. Maxim Volkov was second only to the president, Gideon Alexander Reznikov. If anyone could force the Authority sector to surrender, it was him.

"Okay, so let's assume that by some miracle, you get in, fight your way through Elysium and manage to collar Maxim Volkov, then what?" Trip said. He was back over by the keg, refilling his pint glass. "How do you get out again?"

"That should be the easy bit," Elara said. The computer program had advanced to its final part and was showing a representation of one of the regents' villa pods, with a compact submersible vehicle docked to its side. "Once we have Volkov and anyone else we can lay our hands on, we commandeer an escape sub and let it navigate through the minefield, as it's programmed to do. The difference is that as soon as the sub pops its head above the surface, we'll have a small army of Metals there waiting to spirit us away to Metalhaven."

"But won't there also be small army of prefects?" Trip asked, froth again covering his top lip.

"Hopefully, fewer than would normally come, because of the reduced number of officers, but you're right that it's unlikely we'll get away without a fight," Finn admitted. "Hopefully, Scraps can hack the sub's nav system and surface us somewhere different to where the prefects are expecting, but either way, it's a sure bet they'll try to stop us."

"We'll have a truck standing by to take us back to Metalhaven," Elara added. "And it's not just any truck, either."

Finn frowned. "Why, what's special about it?"

"You'll see," Elara said, smiling. "It'll be a pleasant surprise."

Finn grumbled under his breath. He wasn't a fan of surprises, but he did trust Elara, and he was also already tired of discussing the plan. All he wanted to do was get going.

"By the time the prefects know what's happening, we'll be long gone." Elara continued, before shrugging. "Or, at least, that's the plan."

Trip raised an eyebrow again, though it seemed to be an involuntary reaction, then hid behind his pint. Finn wasn't sure whether it was his third or fourth, but Trip didn't appear any more drunk than usual.

"So, what do you think?" Elara asked.

"It sounds like you have it all covered," Trip replied, still hiding behind his glass. "Why does it have to be you two, though? Couldn't we smuggle the General and some of his soldiers into Seahaven, rather than risking the Hero and Iron Bitch of Metalhaven?"

"It has to be us," Elara said, switching off the computer. The screen went black, and their faces were all suddenly cast into shadow from the little moonlight that was managing to break through the dense clouds that had gathered over the city. "Riley's troops are fine soldiers, but they don't have the skills that Finn and I do. And they don't have our gear either."

Trip nodded. "I'd like to say I wish I was coming with you, but this time I don't. I can understand why no-one has ever broken into the sub-oceanic complex before. It sounds impossible."

"That's the reason no-one has ever tried before," Elara said, refusing to be dragged down by Trip's pessimism. "And that's the reason why this is going to work. Ivan Volkov may know what we're planning, but he'll be just a skeptical as you are. He won't believe we'll really try, and that's why this is going to succeed. We'll take the regents by surprise, and by the time the Authority sector learns what we've done, Maxim Volkov will be ours."

Suddenly, the main communications console booted up and an alarm blared from its speakers. Briggs and Xia sat bolt upright and scrambled out of their cot beds, wearing only the undergarments that went beneath their Metalhaven overalls. Xia jumped into the hot seat and silenced the alarm while

Briggs stood behind her, chin in his hand and a concerned look furrowing his brow.

"What is it?" Finn asked, abandoning their computer terminal, and hustling behind Xia and Briggs. Scraps and Chiefy had also been roused from their sleep-state and were making their way over too.

"Prefect skycars have been sighted coming this way," Briggs said. "It looks like they're coming in from the direction of Volthaven, headed for the north gate near Reclamation Yard seven. It's where we're most vulnerable."

"Then we have to get to Yard seven," Finn said, rushing to collect his laser cannon, but Elara grabbed his arm.

"No, wait, this is exactly what we need," Elara said. "This attack is a perfect distraction. If we leave now, we can get into Seahaven without arousing suspicion."

"But they need us," Finn said, unwilling to abandon Metalhaven in its hour of need.

"We can handle the prefects," Briggs said, and Xia nodded. "Elara is right, this is your best chance. I'll signal the Metals in Seahaven to get ready."

"Are you sure?" Finn asked. He was watching the formation of skycars approach, fast and low over the vast fields of solar panels that provided Zavetgrad with the bulk of its energy. "There could be hundreds of prefects in those skycars."

"And there are thousands of us," Briggs hit back. "Let the fuckers come. We can handle it."

Finn gritted his teeth then looked to Trip, who nodded his agreement. Scraps was already waiting on Elara's shoulder and Chiefy stood to her side. The only one who was hesitating was himself, but seeing the faces of the other

Metals, determined and ready in spite of the odds against them, his doubts vanished.

"Then we go," Finn said, snapping his laser cannon to its magnetic holster. "And we don't come back until we have Maxim Volkov in chains."

8

RIVER OF GOLD

Rebel operatives rushed into the office suite and took up their posts, stirred into action by the warning alarm that had sounded all across Metalhaven. Briggs immediately took charge and began to coordinate the flow of information between the command center of the Metals who were in command of the thirteen reclamation yards. Finn couldn't help but be impressed with how orderly it all was. If the Authority forces were expecting to face off against an unruly, disorganized mob, they were going to be in for a surprise, he thought.

"Briggs and I will stay here, but Xia will lead you to the sewer entrance," Trip said, as Finn and the others squeezed past the incoming traffic and moved into an adjacent room, where their gear had been stowed. "Then once you're in Seahaven, two Metals will meet you and guide you to the secure harbor. Make sure you remember the correct codeword, or I can't promise they won't try to slit your throats."

"Don't worry, we're ready," Finn said, collecting his

baseball bat and attaching it to his magnetic back-scabbard. His laser cannon was already secured on his hip.

Elara still had the black combat knife that General Riley had given her, but with her crossbow pistols long gone, she had chosen to take Tonya Duke's shotgun as a weapon. Finn frowned at the powerful firearm, as Elara slung it then fastened a bandolier of ammunition around her waist.

"Don't you think Dragonfire rounds might be a little conspicuous?" Finn asked, remembering how Inferno had lived up to her name during Elara's trial, by setting fire to half of Yard four.

"Don't worry, this is just buckshot," Elara said, helping to set Finn's mind at ease. She then picked up a sub machine gun and loaded a magazine of tranq rounds. "Don't forget these," she added, waving a spare magazine at Finn. "I'm more than happy to blast prefects and foremen, but the servants inside the sub-oceanic complex are as blameless as the workers in the city."

"I'm actually surprised you remembered," Finn replied, taking an equivalent weapon along with three magazines of stun rounds. "Restraint is hardly your strong suit, not that I'm complaining, of course."

"You have no idea how restrained I've had to be during all the years I've been The Shadow," Elara said, checking and tightening all her straps. "But this isn't restraint, it's basic humanity. If we lose that, we're no better than the golds."

"Must go...," said Xia as the building shook from rocket strikes that were already landing in yard four. "Skycars close..."

Finn nodded then he and Elara headed for the door, with

Chiefy stomping behind them. Scraps was perched on the bigger robot's shoulder.

"Speaking of things that aren't exactly inconspicuous, what about him?" Trip said, rapping his knuckles on Chiefy's powerful metal arm. "You two might have stealth fields, but the Seahaven prefects are sure going to notice a seven-foot robot stomping around."

"I can be stealthy too," Chiefy said, turning his head toward Trip and smiling. Like Finn, the former Metalhaven worker looked uncomfortable standing so close to a machine that would normally have bossed him around. "Please allow me to demonstrate," Chiefy added in a perfectly amiable tone of voice.

A compartment in Chiefy's chest popped open then Scraps clambered inside and shut the hatch. An observation slit like a peephole in a cell door allowed the smaller of the two robots to keep watch. Then Chiefy was enveloped in a shimmering haze of light before disappearing from view.

"Impressive," Trip said, as Chiefy deactivated his stealth field and rematerialized. "You've thought of everything."

"I hope so," Finn said.

Xia was already at the bank of elevators, holding the door open. She didn't speak but the anxious look on her surgically reconstructed face made it obvious she was keen to hurry them along.

The elevator ride seemed to take hours, and each time the walls of the car shook from a nearby explosion, Finn worried that the next rocket might hit the gene bank and trap them inside. Finally, they reached the ground floor, and everyone piled outside onto the street, only to be met by a cacophony of gunfire and concussive blasts that were near deafening outside the protective cocoon of the elevator car.

Squadrons of prefect skycars buzzed above the sector, but for each of the attacking craft that swooped in to deploy their deadly ordnance, a dozen laser blasts chased them, sweeping an anarchic pattern of red lines across the sky. One of the AA guns lashed its powerful energy stream across the belly of a skycar, slicing it open like gutting a fish. The skycar crackled and sparked before its rotors stopped spinning and it crashed headlong into a junkpile, adding to the mass of ruined metal that already filled Yard four.

Then another skycar broke formation and attacked, swooping beneath a cascade of red light, and launching its missiles. Finn's heart leapt into his mouth as he realized they were directly in the line of fire.

"Take cover!" he yelled, running and diving behind a prefect guard post. The missiles slammed into the base of the gene bank, carving out chunks of brick and stone that made it look like a giant beast had taken a bite out of the building. A cloud of dust swept over Finn, and he ducked and covered, but still the grit managed to work its way into his eyes and mouth, and he could taste the metallic flavor on his tongue.

"Is everyone okay?" Elara called out, scrambling to her feet, the crook of her elbow pressed over her mouth.

"Okay," Xia said, face blackened by smoke and dirt.

"Chiefy and Scraps are okay," the modified foreman said. It was standing in the middle of the dissipating dust cloud, unaffected by its stifling acridity.

"Ah, fuck…"

The last comment was made by Trip, and unlike the others, he hadn't yet gotten to his feet. Finn ran to the man and checked him over, finding a shard of shrapnel impaled into Trip's back, below the right shoulder.

"Chiefy, I need you!" Finn called out, and the robot stomped over without delay. "Trip's hurt. Check him out."

Chiefy knelt beside Trip and began to examine the wound, assisted by Scraps, who had a more sophisticated array of scanning tools.

"It's bad, isn't it?" Trip said, wincing. "Just tell me straight, metalhead. Am I going to die?"

"Yes," Chiefy said, cheerfully, and Trip's face blanched of all its blood. "But not for another forty or fifty years, longer if you drink less ale."

"What?" Trip snorted.

"All humans eventually die," Chiefy said, clarifying his statement. "But this wound poses no immediate risk of mortality."

Chiefy removed the piece of shrapnel from the man's side, causing him to hiss dramatically, before cleaning and covering the wound with a dressing that Finn considered unimpressively small, considering the fuss Trip had been making.

"So, I'm okay?" Trip said, still unsure.

"Nothing a few pints won't fix," Chiefy replied. The robot smiled at his own joke, though its metal expression looked a little too manic for Finn's liking.

"Looks like you'll live to fight another day," Finn said, helping Trip to his feet.

More rockets slammed into the ground, but the aerial assault was faltering as skycars continued to be lashed out of the sky by intense barrages of laser fire.

"Quickly..." Xia said, waving them on.

"Go on, I'll stay here and do what I can," Trip said, drawing his side-arm.

"I admire your spirit, but I don't think that will do much against prefect armor," Finn said, looking at the weapon in Trip's hand.

Just then, a foreman stomped toward them, and Finn almost blasted the machine in the chest before he spotted the chrome stripe across its forehead that marked the robot as a friendly. It was carrying a modified laser cutter in each hand, firing from the hip at a skycar that was trying to land in Yard four and deploy its troops. The Authority vessel was hit multiple times and exploded like a bomb, scattering wreckage and body parts far and wide.

"I think you might have a point," Trip conceded, frowning at his weapon, which was pitiful in comparison to the laser ordnance the robot had just unleashed. "I'll help coordinate from inside the gene bank."

"Hurry!" Xia called out, becoming more insistent by the second.

Trip ran back inside the gene bank, chased every step of the way by gunfire from another skycar that was also attempting to land in yard four. Finn rejoined Elara and Xia, but rather than leading them away from the Authority forces that were setting down, Xia looked dead set on heading straight toward them.

"Quickest this way," Xia said, struggling to form the words because of her wired jaw. "Must go through yard." She unslung a rifle and began stalking toward the skycar that had now landed and was offloading it prefects.

"That suits me just fine," Finn said, detaching his laser

cannon from its holster. "I was never one to back down from a fight."

"Our fight is elsewhere," Elara said, shotgun already in hand. "But if we can take out a few of these bastards enroute, then I'm game too."

Finn followed Xia's lead, having to move fast in order to keep pace with her. She may not have worn the uniform of a Haven soldier, but Xia was every bit as skilled and tenacious as one of General's Riley's crack personal unit.

Up ahead, the prefects had disembarked and were forming up into squads, ready to move on the gene bank, but the armor-clad officers hadn't seen Xia and the others coming, and their assault took the Authority troops completely by surprise. As a Metalhaven native, Finn was able to use the terrain to his advantage, but he wasn't interested in stealth. That would come later. Now was the time for shock and awe.

Standing atop a junkpile with Elara by his side, Finn's unique prosecutor armor caught the light of hundreds of laser blasts, causing it to shimmer like molten rock and give him the appearance of a demon. The prefects cried out in alarm and tried to regroup but Finn already had them locked in his sights, and he rained down cannon fire like a one-man army. Elara's shotgun boomed almost non-stop as they stormed toward the Authority soldiers, mowing them down at the same time as shrugging off incoming fire, which rebounded off their armored bodies like sunlight off a mirror.

Xia and Chiefy followed in their wake, stepping over the dead and dying and advancing toward another squad of prefects that had managed to crash land their skycar on the northern edge of Yard four. Xia and Chiefy stayed back, picking off targets with precisely aimed shots, while Finn and Elara focused on the main body of troops, who were led by a supervisor, a senior officer who would one day assume the title of Head Prefect.

Drawing his baseball bat from its back scabbard, Finn accelerated into a charge, dodging and weaving a path toward the prefects, while Elara laid down a blanket of covering fire that left the squad panicked and in disarray. The troops re-routed but the supervisor held his ground, firing at Finn while yelling, "For Zavetgrad!" at the top of his lungs. Bullets thudded into Finn's body, but his armor held fast. Then the supervisor's weapon clicked empty, and the officer's eyes grew wide, but the man's terror was short lived, as Finn cut him down with a savage blow to the face which pancaked the supervisor's genetically perfect nose flat.

"Clear," Elara called out, choosing to save her ammo instead of firing at prefects who were fleeing.

"Here!" Xia mumbled, hauling sheets of rusted metal and lumps of broken machinery away from a section of wall at the edge of the yard.

Chiefy went to help and thanks to the robot's mechanical might, the debris was quickly cleared away, revealing the bare ground beneath the junkpile for the first time in what was probably decades. At first Finn didn't see anything, until Xia brushed away the dirt and mud to reveal a heavily tarnished metal cover concealing an entrance into the disused sewer system. Chiefy forced his fingers around the handle, which was caked in thick mud, then lifted the solid iron cover, and set it down beside Xia with a weighty thump.

"This is the entrance?" Finn asked, and Xia nodded. He looked into the opening, though all he could see was an inky blackness, like he was looking into oblivion itself. "I was hoping for something a little less claustrophobic."

Xia raised an eyebrow but didn't pass comment, then the sound of gunfire closing in on them made the decision for him, and Finn eased himself into the opening, carefully feeling for each rung of the ladder, which were slippery with ice that had formed a century earlier. Inching himself deeper, Finn distracted himself from the prospect of falling to his death by watching the carnage that continued to unfold throughout Metalhaven. Prefect skycars were still buzzing around the sector, some trying to land on rooftops and others strafing the defending Metals and workers with a combination of machinegun fire and rockets, but for every attack there was a counterattack. Laser blasts lit up the sky, tearing holes into the attacking craft and forcing others to withdraw, while the few prefects that had managed to set foot on the rooftops of tenement buildings and recovery centers were met with a mob of chromes. The workers drove the prefects back with improvised weapons then hurled the petrified officers over the sides of the building to their deaths on the frozen streets below.

We're doing it... Finn thought, as he realized that Metalhaven wasn't merely surviving the attack, but resoundingly winning it. *They still believe...*

Elara climbed down after him, then darkness enveloped the shaft, as Chiefy climbed onto the ladder and dragged the iron manhole cover back into place, sealing them in. The robot's floodlights suddenly switched on, temporarily blinding Finn, and forcing him to squeeze his eyes shut. When his head had stopped pounding and his vision had cleared, he looked down and was just about able to make out the bottom of the shaft.

"This is deeper that I thought," Finn said, resuming his careful descent. "These tunnels must have been here since the time Zavetgrad was first founded."

"They have," Chiefy said, his huge metal feet clanking against the rungs like a hammer striking an anvil. "This was the main sewer that carried effluent from the Authority sector out to sea."

Finn snorted a laugh. "That's great. I hope no-one flushes while we're down here."

"Don't worry, it's disused," Elara said. She stopped and looked up at Chiefy. "It is disused right? Because I'm not wading through solid-gold shit for anyone or anything."

"This sewer has not been used for at least one hundred years," Chiefy said, and Elara breathed a sigh of relief, as did Finn. "There is nothing down here, apart perhaps from radioactive mutant rats." Finn stopped climbing, suddenly frozen with fear. Then he saw the robot's mechanical features smiling down at him. "That was a joke. How did I do?"

"Hilarious," Finn said, sarcastically.

"How about you stick to fixing and building things?" Elara added, less charitably.

"As you wish," Chiefy answered, cheerful as ever.

By the time Finn reached the bottom of the shaft, his fingers were throbbing with pain. He stepped away from the ladder to allow Elara to climb down next, shaking his hands in an effort to pump some blood and life back into them.

"How far until we reach Seahaven?" Finn said, peering into the darkness, but he could barely see more than ten meters ahead.

"It should take thirty minutes at a brisk pace," Chiefy replied, dropping down into the sewer with a heavy thump that reverberated along the ancient tunnel with a ghostly resonance. "This is a direct route."

Finn nodded then dusted down his hands and sucked in a breath of the stale air, which made him retch and gag like he'd taken a bite of rotten algae bread. The smell was like nothing he'd experienced before, a heady mixture of musty, earthy odors from mold and mildew, combined with the sulphurous, foul stench of bog water and putrefied sewage.

"I vote that we make it a very brisk pace," Finn said, covering his mouth with his arm.

"At least this proves that golds are no different to us workers," Elara said, fighting ahead, though her eyes were watering. "Their shit stinks the same as ours."

Chiefy laughed. "Good one!" the robot said, patting Elara on the shoulder. The machine's chipper mood could not be dulled by the smell since the robot didn't have a nose. "Follow me, I know the way!"

Chiefy's long stride and relentless robotic pace meant that they covered the distance to Seahaven in twenty minutes flat. Reaching the foot of another tall ladder, Finn risked taking a deeper breath to recover from the brisk walk, and was pleased to discover that the smell was less vile. Then he heard something, like the sound of wind whistling under the door to his old Metalhaven apartment, and he closed his eyes and concentrated on the sound.

"It's the sea," Elara said, grabbing a rung of the ladder and preparing to climb. "We're close to the Davis Strait."

"I've never heard the sea before," Finn said, now able to

pick out the ebbs and flows of the tide, as it pushed water back and forth, in an endless cycle. "It's peaceful."

"What it is, is freezing cold," Elara said, beginning her climb. "Trust me, if we survive this crazy mission, you'll never want to see it again."

Finn followed after Elara, but the climb was shorter than their plunging descent had been, and before long they had reached the top. Elara removed her knife and hammered three times on the metal cover, as she had been instructed to do by Trip and Briggs, then waited. No-one answered.

"Try again," Finn whispered, and Elara knocked three more times, but still there was no reply. "Maybe we're early?" he suggested.

"Perhaps, but we can't just hang around here," Elara said, sheathing her blade. "Give me a hand with this."

Finn climbed the ladder and squeezed in beside Elara, bracing his back against the shaft, and placing both hands onto the cover. He counted to three and they both pushed, but even with their combined strength, the iron lid barely moved. Eventually, their efforts heaved the slab back far enough for Elara and Finn to climb out, and emerge inside what appeared to be the alleyway behind a tenement block.

"We should activate our stealth fields," Elara said, before vanishing and becoming little more than a shimmering blur.

Finn cloaked too then they both waited as Chiefy hauled his sizable metal frame out of the shaft and replaced the cover while barely making a sound. The robot then stood bolt upright and his head turned on a swivel.

"Someone is approaching from the southeast," Chiefy said. "Two contacts, moving fast."

"Cloak yourself and take cover," Finn said. Chiefy nodded, then vanished.

"Stay here, I'll try to get behind them," Elara said.

Finn nodded, even though Elara couldn't see him, then drew his knife and waited. He looked for footprints in the snow that might have revealed where Elara had gone, but his partner had covered her tracks and slipped away without a trace. Then he heard muffled footsteps and muted voices coming from the alley, and he pressed his back to the wall, knife held ready.

"Where are they?" a voice said. It was a woman, and she sounded young.

"Maybe we're in the wrong place?" a second woman replied.

Finn glanced around the corner and spotted the two workers. In addition to their Seahaven blue overalls and thick coats with a waxy, water-repellant covering, they were wearing anxious expressions.

"The Metalhaven contact said they should already be here," the first woman added. "They shouldn't be hard to spot. They have the most famous faces in Zavetgrad!"

"It might be the last face you see..."

Elara deactivated her stealth field and materialized behind the first woman; knife held to her throat. Finn decloaked and stepped out, laser aimed at the second woman, who had been reaching for a blade until she'd found herself staring down the barrel of his cannon.

"Haven..." Elara said, whispering the first part of the secret code word.

"...is our future," the woman replied, managing to stay

cool, despite the combat knife that was pressed against her carotid artery.

"You took your time," Elara said, casually sheathing her knife.

"The patrols are heavy tonight," the woman said, massaging her neck. Elara had drawn blood. "I'm Kira, and that's Shauna," she added, indicating to her companion with a trembling hand. "We'll take you to the secure harbor."

"Thank you," Finn said, lowering his weapon. "I'm Finn and that's Elara."

Both Seahaven women looked at each other and laughed. "We know who you are," Kira said, teasing Finn, but not in an unkind way. "Everyone knows the Hero and the Iron Bitch of Metalhaven, even us sea folk."

9

SEAHAVEN BLUES

The two Seahaven Metals, Kira and Shauna, guided Finn and the others through the backstreets of the coastal sector. Finn and Elara kept their stealth fields deactivated in order to conserve power, and instead relied on Scraps' ability to hide them from the Authority's prying electronic eyes in the sky.

No-one said a word, with the exception of Kira, who occasionally whispered directions or spoke in hushed tones to warn Finn and the others of a prefect patrol that was close by. Finn didn't mind the quiet because it allowed him time to reflect, and also to take in his new surroundings. He'd never been to Seahaven and what he'd seen of the sector from the air during his escape from Zavetgrad hadn't been much. On the ground, however, it was starkly different to Metalhaven, and had he not already known it was part of Zavetgrad, he might have believed they were in a different city entirely.

The tenement blocks were squat and wide, and somehow even uglier than the buildings Finn had lived in, their walls tarnished and weathered from the constant battering of salty sea air and spray from the Davis Strait. Even the recovery centers and wellness centers were unique, both built from a local stone that was heavy enough to withstand the near constant rain and frequent storms that Seahaven was subjected to. Most buildings were at most three storeys tall, but the sector was spread out across the sweeping, rocky coastline, which meant there was no need to expand upwards. There was already plenty of space for everything that the sector needed and more.

Finn stole past one of the recovery centers, which was closed due to it already being past curfew in the sector, but he wished he could have walked through the door and ordered a pint. The stone walls and small windows, lit by a flickering orange fire, made the place look cozy and welcoming, far more so than the sterile recovery centers in Metalhaven, which were slab-like and crude in comparison. Even the gene banks and prefect hubs had a quaint, rustic charm about them, and in finer weather, with the sun shining, Finn imagined that Seahaven would even put the Authority sector, with its gaudy golden streets and ostentatious architecture, to shame.

"Wait-wait!" Scraps' warning made everyone stop and take cover against the wall of a wellness center. The robot was still hidden inside Chiefy's chest compartment, though the peep hole was open, allowing the machine to look out with his eyes, as well as his sensors. "Prefect patrol coming!"

Kira glanced around the corner then her neck snapped back as if she'd been kicked in the face, and she hurriedly backed away. "Shit, it's two prefects and two foremen," she whispered, her hand reaching for a knife hidden in the pocket of her waxy overalls. "They're not on an assigned patrol route, at least not one we knew of."

"Did they spot you?" Elara whispered, and Kira shook her head, though she appeared uncertain.

Finn held his cannon ready, while also watching Scraps through the little viewing slot in Chiefy's chest in case the robot sounded another warning that would compel him to act.

"Unauthorized movement detected," came the voice of one of the foreman robots, which echoed off the stone walls and reached Finn's ears clearly, as if the machine was within spitting distance of him. "Direction, seventeen meters southwest of our location."

"What kind of movement, you dumb machine?" one of the prefects replied. "Because it's too fucking cold and too fucking late into our shift to go chasing after rats."

"The signal is too large to be rats," the foreman answered, its logic processor taking no offense at the prefect's sniping reply. Finn thought it sounded like an old gen-three model, which would make it slower and easier to handle than the newer machines. "I estimate an eighty-percent chance that it is curfew breakers."

"Fucking rebels more like," the second prefect said. Finn heard the metallic clicks of weapon safeties being snapped off. "How many are we looking at?"

The heavy thud of robot feet stomped closer. Finn slid his finger onto the trigger of his cannon then looked at Elara, who had her shotgun ready, but her eyes told him to wait.

"There are two distinct contacts," the foreman replied. "A biomechanical analysis suggests they are females."

"Shall we call for backup?" the first prefect asked, but his partner snorted with derision.

"Backup, for a couple of women?" the officer scoffed,

displaying the sort of macho pride that Seahaven prefects were famous for. It was the only sector where no women served as officers. "Can you imagine the shit we'd get from the men, if we called in backup to deal with a couple of girls? They'd laugh us out of the prefect hub, you pussy!"

"Fine, then send the two foremen in first," the other officer replied, sounding offended and embarrassed. "If these blue bitches have claws, let them scratch at metal eyes first, rather than ours."

"Such tough guys…" Finn whispered, and he considered switching his laser cannon for his baseball bat to make things more up-close and personal.

"Pretend to surrender," Elara whispered to Kira and Shauna, who both looked like they were ready to charge out and fight, despite their knives standing no chance against seven-foot-tall, armored robots. "We'll get behind the prefects and take them out, quietly."

The two Metals nodded and hid their blades, before walking out into the street with their hands held in the air.

"Stop right there!" the foremost of the two robots demanded. "You are out after curfew and under arrest!"

"Ready?" Elara whispered to Finn. She'd replaced her shotgun with a knife. "We take out the prefects first, then hope Scraps can shut down the foremen and save us having to fight them too."

Finn nodded then turned to Chiefy. "Cloak and stay close to Kira and Shauna. If this goes sideways, you'll need to protect them."

"Understood," Chiefy said, with unflappable robotic cool.

Finn smiled at Scraps through his peep hole window.

"You'd better seal yourself up tight, pal, we don't want you catching a stray bullet," he said, tapping the metal door on the compartment his robot buddy was hidden inside. "But hack the foremen and shut them down if you can. If we're forced to fight them, we risk alerting the entire sector."

"Okay-kay..." Scraps said, saluting. "Scraps try but firewall strong!"

"I know you'll do your best," Finn said.

Scraps nodded then the peep-hole door was slammed shut, and Chiefy activated his stealth field and slipped away, ready to provide back-up for Shauna and Kira.

With his own stealth field activated, Finn followed Elara, placing his feet exactly inside her footprints to hide his trail, until they'd circled around the prefect patrol and were stalking up behind the two officers, who were oblivious to their approach. The prefects had Shauna and Kira on their knees in the snow with their hands pressed to the backs of their heads, while the foreman stood watch behind them. Each machine was armed only with their robotic fists, though these alone could shatter brick with a single punch.

"Did you think you could get away with being out after curfew?" one of the prefects said. Finn recognized the voice as belonging to the first of the two officers who had spoken. "We can smell your fishy stink a mile away, blue bitch!"

The two officers laughed, one jostling the other with his shoulder. The first prefect, who appeared the more natural leader of the two, then aimed his rifle at Kira's head.

"Are you one of the rebels?" the man said, his tone suddenly darker. "Because I'm thinking that's why you're out after curfew."

"Thinking isn't exactly your strong suit, is it?" Kira replied, with a smirk.

Finn admired the woman's ballsy comeback, which was the sort of backchat he would have given the prefect in her place, and it got Kira the exact same response. The back of the prefect's hand flew and struck her clean across the side of her face, hard enough to knock her sideways. She recovered quickly and spat blood into the snow before staring into the officer's eyes with a look of raw hatred.

"Speak out of turn again, and I'll have the robot hold you down while I teach you some manners," the prefect snarled, in a sinister tone that turned Finn's stomach. The officer removed his faux-leather glove then grabbed Kira's chin and forced the woman to look at him. "I'll make your bitch friend watch before screwing her too."

"You won't do shit," Kira said, pulling her head away from the prefect. She spat on his boots, and the officer's hand tightened into a fist. "Do you want to know why?"

"Why?" the prefect said, removing his belt and coiling it around his hand.

"Because in a few seconds, you'll be dead…"

Elara decloaked behind the prefect and slit the man's throat. The officer grabbed his neck, eyes wide with surprise, but the cut was deep, and blood gushed from the wound, spraying the prefect's partner.

"What the fuck?!" the second man cried, gawking at the blood like it was venom.

The officer raised his nightstick to strike Elara, and Finn made his move, pulling the man into a choke hold, and squeezing with such force that he heard the prefect's windpipe collapse with a guttural crunch. Tossing the man to the ground, he drew his laser cannon and aimed it at the closest of the two foremen, but the robots had seized Shauna and Kira, and were using the women as human shields.

"Halt!" the lead foreman shouted, lifting Kira high so that only the tips of the woman's toes remained on the ground. "You are Finn Brasa and Elara Cage, wanted traitors. You are under arrest!"

"Scraps, any time now!" Finn called out, but there was no response and Chiefy remained cloaked.

"I cannot contact the prefect hub," the second foreman said, striking the side of its head with its hand, in an effort to unscramble it circuits. "I am being jammed. Source, unknown."

"Not unknown..." Chiefy de-cloaked behind the lead foreman and punched his fist through the back of the robot's head, before yanking out its FLP, along with a cluster of wires and associated circuits boards. "I am jamming your signal."

The second foreman dropped Shauna like a hot coal then grabbed Chiefy's shoulders and smashed the robot against the wellness center. If it had been a Metalhaven building, the two machines would have gone crashing through the wall, but it took more than two warring robots to shatter Seahaven's heavy stone blocks.

"I can't get a shot!" Finn said. "Scraps, you'll have to shut it down!"

Finn tracked the two machines with his laser cannon as they engaged in their brutal mechanical tug-of-war, but he couldn't risk hitting Chiefy instead of the foreman. The two robots continued to brawl, each taking turns to slam the other against the stone walls of nearby buildings, like a wayward ground car bouncing off crash barriers as it careered out of control.

Finn moved closer, trying to minimize the chance of friendly fire, then the robots whirled past him like a tornado, knocking him off his feet. Elara stood in their path, shotgun aimed, but before she could squeeze the trigger, Chiefy finally broke the warring foreman's hold, before grabbing his opponent's head and squeezing like a pneumatic press. The screech of contorted metal made Finn wince, like someone raking their fingernails across tank armor, then the robot's circuits were crushed, and it collapsed in a heap on top of the two dead prefects.

"It's a wonder the whole of Seahaven didn't hear that," Finn said, helping Shauna and Kira to their feet. "Scraps, did you manage to block all the outgoing transmissions?"

"Yes-yes!" Scraps said, peeking through his peep hole. The robot then looked down and his little voice trembled. "Scraps sorry about hack. Firewall too strong!"

"You'll get it, pal, don't worry," Finn said, rapping his knuckles on the compartment where Scraps was hiding. The door was dented and scraped but Chiefy had escaped the battle with the robot-equivalent of a few cuts and bruises. "And good work, Chiefy. You're a hell of a fighter."

"Thank you, though I would rather not do that again," Chiefy answered. "Had that foreman been a Gen-Six or higher, I may not have been so fortunate."

Finn nodded then looked at the pile of bodies on the ground, a mixture of broken flesh and metal, and he realized that despite their close call, fortune had favored them. They were still alive and, more importantly, they remained undiscovered.

"It won't be long before these prefects are missed," Kira said, as she and Shauna started dragging the bodies off the street and behind a row of trash containers that had been pushed up behind the wellness center. "And when they don't check in, every off-duty prefect in the sector will be called up to sweep the streets."

"Scraps, is there anything you can do?" Finn asked, while helping to drag the second dead prefect into concealment.

Scraps thought for a moment, then the compartment door in Chiefy's chest popped open and the robot flew out.

"Can't hack foreman but can hack C.O.N.F.I.R.M.E.," Scraps said, interfacing with the police computer on one of the prefect's wrists. "Scraps have recording of bad-man voice. Make fake response."

"Good thinking, pal," Finn said, figuring that Scraps' idea would at least buy them enough time to infiltrate the sub-oceanic complex, after which it didn't matter if the officers were discovered.

"We're running behind schedule," Kira said, using her hands to shovel snow over the bodies to hide them. "We need to reach boathouse four-nine to collect your equipment before you move on to the secure harbor."

"We're right behind you," Finn said, closing the compartment door behind Scraps after the robot returned to his cubby. "Let's hope we don't run into any more patrols."

The group hustled across the cobblestoned streets, using the dark alleys and thick, obscuring walls of the squat Seahaven buildings to weave a path toward boathouse four-nine. This was where the lifesaving equipment that would protect them during and after their icy swim to the ingress point was stashed, and they couldn't proceed without it.

Despite Finn's wishful thinking, they still had to stop and hide from three more prefect patrols on the way, but thanks to Scraps' electronic subterfuge, they weren't discovered, and finally the boathouse came into view ahead.

The sky had darkened in the time it had taken the party to traverse Seahaven from west to east, and the weather had turned for the worse too. Squally winds whipped through the streets and inside Finn's armor, saturating his prosecutor base layer with ice cold water, while powerful waves smashed into the harbor, lashing them with salt-water spray that stung his face like molten splinters of metal. Finn welcomed the shelter of the boathouse when he arrived, but he knew that his reprieve from the storm would only be temporary, because the next stage of their mission involved a potentially deadly swim out to sea.

"Your bag is just in here," Shauna said, squeezing water from her hair. "We hid it underneath the floor…"

Shauna's voice trailed off and Finn walked into the boathouse to find that the floor had already been pulled up and their bag was sitting out in the open. Two prefects and two foremen stood over the treasure, as surprised to discover Finn and the others in the boathouse as he was to see them. For a second, no-one moved, as if shock had short-circuited their brains, human and electronic alike, then the prefects reached for their weapons, and Finn was jolted into action.

Snapshooting with his laser cannon, he blasted the head of the closest foreman while Kira and Shauna dove at the prefects and wrestled them to the ground. Elara unloaded her shotgun at the second foreman, but the buckshot rattled off its armored shell and scattered like hailstones off a window. Stomping toward her, the machine swept Elara aside with its hefty forearm, sending her crashing into a stack of crates, which collapsed under the mass of her prosecutor armor. Finn aimed and fired two short bursts, drilling a hole in the back of the robot's head, and destroying its FLP, before turning his cannon onto the prefects. Shauna was on the ground, dazed and bleeding from a cut to her head, but the prefect she'd fought was dead, a knife plunged into the man's eye socket all the way to the hilt. Kira had less been less successful. The prefect had disarmed her, and the woman had been placed into a choke hold, with a pistol held to her head.

"Stay back or she dies!" the prefect yelled, his eyes wide and wild. The man's hand was trembling, and his finger was on the trigger, adding pressure.

"Think this through, fucker!" Finn said, keeping his laser trained on the man, but the prefect was using Kira as a shield, just as the foremen had done earlier. "There are four of us, and only one of you. You can't win."

"Five!" came a little voice from inside Chiefy's chest.

"Five of us, and one of you," Finn said, correcting himself for Scraps' sake, though he hardly felt it necessary. "And we're jamming your comms, so you can't call for help."

"They'll still come looking!" the prefect shouted, as Elara got to her feet and stalked closer. "Soon the whole prefect division will be out looking for you!"

Kira struggled in the man's grasp and the prefect tightened his stranglehold on her, while adding even more pressure to the trigger of his pistol. Finn stopped dead and Elara did too, knowing how close the woman was to being shot.

"Kill her, and you're next," Elara said, switching the hold

on her knife, ready to throw it. "The only way you walk out of here is by letting her go."

"Do you think I'm stupid?" The prefect laughed, bitterly. "I know who you are, and I know you won't risk this bitch's life. Now drop your weapons!"

Suddenly, Kira bit the prefect's hand in an effort to free herself, but the officer's cry of pain was drowned out by a single gunshot. When the report of the weapon had faded, someone was still screaming, but it was Shauna, not the officer who had just shot her friend and partner dead. Elara released her blade and it thumped into the prefect's neck like a harpoon. The officer fell, but Elara wasn't finished. She cried out in anger and frustration, then dropped on top of the officer and drove the knife deeper into the man's flesh, while glaring into the officer's eyes until the light behind them had bled away. A dread silence followed, then the prefect's C.O.N.F.I.R.M.E. device crackled, and a message came through, loud and clear.

"SH-776 respond... SH-776, we have reports of gunfire at your location. Check in, over..."

"Scraps, can you reply?" Finn said, turning to his buddy, but Shauna spoke up first.

"There's no time, you have to go!" Shauna said, picking up the bag and shoving it into Elara's hands. "Even if you do answer, they'll still send a squad. They're probably already on the way."

"But what about the bodies?" Finn said, glancing at Kira then having to turn away. Her wound was too gruesome to look at.

"I'll stay and surrender," Shauna said, picking up the prefect's pistol then replacing the false floor where the bag had been hidden and covering it over with dirt. "I'll say I did this. Then they won't be looking for anyone else."

"But they'll send you to trial, or just straight-up execute you for being a Haven operative," Finn said.

"There's no time to debate this, you have to go, now!" Shauna said. She knelt beside her friend, a hand resting on her back. "This is the only way."

Finn looked to Elara but the cold green eyes staring back at him belonged to The Shadow. She nodded and Finn forced down a dry, hard swallow.

"Just make this count, okay?" Shauna said. Already, Finn could hear the scuffle and thud of footsteps coming their way. "Make sure it's not for nothing. Metal and Blood."

"Metal and Blood," Finn repeated, and so did Elara.

They activated their stealth fields and vanished, before slipping out into the stormy night. Finn stopped and turned back, seeing a dozen prefects barge into the boathouse, weapons raised and barking orders at Shauna, her hands already held up in surrender. It felt cowardly to run and he hated himself for doing it, but he hated more that he knew it was the right decision. Shauna and Kira had given their lives for the chance that others could live free. There was no greater sacrifice. The obligation was now on him and Elara to make sure they hadn't died for nothing.

10
CAT AND MOUSE

Finn crouched beside the electrified fence that surrounded the secure harbor area. On the other side of the fence, guarded by special prefects and foremen, was the ferry that linked Seahaven to the ingress point, and the only way inside the sub-oceanic villa complex that was home to Zavetgrad's regents. Elara arrived next, followed by Chiefy, who was somehow able to move while barely making a sound, despite his lumbering metal frame.

"It looks like we got out just in time," Elara said, looking back toward the boathouse where Shauna had surrendered to the Authority. "I count at least twenty prefects now, just to arrest a single woman."

"They're looking for us," Finn said, checking that his stealth field was still actively concealing him from sight. "Or, at least, they're looking for Shauna's accomplices. There wouldn't be that many prefects if the Authority believed that she and Kira were acting alone."

"Let them search, they won't find us now," Elara said, dismissively. "By the time Shauna talks, we'll be long gone."

"Do you think she'll give us up?" Finn said, suddenly worried that the small army of prefects would start running in their direction.

"She won't want to, but she'll crack in the end, especially if the special prefecture gets their hands on her," Elara replied.

Elara's comment could have been construed as a criticism of Shauna's resilience and commitment to the cause, but there was no judgement implied in her analysis. She was simply stating the facts as she saw them. As someone who'd had first-hand experience of a special prefect torture cell, Elara knew better than anyone the lengths that the Authority's secret police would go to in order to extract information.

"You didn't give in; maybe she can tough it out too," Finn said, unwilling to write Shauna off so easily.

"I told them truths mixed with lies, and that was enough to keep Commissar Jones guessing," Elara said. *The truth mixed with lies...* Finn remembered. This had been the advice his former mentor had given him to confound the Authority's loyalty tests. "But the difference between me and Shauna is that I knew I was dead no matter what I told them. They'll feed her hope; hope that the pain will end and that she'll be allowed to live. It will be that hope that breaks her."

"It's not right that we're leaving her," Finn said, angry and ashamed about running out on the Haven operative. "She's sacrificing herself for us."

"She knew what she was getting into," Elara replied, countering Finn's emotional outburst with ice cold logic. "We can't save her, but if we do this right, we can save the tens of thousands of other blues in this sector. Focus on them, because like it or not, Shauna is already dead."

Finn turned away from the hustle and bustle outside the

boathouse and tore open the holdall they'd recovered, taking out his frustrations on the fabric instead of the prefects. Inside was the equipment they needed to survive the deadly two-hundred-meter swim from the secure harbor to the ingress point, but the only object he recognized was a wire cutter.

"Buddy, what the hell are we looking at here?" Finn said.

Removing the wire cutters and setting them aside, Finn sifted through the remaining contents of the holdall, finding four vacuum-packed bags that could have contained anything, and a box of medical syringes. Two syringes contained a pastel blue liquid, while the other two were filled with a milky white substance.

"Cryoprotective agent first," Scraps said, the little robot's voice coming from seemingly out of nowhere. "White syringe. Inject into neck. Help fight cold."

Finn nodded then removed one of the two syringes. "You do me, and I'll do you," he said, pointing his syringe at Elara like a gun. "We'll have to decloak first."

Elara hesitated then dropped her stealth field and tentatively leaned toward him, pulling her hair back so that Finn could reach his target.

"If this hurts, I promise that yours will hurt more," Elara said, and Finn knew that it was no idle threat.

"Not there!" Scraps called out, and Finn jerked the needle away, hand shaking. The robot projected a narrow beam of light below Elara's right ear, where her jaw met her neck. "There!"

"Thanks, pal," Finn said, swallowing hard then adjusting his aim accordingly. He drew in a deep breath then inserted the needle and pressed the plunger. Elara winced and he heard her suck in air through her teeth.

"See, not so bad right?" Finn said, hopefully.

Elara glowered at him then grabbed his shoulder and yanked him closer. Finn didn't even have time to think before the second needle had pierced his skin and the milky substance was pushed into his blood stream. Pain raced through his head and neck, worse than any hangover, then the needle was removed, and it was like his brain was floating on a cloud.

"Ow..." Finn said, while rubbing the injection site. The pain had already dissipated, but he wanted to make a point. "Something tells me that was worse for me that it was for you."

"Actually, according to my bio-readings, Elara's pain response was greater," Chiefy said, cheerfully. Elara snorted a laugh and Finn glowered in the direction where he thought the robot was lurking. He couldn't see Chiefy because his stealth field was still active.

"What's next?" Elara said, replacing the empty injector into the box.

"Next, you swim-swim!" Scraps replied.

"We have to reach the jetty first," Finn said, pointing out that Scraps was getting ahead of himself. He grabbed the wire cutters and studied the electrified fence, which was humming with ominous intent. "Can you shut this down? I don't want to get cooked before I get frozen."

"Yes-yes! Scraps said. "Power down for two min-mins!"

Finn nodded and inched closer to the fence. "Let me know when..."

The hum suddenly stopped and the air surrounding them was less charged, like the calm after a storm.

"Go!" Scraps called out.

Finn touched the wire cutters to the fence, half-expecting to be blasted with a jolt of electricity potent enough to power a foreman, but the jaws of the cutter and fence merely collided with a tuneful clink. Conscious that the clock was ticking, Finn began cutting open the links, working in a straight line from the base of the fence to just under a meter from the floor before switching directions and cutting across at right angles.

"One min-min!" Scraps said, his anxious little voice stressing the urgency.

"That should be enough," Finn said, tossing the cutters into the bag then pulling back on the fence and tearing it open. "Go!"

Elara dove through first, slipping inside the harbor without making a sound, before pulling the holdall through after her. Finn went next, his wider shoulders scraping against the severed wire links, then Chiefy followed, but half-way through, the robot was stuck.

"I require help..." Chiefy said, struggling to free himself, but the more the robot wriggled, the more caught up he became.

"Forty seconds!" Scraps screeched.

Finn grabbed the snips and began furiously cutting, while Elara sawed at the metal with her combat knife. At the same time, Chiefy continued to push himself forward, until the fence burst open, and the robot clattered inside the harbor, sounding like a stack of pots and pans falling off a kitchen counter.

"What the fuck was that?" a voice called out. Then Finn heard prefect jackboots clomping in their direction.

"We have to move!" Elara whispered.

Elara activated her stealth field and Finn saw her footprints in the snow, heading away. He was about to follow when he remembered that the fence was still torn open, like a gaping wound. If the prefect saw it, they'd be discovered. Thinking on his feet, he caught the bottom of the fence in the mouth of the wire cutters then dug the tool into the ground, using it like a fence post. Then the power switched back on and a jolt of current threw him clear. He blacked out for a moment before coming to and discovering that he was being dragged across the ground.

"What the hell was that?" a second prefect called out.

"Looks like nothing," the first voice that Finn had heard replied. "Probably just some dumb seabird flying into the fence. Happens all the time."

The second officer laughed. "Stupid animals. It's no wonder they're almost extinct."

Finn heard the clomp of jackboots moving away and breathed a sigh of relief. Then he saw Elara looking down at him, her stealth field deactivated, and he realized that he was lying on his back, with his head in her lap.

"Can you move?" Elara asked.

Finn waggled his fingers and toes and discovered that he could. "I took a pretty big jolt from that fence, but I think so."

"Good, then get the hell off me," Elara snapped.

Finn rolled to the side and scrambled to his knees. He'd hoped that his stealth field had hidden his blushes, but the electric shock from the fence had disabled the system.

"At least getting past the guards should be easy," Elara said. "They're using image intensification, but the modifications that Scraps made to our armor should keep us hidden."

Finn nodded then tried to re-activate his stealth field, but the system wouldn't initialize. He tried it again, but still nothing.

"I think we have a problem," Finn said, trying for a third time to cloak himself, without joy. "That jolt from the fence has fried my stealth field. I'm visible."

"Scraps, can you fix it?" Elara asked the robot, who was peering out from behind his peep hole in Chiefy's chest, but the machine shook his head.

"Not here, not yet," Scraps replied.

"Then we'll just have to sneak past them the old-fashioned way," Elara said, undeterred by the setback. "How many prefects are inside the secure harbor?"

"There are eight special prefects and four modified foreman robots," Chiefy answered. "I have observed their patrol pattern and there is no way to reach the jetty without being seen. In fact, we must move location within the next sixty seconds to avoid being discovered here."

"We could fight them," Finn said, suggesting a more drastic option. "A surprise attack might let us take down the four foremen and one or two prefects. After that, my chits are still on us coming out on top."

Elara considered the idea but shook her head. "There's no way we could take them all out before someone raises the alarm. Even if we made it into the water, we'd be easy targets. We have to do this quietly, somehow."

"We must move..." Chiefy's interruption was sudden and urgent. "Follow my steps exactly, and do not deviate."

The robot counted down from three on its fingers then stepped out into the open. Finn followed and his heart leapt into his mouth as he saw the back of a prefect, marching in the opposite direction. A single glance behind was all it would take to be discovered, but the officer continued his patrol, oblivious.

"Wait seven seconds, then follow me," Chiefy said.

Elara was bunched up behind him, clinging to Finn in order to occupy the least space possible. Then Chiefy marched ahead, again stepping out in full view of anyone that might have been looking, but the timing was precise, and they were obscured again before inquisitive eyes could spot them.

"We can't keep dancing around like this," Finn said, still huddled close to Elara. "One mis-timed step and this is over."

"Scraps has plan!"

"We have thirty-nine seconds before we must move," Chiefy cut in. Finn was getting tired of the deadlines, but time was now their enemy, and it was constantly harassing them.

"Let's hear it pal, and quickly," Finn said.

"Scraps finally hack foreman firewall!" Scraps said, excitedly. "Use foreman to distract guards."

"It would have to be subtle," Elara said, latching onto the idea like the lifeline it was. "The distractions have to be believable."

"Scraps can do it!" the robot said, confidently. "Scraps tell Chiefy. Follow Chiefy's lead..."

"We must move in ten seconds," Chiefy announced, and

the countdown set Finn's heart racing. "Awaiting instructions…"

"Wait-wait!" Scraps said. "Don't move!"

"Five seconds…"

Finn saw a special prefect march around the corner, heading straight for them. The officer had his eyes down and was struggling to light a cigarette due to the wind and rain that was attacking the flame from his lighter. Then the end of the stick finally burned brightly, and the prefect sucked in a lungful of smoke, when a call came over his comm.

"SP423L, you have an urgent call waiting in the guard house," the voice on the comm crackled. There was an ominous pause, then the caller added, "…it's your paramour."

"Celine?" the officer said, spinning toward the guard house with his back to Finn and the others. "What the hell does she want?"

"I don't know, I'm not your goddamn messenger boy," the voice on the end of the line snapped. "You'd better take it before the supervisor finds out. You know how he hates personal calls when we're on duty."

"Yeah, alright," SP423L replied. "I'm heading there now." The prefect broke into a jog then disappeared inside the guard house.

"A call from a paramour is that your idea of a subtle distraction?" Elara said.

Scraps shrugged inside his cubby. "Worked, didn't it?"

Elara considered arguing but the fact was that Scraps' little ruse, whether subtle or not, had saved their asses.

"Okay, what now?" Finn said.

"In five seconds, move directly ahead," Chiefy replied,

speaking on behalf of Scraps. "Walk in my footsteps and do not deviate."

Chiefy marched out ahead and Finn could see the jetty and the ferry at the end of the harbor. Then a foreman turned the corner and began walking straight toward them.

"Scraps!" Finn hissed. How the robot had not already seen them, Finn didn't know. "Scraps, what's going on?"

"Keep walking..." Chiefy said, calmly.

The enemy robot continued to march toward them before making a sharp left turn and colliding with a prefect that was headed in the opposite direction. It was like being run over by a freight train and the officer was knocked to the flat of his back.

"What the fuck!" the prefect yelled, struggling to get up. The man's visor was smashed, and the sudden impact with the concrete floor had left the man winded and dazed. "Are you malfunctioning?"

"Yes, I require maintenance..." the foreman replied, flatly. The machine then grabbed the officer and hefted the man off the ground, keeping his face turned away so that Finn could slip past unseen. "Are you damaged?"

"Put me down you heap of scrap!" the officer snarled, legs and arms flailing.

Another prefect came running to the man's aid, and tried to wrestle his comrade out of the robot's clutches, but by the time the foreman had released the officer, Finn and the others were long gone.

"What next?" Finn whispered.

"Just keep walking," Chiefy answered, but through the glass windows of a storm shelter, Finn could see two more prefects approaching. The men were chatting idly to one another.

"What about those two?" Elara said.

"They will not be a problem," Chiefy replied, coolly.

Finn felt like he was voluntarily walking off a cliff, and every instinct in his body told him to duck and run for cover before he was discovered. Then a foreman on the other side of the harbor called out to the officer.

"Alert!" the robot said, severely. "Intruder detected!"

The officers threw down their cigarettes and ran toward the machine that had raised the alarm, and Finn breathed a sigh of relief. Seconds later, his boots had trampled over the officers' still-smoldering cigarettes and the jetty was within reach.

"Where? What did you see?" one of the two prefects yelled, aiming his rifle into the darkness beyond the electrified fence.

"There, on the beach," the foreman said. A powerful torch beam emanated from the robot's eyes and illuminated a section of the rocky beach in a severe white light. The two officers edged closer to the fence and raised their visors.

"That's a fucking seal, you moron!" one of the prefects barked, before smacking the robot across the back of the head. "Shit, I'm done with these foremen. When does our request for evaluator robots get actioned, so we can send these junkheaps back to the fisheries?"

"I don't know, Jenkins put in the form yesterday, so hopefully soon," the other officer replied, before glaring at the foreman. "Shut off that damned beam, it's giving me a headache."

The foreman complied and the two-prefects returned to their regular patrol route, but Finn was now able to watch them from the safety of the ferry boat. They'd reached the jetty and the water's edge, but while this should have given Finn cause for celebration, he felt only a deep sense of dread, because next came the hardest part of all. Two hundred meters of freezing cold water separated them from the ingress point leading inside the villa complex, and Finn still didn't know how to swim.

"Are you ready for this?" Elara said, handing Chiefy the holdall, which the machine strapped tightly across his back.

"The last time either of us went into the water, things didn't quite work out as planned," Finn said.

"Third time's a charm," Elara replied, grabbing a hold of the steel rope that permanently tethered the ferry to the ingress.

"What does that mean?" Finn asked. He inched himself toward Elara and the waves lapped over his legs, pouring ice-cold water into his boots. It felt like walking bare foot on razorblades.

"I don't really know, it's just something I used to hear the golds say," Elara answered. She was waist deep now and her voice was tight in her throat. "I think it means third time is lucky."

"I hope so." Finn grabbed the steel rope and suddenly he was neck deep in the water. He felt like he couldn't breathe. "Last one to the ingress buys the beers back home..."

Elara went first, pulling herself forward, hand over hand, as waves crashed into them, swallowing them whole. He lost sight of Elara several times, and each time he almost panicked, before her head bobbed back into view.

"Remember... we only... have... a few... minutes..." Elara

said, struggling to form the words through chattering teeth. "Too long... in the water... and our bodies... shut down..."

Finn didn't need reminding, but he couldn't answer Elara because the breath in his lungs was consumed by the effort of dragging himself toward the ingress.

"You are doing well," said Chiefy, with irritating exuberance. "We are more than half-way across. Keep going."

Finn wanted to respond with a wise-ass remark, but he still couldn't speak. Then he saw the ingress ahead of him, poking out of the water like a miniature island, and he was spurred on to climb faster. A buzzing noise suddenly filled his head and at first he wondered if it was just the rapid-fire chattering of his teeth, until a searchlight blazed from above them and a jet-black prefect skycar descended toward the secure harbor.

"Wait!" Chiefy called out.

"We... don't have... time..." Elara said. Her lips were blue, and her body was shaking violently. "We have... to get out... of... the water..."

"You must wait," Chiefy said, more urgently. "If we move, we will be discovered."

The skycar continued to hover above them but the searchlight wasn't scouring the ocean. Instead, it was aimed at the boathouse where Kira had been killed and Shauna had surrendered. *They've come for Shauna...* Finn thought. He tried to speak the words, but it was impossible.

"Wait..." Chiefy said. "Sixty seconds..."

Finn clung on to the steel rope though he could no longer feel his fingers, then watched as the skycar began to land. Shauna was being marched onto the seafront by a dozen regular prefects, who were preparing to hand over the rebel to the Authority's devout enforcers.

"It's okay... it's leaving..." Finn said, though the words came out as an incoherent mumble.

Elara didn't answer and Finn turned to check on her just in time to see her fingers slip away from the steel rope. He scrambled toward her, but he could barely cling on, and a second later he was loose in the water too, the weight of his armor pulling him under. He saw Elara sinking beneath him and he thrust out his hand, catching hold of the rifle strap that was holding her sub-machinegun to her back. He tried to kick his legs, but the combined mass of their armored bodies was too much, and they continued to sink. His eyes began to close, and he could feel his hold on Elara slipping. Then he was grabbed by the collar and pulled to the surface, as if someone had strapped a Nimbus rocket engine to his feet. Somehow, he'd kept hold of Elara, but she was pulled from his grasp by Chiefy, who held her snugly under his other arm.

"Standby, I will get us to the ingress," the robot said.

Finn tried to ask how, then Chiefy turned onto his back and kicked his legs so fast they were a blur. A bow wave formed in front of the robot's head, like a skycar punching through foggy air, then the robot spun over, grabbed a ladder, and began climbing. Finn was slung over the machine's shoulder, while Elara hung limply from Chiefy's free hand, like a slaughtered animal being carried to market. Both were unceremoniously dumped onto the artificial island then dragged inside a porch, which covered the door into the ingress point.

Finn couldn't move, and his body was numb, like it had had already died and his brain had yet to catch up. The holdall was torn open and Chiefy injected Elara with the blue compound, before the second dose was thrust into Finn's neck. The needle should have hurt like hell, but he felt nothing. Then heated blankets were removed from their vacuum sealed pouches and Finn was enveloped in a suffocating warmth, like being covered in hot treacle. Elara jolted awake then coughed and wheezed like she'd just smoked three packets of Metalhaven cigarettes, one after the other. She looked like death warmed up, but she was alive. They were both alive. They'd done it. They were at the ingress, further than anyone had ever gotten before, but this didn't comfort Finn as much as it should have done. Elysium, the regent's playground, awaited them, and he was genuinely fearful to discover what horrors lurked beneath the icy water.

11

NIGHTS IN CHIFFON

Finn and Elara huddled together underneath the heated blankets while Chiefy prepared the DNA key they needed to open the ingress point. The drug the robot had given them to combat the crushing cold was already taking effect, while the heated blankets rapidly dried their armor and prosecutor base layers. Steam was gently rising from their intertwined bodies, but they remained tucked inside the entryway to the ingress point and safely out of sight of land.

"This would be romantic if we weren't half frozen to death..." Finn said, managing to smile at Elara without his teeth chattering.

"Cool your jets, hot shot, and concentrate on not dying," Elara replied, with typical stoicism. She was smirking too, and though it could have been an involuntarily muscle twitch caused by the drugs, Finn chose to believe otherwise.

"Both of your vital signs are stabilizing nicely," Chiefy cut in. He had the DNA key in his hand. The holdall that had contained the blankets and meds was now empty and had been discarded into the Davis Strait, where it had sunk like a stone. "I believe we are ready to progress."

"Thanks, Chiefy," Finn said. He rapped his knuckles against the robot's steel shoulder. "Not just for helping us to get this far, but for saving our lives back there. If it hadn't been for you, we'd be fish food."

"Yes, that is quite correct," Chiefy said, cheerfully. "I am a hero."

Elara raised an eyebrow at the machine. "And so modest too..."

"It actually makes a change for someone other than Scraps to be the hero," Finn said, peering through the open peephole at his buddy. "How are you doing in there, pal?"

"Scraps wet," the robot replied, grouchily. "Wet and cold. Scraps no like..."

"I'm one hundred per cent with you," Finn replied, though ironically at that moment the heated blanket was starting to become uncomfortably hot. "I'm willing to bet a week's worth of beer chits that the Regents have the temperature inside their villa complex set to a tropical level, so we'll be warm again soon."

"Let's find out, shall we?" Elara said.

She took the DNA key from Chiefy and approached the control panel of the ingress point. Besides a hefty steel door that looked like it could repel a nuclear blast, the control panel was the only other object inside the enclosed porch. A glass panel covering the computer screen to protect it from the inclement weather slid open and the device powered up. The screen displayed the emblem of the Authority. It was a fussy design encompassing elements of the nine district sectors of Zavetgrad set beneath the looming presence of Nimbus. The President's face was integrated into the image of the space citadel, appearing regal, stately and, above all, obnoxiously arrogant. It was the only image of Alexander Gideon Reznikov that Finn had ever seen, and it adorned everything from beer chits to the number plaques that were screwed into Metalhaven's apartment doors, so that there was never any escape from the President's imperious eyes.

"Awaiting DNA verification," a computerized voice said. It sounded like an evaluator robot, one of the Authority's mechanical loyalty officers. "Please confirm your identity within thirty seconds or security procedures will be enacted."

"What kind of security procedures?" Finn wondered, as Elara presented the DNA key to the scanner.

"That kind..." Elara said, and with her free hand, she pointed to the ceiling of the enclosed porch. Four laser emitter barrels were aimed at them, ready to incinerate anyone stupid enough to attempt unauthorized entry.

"We'd better hope the DNA key works then," Finn said, but he was conscious that ten of the thirty seconds had already elapsed. "It *is* going to work, right?"

Elara and Finn both looked to Chiefy, who simply shrugged then lowered his chin to look at the open peep-hole door in his chest. All three of them then looked to Scraps to provide the answer, and some reassurance.

"Key will work-work," Scraps said, nonchalantly. "Ten seconds!"

"That's cutting it awful close, pal," Finn said, glancing up at the laser barrels. He could see them starting to glow hot, in readiness to burn a hole in his skull.

"Please provide verification within the next ten seconds,

or security procedures will be enacted," the computer voice said, this time more urgently.

"We might need to bail..." Elara said. She adjusted the angle of her body and looked ready to make a desperate dive out of the porch area.

"Wait-wait!" Scraps insisted.

"Five seconds..." the official computer said.

"*Scraps!*" His robot pal didn't answer, and Finn was about to make the dive back out in the wind and rain when the computer bleeped, jauntily.

"Welcome home, your excellency, Maxim Volkov, Regent of Spacehaven and Mayor," the computer voice said. "It is wonderful to see you again. I hope you had a pleasant visit to Zavetgrad."

"Shit, even the computers kiss that bastard's ass," Finn said, nauseated by the machine's saccharine tone of voice.

The slab-like steel door then began to trundle open. Due to its heft, the gears and motors required to operate it were powerful enough to run a Stonehaven excavator machine, and the floor rattled beneath their feet. Finally, after a full thirty seconds, the door had opened far enough for them to slip inside. At first, Finn was glad to get out of the wintry night air, but as the slab began to grind shut again, a stifling sense of claustrophobia overcame him.

"I imagine this is what being entombed feels like," Finn said, hugging his arms around his body, and staring at the steel walls, which felt like they were closing in on him.

"If this was a tomb, we'd already be dead," Elara replied. The Shadow was asserting control of her psyche, as she mentally prepared herself for the fight to come. "But by the time we're finished with this underwater circus, it will be a tomb for some."

The elevator began to descend but the speed of travel felt sedate compared to what Finn was expecting. He'd imagined that the Regents would have been itching to return to their villas, after their time spent slumming it in Zavetgrad, but the slumbering pace contradicted this.

"Why is this taking so long?" Finn asked, since the question was gnawing at him.

"Level one of the complex is fifty meters below the surface, which requires this elevator car to be pressurized," Chiefy explained. "The rate of descent is to allow your bodies to acclimatize and adjust."

"Don't complain, it gives us time to warm up properly, and get ready," Elara said. She had shed her heated blanket and had equipped her submachine gun. "Remember we'll exit into the servants' quarters, so tranq rounds only, unless we meet heavier resistance."

"I just wish we knew what sort of 'heavier resistance' we might run into," Finn said, also readying his weapon.

The elevator car suddenly thumped to a stop and the door began to whir open. Finn and Elara moved to either side, ready to burst out and surprise anyone who might have arrived to greet them.

"Sweep and clear, just like we trained in the barracks," Elara said.

Finn nodded. They'd practiced the drill so many times he was sure he could do it blindfold. The door continued its gradual movement and Finn was about to jump out first when Scraps called a warning.

"Wait-wait, security camera!" the robot yelled. He pushed

open the compartment and leapt out of Chiefy's chest, taking flight using his rotor. "Facial recognition!"

"Shit!" Finn cursed and ducked back into cover. "A DNA key can't hide the fact we don't look like Maxim Volkov. Can you hack the system?"

"Yes-yes, working..." Scraps said.

The little robot had already torn open a panel inside the elevator and was plugged in to the circuits, working furiously to tap into the security system. Meanwhile, the door had opened fully, requiring Chiefy to squeeze in beside Finn. The car was only big enough for four at a push, and the foreman's hulking frame was crushing Finn against the wall. A scanning beam probed the car, finding nothing. A buzzer then sounded, angry and abrupt like a warning klaxon, and the doors began to close.

"System malfunction detected, entering failsafe mode," the computer voice announced. "Elevator car will be locked down in thirty seconds. Please alight immediately."

"What's happening?" Finn demanded. "Why are the doors closing?"

"Oops..." Scraps replied, side-eyeing Finn, guiltily.

"Oops? What the hell does 'oops' mean?" Elara cut in.

"While trying to tap into the security cameras, Scraps has inadvertently corrupted a section of the ingress system's programming," Chiefy explained, still altogether too cheerful for Finn's liking. "You must brace the door. If it closes, even I will not be able to force it open again."

"What if we can't brace it? Do we end up back on the surface level?" Elara asked.

Chiefy shook his head. "If the door closes, this shaft will be purged."

"What the hell does that mean?" Finn asked. He was imagining a dozen different scenarios, all of which ended up with them being washed up on a rocky beach, and he quickly backtracked. "Never mind, I think I get the idea."

"I don't have anything to brace the door," Elara said, considering using her combat knife, but even the hefty weapon wouldn't be enough.

"I do," Finn said.

Reluctantly, he removed his baseball bat from his back scabbard and let out a remorseful sigh. "This thing has saved my ass almost as many times as Scraps has. It hurts to let it go."

"Trust me, being flushed into the Davis Strait, fifty meters deep, will hurt more," Elara pointed out. "Jam it in there. I'll buy you another bat when we reach the Authority sector."

Finn sighed again then slid the weapon into the track that the door was following, careful not to let the cameras outside see him. A few seconds later the slab of steel butted up against it and the gears and motors began to groan and murmur, like Finn during one of his frequent nightmares. He was about to utter the words, "It's working!" when the narrow end of the baseball bat nearest to the handle began to warp. Everyone watched and waited with bated breath, hoping that the weapon that had crushed the skulls of prefect and foreman robot alike, would hold up to yet another test, when the screech of tortured metal cut through Finn like a knife, and the bat buckled.

"Scraps, we need that hack!" Finn called out. The door was three quarters shut already.

"Now-now!" the robot yelled, before zooming through the opening.

"Chiefy, you first," Finn said, conscious that the larger of their two robot companions was also the least flexible.

Chiefly squeezed his frame through the opening, while Finn and Elara shoved from the other side, causing yet more tortured screams to attack Finn's ears, as the door and Chiefy's body grated against one another. Finally, the robot was through and Chiefy clattered to the floor on the other side in an inelegant heap.

"Now you," Finn said to Elara.

Elara jumped through and Finn followed a heartbeat behind her, but the door closed against his chest armor, and he was trapped. Elara grabbed his arm while Chiefy braced the door and employed all of his robotic might to resist the more powerful motors that were now being employed to crush Finn like the trash compactors in Yard nine. There were more tortured squeals then Finn was finally freed, and he fell into the servants' quarters, landing even more inelegantly than Chiefy had done.

"Are you alright?" Elara asked, hauling Finn to his feet.

"Yes, I think so," Finn said, feeling a stabbing pain in his chest where the door had almost cracked his sternum like rotten wood. Behind them, the door had closed, and he could hear the sound of icy seawater rushing inside the elevator car. "That was close. Too close..." Finn said, as the 'purge' began in earnest.

"We're not clear yet..."

Elara grabbed Finn's shoulder and twisted his body so that he was facing into the room. One of the regent's servants had entered the arrival hall and was standing, open mouthed, gawping at them like they were extra-terrestrials. The woman was wearing a white chiffon dress, split to the hip on one leg, and nothing else, not even shoes. The only hint of color, besides the color of her skin, was her striking azure blue eyeshadow that marked her out as a servant of Seahaven's Regent, Cedric Brathwaite.

Elara reacted instantly, shooting the woman with a tranq round before she could speak, scream, or otherwise raise the alarm. Two more servants came running, alerted by the commotion, and Elara put them down just as swiftly. They were young men, both wearing white chiffon shirts and shorts that concealed so little of their bodies that they may as well have been naked.

"We need to hide them," Elara said, hustling to the arched doorway that led to the arrival hallway and checking outside. "Scraps may have the security cameras fooled, but whatever robot servants the regents have employed won't be so easily duped."

With the help of Chiefy's mechanical muscle, the bodies of the three servants were tucked behind statues of the regents, past and present, which lined the arrivals hall and the walls of the servants' quarters beyond it. Elara continued to keep watch, but the underwater domain fell still and calm, oblivious to the turmoil that was engulfing the city fifty meters above them.

"The offices of the regents are up ahead, through that glass tube," Elara said, nodding toward the far end of the servant's module. "Move fast but stay quiet. According to Pritchard, there are dozens of servants for each regent, and we can't knock them all out."

"If there are so many of them then where are they?" Finn whispered, following behind Elara as she stalked out ahead of the group. "It's too quiet, I don't like it."

"I believe that this facility is operating on Nimbus time, which would make it late evening here," Chiefy said, also managing to creep forward without making a sound. The robot then pointed to a clock on the wall, which read *24:12*.

"Twenty-four hours and twelve minutes?" Finn said, blinking a few times to make sure his eyes weren't playing tricks on him. "But that doesn't make any sense."

"The president considers himself indifferent to the guiding influence of planets and stars," the foreman explained, and Finn snorted a laugh. This sounded perfectly on-point for humanity's most arrogant man. "A Nimbus day is therefore based on the male circadian period, your natural body clock, which for men is twenty-four hours and nineteen minutes long," the foreman added.

"And it's not the same for women?" Finn asked, curious as to why Chiefy has stipulated a male circadian cycle.

"No, a woman's circadian cycle is twenty-four hours and nine minutes long," Chiefy replied. "I do not know why the male cycle was chosen for the length of a Nimbus day."

"It's for the same reason there are no female regents," Elara cut in. "Zavetgrad was founded by men and has always been ruled by men. We inherited that trait from the old world."

The sound of voices up ahead alerted them to more servants, and Elara took cover, directing Finn toward another statue of a long-dead regent on the other side of the corridor. They waited, weapons raised, but the servants didn't notice them, and after a while split off and entered their own personal quarters to retire for the night.

Finn moved out from behind the statue, which depicted a former Regent of Makehaven in a contemplative pose, reading a book held outstretched in one hand. It was only then that he realized that the face of every statue in the long hall was also that of a man. In Metalhaven, men and women were equal in every regard, from shift hours, the quantity of ale they were expected to chug after a laborious day's work, and the forced donation of seed or eggs to fuel the great Nimbus project. This equality hadn't been for noble reasons, but because it was simply the most efficient use of available resources. The aristocracy – those who ultimately benefited – were all drawn from a small pool of men who had founded Zavetgrad after the war. They had been the very worst of humanity then, and their progeny were no better.

"We're almost through this section," Elara said, rousing Finn from his dark daydream. "Once we're inside the connecting tunnel, it won' take long to reach the offices of the regents, and from there it's a straight line down into Elysium."

The group continued, occasionally forced to stop while another chiffon-wearing servant returned from duty, only to be replaced by another, fresher model that was almost indistinguishable from the last. Finn started to recognize a pattern. Volthaven's Viktor Kozlov liked them dark and predominantly male, while Stonehaven's Yuki Tanaka preferred a more androgynous look for all of his servants, who each wore a long, floaty gown, regardless of their gender. However, it was the servants belonging to Gabriel Montgomery that stood out the most. Finn had detested Metalhaven's regent from the first moment he'd seen the man, but now his loathing reached new heights. Montgomery evidently liked them very young – workhouse young – and Finn felt sick to even think about what the bloated bastard did within the cloistered walls of his underwater domain.

Finally, they reached the end of the servant's quarters, and a great glass tunnel extended out into the ocean, like a hole in the water. Finn took a tentative step inside, and it was enough to distract his harassed mind from thoughts and plans of murdering his former Regent in the most painful and humiliating way possible.

"Stop!"

Finn looked up from the watery abyss and saw a robot standing on the boundary where the servant's quarters met the tunnel. The machine was based on a foreman, but its contours were curved, rather than square-edged, and its face had been sculpted, rather than left as a crude approximation of human expression.

"You are intruders! I am raising the alarm," the housekeeper bot announced.

Finn's heart raced and he drew his laser cannon, ready to blast the robot's FLP to pieces, even though he knew the chances of him doing so before it could send an alert were almost none. Then he saw Scraps, perched on Chiefy's shoulder with a wide grin on his face, and he knew they weren't in any danger.

"You are interrupting my communications systems," the housekeeper said, twisting its artful mechanical features into an aggravated frown. "Refrain at once, or I will be forced to use violence!"

The robot's hands suddenly flipped open at the wrist and two electrified nightsticks extended from the base of its forearms. The housekeeper then adopted a combat stance, ready to employ its deadly weapons, but Finn coolly lasered the robot in the head before it could take its first swing. Sparks flew and electrical arcs leapt from the housekeeper's crippled frame before its motors expired and it collapsed under its own mass.

"At least now we know what sort of resistance we're looking at," Finn said, snapping his laser back onto its holster. "If these prettied-up hunks of crap are all the regents have to throw at us, then capturing Maxim Volkov should be a breeze."

"I hope you're right," Elara said, kicking the twitching machine with the toe of her boot to make sure it was down for good. "But something tells me that this place has a few more surprises to throw at us yet."

12

A MUSEUM FOR ONE

The tunnel connecting the servants' quarters to the offices of the regents was two hundred meters long and built entirely from glass. At first, Finn couldn't understand how the structure was even possible. It seemed magical, as if a sea god had drilled a hole through the ocean and kept it from collapsing under the mass of water above them through use of a supernatural power. Then, as he took his first tentative steps inside the transparent tunnel, he started to see the complex matrix of scaffolds and braces that rose from the structure below and held the tunnel in place, and this gave him the confidence to continue. Engineering was something Finn Brasa could trust. Engineering was physical and real. Engineering determined what could be made and what could be broken. From the gleaming gold of the Authority sector to the omnipresent, looming gaze of Nimbus, the Regents of Zavetgrad were skilled illusionists, able to present the appearance of greatness at every turn, but the truth was that there was nothing special about their sub-oceanic complex. It was just metal and glass. It had been built and that meant it could be torn down.

"There's still so much life in the ocean," Finn said, stopping at the mid-way point to watch a sea creature that was three times the size of a skycar soar above the glass tunnel. Its black and white patterning and sheer size were striking, and Finn remembered seeing a picture of the creature on the data device he'd kept hidden in his old Metalhaven apartment, but he couldn't remember its name. "Maybe this planet isn't quite as dead as we thought," he added, wistfully.

"At least not down here," Elara said. She was following a shoal of fish on the other side of the tunnel that were carefully avoiding the titan-like monster that Finn was watching. "Maybe the Last War only polluted the land and sky, and everything under the sea carried on oblivious."

"I hope so," Finn said, earnestly. "If life can survive down here, maybe the rest of the planet can heal too."

They continued to watch the underwater ballet in silence for a time, until Elara spoke into Finn's ear and made him jump. As usual, he hadn't noticed her creep up behind him.

"Isn't that a whale?" Elara said, standing behind Finn and watching with him as the black-and-white creature looped around the tunnel, as if watching them right back.

"A whale, that's it!" Finn said, snapping his fingers. "The name was on the tip of my tongue."

"Orcinus Orca... Killer whale!" Scraps said, leaping from Chiefy's shoulder to Finn's. The robot then shrugged. "But actually dolphin."

"I don't care what it is, it's beautiful," Elara said, as the majestic creature did another loop, showing off its distinctive pattern. "And there's not a lot of beauty left in this fucked-up world."

"Oh, I don't know about that," Finn said, side-eyeing Elara and grinning. "At least not from where I'm standing."

Scraps giggled and Chiefy was forced to look away, as if trying to hide his blushes, while Elara just rolled her eyes at Finn and shook her head.

"I think that's enough nature watching, stud," Elara said, pressing the DNA key into Finn's hand then nodding toward the pressure door at the far end of the tunnel. "We have an appointment with the Mayor and Regent of Spacehaven, and I don't want to be late."

Finn inserted the DNA key into the scanner and a pressure hatch hissed and began to slowly swing open, like a vault door. A heady waft of perfumed air floated through the gap, reminding Finn of the art galleries and promenades in the cultural quarter of the Authority sector, which constantly burned incense to mask the acrid stench of industry from Makehaven's towering factories.

"Why is there only a door at this end?" Finn asked, glancing back toward the other side of the tunnel to pass the time while the hatch lumbered open. "The servants' quarters are completely exposed to the tunnel, but the Regent's offices are sealed."

"It's probably a failsafe measure," Elara said. She had her shotgun in hand and was poised to enter the office section first. "Considering that the only way into this place is through the servants' quarters, if there was ever a mass break in, or a revolt, they could just blow this tunnel and cut off the outside world completely."

"And drown all of their servants?" Finn asked.

Considering that the regents had hand-picked their slaves, he'd assumed they were treated better than sector workers, at the very least. "That's dark, even for a regent."

"Don't kid yourself that they actually give a shit about these people," Elara said, flatly. "Remember that there are thousands more kids in the workhouse, ready to take their place. These aren't people to the regents, they're property."

Elara stepped through the hatch first, training her shotgun dead ahead but the lights in the entrance foyer were dimmed and there was no-one to be seen, human or robot. Finn followed, with Chiefy and Scraps a safe distance to their rear, and the hatch door closed and sealed behind them with a hiss.

"Looks like no-one is home," Finn said. He turned to Scraps, but his robot buddy already had his scanner dish extended and was actively probing the area ahead of them. "What do you reckon, pal? Are we safe to go on?"

Scraps' little metal eyebrows were twisted into a frown and the robot was concentrating hard. If he'd had a tongue, Finn imagined that it would be protruding out of the corner of his mouth, like an artist in deep contemplation of his work.

"No people," Scraps said, though the statement was made without the absolute confidence Finn was used to hearing from the robot. "But... something else."

"Something else? What something?" Finn asked. Suddenly, he felt like there was an assassin lurking in every dark corner, waiting to strike him down.

"Not sure," Scraps replied. "Be careful..."

"That goes without saying, pal," Finn said, patting the robot on the head. "Keep your scanners primed, though. I don't like surprises."

Scraps nodded then tucked himself in behind Chiefy's head, choosing to stay out in the open rather than remain inside the other robot's chest compartment. Finn nodded to Elara, and they continued through the foyer, moving side-by-side and not making a sound. Before long, they'd reached a stone portico topped with a temple pediment that matched the entrance to the mayor's official building in the Authority sector. It was fifteen meters tall and blended seamlessly into the walls of the sub-oceanic complex. Above it, the ceiling had been adapted to look like sky, complete with clouds that swirled and floated across the false horizon. Had Finn not known that there were fifty meters of ice-cold seawater above them, it would have been easy to believe they were back on land.

"How the hell did they build this?" Finn wondered, stepping through the portico and into a vast hall, lined on either side by stone pillars that jutted up from the polished marble floor and pointed to the false sky. Between each pillar was an office, but the word 'office' hardly did justice to the size and grandeur of each palatial room. "It's like something out of a dream."

"I remember Chief Prosecutor Voss talking about this place," Elara said, also captivated by the space. "He used to boast that the Regent of Seedhaven had once showed him an image of his office and what the regent had called their 'Cathedral'. I thought he was full of shit at the time, but Voss described it just like this. No-one believed him because it sounded impossible."

Finn's awe at the majesty of the Regent's Cathedral quickly changed to anger. For more than two centuries, the workers of Zavetgrad had endured living conditions that were little better than a slum, while the golds had luxuriated in their gleaming apartments and cafes, but the sub-oceanic complex made even the Authority sector look plain in comparison.

"How many oranges from Stonehaven broke their backs to build all this?" Finn wondered. If he'd still had his baseball bat, he would have gone on a rampage, smashing everything in sight. "How many workers died so that these aristocratic fuckers and the bastards that came before them could have all this?"

"Three thousand…" Scraps said.

Finn turned to his robot pal and frowned. Scraps had spoken the words forlornly, out of character with his usual verve.

"Three-thousand what, pal?" Finn asked.

"Three-thousand workers," Scraps said. "That how many died. Complex computer said so."

It took Finn a moment to process what Scraps had said. He understood the number and what it meant, and he felt like he should say something in response, but his mind was blank. There were simply no words that could make sense of something so senseless.

"Let's find Volkov and get out of here," Finn said, his skin suddenly cold.

Finn continued inside the cathedral, but he felt sick and disgusted at himself for being thrilled by something that had been built with the blood and sacrifice of people just like him. It wasn't a cathedral but a graveyard, haunted by the ghosts of Stonehaven workers that had been used and discarded like trash.

Elara stopped at the first of the eight offices, each of

which was marked by its own grand entrance and unique design. Just as each regent had different proclivities when it came to the age and appearance of their servants, it was clear that they also had different tastes when it came to architecture and decoration. Finn recognized some of the styles from his studies on his data device. One office was done in a Scandinavian style, clean and simple, while the neighboring space was a dark and moody gothic nightmare. Another was decorated in an art deco style, while the office opposite to it channeled the English regency period. But while each office was unique, they were all equally resplendent.

With his anger still raw, Finn had no interest in visiting any of the spaces, and he relied on Scraps' scanners to confirm that each office was unoccupied. He was about to walk past the English regency office when he spotted a painting on the wall just inside the entrance. Set inside an ornate wood frame, it was a life-sized portrait of a man wearing a lavish military dress uniform, replete with more medals than the red coat could reasonably fit, set against the background of a grand stately home. It looked hundreds of years old, but the face of the man was familiar, and it made Finn stop and take notice.

"What is it?" Elara asked, curious as to why Finn had paused to look at the painting.

"I don't know, there's just something about this man," Finn said, rubbing his chin and scrutinizing the painting like an art critic. "It's like I've seen him before."

"You have," Elara said. "It's the Regent of Metalhaven, Gabriel Montgomery."

As soon as Elara had said the name, it was like a switch flipped in Finn's brain, and it was suddenly so obvious. The painting itself was ancient but now it was clear that the original face and head had been swapped through some act of digital trickery and replaced with that of Montgomery. The more he looked the more obvious and fake the forgery seemed, to the point of being comical.

"This must be Montgomery's office," Elara added, heading into the space. She snorted a laugh. "The bastard fancies himself an English lord, though I guess that tracks. He always was a pompous ass."

Like in the background of his doctored portrait, Montgomery's office was designed to represent a Victorian English stately home, decorated in the Regency style of the time. The sprawling space, which was four times the size of a Metalhaven recovery center all on its own, was inspired by the architecture of ancient Greece and Rome. Everywhere Finn looked there was fine furniture in a rich, dark wood covered in exquisite linen upholstery, bookcases reaching ten meters high, rows of oil paintings depicting fusty, long-dead aristocrats, and dozens of ornate statues and figurines, all set to a muted color palate of pastel blues, grays and creams.

"Looking at all this, you might be forgiven for thinking that Montgomery had taste," Elara said.

Finn was irritated by the compliment, however backhanded it may have been, but morbid curiosity compelled him to follow Elara inside. He was still repulsed by the extravagances that the regents had surrounded themselves with, at the literal cost of lives, but this was personal. Montgomery was not only the regent of his home sector, but the man who had approved and overseen his sentence to death by trial.

"For someone who is supposedly focused on the future of humanity, Montgomery sure seems stuck in the past," Elara said, running her finger across an oak side table with a gadroon border and bowed legs that stood on lion-paw brass toe caps.

"Where the hell did he get all this crap?" Finn said, more struck by 'how' rather than 'why' Montgomery had chosen to surround himself with relics from the past. "Did he have it manufactured based on archive images and carted down here from Makehaven just to satisfy his ego?"

"I do not believe so…"

It was Chiefy who'd answered the rhetorical question, and it took Finn a moment to locate the robot before he found the foreman admiring a painting on the wall behind Montgomery's oversized desk. Scraps was sitting on the bigger robot's shoulder, equally rapt by whatever Chiefy had found.

"Why do you say that?" Finn asked, sidling up beside the machines.

"Because of this…" Chiefy replied, pointing to the painting.

Finn looked at the canvas but could see nothing about it that made it more special than the multitude of other remarkable objects in the office. Elara joined him and they regarded the painting together, trying to unlock its mysteries. It was a landscape image of burned oranges and warm yellows that featured dozens of what Finn guessed were deer or stags in various poses. Some were resting on the sunlight-toasted grass, while others meandered across the hills, perhaps seeking shelter beneath the tall trees. In the foreground to the right, two white bucks fought, heads bowed, and horns locked, watched by an entourage of other deer, who seemed to be captivated by the struggle, like workers in a recovery center, watching two chromes punching each other out for no good reason. Then he realized that some of the figures were not in fact animals but people, dressed in white outfits. They were playing what appeared to be a ball game of some sort, though Finn had no idea what.

The entire painting was perhaps little more than a meter and a half wide, and the cracked and yellowing varnish made it look old and tired. At first, he'd considered the scene to be dull and boring, like the stuffy portraits of dead men and women that adorned other parts of the office, but the more Finn looked at the painting, the more it revealed, and it struck him that he'd been staring at it, enraptured, for several minutes.

"I like it," Elara said, eventually breaking the silence. "I don't know why I like it, but I do."

"Maybe because its alive," Finn said. He agreed with Elara's assessment and had been asking himself the same question. "It's warm and comforting and peaceful. I don't know when or where this was painted, but I know that it was a happier time."

"It is by an artist called Joseph Mallord William Turner," Chiefy said. The robot appeared pleased that Finn and Elara were appreciative of the work. "It is oil on canvas and was painted in England in around eighteen twenty-seven."

Finn finally tore his eyes away from the painting and frowned at Chiefy. "Are you saying this is an original?"

The foreman robot nodded. "Some of the objects in this room are recreations but many of the artifacts are genuine, like this Turner. According to Scraps, they were brought here after the last war, by the robot crews that were sent out across the planet to recover the detritus of war that now fills the reclamation yards of Metalhaven."

Chiefy returned to studying the painting. Whatever circuits and transistors the image had stimulated in its FLP appeared to be making the robot happy. He'd never thought it possible that a foreman could feel, but then Chiefy was no ordinary foreman, just as Scraps was far more than a collection of electronics stuffed inside an old oil can.

"These objects were priceless even before the apocalypse," Elara said. She now had her arms folded across her chest. "This isn't an office, it's a museum. A museum for the sole amusement and benefit of one man."

Suddenly, Scraps' radar dish spun around and pointed toward the entrance to Gabriel Montgomery's office.

"Danger!" Scraps called out, his body whipping around to face in the direction his dish had been pointing. "Someone coming... Wait-wait... Two-people coming. Arriving from Elysium!"

"Human or robot?" Finn asked.

Scraps had to think hard before answering. Whatever had been perturbing the robot ever since they'd entered the office complex was still causing him to hesitate.

"Human..." Scraps finally answered.

Finn felt sure there was a 'but' coming, but Scraps didn't say anything more. Then he heard the whir of gears and pulleys and the ping of an elevator car arriving somewhere out in the Regent's Cathedral.

"With any luck, it'll be Volkov," Finn said, grabbing his submachine gun, which was still loaded with tranq rounds.

"I hope you're right, but I doubt we're that lucky," Elara replied, stealing ahead and peering through the entrance.

The sound of laugher filtered into the room, then Finn heard two men chatting and joking, like they didn't have a care in the world. He closed his eyes and listened, but neither sounded like Maxim Volkov or Gabriel Montgomery, and they were the only two Regents he could recognize by voice alone.

"It's Yuki Tanaka," Elara whispered, picking out the Regent of Stonehaven. "And I think the other is Vadim Ivanov, Autohaven's regent."

Finn cursed under his breath. Neither were the man they wanted, but capturing two middle-ranking regents was still better than none.

"They'll do for now," Finn said, preparing to move on Elara's word. "Maybe they can lead us to Volkov, so we can grab him without having to chase the bastard all over Elysium."

"Your stealth field is still damaged, so I'll take them," Elara said. "But stay close behind me, as close as you can without being seen. We still don't know what other defenses the regents might have set up."

Finn nodded then Elara activated her stealth field and vanished in a shimmering blur of movement that sped outside into the Cathedral. Finn followed, though he could no longer see Elara, and hugged the walls, using the tall pillars and statues of old regents for cover. He watched as Tanaka, who was wearing a fine, linen two-piece suit led Ivanov, who was simply in a bathrobe, into one of the offices that they'd yet to search, a stark industrial space that was minimal to the point of being almost empty. Tanaka went to a well-stocked bar, still laughing and joking with his fellow aristocrat, and poured a dark amber liquid from a crystal decanter into two glasses that sparkled and shone like diamonds. Finn moved as close as he could without risking being discovered and aimed his submachine gun at Tanaka. Then the square entrance to the office lit up red and an alarm sounded. Beams of light pulsed from emitters in the ceilings and Elara's stealth field was disrupted, forcing her to de-cloak. For a moment, Tanaka and Ivanov simply stood in open-mouthed astonishment, then Elara raised her weapon and fired, hitting Ivanov in the chest and sending the regent crashing to the ground, his crystal glass shattering into a million tiny fragments.

Tanaka dove for cover as Elara pounded the bar with tranq rounds, destroying dozens of decanters and bottles, some of which looked as old as the Turner painting in Montgomery's office. Finn raced up to lend aid, but the Regent of Stonehaven had a keen sense of self-perseveration and had managed to squirrel himself behind a solid steel bookcase that looked hardy enough to withstand any onslaught.

"Go left, we'll catch him in a crossfire," Elara called out.

Finn nodded and was about to move when Tanaka yelled, "Emergency Lockdown! Custodian, protect us!"

"Wait..." Elara said, grabbing Finn's shoulder and holding him back as a seismic thump resonated through the floor. "I don't like this."

Tanaka darted from the bookcase and hid behind the bar before Finn or Elara could get another shot off, then dragged Ivanov's paralyzed body into cover.

"Danger!" Scraps called out. He and Chiefy were just outside. "Robot coming! Unknown model!"

"Back up..." Elara said, pushing Finn toward the door.

"Whoever you are, you're dead!" Tanaka yelled. Finn could see the man's head poking above his bar, eyes wild with rage. "You're fucking dead, do you hear me! No-one comes here. No-one!"

"Behind!" Scraps called out.

Finn and Elara spun around in time to see a section of the floor in the middle of the Regents' Cathedral slide open like a trap door. A rumbling sound like a dozen Makehaven ale trucks speeding down the autoway shook their bones, then a robot was lifted into the room from a hidden compartment below the floor. The face was angular and severe, like the evaluator robot that had interrogated Finn as an apprentice, but this machine was eight feet tall and armored like a tank. There was another thump as a relay switched, and Finn felt the surge of power as if he'd been punched in the chest. The robot's eyes glowed red like laser light and a spear the length of Finn's entire body crackled with electrical energy, before the custodian jumped down from its dais and advanced.

13

I AM FREE

Scraps leapt from Chiefy's shoulder and flew toward Finn, rotors spinning and arms flailing in terror, but Chiefy did not turn and run. Instead, the modified foreman faced down the custodian, and stood between Finn, Elara, and the other robot, blocking the door to Tanaka's office like a sentry.

"You're dead, do you hear?!" Tanaka roared. Finn tore his eyes away from the custodian and saw that Tanaka had used the distraction to drag Ivanov to an escape elevator behind his desk. "How dare you violate our cathedral! This sanctuary is for regents!"

The door of the escape elevator began to close, and Finn panicked, realizing that if Tanaka reached Elysium, he would alert all the other regents, including Maxim Volkov. And if the mayor escaped, their only chance to capture him was gone too. Risking an electrified blast from the custodian's spear, Finn shot up and aimed his submachine gun at the elevator. Flipping the selector to automatic, he unloaded the entire magazine of tranq rounds, hitting metal, walls, statues and, eventually, Tanaka himself. The regent spasmed, first with pain then with nerve convulsions, as the tranq rounds ricocheted off the inside walls of the elevator and thudded into the man's body. The door had closed before Finn could confirm that the Regent of Stonehaven had been knocked out, but he felt sure that he'd tagged his target. However, Tanaka and Ivanov were no longer their primary concern.

"I think I stunned Tanaka, so we still have a chance, so long as we can get past that thing," Finn said, ducking back into cover beside Elara.

"It'll have to get past Chiefy first," Elara said.

Finn admired her confidence in the robot's fighting ability, but even Chiefy looked puny compared to the monstrous contraption that Yuki Tanaka had unleashed. Yet, despite its fearsome appearance, the custodian was no mindless killing machine. With Chiefy blocking its path, the custodian held back and waited, studying its new opponent with its laser red eyes. Whatever processors and circuitry fizzed inside its tank-like armor was intelligent enough to know that Chiefy was no push over.

"Stand aside," the custodian demanded. It spoke with an insistent, thunderous voice that shook the air.

"Request denied," Chiefy answered, with matching firmness.

The custodian growled like one of the mutated wolves Finn had encountered in the wilderness beyond Zavetgrad's boundary fence, then the machine began to pace up and down in front of Chiefy, scrutinizing its opponent with a malignant intelligence.

"Foreman-class, Gen-Five. Modified code base. Inferior technology." The custodian stopped pacing, though electricity continued to crackle and dance across the blade of its spear, impatient to unleash its violence. "Threat assessment... negligible."

"Your analysis is flawed," Chiefy said, adopting a fighting stance. "I will reeducate you."

The custodian laughed, and the sound filled the regents' cathedral, sending a chill racing down Finn's spine. Then, inexplicably, the combat machine lowered its spear and beckoned Chiefy on.

"Wait-wait!" Scraps yelled. The smaller robot was hiding behind a bust of Yuki Tanaka. "Trap!"

Scraps' warning came too late. Blue laser beams tracked Chiefy as he charged toward the custodian, then a thump pounded the floor, like the sound of an emergency generator kicking into life, and a flash of blue light, like an aurora, surrounded the foreman. A sudden silence followed, and Finn felt a stabbing pain shoot through his head, then Chiefy crashed to the ground, stiff and lifeless, as if a power switch had just been flipped to off.

"EMP burst!" Scraps said, still hiding behind the bust. "Chiefy disabled!"

The custodian reached down and picked up Chiefy by the scruff of his neck, like a kitten, and peered into the robot's dead eyes.

"Inferior..." the custodian growled.

The guardian machine flung Chiefy aside, sending the robot's metal body sliding and screeching across the marble floor of the cathedral. He came to rest, stiff as a corpse, inside the gothic-inspired office belonging to the Regent of Seedhaven, Theodore Westwood.

"We take it together," Elara said. If Chiefy's straightforward defeat had dented her confidence, she was not showing it. "We aim for its head and destroy its processor. It might be big, but it's just a box of circuits, like every other robot."

"This isn't like any robot I've seen before, and I thought I'd seen them all," Finn said, dialing the power level of his laser cannon to maximum before meeting Elara's eyes. "But say the word and I'm with you."

Together, Finn and Elara moved out from behind Yuki Tanaka's desk and marched toward the custodian, all guns blazing. The sound of Elara's combat shotgun was deafening, and each blast of the weapon was reinforced and reflected back at them by the walls of the cathedral space, which had the resonant acoustics of its pre-war namesake. Finn's laser flashed in near silence, though at maximum power, each burst of light was blinding, like a lightning strike.

The custodian braced against the onslaught and extended a shield from its left forearm that repelled Elara's shotgun blasts and absorbed Finn's laser energy, leaving the combat machine intact. The electrified spear was slashed at Finn, and he managed to block with his vambraces, but the impact sent him crashing back into Tanaka's office. His armor insulated him against the shock but electrical arcs from the weapon had lashed his face and neck, leaving whip-like marks across his skin.

Elara rolled beneath the robot's next attack and unloaded the last of her shells, but the robot protected its face and head, while its dense armor soaked up the damage like a sponge. Elara was caught then thrown through the air like a rag doll, and sent crashing through Tanaka's desk, which despite its steel frame and industrial build, collapsed like a house of cards.

"Custodian too strong!" Scraps cried, flying to Elara as Finn helped her from beneath the wreckage. She was dazed and bleeding, and mad as hell. "We must escape!"

"Then find us a way out!" Finn cried back, helping Elara deeper inside the office, as the custodian stomped toward them with measured and unhurried steps.

"Elevators locked down!" Scraps answered. The little robot was frantic. Losing Chiefy had dealt him a shattering blow, as crippling as any blast or slash from the custodian's electrified spear. "Scraps scared!"

"I'm scared too, pal." Finn set Elara down and tore his med-kit from a webbing pouch, tipping the contents onto the steel-tiled floor. "But we need you. We have to find a way to beat that machine or we're all dead, do you hear?"

Scraps nodded but the robot was shivering with fright. Finn pressed a stim injector into Elara's waiting hand then grabbed hold of his robot, squeezing tightly to absorb the tremors rattling his oil-can body.

"You've got this, pal, I believe in you," Finn said.

"Can't hack!" Scraps cried, throwing his arms out wide. "Custodian too strong!"

The arched doorway leading into Tanaka's office was smashed open to allow the custodian to force its way inside. The machine then threw tables and chairs aside and crashed through statues like they were made of paper, before turning its red eyes toward Finn.

"Intruders..." the custodian, growled, its eyes flashing brighter.

Finn looked for a way out but there was none. The offices of the regents were each entirely self-contained, and by herding them back inside Tanaka's office, the custodian had cornered them like prey.

"Then try to help Chiefy," Finn said, turning back to his robot buddy. "He's still our best shot against that thing. If you can get him back online, we have a chance."

Scraps glanced across to the custodian, who continued its measured advance, while smashing through anything that stood in its path like a bulldozer.

"You can do it, pal," Finn said, as Scraps' trembling mechanical eyes remained fixed on the fighting machine. "You have to..."

Scraps nodded, then his rotors spun up and a frightened but determined look was set on his face. Then the robot accelerated like a cannonball, straight at the custodian, who stopped and raised its shield, unsure as to whether Scraps was committing hara-kiri as a flying bomb or was trying to escape. The monstrous machine swung its spear at Scraps, like it was trying to swat a fly, and Finn held his breath as the electrified blade sliced through the air inches from the little robot's body. Electrical arcs crackled between the tip of the weapon and Scraps' body, and for an agonizing moment he faltered, his course erratic like a skycar flying through heavy turbulence. Then he was through, and Finn breathed again.

"What good will getting Chiefy back online do us?" Elara said. The meds had done their work, and she was recovered. "The custodian will just hit it with another pulsed EMP and knock him right back on his ass."

"Not if we destroy the emitters," Finn said. He had the bones of a plan in his mind, but it was sketchy at best. "First, we have to get out of here, but that robot is blocking our only exit."

Energized and bolstered by the stim, Elara rapidly assessed their position and their options, her head on a swivel. Then she banged her fist against the wall where Finn had unceremoniously dumped her, and it sounded hollow, like a drum.

"How much power does your laser have left?" Elara asked.

"Not enough to beat that," Finn said, looking at the Custodian. It had almost cleared a path and he could practically feel the heat from its laser bright eyes burning into him.

"It doesn't need to," Elara replied. She grabbed Finn's laser and switched the setting to cutting mode, before handing him her shotgun and tearing the bandolier of cartridges away from her body. "Keep it busy."

"Why, what are you going to do?" Finn said, hastily shoving cartridges into the weapon.

Elara stood up and aimed the laser, but instead of pointing it at the custodian, she leveled the weapon at the wall.

"I'm going to make us a new door," Elara said.

Laser light burst from the barrel of the cannon in a tightly confined beam, and the wall between Yuki Tanaka's office and the adjacent space began to melt. The sharp clatter of marble being smashed, and the taut screech of metal being wrought out of shape spun Finn around, and he found that the custodian was almost on top of him. The spear was thrust at his chest, and he deflected the blade on pure instinct, but while his reaction spared him from being impaled, the electrified weapon gripped his body with powerful convulsions. It was a familiar pain, one he'd experienced almost every day of his working life in the reclamation yards of Metalhaven, at the end of a prefect's nightstick. It didn't make him afraid. It made him angry.

The custodian swung again, and Finn ducked under the crackling blade, but this time he didn't retreat – he attacked. To anyone watching, choosing to stand toe-to-toe with an eight-foot killing machine would have seemed like madness, when the sensible choice was to fall back. They would have asked Finn, why?

Because fuck them, that's why...

Finn was so close to the machine that he could smell the mineral oil that lubricated its gears, and feel the the heat pulsing from its power cell. He swung the combat shotgun at the back of the machine's leg and through a mixture of good timing and good fortune, caught the custodian off balance. Its mechanical knee buckled, and the monster crashed into the steel tile floor, denting and scraping the panels as it thrashed and clawed in a desperate effort to right itself. Finn spun the combat shotgun back into his grip and unloaded its buckshot cartridges into the machine, first aiming at it head, which the custodian protected, before blasting any part of the robot that was visible and vulnerable. Sparks flew and shot bounced all around the office, shattering mirrors, vases, paintings, computer screens and even scratching the paint on Finn's armor, but the one thing that remained undamaged was the custodian itself.

Howling and hissing like a beast, the machine thrashed an arm at Finn and struck him cleanly across the chest. His armor held but the blow was ferocious and sent him crashing into the wall that Elara had been cutting through with Finn's laser. The steel panels gave way and he tumbled into the gothic office, finding himself flat on his back and staring up at gargoyles, skulls, vampires and demons, all with twisted expressions, like they were laughing at him.

"You almost had it," Elara said, suddenly appearing above him and blocking his view of the ghastly office.

"Almost isn't good enough," Finn said, wincing as she hauled him to his feet. If it hadn't been for his armor, his sternum would have been squashed against his spine. "I blasted that thing point blank and it shook it off."

"Not quite," Elara said.

She nodded toward the hole in the wall that Finn's body had created, and he saw that the custodian's spear was no longer the only object that was arcing tendrils of electricity. Finn's attack had bust open the machine's chest cavity and damaged its motor functions, but not enough to stop it. It was barely enough to slow it down.

"Where's Scraps?" Finn asked, hurrying away from the custodian to buy themselves more time. "We need Chiefy if we're going to stand a chance."

"He's over by the door to this office, but Chiefy is still down," Elara said. They were both hobbling now, as if they were on the final leg of a grueling march across the frozen wastelands of post-war Northern Canada. "See what you can do to help, while I take out the EMP pulse emitters in the cathedral."

Elara released Finn's arm and without her support, he dropped to one knee, more exhausted than he realized. Elara stopped and turned back to help him, but Finn shook his head.

"No, go on, I'll be fine," Finn said, waving her away. "Destroy the emitters. If they're still active when Chiefy wakes up, that contraption will just knock him out again."

Finn reached for his med kit, but it was already gone; he'd tipped the contents onto the floor of Tanaka's office when helping Elara. Then he felt a sharp prick to his neck, and he slapped his hand to the site of the pain, like he was trying to swat a mosquito, but Elara had already drawn the needle out of his skin.

"That's a triple dose," she said. It was like she'd teleported across the room. "It'll make you feel incredible for a couple of hours, then give you a four-alarm hangover from hell."

"If I'm still alive tomorrow, remind me to thank you," Finn said. He didn't know what Elara had stuck him with, but it felt good.

Elara ran outside and before long, the gothic office was lit up by flashes of red laser light, as she set to work destroying the EMP pulse emitters. Finn climbed to his feet, and reeled as the drugs took effect, rapidly abolishing his aches and pains and flooding his muscles with concentrated energy. He felt like he could take on a hundred custodians all by himself, but his narcotic-inducted euphoria was not enough to overcome reason. He had tried to one-on-one the custodian and failed. Next time, he was going to have help.

Hurrying to Scraps, Finn ran past a display of gothic armor and weaponry that dominated an interior wall inside Theodore Westwood's office. There were suits of armor, swords and shields, and everything in-between, enough to equip an army. Finn pulled a longsword from the wall then yanked a halberd from the grip of an armored mannequin, before resuming his charge toward his two robot companions.

"Intruders!" the custodian yelled, as it tore the gash in the wall wider with its bare hands and began to pull itself though.

Finn had perhaps a minute to spare, assuming his luck held out.

"How are you doing, pal?" Finn said, crouching beside his buddy and the disabled foreman.

"Close-close!" Scraps said, without looking up. He was working furiously to repair the disabled robot, and Finn could see components littering the floor around the foreman's body, taken from computers and devices in the office, and perhaps even from Scraps' own circuits. "Two min-mins!"

Finn knew that was too long, but he didn't want to discourage Scraps. Instead, he peered inside Chiefy's flipped open cranium and tried to help diagnose the problem.

"What do you need?" Finn said. His mind was racing, and he couldn't think straight.

"Master fuse!" Scraps said, pointing to the device. "Can't replace. Can't find!"

Finn suddenly knew what to do because he'd done it before. Scraps was based on a heavily upgraded Gen-Three Foreman Logic Processor that Finn had stolen from a damaged machine. In the process of learning how to repair the robot, he'd worked out a hundred ways to improvise around problems just like the one Scraps was facing.

"You don't need it, pal," Finn said, thrusting his fingers inside the foreman's head and adjusting wiring terminals, switch positions and components orders. "There, that should do it!"

Scraps scowled at the changes Finn had made, then scowled at Finn. "That bodge-job! Finn a hack!"

"I'm the hack who built you," Finn hit back. The stone floor was shaking now, and Finn could feel the custodian's eyes on his back. "Turn him on and cycle his operating system. It'll work, I promise."

Scraps still looked skeptical then the little robot's eyes widened with fright. "Look out!"

Finn had seen the custodian out of the corner of his eye, and he was ready. Raising the longsword, he parried the spear thrust then countered, stabbing his sword into the killer machine's torn-open chest cavity. Electricity crackled and the robot howled before it pulled the blade from its body and shoved Finn back.

"Cycle his power!" Finn called out to Scraps, while backing away into the cathedral space outside the office. "Do it now!"

The custodian accelerated, swinging its electrified spear with blistering speed. In his amped-up state, Finn could block some but not all of the attacks and he was struck to the ground by a pulverizing blow that sent his sword skidding across the marble floor like a hockey puck. The spear loomed above him and Finn raised his hands in a desperate attempt to defend himself, then blasts of red laser light slammed into the custodian's head and body and drove it back. Elara advanced, sensing the kill, but the custodian grabbed her armor and lifted her off the ground like she weighed nothing.

The spear was drawn back, and Finn clambered toward Elara, hands outstretched toward her and crying her name, then the blade of a halberd sliced through the custodian's arm, and Elara dropped to the ground. The custodian roared and spun around to face its attacker. Chiefy was standing tall, medieval weapon in hand and mechanical eyes narrowed. For the first time since the foreman had been unchained from the

Authority's strict programming parameters, Chiefy was pissed.

"You will not harm my friends..."

The custodian laughed, mocking the smaller robot. "You have no friends. You are a labor model. An automaton. Defective. Inferior."

"My name is Chiefy," the foreman said, halberd ready to strike. "And I am not inferior. I am free."

The custodian darted toward Chiefy and at the same time, the foreman swung the halberd. The two machines clashed, and, in the blink of an eye, it was over. The custodian's head fell from its broad metal shoulders and thudded into the marble floor, cracking the stone like glass. Finn cried out in joy and relief, and climbed to his knees, but his exhilaration was short lived. The custodian's electrified spear had been impaled through Chiefy's power core, destroying the brave robot's beating heart.

14

OUT OF DANGER

Chiefy was still functioning by the time Finn had finally managed to drag his weary body off the floor to reach him, but the robot was paralyzed by electrical pulses that were emanating from the custodian's spear. Scraps came flying over, his little eyes wide with fear, but Elara leapt into the robot's path and plucked him out of mid-air like a ball before he could reach Chiefy and be caught in the web of energy that had gripped the foreman.

"No!" Scraps cried, reaching out to Chiefy. "Help him!"

"We will, pal, don't worry," Finn said, trying to offer reassurance, but he was painfully aware that he was giving false hope. The damage Chiefy had sustained was critical and far beyond his ability to repair without the aid of a full workshop.

Tiptoeing around the two warring machines, which were still frozen in place at the moment they had struck and disabled one another, Finn searched the handle of the electrified spear, looking for a way to disable it. Then he saw the switch on the grip just above where the custodian's sole remaining hand was holding the weapon's shaft. He tried to reach it, but it was like touching a live wire and the pulses of electrical current beat him back.

"Try this," Elara said, offering Finn her knife.

He took it and aimed the tip of the long blade at the shaft of the spear before stabbing it at the switch and making contact. A low, descending thrum resonated throughout the regent's cathedral as the energy core of the weapon shut down and the electrical arcs finally dissipated.

"Thank... you..." said Chiefy. His body was still frozen, but his mechanical eyes and mouth were able to move, albeit sluggishly and with great effort.

"Chiefy okay!" Elara released Scraps and the robot leapt onto Chiefy's shoulder. "Chiefy still active!"

Elara met Finn's eyes and, in that fleeting, imploring glance, he understood the question she had asked, without speaking the words: was Chiefy damaged beyond repair? The look he returned answered her question, and Elara's eyes fell to the floor.

"Finn fix!" Scraps added, turning to Finn. The hopeful smile on his buddy's face was soul-crushing. "Finn clever!"

"The damage is too bad, pal," Finn said, and Scraps began to tremble. "There's nothing I can do for him here."

Scraps whimpered then turned to Chiefy and hugged the robot's head so tightly that his fingers squealed across the metal. Finn felt sick. He hated that he could do nothing for the foreman who had saved them, but he hated more that he'd crushed Scraps' hopes and caused the robot pain.

"Did I... win?" Chiefy said, his eyes flicking across to Finn. "Are you... out of danger?"

"You got him," Finn said, smiling at the foreman. "Took his head clean off, in fact."

"Good!" Chiefy replied. He smiled, but the robot's mechanical mouth was twitching and the lights behind his eyes were flickering softly. "Thank you... for my life. It was... fun..."

Chiefy's final word trailed off then repeated on a loop, "fun, fun, fun, fun...", fading in volume each time until the residual power flowing through his circuits was expended and the robot shut down.

"No!" Scraps cried, climbing onto Chiefy's head, and throwing open the cranial section to access the robot's brain. "Chiefy can't die! Scraps need Chiefy!"

Images of Owen invaded Finn's thoughts, and he wanted to look away, but he knew that would have been spineless. Instead, he moved to his friend's side and rested a hand on Scraps' head.

"He's gone, pal," Finn said, softly, as his friend trembled. "I'm sorry."

Scraps jumped into Finn's arms, and he hugged the robot tightly as he sobbed his dry tears onto Finn's cold, armored shoulder. Never in all his life had we wanted to tear down the Authority more than he did in that moment.

"Maybe he's not gone completely," Elara said. She was standing over Chiefy, looking inside the robot's opened head. "Can't you salvage some components and bring them back with us? Chiefy's body may be broken, but his mind is intact."

"Yes-yes!" Scraps said, suddenly smiling and alert. "Finn remove FLP!"

Finn considered the idea and while he couldn't be certain

that the FLP had survived the electrical shocks that had crippled Chiefy's body, he agreed there was a chance.

"We can give it a go," Finn said, placing Scraps back onto Chiefy's shoulder. "Let me try to prise this thing free," he added, employing Elara's black combat knife in another non-lethal action.

"While you're doing that, I'll try to work out how we get from here into Elysium," Elara said, looking around the cathedral, which was now littered with the wreckage of their battle with the custodian.

"I think I hit Tanaka with at least a couple of tranq rounds before he escaped, so he and Ivanov should still be out cold for a few hours," Finn said, while working to remove Chiefy's FLP. "Even so, we should hurry. There's still a chance they'll be discovered, or that they already have been. The longer we wait, the less likely it is we'll find Maxim Volkov."

Elara nodded. "I'll check Theodore Westwood's office," she said, heading back into the gothic space. "These are supposed to be places of work, so you'd think the bastard has a computer terminal, at least."

Finn didn't see Elara leave because he was still too engrossed in his work. Removing FLPs was not an easy task, and despite the fact it required poking around inside the robot's brain, it was also not a delicate operation. It required force, and no small amount of luck.

"Got it!" Finn said, as the FLP sprang from it socket. He lifted the chip out using the tip of the blade then snatched it between the forefinger and thumb of his other hand before it fell and was lost inside Chiefy's head. "Open wide, pal, you need to take care of this until we can get back to Metalhaven."

Scraps opened his mouth and Finn fed the FLP to him for safekeeping, before he dove back inside the robot's head, looking for memory chips. Many of the circuits and ICs were already fried, but the Makehaven crews that built foremen were good at their jobs, and they always protected the core components more carefully.

"Here, swallow this too," Finn said, posting Chiefy's short-term memory chip into Scraps' mouth. "His archive memory is shot, so you'll have to re-educate him, but the short-term chip looks good, so at least he'll come back as himself. Assuming we can fix these chips into another foreman's body, of course."

"Not if, when!" Scraps said, swallowing the chip. "Finn rebuild Chiefy! Finn clever!"

Finn laughed and patted the robot affectionately. He appreciated the absolute faith that Scraps had in his abilities, and the fact the robot was feeling positive again, but the weight of the task was heavy, and he hoped he was up to it.

"Hey, if you're done playing robot doctor, I need you over here," Elara called out.

Finn started toward Westwood's office, but Scraps jumped onto his shoulder and pointed back toward Chiefy.

"Don't leave like that..." the robot said, forlornly. "Looks bad."

Finn turned back to the warring duo and understood Scraps' point. It didn't seem right to leave Chiefy in such an inelegant pose. Prising the custodian's metal fingers free from the shaft of the spear, Finn then shoulder-barged the massive robot and sent it toppling to the marble floor like a great oak that had been felled. With more care, he then removed the spear from Chiefy's chest and took the weight of the robot's body onto his shoulders, which was much heavier than he was expecting. Groaning and gurning from the strain, he managed to lower Chiefy to the ground, then lay one hand atop the other in a respectful pose that was more befitting of the honored dead.

"Hey, I'm still waiting!" Elara called out.

"You go, pal," Finn said, shaking out his arms and legs. "I just need a minute to recover."

Scraps nodded but before he left, he dropped onto Chiefy's chest and hugged the robot a final time, before wiping a finger underneath a dry eye and zooming away without looking back. In many ways, Finn envied his little robot pal. His modified Foreman Logic Processor, augmented with additional CPUs and components that Finn had saved from reclamation yard seven, processed life thousands of times faster than his own, organic brain did. Scraps had already grieved, already suffered, and already come to terms with his loss, aided by the hope that Chiefy could yet be reborn. In contrast, Finn still woke at night, sweat beading his brow, and with the image of Owen Thomas burned into his eyes. *Maybe that's how it should be...* Finn thought. *Maybe that pain is all I have left of him.*

Finn was about to leave when his eyes were drawn to the spear on the ground. He picked it up and it was far too large for him to brandish effectively, but there was something compelling about the weapon, and with his baseball bat crushed, he needed something else to wield. Then he saw his laser cannon on the ground, where it had fallen after Chiefy had cut off the custodian's hand, forcing it to drop Elara. He recovered the cannon and checked the charge level. It was just enough.

"Finn, where are you?" Elara called out, impatiently. "We need to hustle."

"I'll be there in a minute!" Finn called back, while using his laser to slice through the lower part of the spear's shaft, careful to avoid destroying any important electronics.

The metal was an alloy that Finn didn't recognize, and it took everything his laser had left to cut through it, but finally he was done. Snapping his cannon to its magnetic holster, he picked up the shortened spear and flourished it, as he'd been taught to do during combat training at the prosecutor barracks. Removing a chunk of the metal had actually given it better balance, and it felt natural in his hands. Then he saw the switch on the handle and his thumb slid onto it.

"I might fry myself, but what the hell..." Finn said.

The weapon activated and the tip of the spear crackled with the power of a dozen prefect's nightsticks. The handle was insulated, and Finn was able to spin and swing the spear without electrocuting himself. It felt good, it felt right, and he couldn't wait to use the weapon on an unsuspecting prefect. *Let's see how you like it, you sadistic fucks...* Finn thought, eager to deliver some righteous payback.

"Are you still on this mission or not?"

Elara was standing at the entrance to the gothic office, hands on hips. Her scolding tone of voice and fierce expression were more terrifying than any custodian robot, and Finn set off toward her at a fast jog.

"Sorry, I was just sorting myself out with a new weapon," Finn said, showing Elara the spear. She gave an appreciative nod then tapped at something new that was attached to her hip.

"You're not the only one who's been shopping," Elara said, turning her right hip to face him.

"Do you think Westwood will mind?" Finn smiled at the crossbow that Elara had removed from the regent's display of gothic weaponry.

"I'll be sure to ask his permission, when I see him," Elara replied, and from the ominous tone of her voice, Finn had a sneaking suspicion that asking permission actually meant shooting the man with his own weapon.

"You'll still need a weapon for when things get more up close and personal," Finn said, gesturing to the long wall of gothic weaponry.

"Pick something for me," Elara replied, before folding her arms expectantly. "I'd be interested to see what you choose."

Finn accepted the challenge and promenaded in front of the wall to get a closer look at the selection on offer. There were swords, axes, daggers, maces; everything a medieval army could want. Then he spotted an axe with a forge-blackened two-sided head, which looked sharp enough to cut steel. It's haft was about half-a-meter long and made from a dark wood, wrapped in black leather. A raven, with its wings spread in a threatening pose, was embossed into the blade.

"How about this?" Finn said, removing the axe from the wall. It felt weighty, but not too heavy that it couldn't be wielded with speed and force.

He offered the axe to Elara, presenting it like a squire might present a sword to his knight, and waited for her reaction. To his surprise, he found himself feeling anxious about whether his choice of weapon would meet with his former mentor's approval. Sensing this, Elara drew out the ceremony, torturing him by making him wait. Then she smiled and took the weapon, before admiring it as a craftsman might admire their work.

"It's perfect," Elara said, giving the axe a few test swings. "Perfect for removing Volkov's fat head, that is."

Finn laughed. "Stick to chopping off a hand or something less vital, at least until we're done with him."

"Look-look!" Scraps called out, distracting them both from murderous thoughts.

The little robot was perched on Westwood's gothic inspired desk, replete with gargoyles carved into the knee of each leg. The regent's computer terminal was active and the light from the screen was casting threatening shadows all around the office.

"Are you in?" Finn asked, and the robot nodded, impressing him. "That was quick."

"Volkov DNA!" Scraps said. "Like skeleton key."

The word skeleton made Finn suddenly aware of the dozens of frightening statues and paintings inside the gloomy office, all of which were representations of people and creatures that were dead, dying, or death personified. An intimidating nine-foot statue of the grim reaper himself was poised behind Westwood's desk, complete with scythe. Finn could barely stand to take his eyes off it, for fear that the blade might strike and claim him.

"Can you shut down all the escape pods in the regent's villas?" Finn asked. "If Volkov has gotten wind of what's happening up here, we need to make sure that coward can't run."

"Already done-done!" Scraps said, pleased with himself.

"Great work, pal," Finn said, banging his fist on the desk, and causing a stone-carved skull to roll over. "What else can you do from here?"

"How about tapping into the surveillance and security systems in Elysium?" Elara suggested, sliding the haft of her axe through a belt loop on her webbing. "Fighting a single custodian is more than enough for one trip to paradise."

"No cameras," Scraps replied, shrugging. "No security."

"There's no security at all in Elysium?" Finn asked, wanting to make sure he'd understood correctly.

"Nope-nope!" Scraps said. "Weapons not allowed. Cameras not allowed." The robot grinned. "Regents like privacy."

"I'll bet they do, the perverted fuckers," Elara said, with deep resentment.

"How about access routes into Elysium?" Finn said trying not to think of all the sordid perversions that the regents delighted themselves in, free from the scrutiny of the outside world. "Tanaka had an elevator in his office. Maybe we can use the same one to enter Elysium?"

Elara nodded her agreement. "It would help to know if their unconscious bodies are still there, because if they're not, we can expect to meet resistance once we reach the middle level."

Finn frowned. "But resistance from who and what? If there's no security in Elysium, who will try to stop us?"

Finn and Elara both looked to Scraps to provide the answer, but the robot just shrugged. "No ask me..." he said, unhelpfully. "Scraps don't know!"

Elara rolled her eyes and sighed, then she too shrugged.

"Then there's only one thing for it," she said, fingers drumming against the frame of her new crossbow. "It's time we paid a visit to paradise."

15

ELYSIUM

Finn waded through the wreckage left behind after the custodian had bulldozed through Yuki Tanaka's office, and found the elevator that the regents had used to escape into Elysium. Like many of the doors they'd come across inside the sub-oceanic complex, it was accessible only through use of a DNA key. Once again, Ivan Volkov's blood, identical to his father's, functioned as a skeleton key that allowed them into places that no-one from Zavetgrad had ever seen before, either worker or gold.

"The bodies are gone," Finn said, as Tanaka's elevator reached them, and the doors opened with a tuneful ping. He checked inside, finding evidence of the tranq rounds he'd sprayed into the elevator car as Tanaka and Ivanov made their escape. "I was sure I hit that bastard, but if I did then he should be here."

"It's possible that one of those housekeeper robots found them," Elara said, stepping inside next to Finn. "It's probably not the first time they've come across one or more of the regents, blind drunk or passed out from drugs, or both."

"I hope you're right, because if Volkov has already fled to his villa and found a way to reactivate his escape sub, I'll be pissed."

"Language..." Scraps scolded him.

Scraps was perched on Elara's shoulder and looked in good spirits, despite the trauma of Chiefy's destruction. The foreman robot's FLP and short-term memory chip were inside his belly, providing the possibility for a future robotic rebirth, and this was enough to give the robot hope. And hope was a powerful ally, for robot and human alike.

"Sorry, pal," Finn said, looking suitably repentant.

"I hope you're not squeamish," Elara cut in, hitting one of only two buttons inside the elevator, which was simply marked with the letter "E" in an elaborate script font. "Whatever we see inside Elysium is likely to be an eye opener."

The elevator descended and, as with the journey from the surface to the servant's quarters, progress was slow and steady to allow their bodies to adjust to changes in pressure. Then when the car finally thudded into position and the doors began to open, accompanied by another tuneful ping, Scraps took Elara's advice and covered his eyes with his hands. If the situation hadn't been so tense, Finn would have laughed. He empathized with the little robot not wanting to witness the debaucheries of Elysium, and if he didn't need to be alert to danger, he would have shielded his eyes too.

"Scraps, start scanning," Finn said, inching through the door with his submachine gun held ready, since his laser was out of power. "If there are any more custodians lurking down here, we need to know before they jump out and spear us."

"Scraps already scanning," the robot replied, now peeping through his fingers. "But no custodians."

"What about other robots?" Elara added, stalking ahead and covering the corridor outside the elevator with her weapon.

"Robots, yes-yes..." Scraps said, with a wary tone. "Housekeepers. Maybe others."

This last part caused Finn to pause and turn to the robot. "What others, pal? The last time you had a strange feeling, an eight-foot murder-bot came after us."

"Not sure," Scraps replied, scowling. "Different, but not murder-bots."

Finn blew out a sigh and looked at Elara, who merely shrugged off Scraps' comment.

"We'll just have to find out when we find out," she said, with a resigned air. "But my chits are on it being something freaky and perverted, rather than deadly."

Finn laughed. "I'm not sure if that's better or worse."

His pulse quickened as he followed the corridor from Tanaka's elevator and got his first look at Elysium. It took his breath away, and for a time, Finn forgot where he was and the potential dangers that lay ahead, and simply gazed in awe at the space. Elysium was oval shaped, like an enormous golden egg, but it wasn't only the walls that were curved; there wasn't a straight edge to be seen anywhere. Structures floated in midair like clouds and Finn couldn't see how they were held up, while sinuous openings like the mouths of conch shells hinted at hidden rooms and alcoves secluded all across the sweeping space. Likewise, the corridor that had led them from Tanaka's elevator had looped around in a spiral, concealing the entrance from Elysium and helping to maintain the illusion of a seamless, flowing space, sealed from the outside world, like a womb. It was like nothing on Earth, and as ridiculous as it sounded, Finn wondered whether the elevator ride had transported them to another planet entirely, or maybe even to Nimbus.

"Is this Elysium?" Finn asked, still in awe of the space.

"It must be," Elara said, equally struck by the strangeness and beauty of the place.

"What's that noise?" Finn asked, taking baby steps forward. "It's familiar but I'm not sure why."

He hadn't noticed until then, but now Finn realized that the sounds had always been there, from the moment the elevator doors had opened, lurking in the background like the white noise of a busy mind.

"It's music," Elara answered. There was a yearning in her voice, and she was momentarily lost in the moment, the sounds carrying her away like snow in the wind. "Only regents are allowed to hear it. I got a taste of it once when the Regent of Volthaven arrived in his skycar to begin a trial ceremony. The door opened and for few seconds, I heard it. It was just like this."

Finn closed his eyes to free himself of distractions and focus only on the music. He'd read about the art on his data device, but the relic's speaker was smashed and so his knowledge was academic, but the more he listened, the more he understood how poorly the words matched the reality. Music could not be described, he realized. It had to be experienced.

"Keeping this from us is just another spiteful cruelty the regents have inflicted on Zavetgrad," Elara said, her head gently swaying in time with the notes, as violin and cello weaved a tapestry around them both, ensnaring them like a spider's web. "I don't know how the countries of the old world could have ever been at war when something this beautiful connected them."

Finn didn't answer because he didn't have the words to express how he felt, and with each new instrument that merged into the symphony, he found himself becoming more and more detached, like he was falling down a well that had no bottom. The music didn't just surround him, it was part of him, like every surface in Elysium resonated with its dreamlike allure. The music continued, unhurried and unaware of the violence its curators had perpetrated upon the world, like it originated from a different reality, one where death and misery didn't exist. Piano and drums added comfort and depth, like a warming liquor, while the interplay between wind and string instruments was like a conversation between lovers who knew one other so instinctually that they could finish each other's thoughts and sentences. Listening to the music was like being immersed in warm water, and for those precious few minutes, Finn forgot about Metalhaven, Owen, the trials, and the suffering of hundreds of thousands of workers, and was transported to a place of pure bliss, a refuge from the bitter reality of the world. But like all dreams, it had to end.

"It almost makes me not want to crush this place and send it crashing to the bottom of the ocean," Finn said. He opened his eyes and saw that Elara was looking at him, wearing a quizzical expression. "I said 'almost'," he added, just to be clear that the music had not pacified him completely.

"Let's find Volkov and get back to Metalhaven," Elara said, though Finn could hear the regret in her voice too. Like him, without the gnawing tug of conscience holding her back, she wouldn't leave either.

Scraps guided them, using his scanners to locate which of the alluringly curvaceous openings led to the villa pods, and it didn't take long for their pre-conceptions of Elysium to be confirmed. A stage floated past them, supported by the mysterious force that kept the other structures airborne, and Finn and Elara were compelled to stop and stare. The platform was filled with naked men and women, some of whom danced to the music that permeated every square inch of Elysium, while others frolicked and cavorted, either intertwined in acts of sexual pleasure, or pleasuring themselves while watching the others dance.

"What the fuck..." Finn said, wanting to look away but finding it impossible to do so. "But there isn't even anyone watching them?"

"Not people..." Scraps said. He was still on Elara's shoulder but was facing away from the debauched performance. "Robots..."

"These are robots?" Finn said, pointing to one of the dancers, who was gliding across the stage in front of him, seemingly oblivious to his presence.

"Yes-yes," Scraps said. "We go... Scraps no like."

Finn turned back to the performance, open mouthed, then he noticed the artificial shine behind the dancers' eyes, and the almost imperceptible seams in their glistening synthetic flesh, where one thrusting body part joined another. Before long, he recognized patterns in the motions of those engaged in the orgy, like a song on repeat that once ended, simply rewound and started all over again. The stage then rose higher and began to orbit Elysium, while the enactment continued unabated.

"That was... weird," Elara said. There was a touch of rouge to her cheeks and Finn thought that it was probably the first time he'd seen her shocked by anything. "I vote we avoid the robot sex orgies from this point on."

"Scraps agrees," the robot said, carefully adjusting his position on Elara's shoulder so that he couldn't see the floating stage. "This way," he added, pointing toward a stream that meandered the full length of Elysium, across its longest point. "Villas not far."

Following the stream led them to a sunken island, and a path that swept back on itself and corkscrewed beneath the flow of water, which continued overhead, guided by a crystal-glass channel that was so pure it looked like the water was floating in mid-air. Finn saw a woman standing by the side of the path, wearing a silk toga that exposed her breasts and left little of the rest of her body to the imagination. She didn't look at him as he approached and simply smiled before holding out a fluted, crystal glass filled with a sparkling amber liquid that Finn recognized as champagne, or a close equivalent. Other men and women stood waiting further along the path, dressed similarly and also staring blankly ahead. Finn's first thought was that they were also automatons, but as Finn stood in front of the woman, so that she had no choice but to look directly at him, he knew that she was real. The veins in her neck began to thump harder and faster, her breathing accelerated, and her muscles became taut. She was a servant, and she was suddenly petrified with fear.

"We're looking for Maxim Volkov; tell me where he is,"

Finn said. He spoke the demand with an even but firm tone, yet the woman simply stared blankly ahead, as if looking through him. "Maxim Volkov..." Finn repeated, more sternly. He didn't want to scare the woman, who was just as much a victim of the regents as the workers of Zavetgrad were, but he also needed an answer. "Tell me where to find him, now."

The woman said nothing but drew back the glass of champagne and hugged it to her naked chest, as if to stress the point that it wasn't for him. Finn sighed then stepped aside, and let Elara take his place.

"Volkov..." Elara said, more forcefully than Finn. She reached out and lifted the woman's chin, but still, she did not meet their eyes. "You just have to tell us where he is, and we'll leave you alone."

The woman did nothing and said nothing, and Finn imagined that no amount of coercion would produce a different result.

"There's no point," Finn said, turning back to the path. "We're like a different species to them. All they know is what the regents have conditioned them to think and do."

Finn continued along the winding path, walking past other servants who also offered drinks before realizing that it wasn't a regent standing before them, and shrinking back into their alcoves, chins tucked into their chests. Climbing out the other side of the sunken island, Finn found himself in front of another stage, though this one wasn't floating, nor was it filled with cavorting robots. Instead, a single man – Finn thought it was a man not a machine, because he couldn't see any seams in his naked flesh – was reciting a speech that sounded almost musical in its meter but had no instrumental accompaniment. The language was also strange, and many of the words made no sense. The he heard the phrase, "Friends, Romans, countrymen; lend me your ears..." and a memory stirred. "I come to bury Caesar, not to praise him..." the man went on, and suddenly Finn understood what was happening.

"He's an actor," Finn said, to a consternated-looking Elara. "It's a kind of storyteller."

"And who is Caesar, the person he's telling a story about?" Elara asked, as the orator continued with his performance, focusing into the near distance, either unaware of them or ignoring them. "He sounds like someone important."

Finn shrugged. "I think he was a politician, like the regents," he said, trying to remember what he'd read about Shakespeare on his data device. "He was murdered, by those closest to him."

"Why?" Elara said, and again Finn shrugged.

"Maybe he was too powerful, or maybe he was just corrupt and useless, who knows," Finn said. "It's strange that the regents would have this performed for their amusement, knowing how many people want them dead."

"Maybe they think they're better than him," Elara suggested. "Caesar must have been significant to have a story told about him, especially one the regents thought important enough to save. It wouldn't surprise me if Volkov and his cronies got some perverse amusement from knowing they'd outsmarted such a famous man."

"Maybe," Finn said. "All I do know is that this speech isn't going to help us find Volkov."

They turned from the actor and continued in the direction that Scraps had indicated, while the performer enthusiastically delivered the line, "O judgment! thou art fled to brutish beasts, and men have lost their reason…"

While they walked, Finn wondered if Elara had given the regents too much credit in their choice of entertainment. To him the performance was nothing more than spectacle for spectacle's sake, like the robot orgy and the pointlessness of having servants waiting all day just on the off chance of serving their master a drink, as he strolled through the pointless sunken island, beneath a pointless undersea river, in an utterly pointless place.

Passing through one of the conch-shell openings in the wall, they came across what appeared to be a dining hall. Gold tables were filled with food and drinks that would put even the cultural quarter's best eateries to shame. Then he noticed that each table was staffed by a housekeeper robot, and Finn reached for his weapon before realizing that the machines were immobile, like statues.

"Why haven't they reacted to us?" Finn said, weapon still held ready.

"Did you do this?" Elara asked Scraps, who was still on her shoulder.

"Nope-nope!" Scraps replied. "Housekeepers in passive mode. No scanning."

Finn huffed a laugh. "The regents truthfully never expected anyone from the outside to reach Elysium. They think they're completely safe down here."

"Well, they were wrong," Elara replied, darkly, while searching their new location with scowling eyes "The question is where the hell are they all?"

"That way!" Scraps said, pointing toward a corner of the

room that was obscured in a cloud of smoke, like a thick morning fog.

Finn smelled the air and the scent was familiar as was the taste on his tongue; acrid, bitter, but also somehow compelling. He walked toward the smoke-filled corner, as if drawn to it by a mystery force, and the closer he got, the stronger and more compelling the aromas became.

"It's a drug den," Elara said, wafting the smoke from her eyes. "There are places like this in the Authority sector, if you know where to look."

Finn raised an eyebrow in Elara's direction, and she frowned at him. "I didn't go looking if that's what you're thinking," she said, pointedly. "But Chief Prosecutor Voss could be found inside one most evenings, and when he summoned you for some bullshit reason or another, you had to go." Elara looked around the den, but the extensive range of narcotics appeared to shock even her educated eyes. "I've never seen anything quite like this, though. I don't even know what half the crap in here is."

Scraps flew from Elara's shoulder and landed on one of the tables, which was littered with used needles, pipes, and half-smoked, hand-rolled cigarettes.

"Opium… henbane… LSD… N7… cocaine… Rapture…" Scraps said, pointing around the room while reeling off a list of narcotics, some of which were as old as the Shakespearean play the actor had been reciting, while others were new and unknown even to Finn and Elara. "Look-look!" Scraps added, pointing to a tank in the middle of the den, which was glowing blue with bioluminescent organisms, some of which Finn recognized from inside the caves that ran beneath Zavetgrad.

"Are those radioactive critters the source of some of these drugs?" Finn asked, and Scraps nodded.

"Dangerous..." the robot said, in a cautionary tone. "Powerful."

Finn moved closer to the tank and tapped on the glass, causing the little critters to scurry around inside. Then through the bubbling blue soup, he saw a pair of feet, and his heart leapt into his mouth.

"Elara!" Finn said, snapping his submachinegun out front and orbiting the tank so that he could confront the owner of the feet, but the man was out cold, sprawled in an armchair, wearing only a bathrobe.

Elara darted around the other side of the tank, crossbow aimed first at the unconscious man, then at another who was lying flat on a red leather couch.

"It's Ivanov and Tanaka," Elara said, recognizing the men before Finn had worked it out. "But how did they get here?"

"Maybe it was like you said," Finn answered, while kicking Ivanov's feet, but the man was dead to the world. "The housekeeper bots found them passed out in the elevator and brought them here. It could be that this is where they were hanging out, before deciding to go to Tanaka's office."

Finn reached down and took Ivanov's pulse, and the man groaned and stirred as he did so.

"Shit, I think they're coming around," he said, jolting back and aiming his weapon at the man. "I can stun them again, and we can come back later, once we've found Volkov."

"No need," Elara said. She squeezed the trigger and a crossbow bolt thudded into Ivanov's neck, sinking four inches deep. "We don't need these two, and we certainly don't need them getting in our way."

"Elara, what are you doing?" Finn said, shocked by the sudden act of murder, but Elara ignored him, reloaded her crossbow, and strolled over to Tanaka on the sofa. "Elara, we came here to capture the regents," Finn added, as she aimed her weapon at the Regent of Stonehaven. "What use are they to us dead?"

"These two are no use at all," Elara said. "We leave here with Volkov, and anyone who comes willingly once we've captured him. The rest, I couldn't give a fuck about."

She fired a bolt into Tanaka's neck and the man grunted and croaked, while his hands pawed pathetically at the shard of metal that had punctured his flesh, but the lingering effects of the tranq rounds had robbed Tanaka of any chance he may have had of saving himself.

"Volkov, or nothing," Elara said, reloading her crossbow for a second time. "That's what we agreed, remember?"

Finn sighed heavily and nodded. He didn't like the path that Elara was leading them both down, but he also couldn't stand to leave the regents alive in such a place. Maybe if recitals of their deeds were to be performed in the future, history would not look favorably upon what they had done, perhaps like Caesar, but if that was to be their story, then so be it.

"I remember what we agreed," Finn said, reluctantly. "We leave with Volkov or nothing."

"Someone coming!" Scraps called out, zooming back onto Elara's shoulder.

"How many?" Finn asked.

"Twenty-four!" Scraps answered, and Finn cursed under his breath.

"Robots, humans?" Elara asked. "Are they armed?"

"Humans," Scraps said. "Unarmed..."

The voices grew louder, then the six remaining regents walked out from one of the curvaceous openings in the wall, surrounded by an entourage of young men and women, naked apart from towels that were loosely wrapped around their waists or tossed casually over their shoulders. Their bodies were wet, and their smiles were broad, as they laughed and joked and teased one other for the amusement of the regents, who stroked, fondled and kissed the servants as they danced around them.

From his swagger and confident manner, Maxim Volkov was naturally the leader of the group, and the Regent of Spacehaven and Mayor turned toward the drug den. At first his eyes were focused on the breasts of a servant girl, who was teasing him with enticing glances and coquettish gestures, until the young woman saw Finn and Elara, and screamed. Volkov and the others stopped dead, their eyes wide. Then they ran.

16

SECRETS AND DOUBTS

Elara drew her crossbow and tracked Maxim Volkov as he fled, but the twenty servants who'd exited the bathhouse with the regents had formed a human shield wall, arms interlinked, and were obstructing her aim.

"We need Volkov, the others don't matter," Elara said, still trying desperately to get a clean shot, but she held her fire, rather than risk hitting and killing a servant.

"I'll try to clear you a path," Finn said, advancing side-by-side with Elara.

Finn aimed his submachine gun into the crowd and began firing tranq rounds at the servants, targeting the exposed flesh on their thighs and stomachs to minimize the risk of serious injury. Bodies fell but the resolve of the servants to protect their masters remained unbroken, and by the time the shield wall was broken, Maxim Volkov and the other regents had fled into cover.

"Shit, I've lost him!" Elara cried, pushing her way through the few servants who had remained standing, while they clawed at her armor and tugged at her ankles, begging her to stop. "Do you see him?"

Finn searched the room, beginning with the rows of tables filled with food and drinks that were still being manned by a small army of stationary housekeeper bots. He spotted Volthaven's regent, Viktor Kozlov, and Amir Kahn of Makehaven, but neither were of crucial importance. Then Maxim Volkov's officious, booming voice filled the room, though still Finn couldn't see the man.

"Housekeepers!" Volkov roared. "Override core protocols, authorization Volkov-six-nine-Gideon-two-alpha!"

The dozens of servile robots suddenly straightened to attention, as if they were cadets and a Head Prefect had just marched onto the parade ground and barked an order.

"Load Defense Program from MROM..." Volkov added, though still Finn could not see him. "... then destroy base memory blocks, and kill the intruders!"

The eyes of the housekeeper bots began to flash vividly, alternating blue, green then red. It reminded Finn of when Scraps would enter periods of deep concentration, processing thousands of possible scenarios in the blink of an eye. Then he remembered something from his studies of robot processing languages and systems that he'd undertaken over the course of years in order to learn the skills he'd need to build Scraps, and he realized they were in trouble.

"Elara, hold up," Finn said, slinging his sub-machinegun and drawing the modified spear from his back scabbard.

"Hold up? But Volkov is getting away!" Elara said, reluctantly halting her advance.

"We'll get him, but right now we have bigger problems," Finn said.

His words were punctuated by the crack of robot feet clashing against the stone floor, then the housekeepers split into two ranks of ten, each marching in time with the other to produce a rhythmic, musical beat.

"Scraps can you hack them?" Elara said, turning to the little robot, who was hovering just to their rear, but Scraps shook his head.

"No hack!" Scraps said. "New programs. MROM!"

"It stands for Mask-ROM," Finn explained, noticing Elara's confused frown. "It's a type of memory that can't be altered, even by Scraps. Volkov just loaded a failsafe program and there's no way to override it."

Elara snorted and hooked her crossbow back on her hip. "There's always one way to override a bot's programming," she said, sliding the double-headed axe from the loop on her webbing. "If we can't hack them, then we smash them."

The first rank of housekeeper robots sprang electrified nightsticks from their wrists and trooped forward, while the rear rank continued to march on the spot, beating the rhythm of their advance, like drummers. The crackle of energy from the energized weapons would have normally sent a shiver racing down Finn's spine, but not this time. This time, he was able to fight fire with fire. He flicked the switch on the handle of his spear, and electricity crackled and pulsed around the blade of the weapon, which throbbed with more raw power than the attacking robots had combined.

Finn took the lead, eager to test his new weapon in anger, and the housekeepers split into pairs, ready to meet his advance. The spear gave him a reach advantage, and he thrust the blade at the closest robot, catching the machine in the chest and dumping the spear's deadly voltage into its circuits.

The robot convulsed and screeched like a boiling kettle before dropping to the stone floor with smoke rising from its fried FLP.

The early victory gave Finn encouragement, and he accelerated his attack, moving with a swiftness that the clunky servant robots couldn't match. He punched through the vanguard and struck down two more housekeepers, as if they had been hit by bolts of lightning. Two split off to attack Elara and Finn allowed himself a moment to watch his former mentor in action, keen to discover whether the weapon he'd selected for her was as brutal as it looked. Elara moved with more grace and fluidity than any fighter Finn had ever seen, avoiding the clumsy swipes and thrashes of the housekeepers then counterattacking with the lethal precision of a scorpion's stinger. Robotic limbs thudded into the ground, leaving crippled housekeepers hobbling and tottering in her wake. She glided past Finn and charged into the second rank of housekeepers, cutting down three before the bewildered machines had managed to process what was happening.

"Can you handle the rest of them?" Elara called out, ducking beneath a probing strike from a housekeeper before burying her axe into the chest of her attacker.

"I can, but why?" Finn said, parrying a blow with his electrified spear and paralyzing the housekeeper in the process.

"Because I'm going after Volkov," Elara said. "We can't risk him getting away."

Finn nodded then searched for Scraps, finding the robot hovering about ten meters above them.

"Buddy, which way did Volkov go?" Finn called out.

"That way!" Scraps said, pointing toward one of the contoured exits.

Elara looked at Scraps, then in the direction the little robot's finger was pointing, before pressing the flat of her boot to the housekeeper's chest and wrenching the axe free. The machine erupted into a fit of sparks and crumpled in a heap, then Elara shimmered into nothingness as her stealth field activated, and the last Finn saw of her was a blur of movement heading away.

"Elara gone!" Scraps said, zooming behind Finn.

"She'll be fine, pal, don't worry," Finn said. The twelve remaining housekeepers suddenly turned their attention to him, and he felt his mouth go dry, regretting telling Elara that he could handle the machines solo. "It's us you need to worry about..."

"Wait-wait, got idea!" Scraps said, then the little robot sped away, leaving Finn to face the re-grouped robot army alone.

"Whatever you have in mind, make it quick," Finn said, slowly backing away from the squad and their crackling, electrified weapons.

"Jump back!" Scraps called out. The robot had torn open a control panel on the end wall, and was interfaced with it. "Behind line!"

"What line?" Finn said, searching the ground, but the patterned marble flooring appeared seamless.

"That line!" Scraps cried.

The robot was bouncing up and down in mid-air while pointing to something Finn couldn't see. Then the ground shook, and the floor began to split apart along the seam that his robot buddy had been trying to point out. Finn almost lost his balance and fell in the yawning abyss below him, but he managed to keep his footing. A waft of hot air then washed over his face, filling his nostrils with a heavily perfumed scent that smelled faintly of cleaning chemicals. He looked down and saw a lake-sized pool of steaming hot water on the sub-level below him, and realized it was the bath house where Volkov and the other regents had been relaxing before he and Elara had broken up their party. It was a steep fall in a deep well, and it filled Finn with dread. His experiences with water thus far had not been happy ones.

"Quick-quick!" Scraps yelled.

Finn looked to his rear and saw that the floor was retracting in multiple places, forming a five-pointed star in the middle of the room. He was in the dead center, and the floor was slowly moving away from him, threatening to leaving him stranded in a central island, along with the twelve robots. He was about to leap to safety when one of the machines grabbed his shoulder and he felt a jolt of electricity grip his muscles. Fighting the pain, he stabbed his spear into the robot, and it exploded away from him as if struck by a cannonball, and fell into the star-shaped pool below. Other housekeepers tried to reach him, wrestling with each other to be the first to reach their target. Some slipped and fell into the water, while others blindly stumbled forward and plunged into the chasm as if unaware that the floor had disappeared beneath them.

"Hurry!" Scraps called out. "Finn-Finn can't swim!"

"I know that, pal!" Finn called back, not welcoming the reminder.

He glanced back at the housekeepers, who were steadily

toppling into the water without any interference from him, then shuffled back as far as the receding floor would allow, to give himself a run-up. Deactivating the spearhead, he threw it like an Olympian athlete, and the weapon thudded into a buffet table like a giant arrow striking a target. He then puffed out his cheeks and sucked in a breath of the steamy, perfumed air.

"Here goes nothing…"

He accelerated into a sprint and pushed off with as much force as his tired legs could manage, but with the weight of his armor and the limited speed he'd been able to build up it wasn't enough. Falling short, Finn's chest thumped into the floor's cross-section, knocking the wind out of him, and he grasped at the stone, desperately trying to cling on, but his fingers were slipping. Scraps flew down and grabbed his armor, before engaging his rotors at maximum power. The downdraught from the spinning blades felt like they were working against him, rather than for him, but the robot's efforts proved just enough, and Finn was able to clamber to safety.

"Thanks, pal," Finn said, rolling onto his back and gasping for breath. "I don't know how many I owe you now."

"Lots," Scraps said, giggling, though the robot also appeared fatigued. Running his rotors at full speed had depleted the energy reserves in his power core. "But Scraps not counting."

"Lucky for me," Finn said, smiling at his friend and savior.

Finn climbed to his feet and hoisted Scraps onto his shoulder before recovering his spear. Also on the buffet table was an ice bucket filled with a bottle of sparkling wine. He picked up the bottle and took a long, deep drink. The bubbles danced on his tongue and the alcohol soothed his frayed nerves. Then the sound of fizzing electronics made him return to the pool. He looked over the precipice and saw that all twelve housekeepers had fallen to their demise, filling the bath house with burned and broken robot parts that had turned the clear water grey with smokey oils and blackened plastics. He laughed and took another swig of champagne before tossing the bottle into the chasm and watching it smash on the head of a robot, like he was christening the maiden voyage of a sailing ship.

"Enjoy your swim," Finn said, and Scraps chuckled.

Finn turned away and headed after Elara, but he didn't get far before he was confronted by a man staring back at him from the other side of the crater. It was the Regent of Volthaven, Victor Kozlov, shivering and dressed only in a towel.

"Stay back!" Kozlov roared. He had a cutlery knife in his trembling hand, and was waving it at Finn like a sword. "I am a Regent of Zavetgrad, and I will be obeyed!"

"Not today you won't, regent," Finn said, starting a slow orbit of the chasm toward Kozlov, who without his fine clothes and army of protectors looked frail and insignificant.

"Stay back, I say!" the man shouted, but Kozlov's voice cracked like old leather, and Finn continued toward him, spear in hand.

"I'll give you a choice," Finn said, as Kozlov backed away, still threatening him with a dinner knife. "You either come with me willingly, or I bring you by force."

"Bring me where?" Kozlov said. The regent hadn't been

looking where he was going and had backed himself into an alcove. "What is the meaning of this outrage?!"

"You're coming with me to Metalhaven," Finn said, cornering the terrified regent. In his armor, Finn towered over the man, who cowered before him like a frightened animal. "You're going to order the special prefecture to surrender Zavetgrad to the people."

"You mad fool!" Kozlov laughed, though it was the cackle of a lunatic. "You have no idea what you're doing!"

"I know exactly what I'm doing," Finn said, electrifying the tip of his spear and aiming it at Kozlov. "I'm removing you from office."

Kozlov laughed maniacally again, and Finn found the man's reaction deeply unsettling. He sensed that the regent knew something Finn didn't, a secret that could negate any victory he believed he had won. He studied the aristocrat, trying to understand him, and the reason for his strange, frightened behavior, but all he saw was a terrified, little man. Under the harsh light of the crackling spearhead, every crease and fold of the regent's jaundiced, bloated face was accentuated, making the man look ghoulish and decayed. In that moment, Finn pitied Victor Kozlov. He was a small, unworthy man, scared and pathetic.

"Laugh all you want, Kozlov, but you're coming with me," Finn said, grabbing the man by the scruff of his neck. "One way or another, the Authority will fall. You can either still be alive to see it, or die here. It's your choice."

Kozlov struggled but Finn was twice as strong, and ten times as determined as the regent was, and he bundled the man out of the alcove and pushed him in the direction he'd last seen Elara running.

"Unhand me!" Kozlov cried, his voice breathless and tense. "Unhand me, I say!"

Kozlov's back suddenly jerked arrow-straight, and the man dropped to his knees, squeezing his hands over his heart. Finn grunted a sigh, realizing that he'd probably have to drag the man, kicking and screaming, but the regent was more than simply defiant, he was in pain. Kozlov then collapsed onto the marble floor, face white and body stiff as a board.

"Cardiac arrest..." Scraps said, whispering the words to Finn.

Finn cursed under his breath and reached for his med-kit before remembering he'd left it on the floor of Yuki Tanaka's office. Powerless to the help the regent, he knelt by the man's side, as Kozlov reached out to him imploringly, eyes bulging from their sockets.

"Will he survive?" Finn asked, taking Kozlov's hand and squeezing it. It was a small act of humanity, though Finn didn't believe the regent deserved it.

"No-no," Scraps said, shaking his head. "Massive attack. Heart failing..."

"He'll never let you have it..." Kozlov wheezed, grinning at Finn through clenched, yellow teeth.

"Who won't?" Finn asked, desperate for the man's secret.

"Enjoy it..." the regent hissed, spiting Finn with his last breath. "... Enjoy it... while you can..."

Viktor Kozlov's eyes went glassy, and his writhing body became still. Finn cursed bitterly then shook his head and stood over the man, hating him more in death than in life. By teasing his secret, Kozlov had robbed Finn of the absolute confidence he'd had that he and Elara were doing the right thing. Unable to stand even looking at the regent, Finn rolled the body to the edge of the star-shaped precipice and hurled it into the pool below.

"Find me another regent, buddy," Finn said, hands on hips, with doubt invading his mind. "Find me one that's still breathing, so I can choke some answers out of them."

17

THE FINAL COMMAND

Scraps led Finn through another of the seemingly endless number of curvaceous doors inside Elysium, and to his surprise, he found that he was walking on grass. It wasn't the brown, threadbare kind that occasionally managed to poke through the poisoned soil of the reclamation yards, but lush, thick and green. The space widened and the ceiling became tall, before blending into the illusion of a sky that was so convincing Finn actually thought he could feel the sun on his face. Then came trees, small, and neatly planted, full of fruits, some of which Finn recognized and others that he didn't. The apples were a vibrant red, and there were oranges too, but a smaller, yellow-orange fruit with a smooth skin was new to him, as was the curious bell-shaped fruit with a leathery, dark skin.

At the far side of the arboretum was a set of garden furniture, as elaborate and ornate as everything else in Elysium. Wicker-framed couches, sofas and loungers were padded with plump cushions fitted with silvery silk covers, while the tables were laden with carafes of fruit juices, liquors and samples of the fruit that were growing on the trees, cut and carefully prepared for a feast.

Theodore Westwood, the Regent of Seedhaven, was sitting on the central couch, surrounded by a dozen of his servants, who clung to his ankles, legs and shoulders, shielding him from the evil outsider who had invaded their perfect garden. Five housekeeper robots stood guard in front of them, hands replaced with nightsticks, which crackled softly, adding a stark, unearthly light to the biblical setting. The dazzling electrical sparks highlighted the seams in the walls and the sprinklers hidden in the ceiling, shattering the illusion of perfection. Suddenly Finn saw the garden for what it was, a barren husk, and a poor imitation of nature's grandeur and beauty. Like the regents, once the façade had been stripped away, all that remained was a rotting shell, barely clinging onto life.

"Whatever you want from me, I won't give it!" Westwood announced, his voice at least appearing strong. "And if you kill me, another of my bloodline will only take my place, and the people of Zavetgrad will be made to suffer greatly for your transgressions!"

At one time, a speech such as the one Westwood had just delivered would have made Finn's skin crawl with fear, but not any longer. With only a sodden towel wrapped loosely around his thin waist, Westwood was no less pitiable than Kozlov had been. The man was tall and skinny, to the point of appearing gaunt, his cheeks sucked in as if the vacuum of space filled his mouth. He looked ill and frail, and above all, frightened.

"Your hereditary privileges end today," Finn said, finger poised on the button, ready to electrify his spear. "There will not be another Regent of Seedhaven. There will not be another regent, ever again."

Like Kozlov, Westwood laughed, but this time Finn was angry, as well as unsettled. *What the fuck do they know? Why is this so funny to them?*

"I admire your courage, Hero of Metalhaven, but it will do you no good," Westwood said, still grinning. "Gideon will never allow Zavetgrad to fall into your filthy hands."

"What does that mean?" Finn said. This was the same threat that Kozlov had made, except Westwood's version was less veiled.

"You will find out, foolish boy," Westwood answered. Then the smile fell from his face. "If you live long enough, that is."

The regent clapped his hands and the housekeeper bots advanced. At the same time, Finn pushed the button on the shaft of the spear to electrify the blade. The robots quickly moved to surround him, but the trees of the arboretum provided perfect cover, and with his reach advantage, the housekeepers didn't stand a chance.

Holding the spear at the base of the shaft, Finn thrust the electrified blade into the chest of the closest machine. The blade barely penetrated its metal shell, but voltage and current were the spear's true weapons and the housekeeper was tormented with an influx of power that exploded the transistors in its FLP and rendered it nothing more than a collection of scrap metal.

The others intensified their attacks, but Finn darted behind a tree, using it to the block the paths of the clumsy robots, while thrashing them down, one by one. As the robots fell, shaking the ground, apples and oranges tumbled onto the perfect grass, some bouncing off the heads of the machines and making them look comical and foolish, as well as inept. Finn realized something then, as he speared the fourth housekeeper robot in the neck and then held the weapon in place, while the machine convulsed and crackled. The defense program that Volkov had loaded into the housekeeper's processors from MROM was as old as Elysium itself. The protected memory blocks had likely been programmed two centuries earlier, and the regents had never thought to upgrade them, because there simply hadn't been a need. Elysium was an impenetrable garden of Eden, or so they had thought. Now, their complacency would cost them dearly.

Striking down the last of the housekeepers, Finn flourished the spear then deactivated it and returned it to his back scabbard. There were still a dozen servants between himself and Westwood, but none of them posed a threat. They were docile and helplessly devoted to their master, and despite knowing that it wasn't their fault, or their choice, to have become these servile concubines, he couldn't help but feel repulsed by them.

"Leave him alone!" one of the servant women yelled, pulling herself in front of Westwood. "Leave! Please!" another cried, a young man of no more than seventeen.

"It's okay, my loves, let me handle this," Westwood cut in.

To Finn's surprise, Westwood stood up and squeezed his gaunt, naked frame past his servants to face Finn directly.

"This is between us," Westwood said, standing tall. "You do not need to harm my servants."

Finn laughed. "What the fuck is this? Compassion?" he said, struggling to believe what he was hearing. "Or are you just trying to protect your property, like any good businessman would?"

Westwood regarded Finn with contempt, like he was a fungus that had infested his plentiful orchard. It was a look he was used to receiving from regents and prefects, but beaten and humiliated as he was, Finn was amazed that Westwood could remain so arrogantly disapproving.

"I am not the monster here," Westwood said, reciting the line with such confidence and elan that Finn almost believed that he was the villain of the story. "Look at what you have done here," the regent added, with a sweeping gesture toward the carnage that surrounded them. "My legacy is one of creation and growth. Because of me, a million people are fed every day, instead of starving to death in this bankrupt world that we regents alone have spared from ruination." He shook his head at Finn. "You believe that you are the salvation of Zavetgrad, but you will be its destroyer, Finn Brasa."

Westwood's words rattled around Finn's brain, and after a lifetime of the Authority's brainwashing and conditioning, he almost believed the man. Almost.

"This isn't just an act to you, is it?" Finn said, understanding something about the regents that he hadn't realized before. "You actually believe your own bullshit, don't you?"

"I know the truth," Westwood said, defiantly. "And the truth is that without the Authority, and without my ancestors, Zavetgrad would not have survived a decade."

"You're wrong," Finn hit back. "I've seen Haven, and I know what life looks like without you." He took a step closer to Westwood, and the servants gathered more tightly around him. "Your reign is over, but you still have a choice. You can come with me, willingly, and help the transition to occur without further bloodshed, or you can die right here, and be buried in your fake garden."

"No!"

A young man rushed at Finn, hands balled into fists, but the charge was frantic and clumsy, and Finn struck the man to the ground as easily as trampling grass.

"Protect the regent!" another yelled, and five more of the servants surged toward Finn, while the others stayed to protect Westwood, like bark surrounding the softer wood of a tree.

Finn electrified his spear and struck the mob down as gently as he could, without drawing blood. Westwood saw his chance and ran, pushing his servants aside and making a dash for the curved exit, but the man's shriveled muscles and diseased organs, neglected by decades of substance abuse and sloth, were unable to carry out the task that the regent's malignant brain had commanded of them. Stumbling on the fallen fruit and broken remains of the housekeeper robots that Finn had mown down earlier, Westwood fell and struck his head on the gnarled roots of the apple tree. At once, the servants broke off their pitiful attack against Finn, and rushed to the regent's side, pawing at the man, and crying out as his blood stained their fingers.

Finn deactivated his spear and sheathed it. He could see the sharp lump of tree root that Westwood had struck his head against, and he feared the worst.

"What's the verdict, pal?" Finn said, as Scraps flew down from his hiding place in one of the orange trees and landed on his shoulder.

"Traumatic brain injury," Scraps said, providing his diagnosis. "Epidural hematoma. Severe."

"So, he's dead?" Finn said, not understanding the technical jargon and latching onto the words 'traumatic' and 'severe'.

"Not yet," Scraps said, "but soon."

Finn shook his head. "If these idiots keep killing themselves, there won't be any regents left to capture." Then he had a troubling thought and glanced at Scraps on his shoulder. "Are there any more left?"

Scraps nodded. "Yes-yes. Amir Khan in drug den."

Finn had to think for a moment before remembering that Khan was the Regent of Makehaven, the sector that manufactured everything from work overalls to foreman robots. He was not someone that Finn had ever had dealings with before, but the man's reputation preceded him. Khan was proud and vain, but Finn had never thought him one of the crueler regents. The trials in Makehaven had generally been swift affairs, with clean outcomes. Khan was a stickler for efficiency, and did not like his sector's workers to be distracted for too long.

"What's Khan doing in the drug den?" Finn asked. Of all the places Khan might have been, this seemed to be the least likely option.

"No clue," Scraps said with a shrug.

Finn sighed again. "Okay, let's see if the Regent of Makehaven will be any more compliant."

He glanced at the bawling mass of servants, who remained bent over Theodore Westwood's body, as the man slowly died. Despite their misplaced devotions, he felt a twinge of sadness for the servants. Their love had been cultivated, like the trees in the incongruous orchard, but their grief was at least real, and grief was something that Finn understood. Even so, he would not shed a tear for the Regent of Seedhaven who, despite claiming to have sustained the lives of millions, had in fact overseen just as much death and cruelty as his contemporaries. Westwood had reaped, not sown, but in death at least his body would serve as fuel to fertilize the fruits in his private orchard. This was the sum total of goodness that the man was capable of.

Leaving the orchard, Finn returned to the drug den, walking past the still crackling and smoldering remains of destroyed housekeepers, and pausing to peer over the star-shaped precipice at the bath house below, where Victor Kozlov was floating, face down in the water. Occasionally, he heard the scurrying of feet and saw a servant, running from one pillar to another, or scampering from an upturned buffet table to the next. They seemed to be following him, though Finn sensed no ill intent. It was like they were watching him, transfixed by this alien invader into their domain.

Reaching the den, Finn found Amir Khan sitting in a grand leather armchair, a glass of whiskey or brandy in his hand. Ten of his servants were seated around him, hands resting on their laps in attentive poses, as if they were waiting for Khan to read them a bedtime story. Yet their attention was not focused on the Regent of Makehaven, but on Finn. Their expectant stares quickly became unnerving, and Finn focused back on Khan, noting the Regent of Makehaven had dressed and was wearing his fine regent's robes. The man's right shirt sleeve was rolled up, and as Finn got closer, he could see that therewas an intravenous line inserted into his forearm.

"You took your time," Khan said, in his silky-smooth voice. "I had expected you to barge in on me much sooner."

"What are you doing?" Finn asked, as the man casually drank from his glass.

"I am denying you your prize," Khan said, cheerfully. There was a glassiness in his eyes and Finn suspected that his aloofness was not natural, but stimulated by alcohol, and whatever narcotic he was pumping into his bloodstream. "You have no doubt already killed my friends, so I am denying you the pleasure of murdering me as well." Khan smiled and shook the line fixed to his arm. "I have already killed myself, and I suspect my death will be much more enjoyable than those of my fellow regents."

Finn glanced at Scraps, but the robot was already conducting an analysis of the substance that was being fed through the tube.

"Synthetic opiate," Scraps said, tapping into the line with a needle-like probe. "Lethal concentration."

"Can it be stopped, or the effects reversed?" Finn asked. Scraps shook his head and Finn growled with frustration, before confronting Khan, hands on his hips. "Why?"

"Ah!" Khan said, using his glass to point at Finn, as if he'd just been duped by a clever trick. "I had hoped you would ask, prior to committing your act of murder."

"I'm not here to kill you, I wanted you as my prisoner," Finn pointed out. "I wanted you to undo all the damage you've caused, but none of you care, do you? You're not interested in anything besides your own power."

"We are not the power here, boy," Khan said, in a deeply condescending tone. "But you will learn that soon enough."

Finn was tired of the regent's riddles, but the biggest conundrum was sitting in front of him.

"I don't understand why you'd kill yourself, rather than accept you've lost, and do fucking good for once in your life."

Khan leaned forward and smiled, before opening the tap on his intravenous line fully.

"Because, my dear hero, fuck you, that's why...."

Khan laughed at the culmination of his carefully prepared slight, then reclined in the armchair, finished his whiskey and closed his eyes. Already the synthetic opiate had flooded his body with the deadly narcotic, and within seconds the man had drifted into a drug-induced coma that would quickly lead to his death.

"I've had enough of this," Finn said, turning his back on Khan. "Let's find Elara, and hope that she's had better luck with Maxim Volkov."

Finn headed outside, but the scuffle of feet behind him made him alert, and he spun around, spear ready. The ten servants were behind him, following on their hands and knees, wary, but not frightened.

"What do you want?" Finn demanded, looking into the eyes of each servant, who stared back at him eagerly. "Your master is dead now," Finn added, pointing at Khan. "You're free."

"What does 'free' mean?" one of the young women asked.

"It means you can do whatever you want," Finn said. "It means you're not servants anymore."

"Are you our new regent?" another asked, a boy of perhaps fifteen.

"There are no more regents," Finn said, stressing the

point as forcefully as he could, without sounding aggressive. "You don't serve any master."

The servants looked deeply confused, and Finn realized that he and Elara had never had a plan for what would happen to Elysium's workers, after they'd deposed the regents. A lifetime of brainwashing could not be undone in a few seconds, and he doubted that anything he said could convey the meaning of the word 'free' in a way that would make sense to them, but he also knew he couldn't just leave the servants to die.

"Take this," Finn said, removing the DNA key from a stow in his armor. "Go back to your quarters on the upper level and use it to open the door that leads outside."

The mere mention of the word 'outside' seemed to strike dread into the hearts of the servants.

"We are not allowed outside," the young woman said, timidly, refusing to take the key.

Finn thought for a moment then changed his tactics. The servants obeyed their regent without question, and in order to save them, he had to do something that went against every natural instinct in his body. In order to free them, he had to become their master.

"You asked if I am your new regent," Finn said, and the woman nodded. "I am more than that. I have replaced all of the others and became the Regent of Zavetgrad, and all its sectors."

The woman seemed buoyed by this, and she inched closer, still on her hands and knees, before touching the toe of Finn's boot.

"Then command us, Regent," the woman said, a smile

curling her lips, relieved that the world made sense again. "Tell us what you want."

"I want you to take this and to leave Elysium," Finn said, again offering her the DNA key. The woman hesitated, but Finn had given a command, and it would be obeyed. "Gather up all of the other servants, and tell them what I told you. Take whatever clothes you can find from the wardrobes of the former regents, and dress warmly, because the outside is cold."

"But, where should we go, my Regent?" the woman asked.

"Take the ferry to land," Finn said. "Then look for those wearing blue overalls, and only those people," Finn said, stressing this part most of all. "Tell them Finn Brasa sent you. Tell them 'Metal and Blood', and that it is my wish that they keep you safe."

The woman nodded, though she was clearly perplexed and frightened. "And then what, my Regent?" she asked.

"Then, when I have finished my work, I'll come and find you," Finn said, resolving in that moment to make sure that the servants were protected. "I'll find you, and I'll teach you what it means to live free."

The woman nodded again, but confusion furrowed her brow. "We will do as you command, my Regent, but I don't understand."

Finn reached down and placed a hand on the woman's shoulder. She did not recoil from his touch, and instead, it brightened her eyes and made her smile.

"In time, you will," Finn said. "In time, you'll be free, and you'll understand, but for now all you need to do is trust me."

The woman bowed her head, then got to her feet, and the

others rose with her. "We will do as you command, my Regent. We will go outside and await your arrival."

Finn nodded and smiled, then turned to leave, but the woman caught his hand.

"What should we call you, my Regent?" the woman said. "We always address our masters by name."

Finn was about to tell the woman that he could call her Finn, when he had a better idea. One that he hoped would inspire them to carry out his orders, no matter how strange and troubling they seemed.

"My name is Hope," Finn said, meeting the eyes of each servant in turn. "You can call me Hope."

18

THE VILLA IN THE OCEAN

Finn followed behind Scraps, who had flown ahead with his scanner dish activated, searching for Elara and the remaining regents, in particular Maxim Volkov. The route led him back into the main cavern, with its meandering river and hovering stages. The various theatrical acts, musical performances, and robotic orgies were still taking place in earnest, their performers unaware that most of their aristocratic benefactors were dead.

Suddenly, Finn spotted a convoy of servants enter the main hall, headed for a bank of elevators that ran up, not down. The procession was led by the woman he'd spoken to in the drug den, and convinced that he was the new and sole remaining Regent of Zavetgrad. Others in the line carried jackets and coats and dozens of pairs of pants, all raided from what Finn imagined was the extensive and unnecessarily large wardrobe of clothes that each regent had needlessly amassed.

"They're actually doing what I asked," he commented to Scraps, as the first of the procession arrived at the elevators and began to dress, replacing scant robes for hardier clothing. "Do you think they'll make it?"

Scraps nodded, eagerly. "Yes-yes!" the robot replied, and his confidence gave Finn hope. "Finn set them free!"

"Not yet," Finn replied, aware that they still had a long way to go before the servants could truly be considered free of the Authority's control. "But they'll at least not be slaves, and that's a start."

The architecture of Elysium had been designed to feel organic and free-flowing, and Finn soon found himself following a sweeping downward path, that undulated in a chaotic pattern, like sand dunes. Eventually, the passageway descended into a long, oblong hallway, that appeared to stretch across Elysium's entire breadth, and provided access to each of the regent's private villas. The wreckage of destroyed housekeeper robots acted like a trail of breadcrumbs, leading Finn to wherever Elara had gone, while in pursuit of Maxim Volkov. The villa belonging to the Regent of Spacehaven was at far end of the oblong hallway, and a travelator was still active, despite there being no passengers for it to ferry.

Finn stepped onto the travelator, grateful to give his feet a rest, and allowed the motorized conveyor to carry him deeper into the passageway. At a little over the half-way mark, Finn saw bodies on the ground. At first, he worried that Elara had given herself over to The Shadow, and had started killing servants as well as regents, but as the conveyor brought him closer to the bodies, he saw that the group of twelve servants were very much alive. They were all on their knees, prostrated as if in prayer, using their white chiffon robes to cover their heads. Soft sobs and sorrowful whispers could be heard from beneath the blanket of fabrics, and Finn noticed that they were all facing in the same direction, toward the northern wall of the oblong space. Finn frowned and looked at the wall, and it was only then that he realized it was made entirely of glass. What looked like hundreds of species numbering thousands of fish and other aquatic creatures flitted to and fro beyond the transparent wall, inside what was essentially a giant fish tank in the middle of the ocean.

"The regents sure love to bottle beauty for their own amusement," Finn said, speaking idly to himself.

He was about to turn away, when he saw water on the floor, pooling close to where the servants were bowed down. His pulse quickened, concerned that Elara's battle with the housekeeper robots had somehow cracked the glass wall, and that the whole weight of the ocean was about to crash in on them, but the pool didn't appear to be getting any larger.

"Where is this water coming from, pal?" Finn said to Scraps.

The robot didn't need to conduct any new scans because Scraps already knew. He pointed up and Finn saw an open panel in the wall that provided access into the giant fish tank. Finn drew his eyes down and suddenly the reason for the water, and for the strange, prayer-like ritual that the servants were performing, became clear. Cedric Braithwaite, the regent of Seahaven, was floating inside the tank, weighed down by a robotic housekeeper that had been tethered to the aristocrat using the belt of his bathrobe. The man's lips were blue from the cold and his eyes had already been eaten by some of the sea creatures that inhabited the tank with him. Others were busy nibbling at his naked, wrinkled flesh, and already his right foot had been picked clean up to the ankle.

"I suppose it's poetical in a sense," Finn said to Scraps,

amused by Elara's chosen method of executing Braithwaite. "He was the regent of Seahaven, after all."

"Elara dark humor," Scraps said, turning his back on the huge fish tank so that he could no longer see Braithwaite being eaten. "Scraps glad she on our side."

"Me too, pal," Finn laughed.

Finn was about to continue his search for Elara, but he couldn't simply leave Braithwaite's servants to continue their senseless act of lamentation. He jumped off the travelator and stood in front of one of them, a boy of about thirteen who appeared to be the lead mourner, and tapped him on the head. The boy looked up, then immediately turned his head away, and shielded his eyes.

"You're the demon..." the boy said, his voice trembling. "Cedric warned us... he said you were here to kill us all!"

"I'm not a demon," Finn said. He was annoyed that Braithwaite had spent some of his final moments poisoning his servants against him, though he also wasn't surprised. "And I'm not going to hurt you, or any of the other servants. I'm your new regent."

The boy hesitated then peeked at Finn through his fingers. Beneath their translucent robes, he could see that the other mourners were also furtively watching him.

"You're a regent?" the boy asked, doubtful but also intrigued.

"There has been a change of government, so I'm now the only regent," Finn said, reprising his white lie from earlier and also embellishing it a little. "And I've decided to close down Elysium, for good."

"So, what is to become of us?" the boy asked, nervous again.

"It'll all become clear, soon enough," Finn replied. He didn't want to get bogged down trying to explain the concept of freedom for a second time. "Just go back to your quarters. You'll find others like you waiting there, with new clothes. They'll explain what to do next."

The boy opened his mouth to speak, but was clearly unaccustomed to questioning the orders of a regent, and so swallowed any objections and climbed to his feet. The other eleven mourners followed his lead. The boy then saw Cedric Braithwaite floating in the tank behind Finn and his skin drained of all its color.

"He's not regent anymore," Finn said, side-stepping to block the boy's view. "Now do what I asked. This is my one and only command to you."

The boy nodded, then gathered his wrappings and began to amble away. The others followed, stumbling and tripping over their own feet and robes. They looked shell-shocked, as if a bomb had landed in the middle of their group and the concussive explosive had blown their eardrums and rattled their brains like ice in a cocktail shaker. He wished he could do more for the servants, but for the first time in their lives, their future was up to them. Some wouldn't make it, but Finn had already learned the hard way that he couldn't save everyone, not even his own best friend.

Picking up the trail of robot breadcrumbs, Finn finally arrived at the elevator door that led down to Volkov's villa. He searched his webbing pouches for the DNA key before cursing under his breath and realizing that he'd given it to one of the servants. Then he spotted that the door to the elevator was slightly ajar, and he inspected it more closely, finding that a robotic arm had been wedged into the jamb to stop it from closing fully. Sliding his spear through the gap, he used the extra leverage to prise open the door and squeeze himself through.

"We're in, but without the key, how do we work this thing?" Finn said to Scraps, while returning the spear to his back scabbard. "I don't suppose you can mimic the DNA key or hack the controls?" he added, hopefully.

"Nope-nope, but no need!" Scraps said, leaping onto his shoulder and pointing to the far wall of the car "Look-look!"

Finn inspected the wall and found the word, "KEY" scrawled in red letters. The bases of each letter had run, as if the ink had been slightly too watery, then he considered the idea that it wasn't ink at all, but blood, and a shiver ran down his spine.

"Is that…"

"Blood," said Scraps, oddly unconcerned by this fact.

"And is it…"

"Volkov's…" Scraps answered, finishing Finn's sentence.

"Then I guess we have our key," Finn said, laughing nervously.

He ran his hand across the letter "K", smearing some of the blood onto his own fingertip, then pressed it onto the scanner. The computer took a moment to process the sample, then the control panel activated.

"Welcome home, your excellency," said a computerized voice in a sultry tone.

"Somehow, I don't think this was a happy homecoming," Finn answered, while pressing the button to set the car in motion.

As with their previous descents, the elevator took several minutes to arrive at its destination, to allow the pressure inside to equalize with the pressure in the villa pod, which was over two-hundred meters deep, on the ocean floor. When the door finally opened, and Finn stepped outside, he wondered if he'd travelled further than he realized, all the way through the center of the earth, and to a green and pleasant land on the other side. The sky was blue and the sun warm, while a gentle breeze blew through an olive grove and kitchen garden, carrying with it first the scent of lavender, a commonly used fragrance in the Authority sector, then more earthy tones from the black soil that had been ploughed, ready for planting. At the end of the garden was a grand stone villa that looked to have been plucked out of time from the age of Roman senators and emperors. Its grand portico echoed the one that stood in the entrance to the Regent's Cathedral on level one, and the building was covered in intricate carvings and lush, green vines that hugged the architecture in a loving embrace.

The fantasy was so complete that Finn almost believed he had travelled through space and time, but like everything else in Elysium, it was a fabrication. Before long he was able to pick out the seams in the digital panels that reproduced the sky and the horizon, and the vents and fans that produced the wind, and the illusion was shattered. Now, instead of a perfect roman villa, Finn saw only a cheap parlor trick, created at enormous expense for the sole amusement and profit of Maxim Volkov.

Pushing through the iron gates at the boundary of the villa, Finn walked through the garden, heady with the scent of herbs and flowers, and climbed the steps to the house. The front door was already open. Finn was nervous to enter, worried to discover what Elara had been doing while he'd been chasing the other regents around Elysium to no profit. Walking into the atrium, he heard sobbing, then saw Gabriel Montgomery, the Regent of Metalhaven himself. The obnoxious aristocrat was tied to one of the pillars that surrounded the impluvium, a pool filled with fake rainwater that had drained off the slanted roof.

Montgomery spotted Finn and his blubbing stopped. The man set his jaw like it was chiseled from stone, while his eyes grew wide and fearful. The regent's robes were cut and bloodied, and it was clear that the man had been beaten. A pit began to form in Finn's gut, but he continued past Montgomery, whose eyes followed him like those of a painting, and toward the triclinium, where he found Maxim Volkov tied to a stone pillar just outside the roman-inspired living room. Elara was sitting on one of the long couches, reloading her crossbow. Three of the bolts were already impaled into Volkov's body, one in each thigh and one in the man's right shoulder, but unlike Montgomery, the Regent of Spacehaven and Mayor was not sobbing. Instead, Volkov was furious with rage.

"You'll get nothing from me, rebel bitch!" Volkov roared as Elara casually wound back the string of the crossbow. "Just shoot the next bolt into my heart and be done with it!"

Volkov saw Finn out of the corner of his eye and the regent's head snapped toward him. To Finn's astonishment, the man laughed.

"Finally, the true architect of this outrage shows himself," Volkov sneered. "Did you enjoy torturing and killing my friends and colleagues, traitor scum? Did it give you satisfaction?"

Finn ignored Volkov and moved close enough to Elara that he could speak to her without being overheard.

"Hey," Finn said. He wanted to say, *"Hey, what the fuck are you doing?"* but chose to save his questions for after he'd gauged Elara's mood, which seemed darker than the black soil in the garden outside.

"Hey," Elara replied, casually, as if they'd just met up for a beer in the local recovery center. "Did you bring any of the other regents with you?" she asked, while fitting a bolt into the crossbow.

"I tried, but they were uncooperative," Finn said, choosing not to go into detail.

"So, you killed them all?" Elara asked, looking up for a moment.

"As it turns out, I didn't have to, but to answer your question, they're all dead," Finn replied. Elara's expression grew curious, but she didn't ask him to elaborate, since she clearly had other things on her mind. "I saw that you turned Cedric Braithwaite into fish food..." Finn added, and Elara laughed and smiled, causing another knot to form in Finn's gut. "That means Volkov and Montgomery are the only ones left."

Finn was trying to subtly make clear that killing the last two regents would do them no good, without having to point it out. He knew that Elara understood the critical importance of recovering Volkov alive, and didn't want to condescend to her by stating this explicitly. Yet, the evidence of her actions thus far spoke to the contrary.

"Maxim and I were just having a little chat, isn't that right, Maxim?" Elara said. She finished loading the crossbow, and rested it on her knee, causally aiming it at the regent.

"Maxim enjoys a little bit of torture, don't you, Maxim? I remember very clearly how you had your pet dog, Juniper Jones, torture me."

"Fuck you," Volkov spat back. "You're a traitor and a terrorist. You got what you deserved."

Elara's finger added pressure to the trigger and a bolt flew, striking Volkov in his uninjured shoulder. The man clamped his teeth shut and hissed with pain, before forcing a grimace-like smile and laughing.

"You think you can break me, girl?" Volkov raged. "You have no idea what you've done. It doesn't matter what happens to me now because you've doomed us all!"

"Why?" Finn said, stepping into the line of fire, worried that the next bolt Elara shot might be the last. "Kahn and Westwood said the same, but why are you all so scared? What are you afraid of?"

"I'm not afraid of anything," Volkov spat, offended at the accusation of cowardice. "But if you think you can free Zavetgrad, you're a fool. There is only one man who decides the fate of this city, and it's not me."

"Reznikov?" Finn asked. The president's name had been brought up previously, by another regent. "But he's in orbit for fuck's sake. What can he possibly do from Nimbus to stop us?"

Volkov laughed again, but unlike the lunatic sniggers of the other regents, Volkov's laughter was wry and stoical.

"What indeed?" the man said, before shrugging his bleeding shoulders. The regent seemed lost in his own thoughts for a time, and when he spoke again, his attitude had shifted. "But what the hell, I'll return with you, if that's what you want," he said, and Elara paused in the middle of reloading her crossbow. "You can bring me to the gates of the Authority sector as a hostage and make your demands. Then perhaps you'll come to understand something of what awaits you, should you manage to storm my golden capital and take control of the city."

"You'll come willingly?" Elara asked, and Volkov nodded. "Why the sudden change of heart?"

Volkov leaned forward and the ropes binding him to the stone pillar bit into his flesh. With four crossbow bolts impaled into Volkov's body, it must have been excruciating, but the regent and mayor endured the pain, baring his bloodstained teeth like a wild animal.

"Because I want to see the looks on your faces when you realize what you've done," Volkov snarled. "I want you to think you've won. Then at the pinnacle of your joy, I want to witness your delicious agony, as you finally understand the futility of your actions." The regent drew back and sighed contentedly. "Yes, I'll come with you, Iron Bitch, for all the good it will do you."

There were now more knots in Finn's gut than there were in the ropes binding Maxim Volkov to the pillar. He looked at Elara, and he could see that murder was still on her mind, but Volkov's shocking offer had jolted her out of her dark funk.

"I don't like it," Finn said. "I know he's trying to fuck with our heads, but the other regents also warned me that we were making a mistake." He glanced at Volkov, who had closed his eyes and appeared indifferent to his fate. "The difference is that they were all terrified. Volkov seems to want us to take him."

Elara was quiet for a time, then she hooked her crossbow to her belt and shrugged.

"We've come too far to turn back now," she said. "We have to follow this through to the end, no matter where that takes us."

No matter where that takes us... Finn repeated in his mind, and his skin felt cold.

"Hey, I don't like where this is taking you," Finn said, finally plucking up the courage to confront her. "You're becoming cruel. Cold."

"This isn't the time, Finn," Elara said, instantly going on the defensive.

Finn stepped in front of Elara in the hope that blocking her view of the tyrannical regent would calm the anger raging inside her, and spoke softly.

"This is the only time we have," Finn hit back. "When I fell, it was you who picked me up, and dragged me out of the pit of self-loathing and anger." He held her shoulders and she tensed up. "You saved me. Let me help you."

For a moment, Elara eased into his hold, and it seemed like she was going to say something. Then she stepped back, out of his grasp, and began to idly adjust the straps and buckles of her gear, while refusing to meet Finn's eyes.

"You can help me by cutting down Volkov and Montgomery, and loading them into the escape sub," Elara said, and The Shadow was back in control again. "We still have a long way to go yet."

19

OMINOUS PORTENTS

Elara muscled Maxim Volkov inside the escape submersible and shoved the man hard into a seat. The Regent of Spacehaven and Mayor hissed with pain and glowered at Elara, though while his hateful stare implied a desire to do her harm, Volkov wasn't foolish enough to provoke The Shadow.

Despite Elara's protests that they should remain embedded into the man's flesh, Finn had removed the crossbow bolts from Volkov's arms and legs and applied simple dressings to ensure the regent didn't bleed to death. Elara had drawn the line at administering any kind of pain medication. *I want that bastard to suffer...* she had told him, and on this matter, they'd agreed. For the hundreds of workers that he had personally sent to their deaths, and for the hundreds of thousands more that had been subjugated and abused at his command, a little pain was the least Maxim Volkov deserved.

Yet while the regent was clearly hurting, Volkov remained unafraid, both of Elara and of the fate that awaited him, should he be paraded into Metalhaven as their prisoner. Finn didn't know whether it was courage or zealotry that kept Volkov from breaking, but it made him deeply uneasy, all the same. He'd believed Maxim Volkov to be the most powerful man in Zavetgrad, and the key to securing control of the city, but now he feared he'd overestimated the mayor's importance, and underestimated the reach of Gideon Alexander Reznikov.

If Maxim Volkov was a rock then Gabriel Montgomery was a blubbering mass of jello. As Finn maneuvered the cowering regent into a seat beside Volkov, the man slipped on the mucus that was dribbling from his nose, as if he had the worst case of flu in human history. Finn had always hated Montgomery, even before the regent had presided over his trial, and he despised him even more now. At least Volkov had shown his mettle by staying true to his beliefs and ideals, as abhorrent as they were, but the Regent of Metalhaven showed none of the toughness that his sector workers were renowned for. Like the other regents, once stripped of their finery and army of protectors, Montgomery was a contemptable piece of shit.

"For fuck's sake, get a grip," Volkov snarled while kicking Montgomery's heels, which was all he could do with his hands tied behind his back. "You're a Regent of Zavetgrad. Act like one!"

Montgomery straightened up and the man's expression became taut like a scolded child, though his lips continued to tremble.

"I'm sorry, I'm sorry, I'm sorry…" the man repeated over and over again, chanting the words under his breath.

Volkov shook his head and turned away. Montgomery's sniveling disgusted the man, and it was suddenly obvious why

Volkov held the position of mayor, in addition to controlling Spacehaven, the most critical sector in Zavetgrad. The other regents had inherited their titles from their fathers, who had inherited them from theirs, and so on down the line to the founders of the Authority. They'd never had to lift a finger to do anything in their lives, and despite their ostentatious offices inside the complex, they'd never done an honest day's work either. The actual running of the sectors was left to the administrative golds, while the regents remained in their sub-oceanic paradise, availing themselves of every pleasure and sin imaginable. Volkov had been no different in this regard, but in one key aspect, he was nothing at all like the other regents. Maxim Volkov was a believer, as fervent in his faith as any of the Special Prefecture. Elara had been correct to state that he was the key because he alone commanded the respect of the Authority's true leader, Gideon Alexander Reznikov.

Or so Finn had thought.

"You can bring me to the gates of the authority sector as a hostage and make your demands..." Volkov has said, after Elara had tortured the man by shooting crossbow bolts into his arms and legs. *"Then perhaps you'll come to understand something of what awaits you, should you manage to storm my golden capital and take control of the city."*

The statement was an ominous portent that echoed the sentiments of the other regents, but while they had appeared fearful of Reznikov, Maxim Volkov seemed eager for the president to act. It was like Volkov was the captain of a maritime ship that had been boarded and overrun by pirates, but rather than surrender, he chose to scuttle the vessel and take his enemies down with him.

"As much as I'd love to see your faces when Reznikov

learns of this disgrace, you'll never make it out of Seahaven alive," Volkov said, grinning at Finn. "As soon as this capsule surfaces, an army of special prefects will pull it from the water. Then this little rebellion of yours will be over, and I'll enjoy planning a very slow, special death for you both."

"That's where you're wrong," Elara said, pressing the toe of her boot into the wound on Volkov's right thigh, and making the man roar with pain. "Scraps has reprogrammed this little boat to surface far away from your prefects."

Scraps growled at Volkov then gave the regent a rude hand gesture that despite being made with feeling, still made Finn smile, because even a very cross and angry Scraps was still endearing.

"We'll see..." Volkov hissed, remaining defiant. "Even if you do avoid my rescue crew, you still have the whole of Seahaven to traverse before reaching your little stronghold. And there are drones watching every square inch of the coastline to stop Haven rebels from landing, so even if we do surface off course, it won't take long for my officers to respond."

"We'll see..." Elara replied, echoing Volkov's words with cool detachment.

Scraps launched the submersible, and the craft began its slow, careful ascent to the surface. Finn checked the control console and saw that their journey time was a little under an hour. This was partly to allow their bodies to acclimatize to changes in pressure, and partly so that they could safely navigate the minefield that protected the regent's sub-oceanic complex.

Elara unhooked her crossbow and sat in a chair opposite Volkov, crossing her legs and resting the weapon on her knee.

A bolt was already loaded, and Finn could sense that Elara was itching for the mayor to give her an excuse to shoot it. Volkov, however, didn't give her the satisfaction, and the man barely said a word for the duration of the ascent.

Finn should have been grateful for the peace and quiet, but silence only allowed the voices in his mind to become louder. Foremost amongst those was the niggling voice of doubt that warned of consequences, as yet unknown. For all of his life, his enemy had been clear to him. Foremen and prefects were dangers he understood and, even though the regents of Zavetgrad were rarely seen outside of trial days, their demeanor on such occasions revealed everything he needed to know about these despicable men. Yet, Nimbus had remained an enigma. Omnipresent in the sky above Zavetgrad, Nimbus had always been watching them. Watching and waiting. Now, Finn sensed that it would finally make its presence known.

Finn had never seen the President of Zavetgrad, at least not for real. The man's face, or what was believed to be his face, adorned the emblem of the Authority, but that was as much as anyone knew, besides the regents. As such, Gideon Alexander Reznikov had become a sort of mythical figurehead, and though it was a crime punishable by trial to take his name in vain, this didn't stop patrons of recovery centers across all work sectors from speculating. Many believed that Reznikov had died years earlier, without a natural heir, while others contended that the man had never existed at all, and that the office of the president was merely a tool the regents used to keep order. Its mystery was its power.

For his own part, Finn had cared little whether Reznikov was real or imagined, because to him it was Nimbus itself that was the greater enemy. Every rocket that launched from Spacehaven removed more of the precious few natural resources that remained on Earth. With each rocket, Zavetgrad was diminished, while Nimbus grew stronger. Eventually, the Authority would have no need for the work sectors and its populations at all. That had always been the Authority's end-game – to create a new civilization in the stars, one where people like Finn and Elara were not only unwelcome, but unnecessary. With their focus on capturing the regents and taking over the city, Finn had all but forgotten about Nimbus. Now he couldn't think of anything else, and it was making him sick with worry. It felt like Nimbus was a sleeping dragon and that their actions were about to awaken it.

"We've got another fifty minutes before we reach the surface," Elara said. As usual, Finn hadn't noticed her sneak up on him. She was reclined against the bell-shaped interior of the pod, crossbow still trained on Volkov. "But that time will pass in a flash, and we need to be ready."

"I hope the Seahaven Metals detected the launch and are waiting for us," Finn said, staring idly out of the porthole window. "For all his bluster, Volkov is right that every prefect in the sector will come after us once we surface."

"Don't worry, the Seahaven blues have prepared a little surprise for us," Elara said, toying with the crossbow while Volkov pretended to ignore her. "I heard Briggs talking about it."

"What sort of surprise?" Finn asked. Elara knew he hated surprises, but he could tell that she wasn't going disclose what she knew.

"It's one you'll like," Elara replied, coyly. "But it's best if you see it for yourself. Then you'll understand."

Finn shot Elara a withering look, but she wouldn't be moved, and he suspected that her cloak-and-dagger behavior was as much to prevent Volkov from eavesdropping as it was to keep the surprise secret. With nothing better to do, he returned to watching out of the window as the pod slowly maneuvered away from Elysium. He'd expected the place to look as wild and as alien from the outside as it did on the inside, but it was disappointingly bland. The complex was a square box that concealed all of the curiosities and extravagances that were contained within it. The same was true of the upper-level offices and the servant's quarters.

Finn was about to turn away when he spotted the ingress shaft that led to the ferry terminal, two-hundred meters out to sea. He could see a light inside it, traveling upward, and he smiled. He didn't know for certain that the elevator was filled with servants making their way to Seahaven, but he hoped so. Even if they did make it, and the blues took them in, adjusting to their new lives would be difficult, perhaps even impossible. *At least they have a chance...* Finn thought. *For now, that will have to do.*

Elara had been right, and the time passed quickly. In what seemed like the blink of an eye, the escape pod had emerged from beneath the ice-cold water of the Davis Strait, and began bobbing up and down in the turbulent waves. Elara grabbed a hand hold and pulled herself to the nearest porthole window, while Finn kept watch on Volkov and Montgomery. The Regent of Spacehaven was alert, perhaps mentally preparing himself for the possibility of rescue or escape, while Metalhaven's former regent remained in a near-catatonic state, babbling to himself that everything was going to be okay. It was only then that Finn noticed the pool of liquid around Montgomery's feet and the yellow stains on his once perfectly white bathrobe.

"Scraps, any sign of the Metals?" Elara said.

"Yes-yes, they close!" Scraps replied. The robot was interfaced with the escape pod's computer. "Outboards active. Reach land in three min-mins!"

The timescale was shorter than Finn had been expecting, and he felt adrenaline begin to surge throughout his body, waking up his muscles and setting his senses on edge. He glanced through the porthole and saw land. It was a shallow, shingle beach where dozens of small fishing boats had been pulled ashore and tied together.

"On your feet," Finn said, turning back to Volkov, who ignored him. Finn drew his spear and whacked Volkov's shoulder with the flat of the blade, causing the man to hiss like a snake. "I said get up."

Grudgingly, the mayor stood, though it was not without considerable effort on account of his injuries. What amused Finn was how Volkov had used Gabriel Montgomery for leverage, grabbing the man's shoulders and pressing down on his hunched over frame, like the regent was just another one of his slaves. The pod then hit the beach and the sound of metal grinding against stone echoed through the chamber. Finn heard voices, then the sound of chains being attached to the pod, anchoring it to the boats on the beach.

"We're secure," Elara said, craning her neck to look through the porthole. "Scraps, pop the escape hatch."

There was a sharp, sudden explosion, and a circular door exploded from the capsule, like it had been fired by a cannon.

Cold, sea air rushed inside, replacing the smell of sweat and urine with a salty freshness.

"Savor your last taste of freedom, traitors," Volkov said. The mayor couldn't straighten his legs or square his shoulders, so he remained hunched over like an old man. "Savor it while you can, because the only way you're getting out of Seahaven is in shackles, or a box."

20

THE SURPRISE

Finn peered through the open escape hatch, but heavy rain and a yawning darkness obscured his view, and all he could see were indistinct shapes and flickering shadows. Then a floodlight switched on, and he was temporarily blinded. Finn's pulse quickened, afraid that a squad of special prefects had intercepted them, until he saw the heavy blue overalls of Seahaven workers, and he exhaled a relieved breath.

"It won't be long now," Volkov said, contemptuously. "Every prefect in Zavetgrad will be out in force, looking for me. A hundred skycars are likely already inbound."

Elara let her hand fly, striking Volkov cleanly across the side of the face, staggering him.

"Keep your mouth shut, unless you want to eat another crossbow bolt," Elara snapped, as Volkov recovered, dabbing his inflamed skin with the back of his hand. "Besides, most of your prefects have been reassigned to Spacehaven or the Authority sector, on the orders of your son, so I wouldn't get up hopes of a rescue."

The insult of being struck incensed Volkov, and for the

briefest moment, the regent considered striking back, but the tyrant managed to rein in his violent urges.

"I'm still mayor, so they'll come for me," Volkov hit back, though it seemed the man was less certain of his privileged status than ever.

"Blood!" came a cry from outside.

"Metal!" Elara called back.

A woman appeared outside the escape hatch, dressed in traditional Seahaven blue. She was drenched from head to toe, partly from having waded out to sea to meet the pod, but also because they'd emerged from the ocean into a heavy storm.

"Quickly, skycars are coming," the woman said, before vanishing as hurriedly as she'd appeared.

Finn glanced at Maxim Volkov and the man grinned, but lucky for him, Elara didn't see it, otherwise the regent would have gotten another smack across the mouth.

"You first," Elara said, shoving Volkov to the shallow ladder that led to the escape hatch.

The regent was suddenly more compliant, perhaps buoyed by the news that his forces were on the way. Even so, his injured thighs struggled to the climb the ladder, and Finn and Elara ended up practically shoving the man through the hatch. Surprisingly, Montgomery was less of a challenge. In his near catatonic state, the Regent of Metalhaven was pliable, like warm algae-bread, and they had little trouble in coaxing him through the opening. Finn followed then helped Elara though, bracing himself against the driving wind and rain. He heard laughter and he turned to see Maxim Volkov looking into the sky. He was knee-deep in the ocean, bathrobe blown open like curtains in a breeze.

"See, what did I tell you!" Volkov cried. The man was shivering violently because of the sub-zero temperatures, but he didn't seem to care. "My prefects are coming, and you will not be able to escape them!"

Two Seahaven rebels hauled Volkov away before Elara had chance to punch him again. Three more dragged Montgomery onto the beach, and the shingles cut the man's feet, leaving behind a watery, bloody trail, which Finn and Elara followed in earnest.

"Are you going to tell me what this surprise is?" Finn said. He could barely open his eyes due to the needles of water that were battering his face.

"It's just up there," Elara said, as the two clung to each other for support. Slippery armor, rain and mossy shingles were not a good combination.

Finn couldn't see what Elara was referring to, but he could see the prefect skycars approaching from the northern edge of the perimeter fence. The flying vehicles had been forced to detour around Metalhaven, which had added a few minutes to their journey, but they were already closing fast.

"How many are there?" Finn asked Scraps, who clung to his shoulder pauldron like a pirate captain's parrot.

"Twelve-twelve!" Scraps called back. "Five min-mins out!"

Finn hoped this was just the robot's usual habit of speaking words twice, rather than there actually being twenty-four skycars, but even if there were only a dozen, that was more than enough.

"You're fucked!" Volkov yelled. The regent was now standing on the concrete seafront, bathrobe still flapping like a flag. "Yours will be the trial to end all trials!"

Elara stormed up the steps to the seafront with the power

of a tidal wave crashing to shore, and punched Volkov so hard that the man was knocked unconscious and sent crashing to the flat of his back.

"Lock him in the rear of the truck," Elara said, directing the command to the female Metal who had first greeted them. She pointed at Montgomery, who cowered before her, covering his face with his hands. "Him too, and hurry."

Finn made it onto the seafront and finally saw the surprise that Elara had been referring to. Their getaway vehicle was a Makehaven ale truck, but the vehicle had been overhauled so heavily that it looked like a tank from the last war. It was covered in heavy armor, including the windshield, which had been replaced by a steel sheet with two slots cut into it so that the driver could see out. The wheels and tires were protected by shields that hung over the arches, and there were platforms around the rear bed that looked like they had been designed for people to stand on, enhancing its carrying capacity. The only part of the truck that Finn couldn't make sense of was the dome-shaped protrusion in the roof of the fixed trailer section.

"I hope it's as tough as it looks," Finn said as the rear doors were swung open and Volkov and Montgomery were thrown inside like garbage sacks. "Who's driving?"

"Me, because I know the way," Elara said, pulling open the driver's side door. "But don't worry, you have the more fun job," she added, pointing to the mysterious dome.

"We have to scarper, but good luck!" The female rebel called out. She and the other blues had gathered on the seafront, ready to slip away through the narrow, cobbled streets. "Me and the rest of the guys had a bet on whether you'd actually pull this off." The woman laughed. "I lost."

"We're happy to disappoint you," Finn said, smiling at the woman. He reached out his hand and she took it. "Metal and Blood."

"Metal and Blood…" the woman replied, then her hand slipped from Finn's, and the rebels ran, any trace of them washed away by the driving rain.

"This will be a bumpy ride," Elara said, sparking the truck's engine into life. It growled like an angry beast, and Finn wondered whether the modifications had extended to beneath the hood too.

Suddenly, bullets began to ricochet off the truck's armor and Finn saw the skycars form up into an attack pattern. Finn jumped into the passenger seat and reached for his seatbelt, but Elara caught his hand.

"Don't bother, you won't be sitting there for long," Elara said. Finn frowned at her, then Elara punched the dividing wall between the cabin and the rear section, and a door flung open. Inside was a cramped passage that led to short ladder.

"What's down there?" Finn asked.

Elara smiled. "A laser cannon; your actual surprise."

She floored the accelerator, propelling Finn into the narrow tunnel before he could ask any more questions. The engine roared and the tires squealed, as the vehicle hurtled along Seahaven's winding roads, bouncing Finn against the walls of the tunnel, and shaking him so badly he didn't know up from down. Nauseous and bruised, he finally reached the ladder and pulled himself up. Bullets rattled off the truck, but he couldn't see a thing, because his view outside was blocked by a circular curtain of metal.

"How do I open this dome?" Finn called out.

Elara couldn't hear him over the growl of the engine, but

Scraps had followed Finn inside, and the little robot knew what to do.

"Pull lever!" Scraps said.

"I don't see a lever," Finn called back.

Suddenly, the truck lurched right, and Finn's head clanged against the metal like a hammer striking a bell. For a second or two, he blacked out, and awoke to the sound of more bullets thumping into the truck's armor.

"There-there!" Scraps yelled, climbing onto Finn's shoulder, and pointing to a red lever. "Pull-pull, quickly!"

Finn found the lever and yanked it, then the curtain of metal that he was cocooned inside burst open and he was exposed to the full force of the driving rain. Elara was hurtling down a slip road toward the main autoway, but a skycar had landed ahead of them to block their path.

"Hold on to something!" he heard Elara shout, and to Finn's horror, the truck accelerated harder, its armored grill aimed directly at the skycar.

Finn grabbed onto whatever he could find, and the truck ploughed through the craft, pulverizing it like a wrecking ball razing an old tenement block to the ground. Finn ducked inside the spherical alcove as wreckage flew over his head. The truck faltered for a moment then began to accelerate again, but as Finn pulled himself back out into the open, he could see smoke rising from the engine bay.

"Why aren't you shooting?" Elara yelled.

"Shooting with what?" Finn called back. "Where the hell is this cannon?"

"The red button!" Elara shouted. "Push it!"

Finn searched around him then finally saw the button, part-buried beneath debris from the skycar that Elara had scrambled like an egg. He hammered it with his fist, then gears and motors began to grind into action, and a double-barreled laser cutter sprang from inside the trailer compartment, mounted on a motorized platform. Grabbing the firing handles, Finn aimed the weapon skyward and fired, sending twin bursts of searing-hot laser energy into the thundery night air. More by luck than judgement, his first shot landed true, and a skycar exploded in a fury of flames, before veering sharply left and colliding with a second, taking it down too.

"I like this surprise!" Finn shouted, grinning from ear to ear.

He aimed and fired again, slicing a deep gouge into another pursuing craft, which lost power and crashed into a gene bank by the side of the autoway. Prefect gunners returned fire, lashing the hull of the truck with heavy machineguns, but Finn didn't care how close the shots came, because he had the bigger gun, and only a bullet to the brain was going to stop him from using it.

Soon the sky was awash with red laser light and orange flames, as skycar after skycar was cut down. It was as natural to Finn as breathing. The cutter, though adapted from a tool into a weapon, was a device he'd used so often it was like an extension of his own body, and he felt as connected to it as his hands were to his wrists. If Elara had pointed to a single raindrop in the sky, Finn could have vaporized it, without a second thought.

By the time nine of the pursuing skycars had been destroyed, the gates to Metalhaven were in sight. More skycars were inbound, some risking flying over the occupied sector in a desperate rescue effort, but those vehicles were cut down by lasers mounted on the rooftops of tenement buildings, recovery centers and gene banks. Finn continued firing too, but his vision had become clouded by smoke from the truck's laboring engine.

"How much further?" Finn called out, ducking inside the truck to avoid the bullets that had left the truck's armor pockmarked and dented.

"We're almost through, hold on!" Elara cried.

Suddenly, foremen ran into the road and threw themselves at the truck, in a desperate, last-ditch attempt to prevent it from reaching safety. Some were crushed beneath the vehicle's heavy wheels, but two managed to cling on, and haul their robot bodies onto the hood of the truck.

"Finn!" Elara yelled, as one of the foremen began to peel back the armored windshield.

Finn's instincts and training kicked in, and he climbed onto the roof of the truck, before drawing his spear and aiming the weapon at the foremen. "Hey, up here!" he called out, waving the electrified spear at them, like he was Zeus, conducting lightning.

The two machines switched their attention to Finn, like wolves that had spotted an easier prey, but their logic processors had made a fatal miscalculation. Finn was not the prey – he was the hunter.

Charging forward, he met the machines as they scrambled over the armored windshield toward him, swiping one into the road with a clean strike that took the robot's head clean off. The second foreman tried to grab him, but Finn's armor was wet and slippery, and the robot's metal fingers couldn't gain purchase. Side-stepping the foreman's lunge, Finn cracked the spear across the robot's back, paralyzing the machine with thousands of volts of electricity. Its eyes went dim and the machine slid off the roof before clattering down the road behind them.

"We're not going to make it!" Elara said. The gates to Metalhaven were already open, but the truck's engine was shot, and the vehicle was slowing to a crawl.

"We'll have to make a run for it!" Finn said, sheathing his spear and climbing onto the side-sill next to the passenger door.

"What about Volkov?"

"Fuck Volkov!" Finn said, pulling the door open and extending his hand to Elara. "Come on, before the last of the skycars make another run at us."

"We can't leave him," Elara hit back, pounding her hands onto the dash in an effort to will the truck to keep moving. "Not after getting this far!"

Finn looked to their rear and the last of the original twelve skycars were already on the ground. Dozens of prefects were piling onto the road, while at least thirty more skycars were coming in behind them. Like Elara, he desperately wanted to make it back with their prize, but he didn't see how it was possible.

"There are too many of them," Finn said, turning back to Elara. "If we go out there alone, we'll be gunned down in seconds."

"We're not alone..."

Through the narrow slits in the battered windshield armor, Finn could see a small army of Metalhaven workers charging through the gate, firing sub-machineguns and laser cutters at the advancing prefects. Three trucks roared past, then two of them swerved hard and crashed into one another, forming a barrier across the autoway. The third u-turned sharply then rammed into the back of their armored truck, before pushing the broken vehicle into Metalhaven. Bullets continued flying in both directions, and Finn saw workers take fire and go down, but the chromes were pulled to safety by their comrades in arms. Then the mighty gates to Metalhaven were slammed shut, and the prefect forces of the Authority were trapped outside.

Finn and Elara collapsed on top of one another, hugging each other tightly. He didn't know whether to laugh or cry, but in the end, laughter won out, and they both broke down into fits of giggles, embracing each other ever more tightly. They had done it. Somehow, they had pulled off the impossible. Yet as great as their achievement was, there was still work to do.

21
AFTER...

FINN PUSHED through the door to the executive office suite on the top floor of the gene bank in Reclamation Sector Four and found Trip waiting for him with a pint of Metalhaven ale in each hand.

"There he is!" Trip said, thrusting a glass into Finn's hand. It was so cold it burned his fingers. "And there she is!" the man added, as Elara entered, somewhat taken aback by the boisterous greeting. "Get that down you, you've earned it!" Trip added, pressing the second pint into her hand, before rushing off to pour himself one.

"I'm not sure I should be drinking with all the other chemicals rushing around my bloodstream, but what the hell," Finn said.

He turned to Elara, intending to chink his glass to hers in celebration of their success, but her pint glass was already horizontal and Finn watched, astonished, as the ale vanished down her throat in seconds.

"I needed that," Elara said, handing the empty glass to Trip and taking the fresh pint that he'd just poured for himself. Slightly bewildered and a little annoyed, Trip returned to the keg, muttering under his breath. "In fact, I could probably drink an entire barrel," Elara added, before belching.

"I don't think I have the strength to carry you out of here, so please don't," Finn said, smiling before taking three long gulps of beer. As usual, the first mouthful tasted foul, the second passable, and the third was like ambrosia itself.

Xia appeared with a med kit in hand, which she set down on the table beside Finn before activating a portable medical scanner that was already set up.

"Finger..." Xia grunted, pointing to the receptacle in the device.

"Whatever you say, doc," Finn said, sliding his index finger into the machine. It pricked his skin, took a blood sample, then the analysis appeared on the screen. Finn wasn't versed in medical jargon, but he noted that many lines and numbers appeared to be in the red. "So, what's the verdict, will I live?" he asked, only half joking.

"Yes," Xia replied, while preparing a series of injectors, some of which had needles that looked painfully long. "Probably..." she then added.

Finn jerked his finger out of the machine and stared at Xia, open mouthed. The woman smiled, at least as best she could considering the metalwork in her jaw.

"Joke..." she said, blushing a little.

"You're a better freedom fighter than a comedian," Finn said. He removed his right vambrace and rolled up the sleeve of his base layer uniform. His blood was pumping so strongly that it wasn't difficult to find a vein. "Make it quick. I hate needles."

Xia shook her head. "Not there..." she said, ominously, before pointing to Finn's backside. "There..."

"That had better be another joke..." Finn said, automatically turning his ass away from Xia so that she couldn't stab it before he had chance to protest.

Xia raised an eyebrow then smiled again. "Joke..." she said, with more wickedness. "Arm will do."

"Thank fuck for that," Finn said, and Elara laughed, though it seemed that she was just as relived as he was.

Despite stabbing his arm instead of his backside, the injections were still deeply unpleasant, but a second blood scan by the computer revealed that the drugs had done their work, and brought Finn's vitals back within acceptable norms. Elara received her injections next, and she didn't flinch once, even as the longest and thickest needles pierced her skin, though Finn put her bravery down to the fact she was already three pints down.

Scraps flew through the door, looking freshly painted and oiled. The robot had been undergoing some maintenance too, and with a fresh influx of power, he was looking sprightlier than ever, at least physically. His expression, however, was dour.

"What's up, pal?" Finn said, rolling down his sleeve and reattaching his vambrace.

"Chiefy..." Scraps said. The robot landed on the table and his head and shoulders sank under the weight of his loss.

"Sorry, pal, I forgot," Finn said. "Let's see what we can do."

Finn knelt in front of the robot then opened the compartment in his chest. It was still damp from the rain and seawater that had worked its way inside, during their race back to Metalhaven. Rummaging around and causing Scraps to fidget and giggle as if being tickled, Finn found Chiefy's Foreman Logic Processor and the chip that contained the robot's short-term memory record.

"I'm sure we can repurpose one of the other foremen to act as Chiefy's new body," Finn said, while checking over the chips. They were intact and appeared to be in good condition. Scraps had looked after them well.

"According to these records, there's a disabled Gen-VII Chief Foreman in storage on floor fifteen," Elara said. She had used the medical computer to search through the gene bank's inventory. "Physically, the machine is in good condition, but its FLP was corrupted, so maybe it would be a good candidate body?"

"Yes-yes!" Scraps yelled, throwing his hands into the air. The robot then plucked the FLP and memory chip from Finn's hands, spun up his rotor, and shot out of the door like a missile.

"I guess he liked that suggestion…" Elara said, smiling at the afterimage of Scraps, who was moving so fast Finn couldn't even hear his rotors anymore.

The main comms terminal began to chime an incoming message, and Xia rushed to the computer, and sat down in front of it.

"Haven," Xia said, waving them over. "Pen and Riley."

Finn and Elara gathered around the terminal, both accepting fresh pints of ale from Trip, whose sole function in the resistance appeared to be ensuring that people never went thirsty, himself least of all. Xia connected the signal and holographic images of Principal Penelope Everhart and General William Riley appeared in front of them. Finn had forgotten about the terminal's ability to generate detailed visual representations of the callers, and the ghostly images took him aback.

"Catch you at a bad time?" Pen asked.

"Not at all, I'm just not used to these visitations yet," Finn said. "It would be nice to see you in person again."

"I wish for that too," Pen said, smiling. "And after what you've just achieved, that may happen sooner than either of us expected."

Finn nodded. "I still can't quite believe we pulled it off, but Maxim Volkov and Gabriel Montgomery are cooling off under guard, a few floors below us," Finn said. "The esteemed mayor is as defiant and belligerent as ever, despite the failed efforts of his prefects to rescue him."

"Maxim is just like his father, or at least the previous clone version of himself," General Riley grunted.

"You knew Maxim's predecessor?" Finn asked, and Riley nodded.

"The Volkov patriarchal line should have ended after the first Volkov was rendered sterile by radiation in the aftermath of the last war, but thanks to cloning, that family has clung on to power for generations," Riley said. "Dimitry Volkov looked and acted just like Maxim, and in a few years, Ivan Volkov will be the same."

"The difference is that Ivan Volkov will be the last Mayor of Zavetgrad," Elara said. Talk of the Volkov family had flared her anger. "And after that, the Volkov line will die."

"Until then, remember why you went to such great lengths to capture Maxim Volkov," Pen said, sensing the dark undertones beneath Elara's comment. "Only he has the Authority to stand down the special prefecture and hand over the Authority to our control. Assuming, of course, he does what we ask of him."

This was the question that had been haunting Finn's thoughts ever since they'd invaded Elysium and turned the regents' personal paradise into a living hell. He'd thought that the mere threat of death would have been enough to compel Maxim Volkov's compliance, but the man seemed to care little for his fate. It was possible that, with a noose around his neck, Volkov would crack and give them what they needed, but Finn doubted it. The mayor's resolve was too strong, and Finn believed that Volkov would rather die than betray the Authority and his president.

"Penny for your thoughts?" Pen said. Finn frowned at the holographic image of the woman. "It's an ancient phrase. It means I'd like to know what you're thinking."

Finn sighed and shrugged. "I don't think Volkov will break," he said, telling it as it saw it. "I think he's too pig-headed and proud."

Though Pen's expression barely changed, Riley wore his emotions on his sleeve, and the man's craggy brow wrinkled in frustration and concern.

"And is this also your assessment, Elara?" Pen asked.

Elara thought for a moment then nodded. "I hate to admit it, but Finn's right. It didn't seem to matter how many crossbow bolts I shot into him, the bastard barely batted an eyelid."

Pen's eyes widened, clearly intrigued and more than a little disturbed by Elara's actions, but she chose to overlook them and stay on track.

"Right now, Ivan Volkov is the key," Riley cut in. Unsurprisingly, he wasn't concerned by the admission that

Elara had tortured the mayor and former Regent of Spacehaven. "Perhaps, we don't need Volkov senior to order the surrender. Maybe we just need to threaten him enough that his clone son cracks and submits instead."

"But you said they're both alike?" Finn said, pointing out the flaw in Riley's logic. "You said that Ivan is just as intransigent as Maxim?"

"I said he will become that way," Riley corrected him. "I knew Maxim as a young man, and youth has a peculiar effect on us all, clones and natural-borns the same. As a younger man, Maxim was a raw nerve, who craved attention, most of all from his own clone father, but the senior Volkov's are incapable of affection, kindness or empathy. That's why they all mature into stone-hard bastards, who care nothing for anyone."

Finn could see the parallels between the young Maxim that Riley had just described and Ivan Volkov, whom he knew all too well from prosecutor training, but he didn't see how any of this would help them.

"If Ivan really does crave his father's approval, then capitulating to us is the last thing he'll do," Finn said. "He'll never win Maxim's respect by rolling over."

"No, but at this moment, Ivan wants something more from his father than respect," Riley continued. "He wants his love."

Elara snorted. "Love? Come on, General, we both know that neither Volkov is capable of that."

"You're wrong," Riley said, sternly. "Young Maxim Volkov was a sensitive man, driven by his passions, but he was also deeply insecure. The man had everything, except the one thing he truly wanted."

"I must admit, I'm struggling to believe that Ivan is that needy," Finn said.

"The Volkovs are raised to be hard and unbending," Riley said. The pushbacks were starting to irritate him, but he would not be swayed from his opinion. "Maxim was treated severely, cruelly even, just as his clone father was before him, and so on to the beginning of the line. Ivan is no different, but as of this moment, he is vulnerable. I tell you, it's our only chance."

Finn and Elara exchanged unconvinced glances, but their objections and concerns didn't matter, because Riley was right – they had no choice but to try. Then Finn had an idea.

"Maybe there's something we can do to tug at Ivan's heartstrings, if he has any," Finn said. The idea of a Roman triumph had always appealed to him and now he would get his chance. "In ancient Rome, victorious generals would have a ceremony to celebrate the success of a military campaign. If we lead a procession toward the Authority sector, with the two regents bound to stakes, as spoils of war, it might be enough to break Ivan's resolve."

"Sounds gruesome," Pen said, disapprovingly.

"Yes, and perfect," Riley said, acting as night to Pen's day.

"It would also serve a dual purpose," Elara added. "It would show all the golds that their revered leaders aren't untouchable gods but just men."

"The special prefects are zealots, and they'll fight on to the last, but the regular officers don't have their fervor," Riley added. The general seemed persuaded. "If we can crack Ivan's resolve and strike fear into the hearts of the other golds, they may well crumble."

"They would crumble more quickly if we had Haven's

soldiers with us," Finn said, looking directly at General Riley as he said this.

"We're working on it," Riley replied. Finn's comment had put the man on notice, and he didn't appreciate it. "For the moment, Zavetgrad's border fence remains an insurmountable barrier, so for now, you're on your own."

"But not for long," Pen cut in, striking a more optimistic tone. "Our soldiers and skycars stand at the ready."

"Then, hopefully, we'll see you soon," Finn replied, smiling.

The principal and the general signed off and for the first time since embarking on their outbound journey to the suboceanic complex, Finn found himself at a loose end. He also discovered that he had an empty pint glass.

"I could use another drink," Finn said, looking for Trip, but the man had vanished.

"Keg," Xia said, pointing to the corner of the room, where Trip's supply of beer was kept. "Empty..."

"Typical," Finn said, setting down the glass on the table with a disheartened thud. "Maybe we can find an open recovery center?"

"I can do one better," Elara said, with a twinkle in her eye. "I found a bottle of brandy in a drawer in one of the other executive office suites. I kept it hidden in case we ever had cause to celebrate." She shrugged. "I think we do."

"Where is it now?" Finn asked. All of the executive suites had been converted when the gene bank had become the resistance HQ.

"It's in my room," Elara said, beckoning Finn to follow. "We can stop by and check in on our guests on the way."

Finn followed Elara out of the office suite and down three

flights of stairs to where Maxim Volkov and Gabriel Montgomery were being held in a converted storeroom, under heavy guard. The Metals guarding the door nodded and grunted acknowledgments as they approached – the men and women had originally been Stonehaven oranges, who weren't much for conversation – and Elara pulled back the bolt on the door. The slab of metal was like a vault, and Finn had to help her to haul it open.

Finn heard Montgomery's mutterings even before he'd stepped inside the makeshift prison cell. The man was lying on a cot, a toilet bucket half-filled at the foot of the bed, stinking the place out like rotten meat. The former Regent of Metalhaven had been insensible ever since his capture, and the man remained in a state of fear-induced catatonia. Maxim Volkov, on the other hand, was sitting up against the wall, arms folded but eyes burning brightly. The conditions of his incarceration had not fazed the man in the slightest, and he remained iron-clad in his defiance.

"How the tables have turned," Elara said, enjoying the moment.

"Fuck you," Volkov snarled in response, before turning his head and staring at the wall.

Elara smiled then closed and bolted the door. Simply knowing that Volkov was still safely locked up was all the reassurance she'd needed.

"I'm impressed," Finn said, as they returned to the stairwell and headed to the floor that had been converted into living accommodation for the senior metals.

"How so?" Elara asked.

"I was half-expecting you to impale Volkov with a few more crossbow bolts," Finn replied, smirking at her.

"He'll get what's coming to him, soon enough," she said, darkly. "Until then, I'm content knowing that he's under lock and key."

They reached Elara's room, and she threw open the door, like a worker returning from a long day at the office, happy to be home. Armor plates then went skidding across the floor, as they were discarded with similar abandon.

"That's better," Elara said, stretching like a cat. Shorn of her armor, Finn could see tears and scratches in her modified base layer, along with patches of dried blood.

Finn began to remove his armor too and stacked it neatly alongside Elara's which remained in a heap where she'd thrown it. Without the dense metal plates and the mass of his spear, which he'd placed up against the wall, he felt tons lighter, and he grabbed hold of a sideboard to stave off the curious sensation that he was floating.

"Pour a couple of these," Elara said, placing the bottle of brandy on the table, alongside two crystal tumblers. "I'm going to take a shower, and try to wash off the filth of Elysium."

"Good idea, you really do stink," Finn said.

Elara stopped dead and glared at him, but Finn simply laughed. Provoking Elara was a dangerous game, but one he enjoyed playing.

"You can shower after me," Elara said, helping herself to quick swig from the brandy bottle before heading into the bathroom. "If I stink, then you reek."

"No need to be petty," Finn said, still teasing.

He poured a brandy and downed it, and the strong liquor took his breath away. Once the burn had subsided, and the fruit flavors began to percolate around his palate, Finn found himself wanting another.

"Whose apartment was this?" Finn asked, inspecting the room, full glass of brandy in hand.

"Who knows, just some random exec," Elara called back. He could barely hear her over the rush of flowing water from the shower. Steam was billowing out from the bathroom. "Your typical entitled gold, I suppose..."

Finn continued to inspect the room, which was a second home for the executive that owned it; a place for them to stay should the hour run late, and they chose not to make the journey back to their primary abode in the Authority sector. The apartment also served as a boudoir where they would entertain, and be entertained, by their paramour. As he thought of this, he found a photograph of the executive in question on a bookshelf, and picked it up. The woman was in her early thirties, plain but pretty enough, Finn thought, with short, chestnut hair and muddy-brown eyes. In another photo, the woman was standing with her paramour, an impossibly good-looking gold with a square jaw and radiant blue eyes.

"Probably a moron..." Finn commented to himself, before laughing at his own joke.

The pair were dressed up, the exec in a slick red dress that hugged her athletic physique, while the paramour wore a suit, exquisitely tailored around his muscular frame, and a white shirt unbuttoned almost to the navel. This did nothing to alter Finn's opinion that the man was a moron.

Finn set the photos down then sidled over to the executive's desk. Elara hadn't tidied anything way, and there were still folders containing paper documents strewn across the industrial glass surface. He picked one up and started reading. It was a record of babies that had been given a genetic rating of five and assigned for transportation to Nimbus. The number was surprisingly small; only one in an entire month. Finn idly wondered who their unwilling and unwitting parents had been, and who these babies might become. *What sort of person will they grow up to be? Will they ever learn about Earth? Will they wonder where they came from?*

Finn sighed and tossed the folder back onto the desk before taking another drink of brandy, which did an effective job of washing the questions from his mind. Then Elara walked back into the room, a towel wrapped around her body, and he almost dropped the glass.

"Is that mine?" Elara said, smiling at him. She seemed to like that she had the ability to strike him dumb.

"It is now," Finn said, handing her the brandy. She took a polite, slow drink, her eyes lingering on him over the top of the crystal glass.

"Your turn," Elara said, nodding toward the shower. Her wet hair sprayed water onto the desk, splattering the documents. "I left a towel out for you."

"Yes, ma'am," Finn said, slipping past her and heading toward the bathroom, while peeling the base layer uniform away from his shoulders. It was stuck on by sweat, blood and dried seawater. "If there's a laundry processor in here, it would be a good idea to wash our base layers," he added, while turning the faucet to start the shower. "There's no point getting clean, only to put these stinking things back on."

"Kick it out to me, and I'll do it," Elara said, gathering up her own base layer. "This is a senior gold's apartment, so everything in here is automated. It will only take a couple of hours to get them washed and returned."

Finn did as he was asked, and Elara peeked at him through the bathroom door, making him jolt back in embarrassment. As he shut the door, he could hear her laughing. The soothing hot water soon made him forget about Elara's brazenness and he spent far longer than he'd planned simply soaking himself. Finally, with his fingers beginning to wrinkle, he shut off the shower and grabbed the towel to dry himself. It was only then that he realized he had nothing fresh to wear.

"Hey, do you think the exec's paramour might have left some clothes here?" Finn said, wrapping the towel around his waist. It barely fit, and he began to wonder whether Elara had given him a small towel on purpose. "See what you can find, but avoid the tight pants and silk shirts, I don't want to look like a gigolo."

Finn pushed through the door to the bathroom and found Elara outside, wearing the svelte red dress that he'd seen in the photograph. His mouth fell open, and Elara laughed, causing the skin on his face to flush hot.

"What do you think?" Elara said, doing a twirl.

"Umm…" Finn realized that his response was lacking, but it was all that he could muster. His brain had lost the ability to process words.

"That good, huh?" Elara said, acting crestfallen, though Finn wasn't too stupefied to know she was playing with him.

"It looks good," Finn said, clearing his throat. "Incredible, actually…" and Elara smiled again. Finn then regarded himself, dressed only in a small white towel. "I don't suppose you found anything for me?"

"We'll find you some clothes after," Elara said, setting the empty glass of brandy down on the side of the sink.

"After what?"

Elara stepped closer then kissed Finn full on the lips.

"After..." she repeated, taking his hand and leading him to the bedroom.

22

THE TRIUMPH

Finn checked his armor one last time, making sure that each section was perfectly seated and that not a single smudge or fingerprint besmirched the freshly painted and repaired panels. His base layer uniform had been washed and returned to him by the automated laundry system in the gene bank, and it felt brand new. He felt brand new too, but his cleaned and repaired armor had little to do with his personal euphoria. That had all been a result of the previous night, the memory of which was still swirling around his mind, tormenting, and tantalizing him like a fisherman's lure. Finn had tried to play it casual come daylight, but he'd struggled to wipe the smirk from his face all morning as the senior Metals finalized preparations to march on the Authority sector.

Elara, naturally, had no such problems and had taken it all in her stride, confidently and without embarrassment. He envied her glacial cool and her confidence, but most of all, he was relieved that there was no awkwardness between them. No regrets. And though her attention had been focused on the triumph, the stolen glances they'd shared during natural lulls in the process were thrilling. And also terrifying. As mentor and apprentice their relationship had been simple, but now it was impossible to deny there was so much more between them than simply a shared goal to tear down the Authority. Love, or what he'd thought had been love, had made a fool of him before, and his rational self was urging him to be cautious, but the truth was he'd fallen for Elara Cage, and he'd fallen hard.

"Hey, you still with me?" Elara said. Like Finn, she was fidgeting with her armor and weapons, getting them just right.

"I'm still here," Finn replied, though in truth he'd been a million miles away. "I'm just worried that this won't work."

"So am I, but Riley feels strongly that young Ivan will crack once he sees his father with a noose around his neck." Elara cocked her head to one side, contemplatively. "In the end, it doesn't matter. Either Ivan Volkov concedes, or we take the Authority sector from him by force. The only difference is how much blood gets spilled."

Finn sighed and nodded. He didn't care for Elara's bleak appraisal, but he didn't disagree with it either. And though he shared Elara's doubts that they could appeal to Ivan Volkov's human side, he had seen first-hand how emotional the young man could be. Ivan's reaction to the deaths of Tonya Duke, Finn's fellow apprentice and Ivan's lover, and Sloane Stewart, the Regent Successor's paramour and bodyguard, had shown that he was capable of deep emotional attachments. Finn had to believe that the prospect of losing his father too would be enough to shatter Ivan's resolve.

The stomp of heavy feet rattled the polished tile floor and Finn turned to see a Gen-VII foreman robot marching toward him, carrying a modified laser cutter that was three times the size and power of Finn's personal cannon. Like his own armor, the robot didn't have a dent or a smudge on him, and his gears and motors sang with well-oiled fluidity. Sitting on the foreman's shoulder was Scraps, restored to his chrome and gold best, a broad smile stretching across his mechanical face.

"Chiefy, is that you?" Elara asked, as the robot halted a few paces to their rear.

"Hello, Elara, it is good to see you again," Chiefy said, nodding his new head. The robot then turned to Finn and smiled. "It is also good to see you, Finn. You look... well."

"Thanks," Finn said, hesitantly. The robot had a twinkle in his eye and a penchant for mischief, courtesy of his programmer, Scraps.

"I am detecting subtle changes to your neurotransmitter levels," Chiefy continued. The fact that Scraps was also grinning concerned Finn greatly. "Increases in oxytocin and dopamine are something associated with romantic feelings." The robot leaned in closer, pretending to speak privately to Finn, despite the fact Elara was well within earshot. "Could it be that you are in love?"

Elara snorted a laugh and Scraps choked down an electronic giggle, though Finn was struggling to find the funny side.

"Don't make me regret pulling that processor out of your old head," Finn said, sternly. He looked at Scraps, and narrowed his eyes. "You and I need to have a little talk..."

Scraps giggled again then held up his hands in surrender. Despite the gesture, he looked entirely unrepentant.

"It's time," Briggs said, poking his head around the door

of the gene bank. "Give the word, and we'll get this underway."

Finn looked to Elara. Despite his fame, Elara was the more senior Metal. It was on her command that they would begin.

"Let's do this," she said. "Begin the triumph."

Briggs nodded then disappeared through the doors, which were thrown open a few seconds later, flooding the foyer of the gene bank with warm, orange light from the low autumn sun. There was a shout of "Metal and Blood!" and Finn recognized the powerful vocal cords of Trip, who had been given the honor of issuing the first war cry, then the air erupted into cheers and shouts. Finn and Elara marched outside in lockstep with one another, their armor gleaming in the sunlight, and the cheers rose to a thunderous roar.

"The Heroes of Metalhaven!" Trip bellowed, and a chant of "Metal and Blood!" started up, muted at first, while he and Elara walked toward the motorcade of armored ground cars, then near-deafening as they climbed onto the bed of a modified ale truck and stood beside the bound bodies of Maxim Volkov and Gabriel Montgomery. The two regents were tied to stakes, actually old iron lampposts that had been recovered from the scrapyards, and set high above the bed of the truck on a platform that had been constructed by workers from Makehaven.

The men were dressed in simple jumpsuits, again fabricated by Makehaven purples, which had been designed to mimic the outfits that offenders were forced to wear during their trials. Montgomery's jumpsuit was Metalhaven chrome, while Maxim Volkov wore white and gold, to represent Spacehaven and the Authority. The figure-hugging outfits accentuated the men's gluttonous physiques, especially Montgomery, who looked like a mewling blob of fat. Though while Maxim Volkov was out of shape, he retained a powerful stature with broad shoulders and a barrel chest. It was clear that the man's body had once been fit and strong, but while he'd allowed his physical conditioning to slip, Volkov's mind was still keen. While Montgomery had already soiled himself, Volkov held his head high, shaking off the insults and rotten lumps of algae bread that were battering his face and body like rain bouncing off a window.

"Chiefy, keep an eye on our guests, will you?" Finn said to the upgraded robot.

"A pleasure," Chiefy replied, before turning toward the captured men and brandishing his powerful laser.

Montgomery turned away, shivering with fear, but Volkov simply laughed and stared at the robot, as if willing the machine to slice him up like scrap.

"Let's go!" Finn yelled, hammering his fist onto the roof of the truck's cab, where Trip was now seated, alongside Xia and Briggs.

The engine fired and the truck lurched forward, to more cheers from the crowd. A hundred more trucks and ground cars, loaded with an army of freedom fighters, joined the procession behind them, as they navigated the streets toward the autoway on the northern edge of Metalhaven, between yards nine and ten. Running alongside the ground cars were fifty foreman robots, the bulk of their available machine force, each armed with two assault rifles, recovered from prefects who had been killed when Metalhaven had fallen. The stomp of their feet on the road were like war drums, driving them forward to battle. The vehicles in the procession had also been retrofitted with laser-cutters adapted to act as anti-aircraft weapons and gun emplacements. Each was capable of destroying skycars and even punching holes into the armored ground cars that the prefecture employed.

Taken together, they presented a formidable fighting force, but Finn was under no illusion that the Authority possessed forces equal or greater in number to their own, with better equipment and better training. Yet, he also knew from his studies of ancient history that battles were not always decided in such simple terms. From the Battle of Thermopylae, where Leonidas and seven thousand Greeks held off hundreds of thousands of Persians, to The Alamo, where a hardened group of Texan defenders held the Alamo Mission against a larger Mexican force, numbers had not always been the deciding factor in a war. What mattered was who wanted victory the most. Who had the heart to fight for what they believed in. The prefects of the Authority were bullies, down to the last man, who had never been challenged or faced the prospect of death and defeat. The chromes of Metalhaven would put their loyalty, and their bravery, to the test.

"Where are they?" Elara said, looking into the sky, which had remained cloudless in honor of their triumph. "I would have expected a dozen skycars to come after us the moment we entered the autoway."

"I don't know," Finn replied, also concerned that their advance toward Zavetgrad's capital appeared to be going unchallenged. "Scraps, are you picking up anything on your scanners? Roadblocks up ahead, or prefects waiting in ambush?"

Scraps was sitting on the roof of the truck's cab and

already had his scanner dish deployed. The robot squinted his eyes in concentration as he set his considerable processing power to the task of finding their enemy, but after a full minute of intense scanning, he came up with nothing.

"No prefects up ahead," Scraps said, shrugging. "No skycars airborne, not anywhere."

"Then where the hell are they?" Finn said, beginning to feel uneasy.

The convoy continued unchallenged and in less than ten minutes they had reached the border gate leading into the Authority sector. To Finn's astonishment, the gate was open and the guards that usually manned the towers were conspicuous by their absence.

"This doesn't seem right," Briggs said. The man had pulled himself part-way through the passenger side window of the cab so that he could speak to Finn. "We should be fighting by now. It doesn't make any goddamn sense."

"Send a squad ahead to check the gate," Elara ordered. "They might have mined the road or laid another trap of some kind."

Briggs nodded, then slid back inside the cab, and Finn heard the crackle of his radio, followed by the muffled sound of his voice. Moments later, a ten-man squad approached the gate, accompanied by two foremen. Anxious minutes slipped by, during which time Finn scanned the walls of the sector and the horizon line, expecting to be ambushed at any moment, but the air was still, and the sector was deathly quiet.

"Nothing!" Briggs said, leaning out of the window again. "Not a goddamn fucking thing. It's like they just left the door wide open for us."

Finn and Elara exchanged anxious looks, but both knew that there was no going back. If Ivan Volkov had laid a trap, they would have to spring it. The alternative was to retreat into Metalhaven, and lose all of the momentum they had built up over the last few days.

"They've invited us in, so it would be rude not to accept," Finn said, trying to sound confident and unflustered.

He may have shared Briggs' concerns, but in the same way that they'd repaired and polished their armor to look unconquerable, it was crucial that Briggs and the other Metals didn't see doubt in his eyes. Rebellions could be as fragile as a house of cards, and Finn and Elara were its foundations.

"Move out!" Briggs yelled, while punching a fist toward the gate, and the convoy started up again.

The rumble of heavy vehicles was not a sound that the golds of the Authority sector were used to hearing. Heavy industry and hard work were things that happened outside of their golden walls, and as the procession advanced toward the Authority central square, the streets emptied, like rats leaving a sinking ship. Curtains twitched and doors and shutters were slammed as the well-to-do citizens of the Authority sector fled from the oncoming horde of invaders. And still there wasn't a prefect to be seen.

"Look, there's a prefect hub," Finn said, pointing to a square building on the junction ahead of them. He banged on the roof of the cab, and Briggs appeared on cue. "Check out the hub, but be careful. They might be waiting inside."

Briggs nodded and relayed the command, then two squads of Metals supported by ten foremen stormed the prefect hub, weapons raised. The shouts, crashes and bangs of doors being kicked in and furniture being tossed aside briefly interrupted the stillness of the autumn evening, then the squad leader emerged, and shrugged.

"There's no-one here!" the leader shouted, rifle slung over his shoulder. "All the ground and skycars are gone too."

"But gone where?" Finn said, more to himself than to anyone else.

"Our recon squad just reported back," Briggs said, hanging out of the window with a radio pressed to one ear. "There's nothing between us and the central square, and it looks like every gold in the sectors has barred themselves indoors."

"What about the central square itself?" Finn asked. The way had been cleared for them, and there had to be a reason.

"There are two TVs hovering in front of the Mayor's building, like the ones they use for trials, but that's it," Briggs answered. "No prefects, no foremen, no bloody anyone!"

"Then we push on," Finn said, assuredly. "Ivan wants us to see something, so let's find out what it is."

The grand motorcade roared ahead, and within a few minutes the armored vehicles had surrounded the Authority central square, laser cutters aimed at every street entrance and rooftop. Trip drove their armored truck directly up to the steps of the mayor's building, and its gold-fronted portico that reminded Finn of the entrance to the regents' cathedral inside the sub-oceanic complex.

"What's the matter, hero?" Maxim Volkov said. "Not quite the welcome you were expecting?"

Volkov was smiling, as if he knew something, though Finn struggled to understand how that could have been possible. He was about to interrogate the regent when the two giant TV screens hummed closer. A hundred rifles and laser weapons were suddenly trained on the screens, but Elara raised her hand, and no triggers were pulled. The screens arranged themselves, one above the other, with the largest screen, a titanic three-hundred-and-fifty-inch monster, adopting the topmost position. The bottom screen flickered, before turning a brilliant, dazzling white, then the face of Ivan Volkov appeared.

"I had expected you sooner," Ivan said, his voice blaring from speakers built into the hovering TV. "But I'm glad you finally made it."

"What's this all about, Ivan?" Finn said. The sheer size of the man's face on the screen was disturbing and off-putting. "Why have you abandoned the sector?"

Ivan snorted then waved a hand dismissively, and Finn noticed that his former co-apprentice was wearing full regent's robes, including the mayor's sash and chain. This fact seemed to amuse his father, who had not stopped smiling since Ivan had appeared on the screen.

"The Authority sector is not important," Ivan replied. "If you had bothered to learn anything about the true nature of Zavetgrad during your brief tenure as a gold, you'd know that."

"Then surrender it to us," Elara cut in. She unhooked the crossbow from her belt and aimed the weapon at Maxim Volkov. "Surrender control of the city to us now, or your father dies."

Finn watched Ivan's face but there wasn't the slightest flicker of emotion. If anything, the man looked bored.

"Then kill him, if you have the stomach for cold-blooded murder," Ivan replied.

Maxim Volkov laughed, and Finn stared at the man in

disbelief, because Ivan's father didn't look hurt or betrayed, but proud, and for a moment, even Elara's usually unshakable poise wavered.

"My orders are to hold Spacehaven, which you should know is the most important sector in Zavetgrad," Ivan continued. He picked fluff from his sleeve, looked at it disparagingly, then flicked it away. "You are welcome to the Authority sector, for all the good it will do you."

"This is madness," Elara snapped, storming toward Maxim Volkov, crossbow still aimed at the man's throat. "This is the most powerful man on the planet, your own goddamn father, and you would just let him die?"

"He *was* the most powerful man on the planet, until he was captured," Ivan corrected her. "As soon as that happened, I became the senior regent."

Finn looked at Maxim Volkov but the smug expression on the man's face told him that the former mayor had known that this would be the outcome from the very beginning. Suddenly, the reason for his compliance and cooperation was clear. Maxim Volkov had known he was dead from the moment they had driven through the gates of Metalhaven, and any chance of escape was gone.

"In any case, because of what you have done, my title and position are ultimately unimportant," Ivan continued, idly checking his nails. "There has only ever been one man who holds power over this city, and the voice of Authority does not speak from the surface of this raped world, but from Nimbus – humanity's future home."

The lower screen dimmed, then the giant TV above it burst into life, bathing Finn and Elara in an intense silver light that forced them to shield their eyes, as if they were looking directly into the sun. Slowly, the light faded, and the face of another man appeared. It took a moment for Finn's eyes to adjust, but he recognized the face at once, because it was the same face that adorned the emblem of the Authority, carved into the portico of the mayor's building.

"I am Gideon Alexander Reznikov, President of the Authority," the man said, though he needed no introduction. "I am here to offer you a chance to end your rebellion, peacefully," the president paused then stressed, "...only one chance."

Finn peered at the face of the president, which was looming over him larger than life, impossibly young-looking but with the presence and power of a god, and he was struck with terror.

"Return to your sectors," Reznikov boomed. "Return control of Zavetgrad to the regents or their successors, and surrender Finn Brasa and Elara Cage to Ivan Volkov so that justice can be served." There was another pause, during which time not a single man or woman took a breath. "Do this and the workers shall be spared. Refuse, and the consequences will be severe."

The silence was deafening then suddenly Elara laughed. Briggs, hanging out of the window of the cab laughed too, and before long hundreds of metals had bursts into fits of laughter.

"Surrender?" Elara said to the young face staring down at her. "We've captured or killed all your regents, and your new mayor has just surrendered the capitol to us. Why should we do anything you demand?"

Reznikov smiled and Finn felt a chill seize his bones. His bitter experiences with head prefects, prosecutors and regents had taught him to know the face of cruelty, but it wasn't until that moment that he saw the face of evil.

"A small demonstration, then," Reznikov said, coolly.

There were anxious murmurs from the assembled freedom fighters, then Scraps' radar dish swung around and pointed into the sky.

"Danger!" the robot yelled.

"What is it, pal?" Finn said, turning to his friend. "What danger? Where?"

Scraps pointed into the sky. "Look-look!"

Finn peered up and at first all he could see were a few thin clouds rolling across the burned orange sky. Then, higher, he saw Nimbus, but for the first time in his life, it was more than merely an inanimate lump of metal in space. Lights flared across its surface, making it look alien and ethereal. Then he spotted a smoke trail and soon others spotted it too. There were cries of, "There!" and "What is that?" but no-one knew the answer. To Finn, it looked like a damaged skycar, spiraling to the ground, but the object was higher than anything he'd seen before.

"Volkov, what's going on?" Finn demanded, turning to the former mayor, who was also looking skyward, but with a smile on his face.

"It's a missile, you stupid fucker!" Volkov said. He turned to Finn and laughed. "And now you understand your mistake. Now, you'll witness what true power means."

"We need to take cover!" Briggs yelled, pressing a radio to his ear, but Finn snatched it from his grasp before Briggs could order a retreat.

"Wait, it's not coming for us," Finn said, tracking the path of the missile.

"Has it misfired?" Elara asked, but Finn's knotted gut told him no.

The missile screeched across the sky above them and smashed into a building a couple of miles away. The shockwave hit them a moment later, blasting Finn's hair back like a strong breeze.

"Oh no..." Elara said, staggering forward and bracing herself against the railings surrounding the truck's platform. "They've hit the workhouse..." She turned to Finn and her face was drained of blood. "The children..." she said, barely more than a whisper. "All of the children..."

In the background, Finn could hear Maxim Volkov laughing, and his legs suddenly gave way, forcing him to hold the roof of the cabin to stay standing. He didn't want to look, but he forced himself to do it, and saw smoke rising from the workhouse, where every child in Zavetgrad lived and trained from age three to thirteen. Thousands of children, all under one roof. And Gideon Alexander Reznikov had just turned their building into a furnace.

23

THE SHORT CUT

Finn was frozen in terror as a thick column of smoke rose into the sky, twisting and coiling like an angry viper. In the background, he could still hear Maxim Volkov laughing and he reached for his spear, ready to shove it down the repulsive man's throat, when the voice of Gideon Alexander Reznikov cut through him like a knife.

"Your choice is this," the president of the Authority said, still looming large above them on the giant TV screen, imperious and unmoved by the atrocity he had just committed. "Surrender to me, unconditionally, or I will raze the city to the ground, killing you and every last worker and gold in Zavetgrad. You have forty-eight hours to comply."

The screen flashed off and hummed away, then Ivan Volkov reappeared on the smaller of the two TVs. The man's eyes were fixed on his father for a moment, before the image of the new mayor looked directly at Finn.

"Release my father, and convey him to the gates of Spacehaven," Ivan said, ignoring the fact that Gabriel Montgomery was also tied to a post beside the former regent.

"And don't try to be a hero and save the children in the workhouse because they're already dead. In an hour, there will be nothing left of that building but blackened brick and bones."

Finn reeled toward the screen, electrified spear in his hand. He almost hurled the weapon at Ivan's face, but he'd held on to just enough of his wits to realize it would have been foolish and futile to do so.

"Fuck you, Ivan!" Finn snapped, aiming the weapon at Volkov's head. His hand was trembling. "How can you do this? They're children!"

"They are surplus to requirements," Ivan replied, unmoved by Finn's outburst. "Everything that is necessary for the future of humanity is already with me, in Spacehaven; we have no further need of workers."

"What the hell does that mean?" Finn said, confused. Reznikov had just ordered their surrender, but Ivan Volkov was still talking as if Zavetgrad was finished, either way.

"Just give me back my father!" Ivan roared, in a sudden flare of anger that Finn had grown accustomed to experiencing from the younger Volkov. It was clear to Finn now that Ivan's earlier aloofness regarding his father's fate had been an act for the benefit of Reznikov. "Deliver him safely, and I'll allow you to scurry back to Metalhaven with your tails between your legs." Ivan leaned closer to the camera and his face, already blown up larger than the side of an ale truck, became distorted and freakish. "Refuse, and the birthing center will be targeted next..." Finn felt a chill rush down his spine; the birthing center was populated by hundreds of pregnant women, all forced to give birth to Zavetgrad's future workers. "Don't think I won't do it, Finn," the new regent growled. "Please understand that your lives mean nothing to me."

The screen went blank, and Finn again had to resist the urge to hurl his spear at the TV. Then he heard a cry of pain, and he spun around to see Elara with her axe pressed to Maxim Volkov's throat. She'd already drawn blood.

"Elara, wait!" Finn called out, darting toward her. Volkov's face was twisted in agony, but the man's eyes remained hateful and defiant. "He's still more useful to us alive. If Ivan learns we've killed him, who knows what he'll do."

"What more *can* he do?" Elara hissed, barley holding back. "They've already bombed the workhouse, and they need the work sectors to keep running, or their precious gold lifestyle crumbles."

Volkov managed a strained laugh and Elara cut deeper, forcing the man to grit his teeth and force out his words through spasms of pain.

"You still don't understand do you?" Volkov said, twisting and writhing like a captured animal. "I told you, but you wouldn't listen..."

Finn put his hand on Elara's arm and added gentle pressure, pulling the blade of the axe away from Volkov's bleeding flesh. Her wrath suddenly was redirected toward him, and Finn could see that The Shadow was fully in control.

"We need him, for now," Finn said. "Ivan wants him back, and that gives us leverage."

Finn didn't care whether Maxim Volkov lived or died and would have been happy to slit the man's throat himself, but Elara was acting on emotion, and they had to think clearly.

Reznikov had outplayed them and what they'd thought was a foolproof plan to take over the Authority had backfired in a horrific way.

"Sir, the workhouse..." It was Briggs. The man had climbed out of the truck's cab and was standing on the sidesill. "It's badly damaged but still intact. Many of the children could still be alive."

Briggs' comment couldn't have been timelier, because it snapped Elara out of her murderous rage like a slap across the face. She brushed Finn off her then spat in Volkov's face. The former regent merely laughed again, and proceeded to lick the dribbles of Elara's saliva into his mouth, flicking his tongue at them like a snake.

"The golds must have firefighting equipment," Elara said, focusing her energies toward a more useful goal. "Find them and get to the workhouse as fast as you can, and organize as many trucks as we can spare to form rescue teams."

Briggs nodded and relayed the order via his radio. The man was about to head off to coordinate the rescue teams when Chiefy grabbed the Metal's arm and held him back. Scraps was perched on the Gen-VII foreman robot's shoulder, sensor dish extended and aimed toward the burning building.

"Wait, there is more," Chiefy said. There was a data flow between Chiefy and the smaller robot, whose staccato statements were less able to convey detailed information verbally. "Scraps had detected radio signals emanating from the workhouse that are consistent with the remote explosive detonators that Stonehaven workers use to collapse condemned structures."

Finn frowned. "Are you saying they planted explosives in the basement of the workhouse?"

"Correct," Chiefy nodded. "A force of prefects has also surrounded the grounds around the workhouse."

"That's what Ivan meant when he said that in an hour there would be nothing left of the workhouse but rubble and bones," Elara cut in. "The missile from Nimbus was for show, to get our attention. Ivan intends to finish the job by bringing the building down from the inside."

Finn cursed and punched the roof of the truck's cabin so hard it dented the metal. He looked around them and saw that Xia and Trip were also outside, hanging off the truck's wing mirrors, ghostly faces staring at him, looking for instructions. At one time, he too might have been paralyzed with fear, but not anymore. He wasn't going to let Ivan Volkov tell him what to do, because fuck him.

"Trip, Xia, we need Haven operatives and Stonehaven workers who understand explosives," Finn said, jumping into gear. "Put the word out, and gather as many as you can. Ivan said we had an hour, but that was five minutes ago. Every second counts."

"You got it, we'll meet you there," Trip said, and the two Metals jumped down and ran toward the other leaders, yelling the new orders.

"Briggs, can you drive one of these trucks?" Finn asked, turning to the former worker from Metalhaven.

"My legs aren't what they use to be, but yes," Briggs replied.

Finn looked at the trucks and ground cars that had assembled in the Authority central square, and his eyes fell onto an armored flat-bed that had a pintle-mounted laser cutter welded to the bed of the truck.

"That's our ride," Finn said, pointing to the vehicle. "You drive and Elara and I will shoot."

Briggs nodded then headed off to requisition the truck that Finn had pointed out. Already, other cars and trucks had assembled, and amongst them Finn could see red and gold fire wagons racing toward the autoway, but the main road took a circuitous route to the workhouse, and Finn didn't want to waste a second.

"What about them?" Elara said, punching the head of her axe into Volkov's sizable gut and causing the man to issue a muted grunt.

"They can stay here," Finn said. "I'll have a squad keep watch on them."

Finn turned his back on Volkov, whose continued efforts to taunt him with strained smiles were drawing out the same murderous impulses that had almost overcome Elara. What bothered him the most was that Volkov was enjoying himself. He was a mad man content to watch the world burn.

"You may as well let them die," Volkov said, his tone bright and almost jolly. Finn gripped the roof of the truck and closed his eyes, trying to calm himself. "Nothing you do now will matter," Volkov continued. "This is the beginning of the end, Finn Brasa." The man laughed, mocking him. "Do you want to know what I find so funny?"

Finn turned back to Volkov and stood in front of the man; spear still gripped tightly in his hand.

"Go on, tell me," Finn said. He knew Volkov wouldn't be quiet until he'd said his piece.

"You're supposed to be the Hero of Metalhaven, the

savior of Zavetgrad," Volkov said, laughing under his breath. "But you haven't saved a goddamn soul, Finn Brasa. You've condemned them all to die."

Finn swung the spear and struck the flat of the blade across the side of Maxim Volkov's head, knocking him out cold. Volkov's body fell limp and tugged against the restraints, but the bonds that fixed him to the pillar held fast. Then he heard the sound of running water and the pungent smell of urine, and he looked across at Gabriel Montgomery. The man was trembling, and a stream of yellow urine was trickling down his leg and meandering across the rusted bed of the truck, following a chaotic path between the rivets and checker-plate pattern stamped into the metal. Yet, however much he despised his former regent, Montgomery's torment gave him no satisfaction. It merely reinforced his fear that Maxim Volkov was right, and that the end of days was coming for them all.

"Briggs is here," Elara said, as the truck with the pintle-mounted laser pulled up alongside their vehicle. "But the rescue convoy is already on the autoway, and if we leave now, we'll get stuck behind them. It could take twenty or thirty minutes to reach the workhouse, and we don't have that much time."

"We're not taking the autoway," Finn said, jumping from one truck to the other, and grabbing hold of the laser cannon. "Chiefy, Scraps, we need the fastest route to the workhouse, through side-streets, back-alleys and whatever you can find. Hell, I don't care if we have to drive the through middle of the cultural quarter, so long as we get there fast."

"I will plot a course," Chiefy said. The robot jumped down, leaping over the second truck in a single bound and landing beside the driver's side door, barely making a sound. "But I suggest that I drive."

"Be my guest," Briggs said, throwing open the door and stepping out. "I've gotten more used to pulling pints than gear levers."

"Scraps navigate!" the smaller robot said, flying inside the truck and interfacing with its rudimentary control systems. "But bad-men in the way!"

"Let us worry about them," Elara said. She plucked Finn's laser cannon from its holster then handed her crossbow to Briggs, along with the bag of bolts. "So long as you keep loading this, I'll keep shooting it."

Briggs nodded and took the weapon, though not without some reticence. "Something tells me I'd have been safer driving this thing," the Metal said, wedging himself into the corner of the flat-bed, bag of bolts in hand.

Finn hammered the flat of his hand onto the cab of the truck.

"You're up Chiefy. Floor it!"

The truck's engine roared, and its tires screeched against the golden bricks of the central square, before it surged forward like a rocket, sending Finn tumbling backward as if he'd been kicked in the chest. Elara managed to hold on to the frame of the headboard, and her dignity, while Briggs slid from one side of the truck's flatbed to the other, like a drunken worker tottering down a frozen street.

Grabbing hold of the laser cannon's pintle mount, Finn dragged himself off the floor and climbed to his feet. Already, the Authority's central square had been left behind, obscured by a plume of dust and black exhaust smoke, and Finn began to regret his instructions to Chiefy, which the robot appeared to be taking literally. The truck was hurtling down a pedestrian side-street with barely an inch of space to either side, heading directly for the public arboretum. It was a place that Finn had visited a number of times with Juniper Jones, and he recalled the bittersweet memory of plucking his first piece of fruit from a tree. It was vivid in his mind, especially because he could see the tree in question through the glass walls of the arboretum.

"Hold on!" the robot called out, brightly.

In other circumstances, Finn might have found Chiefy's cheerfully obvious statement to be funny, but there was nothing amusing about driving headlong at a glass wall at fifty miles per hour. He ducked just as the radiator grille of the truck smashed through the wall, sending fragments of sharp glass flying over his head. The truck lurched to the right, then left, and suddenly its was apples and pears that were raining down on his body, rather than splinters. He lifted his eyes to look ahead and wished he hadn't. Chiefy was threading the truck between trees and bushes with the precision of a surgeon, forcing the heavy vehicle to move in a way that defied physics.

Within seconds, they had smashed through the other side of the arboretum, leaving utter carnage in their wake, but the destruction wasn't over yet. The cultural quarter was ahead, and though the golds had abandoned its cobbled streets for the safety of their homes, the cafés were still set up with their outdoor tables and chairs, while market stalls lined the pretty, golden avenue, filled with scarves and hats, sweet treats and works of art. Chiefy destroyed them all, charging through each display as if he'd been aiming to hit them, rather than avoid them. A pair of fine silken panties smacked Finn in the face and he tore them away, spitting the fibers out of his mouth, before tossing the item of lingerie over his shoulder. He glanced at Elara, hoping that she hadn't noticed, but of course she had and his humiliation was complete. But there was no time for embarrassment, because the truck was nearing the edge of the cultural quarter.

"Bad men ahead!" Scraps yelled, poking his head through the divider between the cabin and the flat bed. "Roadblocks!"

Finn and Elara sprang into action. With the market stalls and café tables in ruin behind them, they were now entering the residential district of the Authority sector, with its wider roads and paths. Smoke from the burning workhouse was directly ahead, but so was a blockade of three prefect ground cars – troop transports in all but name. Each vehicle had ten officers in the back, hunkered beneath armored side-plates, and Finn could see the barrels of their assault rifles poking up like flagpoles. Finally, the skycars that had been conspicuous by their absence up until then began to hum into view, arriving from the direction of Spacehaven. Finn realized that Ivan Volkov had gotten wise to their plan and was trying to stop them from reaching the workhouse and defusing the explosives, but there wasn't a chance in hell he was going to allow more children to die.

Aiming the laser cannon at the middle of three prefect ground cars, Finn squeezed the trigger and lashed pulses of searing hot energy at the vehicle. The ground car's armor melted like ice exposed to a naked flame, then exploded, blowing up a dozen prefects at the same time. Chiefy rammed through the wreckage, chewing it up like grizzled meat, and powered on, but the two remaining ground cars u-turned in the road and pursued.

"You deal with the skycars, I've got these," Elara called out.

Elara steadied herself with one hand on the headboard frame while hammering shots at the pursing vehicles with Finn's laser cannon, but the armored vehicles were tough enough to withstand the barrages. The protective barriers surrounding the troop compartments of the prefect vehicles then dropped and ten officers took aim, but Chiefy swayed the truck from side to side, and the incoming bullets flew wide. Elara's aim, however, was faultless.

Laser shots burned through the prefects' armor like it was made of cheap plastic, while at the same time she speared the helpless officers in the second truck with crossbow bolts, shooting with both hands with equal precision. Briggs reloaded as fast as he could, but the man couldn't keep up with Elara's furious pace, and soon the prefect ground cars had drawn alongside.

"Finn!" Elara called out, and he spun around, lashing a laser blast across the ground car to his right, and splitting the vehicle in half between its front and rear axles. Prefects screamed in terror, and they were flung into the road, while the two halves of the vehicle cartwheeled out of control and smashed into a luxury condo.

Across the other side, foremen had jumped across and Elara was locked in a struggle with one, fighting off the machine's attempts to strangle her. Grabbing the spear from his back scabbard, Finn electrified the blade and speared the robot like a medieval jouster, knocking it into the road. Elara recovered and drew her axe, meeting the advance of two more robots with blinding fury. The black, double-headed blade flashed through the air and the machines were hacked to pieces like rotten wood.

Suddenly, bullets raked across the top of the truck and Finn was hit, but his refurbished armor repelled the metal slugs, and he was unhurt. Replacing the spear in his back scabbard, he grabbed the handles of the laser cutter and wheeled it around to face the trio of skycars that were strafing them. He fired on reflex, hitting the lead vehicle and destroying its port rotors. The craft veered off course forcing one of its wingmen to evade and crash into the third skycar, and soon both were hurtling toward the ground in a conjoined mass. The lead skycar exploded a moment later, the concussive blast shattering the windows in the condos that lined the street. Finn punched the air then his jubilation turned to horror, as the vehicle crashed directly into their path, blocking the road.

"Scraps, Chiefy, we need another way through!" Finn shouted.

"Processing", Scraps answered, through Chiefy had not altered course and they were still racing toward the burning wreckage of the skycar.

"Process faster!"

"Wait-wait!" Scraps said, his little eyes, scrunched up. "Trust Scraps!"

Finn released the laser cutter and grabbed hold of the headboard frame with both hands. Elara was already there, knuckles white and teeth gritted and bared.

"Fifteen meters... left hard!" Scraps screeched.

Chiefy made the turn, crashing into the front of a building before hurtling through its foyer.

"Ten meters, square right, then straight!" Scraps called out.

The truck lurched hard and crashed through another glass frontage, before resuming its original trajectory, but now they were driving down a blind alley.

"Scraps, it's a dead end!" Finn yelled, but the robot's eyes remained scrunched up tightly.

"Fifteen meters, acute left! Then ten meters, square right!"

Chiefy followed the instructions to the letter and the truck smashed through a wall and into the rear courtyard of a restaurant, before lurching right and punching through a set of ornate wooden gates. Splinters scratched Finn's face, but the maneuvers had worked and they were back on a road. Where to, he had no idea.

"The workhouse is that way!" Elara shouted, pointing to their right, where the plume of smoke continued to rise.

"Scraps knows!" The robot replied, waving Elara off. "Two-hundred meters, slight right, then jump-jump!"

"Jump?" Elara and Finn both cried out together.

"Yes, jump-jump!" the robot confirmed. "Must go fast!"

Chiefy floored the accelerator and the truck powered down the narrow road, climbing to thirty, then forty, then sixty miles per hour. The buildings to either side fell away, and the workhouse became visible ahead and to their right. It was an enormous structure, one hundred and fifty meters long and wide, and twenty storeys high, packed with as many as twenty or thirty-thousand children; the true number was not known. The missile from Nimbus had struck the roof in the dead center and the upper levels were ablaze.

Suddenly, another gate was smashed down by the truck's

now mangled and twisted grille, and they turned onto an unfinished slip road that ended suddenly a few hundred meters ahead.

"Hold tight-tight!" Scraps said, tucking himself into Chiefy's lap as the truck accelerated to seventy miles per hour.

Finn was already holding on as tightly as his throbbing hands could manage, then before he had time to think, the truck was airborne. For a second or two it felt like they were floating in freefall, and it was oddly peaceful. Then the truck slammed into the desolate grounds surrounding the workhouse, and its suspension buckled. Chiefy wrestled with the wheel, somehow managing to prevent the truck from spinning out of control and overturning. Eventually, it ground to a halt directly in front of the burning workhouse, smoke and steam billowing from its ruined engine bay. Finn tried to speak, but his breaths were coming too fast and his heart was pumping so hard he thought he was going to die. Eventually, the adrenaline eased, and he managed to say two words.

"How long?"

Scraps pulled himself out of the broken cabin. "Thirty-one min-mins to bombs," the little robot said, mimicking Finn's breathlessness perfectly, as if his oil can body contained mechanical lungs. "Still time!"

24

THE FUTURE PRINCIPAL

Finn helped Briggs to stand, but the man had been thrown around in the back of the truck so badly that he was barely conscious. He grabbed the headboard of the truck with his left hand – his right looked broken – then nodded weakly to Finn to indicate that he was okay. A moment later, the rebel's legs gave way beneath him, and Briggs collapsed onto his ass with an anguished groan.

"I think I'm done," Briggs said, annoyed with himself for being unable to continue.

"Don't worry, just wait for Xia and the others," Finn said, resting a hand on the man's shoulder. "We'll take care of the bombs."

Chiefy kicked the driver's-side door off its hinges, sending it skidding across the asphalt-covered grounds that surrounded the workhouse, then climbed out. Scraps was perched on the foreman's shoulder, sporting some fresh dents and scrapes.

"Scraps has uploaded the locations of the explosives," Chiefy said, while removing a heavy tire arm from the door sill of the truck and brandishing it as a weapon. "There are three charges in total, all in the basement level."

"Then let's move," Finn said, accepting his laser cannon back from Elara. "We can't wait for Xia and the Stonehaven workers to arrive. We have to get in there now."

Finn jumped down, though his legs almost gave way beneath him, then started toward the burning building, but Chiefy extended an arm to block his path.

"I advise caution," the robot said, explaining his actions. "There are prefects ahead, and we will have to fight our way through."

Finn had been so eager to find the explosives that he'd forgotten about the prefects, but now he saw the officers forming up outside the main entrance to the workhouse. There were only twenty in total, and each sported green adornments to their armor, indicating that they were from Seedhaven, notoriously Zavetgrad's least troublesome work sector. The green prefects had a reputation for being lazy, spending their days sitting inside watchtowers in the giant vertical farming structures, eating their way through almost as much produce as the farms manufactured. As a Metalhaven chrome, Finn had naturally never had a run-in with a green, but from the cumbersome fit of their armor and loose formation, he figured their reputation was well earned.

"Ivan must be keeping his best forces, and the special prefecture, back to guard Spacehaven," Finn said, surmising the reason for their lackluster opponents.

"That means he knows we won't surrender," Elara said, sliding a bolt into her crossbow. "And the little fucker is right."

Finn nodded but still something was gnawing at the back

of his mind. *If they know we won't surrender, then why the forty-eight-hour deadline?* The question was driving him mad. *Why not an hour? Why not demand we surrender at once?*

The sound of bolts and hinges snapping, and metal being warped out of shape brought Finn back to the moment, and he saw that Chiefy had torn away the hood of the truck and was holding it like a shield.

"Please get behind me," the foreman robot said.

If Chiefy's command alone hadn't been enough to compel Finn to move, the sound of gunfire certainly was. Finn and Elara slipped in behind the improvised shield and bullets began to rattle off it, but despite the size of the target, Finn could still see rounds skipping off the asphalt well wide of their position. He chanced a look around the side of the shield and the prefects were in disarray. Despite their advantage in numbers and weapons, they looked like rookies who had barely held a rifle.

Chiefy began to advance, slowly at first before building up to a jog and then a run. The gunfire intensified and Finn heard blurted orders and cries of, "Fall back, fall back!", but it was already too late, and Chiefy bulldozed through their ranks like a wrecking ball. The prefects who had survived being rammed, or had gotten out of the way, tried to run, but neither Finn nor Elara were in a merciful frame of mind. Crossbow bolts sank into eye sockets and thudded into necks, while the razor-sharp edge of Elara's double-headed axe dispatched three others. Finn's laser cut down several more as the Seedhaven prefects fumbled to recover their rifle and clear jams, then he holstered the cannon and drew his spear, not even bothering to electrify the blade. That would have been too quick and easy.

Finn stormed toward the last quartet of prefects, impaling one through the gut with a powerful thrust, before whirling the weapon around his head and opening the throats of two more. The last officer threw down his jammed rifle and pulled a knife, though whether the man had chosen to face Finn out of courage or simply because his petrified muscles wouldn't allow him to run made no difference. Screaming like a lunatic, the prefect hacked and slashed wildly, even managing to score a groove across Finn's freshly painted armor before he drove the spear deep into the prefect's chest and electrified the blade to end his suffering.

"The door is locked," Elara said. She was a step ahead of Finn, having already dispatched her prefects. "Chiefy, see if you can break it down."

Chiefy tossed his makeshift shield then shoulder-charged the door and crashed through it. Smoke billowed through the opening, and Finn could already feel the heat from the fires, but he ran inside without a care for his own safety.

"Scraps, why haven't the fire suppression systems kicked in?" Finn yelled. The smoke was already clinging to the roof of his mouth.

"Golds disabled!" Scraps said, and Finn cursed Ivan again. "I fix!"

The robot pulled open a control panel then interfaced with it. A few seconds later, water began gushing from sprinklers on the ground floor.

"There's damage to more than a third of the building," Elara said, reading the panel over Scraps' shoulder. "Half of the suppression systems are offline, and the fires are still spreading."

"We need to find the survivors and get them out," Finn said, heading into one of the assembly halls.

"Finn, wait, we have to disable the explosives first," Elara called after him. "If we don't, then there won't be anyone left to save."

Finn cursed then checked outside and saw that the first trucks in the rescue convoy were starting to make their way off the autoway, but it was a single-track road to the workhouse, and the rescue teams were still at least ten minutes away.

"How long till the charges detonate, pal?" Finn asked.

"Twenty min-mins!" Scraps answered, without any of his typical optimism.

"We can't rely on disarming these bombs, and if we don't start evacuations now, we could lose everyone," Finn said, torn between what to do for the best. "Someone has to stay and help get these kids out."

"I'll help..."

Finn saw a girl in the assembly hall then he noticed that a door had been slid open at the far end, and that other small faces were peering out at him.

"I'm a floor coordinator on ten," the girl continued. Her face was blackened with smoke, and she had burns to her arms and neck. "When the fires started, I brought my wings down here, into rooms and halls that weren't smokey. The governor robots have all left, so on the way down, I told the other floor coordinators to get ready too. I didn't know what else to do."

"You did great," Finn said, rushing to the girl and kneeling in front of her. "How many of you are there?"

The girl shrugged. "Three dormitory floors are down

here, and six more on the levels above us. I couldn't get any higher than fourteen. The smoke was too thick and it was too hot."

"What's your name?" Finn asked. He could sense that the girl was smart and likely a high rating, a double-four at least. The white patch on her overalls suggested that she had already been assigned to Spacehaven.

"Zoe," the girl replied.

"I'm Finn, that's Elara, Chiefy and Scraps," Finn said, pointing to his companions in turn. "We're here to help, but we need your help too. We need you to speak to the other coordinators and lead everyone outside, and we need you to do it fast."

Zoe nodded, but the act of doing so caused her to shudder with pain from the burns on her neck. Finn choked down his anger and was about to tell Elara that'd he'd help Zoe evacuate the survivors when Briggs stumbled through the door.

"I'll get them out," Briggs said. The man had fashioned a makeshift sling for his arm, but from the way the man was walking, Finn figured it wasn't the only bone that was broken. "You lot deal with the bombs."

Finn stepped back and Briggs sank to his knees in front of the girl, groaning and wincing as he did so.

"Zoe, was it?" the man said, and the girl nodded. Briggs removed a tin star from his collar, a simple symbol of his leadership position in the resistance, and pinned it to Zoe's overalls. "You're in charge now, boss, so let's get to it. And once you're all out, you never have to see this shithole again."

"We're being freed?" Zoe asked, a touch of brightness lighting up her blackened face.

Briggs nodded. "That's right."

The girl managed a smile then took Briggs' free hand. Slowly, and with great effort, the man stood.

"This way," Zoe said, dragging Briggs into the assembly hall. "I'll show you..."

The screech of tires alerted Finn to the arrival of another vehicle, and for a heart-stopping moment, he feared that it was a prefect ground car. He ran outside, laser ready, but it was the truck carrying Xia. She was with two other men, wearing orange overalls.

"Pieter," Xia said, nodding to one man. "Francis..." she added, nodding to the other. "They know bombs..."

Finn glanced back along the road and saw that the fire wagons were now on the single-track lane. He could see workers furiously engaged in the effort of deploying the aerial platforms and hoses that would be needed to beat back the fires that were rapidly engulfing the workhouse. There was nothing more he could do outside. Everything now hinged on defusing the charges.

"Then follow us," Finn said, heading back inside the workhouse. "We have three explosives, all in the basement level. Chiefy will show us where they are, the rest it down to you."

Chiefy gave the Stonehaven workers a friendly wave, though they were far too confused and stoical to wave back, then led them into the basement, crashing through the steel barrier with the same ease that his powerful Gen-VII robotic frame had broken through the main entrance. Chiefy's eyes lit up like beacons, lighting the way down the steep metal stairs into the basement level.

Finn followed, laser in one hand and spear in the other, in

case Ivan had prepared any further surprises for them, but once inside the cavernous, open-plan sub-level, all he could see were generators, switch boxes, HVAC controls, and piles and piles of junk that had been dumped there over decades.

"There is one charge in the south-west corner structural support, one directly in front of us, and the other in the northeast corner," Chiefy said, pointing the way to each. "The foundations of this building were built poorly. Destroying these supports will cause the building to implode, though it will be an imperfect demolition."

"Ivan probably wanted it to be messy, the sick fucker," Finn said before turning to the demolitions experts. "Francis and Pieter, right?" he asked, and the men nodded. "You take the northeast and southwest, while Chiefy and Scraps disable the charge on the central support." The men nodded again and hurried away. "And make it fast," Finn called out, stopping them in their tracks. "We only have a few minutes."

Finn didn't specify how many minutes they had, because he didn't know, and part of him didn't want to know. He looked at Scraps, their official timekeeper, and the robot pulled apart his steepled fingers then folded them into the palm of his hand until only four remained. It was less time than Finn had thought.

"The process is quite simple," Chiefy said, while removing the cover on the explosive charge that he had been tasked with defusing. "I should be able to defuse all three charges, if required."

"Let's just start with this one," Finn said.

He appreciated the robot's confidence, but they were less than four minutes from being blown apart and their charred remains buried beneath thousands of tons of rubble. Until the job was done, he could barely take a breath.

Chiefy got started, his large hands working with surprising dexterity given the robot's bulk and utilitarian design. Finn looked for Francis and spotted the Stonehaven worker in the far corner of the basement. He could barely see the man in the gloom, over a hundred meters away. Meanwhile, Pieter had reached the final charge and had set down his tool kit, ready to work.

"Ah, fuck, I've got the wrong toolbar!" Pieter called out. The man stood up, holding a torque wrench which was clearly of no use for defusing a bomb. "I'll need to borrow some from Francis."

Finn was about to yell out, "Then hurry the fuck up!" when Pieter suddenly spasmed and his body went rigid. Scraps became alert and hovered into the air, before shining a torchlight from his eyes into the corner of the room and illuminating a governor robot. The machine, which was a modified foreman programmed to manage the workhouse children, had punched its hand through Pieter's body, like a knife. The Stonehaven worker was lifted off his feet, still too shocked to even cry out, before being torn in half and thrown against the wall.

"Francis, look out!" Finn yelled but it was already too late.

A second governor robot had moved out of the shadows and clamped its hands to the side of the worker's head. Francis screamed, then shrieked as the robot slowly added pressure, until the man's head popped like an egg. Then the two robots turned toward Finn and the others, and charged.

Without a word spoken between them, Elara went north, axe in hand, while Finn electrified his spear and launched the weapon like a harpoon, striking the second robot in the chest, and paralyzing it with pulses of current and voltage that overloaded its circuits.

"Look out!" Scraps yelled, and Finn reeled around to see a third governor. It had been lurking beneath the stairs, lying in ambush like the others.

Finn aimed his laser and fired, blasting the machine's left arm clean away from its body, but the governor was already on top of him, and he was struck hard across the back and sent down. The robot raised its right foot and Finn barely managed to roll out from beneath it before the governor's hammer-like heel slammed into the floor, denting the metal. Scraps charged the governor and clawed at its ocular sensors, but the bigger machine simply swatted him into the corner of the room like he was an irritating fly. Finn could tolerate a lot, but not someone hurting Scraps. He drew his knife, a pitifully inadequate weapon against a seven-foot machine, but Finn was so full of fury that even a simple blade was a weapon of mass destruction in his hands.

Rushing the governor, Finn pounced onto the machine and dragged it down. The robot fought back, cracking Finn's armor with powerful punches and knee strikes, but Finn was blind to the pain. He stabbed his knife into the robot's neck, over and over and over again, until the blade was twisted and dulled, and the handle cracked. Sparks flew and oil splattered from the machine's gears and motors like blood, until Finn had hacked through its control wires and disconnected its machine brain from its body.

"I have disabled the center charge," Chiefy called out, as Finn wiped oil from his face. "I will now disable the second."

Chiefy ran to the southwest corner, where Pieter now lay

dead, alongside a still-active charge. Finn climbed off the frame of the beaten robot and looked for Scraps. The little robot was dented and dazed, but seemed okay.

"How long, pal?" Finn called out. The time left on the clock mattered more than any of their injuries.

"Sixty second!" Scraps said, dusting himself down.

Finn looked for Elara and found her in the northeastern corner of the basement, kneeling beside the final charge. The last of the governor robots lay on the floor between them, Elara's axe still embedded into its machine brain. He glanced back to Chiefy, but there were two hundred meters at least between the two charges, and even a Gen-VII couldn't move that fast.

"Which wire do I cut?" Elara called out. She had Francis' wire snips in her hand.

"Green, blue-green, yellow, red," Chiefy called back.

Elara stared at the device.

"Thirty-seconds!" Scraps squeaked.

"The first three are cut already but there's isn't a red wire!" Elara yelled. "Grey, blue, or black?"

Chiefy stood up. He'd already defused his charge. "I do not know," the robot said, desperately. "You will have to guess."

"Ten seconds!" Scraps said, covering his eyes with his hands.

Elara looked at Finn then back at the bomb before she dove her wire cutters into the device and snipped. Finn waited. They all waited. Nothing happened.

"Finn, Elara?" Briggs voice came booming down the stairs from above them.

"We're here," Finn said, barely able to breathe, let alone talk. "The charges are defused."

"That's great, but we've got incoming skycars," Briggs said, and Finn growled in frustration "They're coming in hot. We need to get you out."

Finn picked up Scraps and passed him to Chiefy for safekeeping, before waiting for Elara. She arrived, and they held each other's arms, touching foreheads together in a moment of shared relief and gratitude that they were still alive, before climbing the stairs. Outside, the fire wagons were in full flow, dousing the flames on the upper floors, while thousands of children stood in neat columns on the asphalted grounds, like companies of soldiers, waiting to be ushered into the trucks that would take them away from the workhouse. Zoe, the girl who had so bravely stepped forward to volunteer, was still helping to coordinate the evacuation, the tin star on her overalls glinting with light from the fire. *A future Metal...* Finn thought to himself, inspired by her courage. *No, a future Principal...* he corrected himself.

Then Finn saw the trio of skycars hugging the inside of the electrified border fence, skirting the edge of the sector, out of range of their lasers. They were jet black, and arriving from the direction of Spacehaven. *Special Prefects...* Finn thought, his gut knotting.

"Is everyone out?" Finn asked, grabbing Xia as she ran past, but the Metal shook her head. "Not all. Many trapped."

"Fuck!" Finn cursed and wheeled back toward the building. The flames were almost out, and the charges were disabled, but still there were hundreds, maybe even thousands of children trapped inside. "We have to get back in there," he said, before starting toward the workhouse.

At the same time, the trio of black skycars began their attack run, launching a barrage of missiles, four from each craft. Finn saw the weapons streak toward the workhouse, but still he ran as fast as he could. In the distance, he heard Elara calling out for him to stop, but he couldn't obey, even though in his heart, he knew he didn't have a chance in hell of saving anyone else. Eyes streaming with tears, he tore ahead, then the missiles slammed into the workhouse building and the explosion blew him backward like a sailboat caught in a hurricane. The last thing he saw was the skycars soaring overhead, laser fire chasing them, before he landed hard on the asphalt, cracked his head, and fell into unconsciousness.

25

ROBOTIC OPTIMISM

Finn picked up one of the thousands of bricks that lay scattered around him amongst the wreckage of the workhouse, then idly tossed it aside. It clacked and clattered down a pile of bricks just like it, before coming to rest beside the burned out remains of a table in what had once been the workhouse dining hall. Around him, hundreds of workers were furiously engaged in the desperate task of digging through the rubble looking for survivors, but after ten hours, little hope remained of finding anyone else alive.

Foremen did the bulk of the heavy lifting, aided by a fresh contingent of robots from the Authority sector that Chiefy and Scraps had hacked and reprogrammed. This included governors, the same machines that had ambushed them in the basement of the workhouse, killing the two Stonehaven workers, Francis and Pieter. Finn had to resist the urge to smash the governor robots to pieces for their part in the outrage, and had to remind himself that the machines were acting without free will, under the control of Ivan Volkov. Even Volkov was a puppet of sorts. Gideon Alexander

Reznikov was the sole architect of the atrocity. He controlled Zavetgrad. He set the rules. He was to blame. Finn was determined to make sure that he saw justice.

"You don't have to be here, Finn," Elara said. Like him she was holding broken bricks in her hands, which were bloody and calloused from the work of sifting through the rubble. "You took a hard blow to the head and should be resting."

"I can't rest," Finn said, throwing another brick aside. "If I close my eyes, all I see is this building collapsing. My fucked-up imagination fills in the rest."

"I know," Elara said, lowering her chin to her chest. "I see it too."

"You are not responsible," Chiefy said. The robot was further ahead, its hands scuffed from tirelessly digging through the rubble. "Without your efforts, there would have been no survivors, but because of you, more than sixteen thousand children are alive."

"But how may are buried under all this?" Finn said, gesturing feebly to the sea of bricks that consumed his view no matter in which direction he looked. "How many did we lose?"

"Surely, those that live are more important?" Chiefy said. "It is the future that matters, not the past."

Finn sighed and looked into Chiefy's bright, mechanical eyes. In many ways the robot was also like a child. Perhaps it was the effect of Scraps' re-programming, but the machine could not help but see the positives in everything. Finn envied his ability to remain optimistic, but it was something he simply couldn't do. He was consumed by his failures, which seemed to mount no matter what he did. His first fuck-up had gotten Owen killed, and as important as his brother in all but blood had been to him, he was just one man. Finn wondered how different things would have been if he'd simply died in the crucible instead of his friend. He wouldn't have become a Prosecutor of Zavetgrad, and he wouldn't have reached Haven or freed his home sector, also at the cost of innocent blood. And he wouldn't be standing on the bones of thousands of dead children now. For all the good he had supposedly done, his actions had simply led to more death and destruction. *Is it worth it?* Finn asked himself. *Am I really making a difference, or just making everything worse?*

"Sir..."

Finn turned to see Trip balanced precariously on the bricks, holding onto a twisted metal beam for support. Behind the man, clear of the rubble, was a ground car, and Finn could just about make out Xia in the driver's seat.

"We've managed to hook up a transmitter and get in contact with Haven," Trip continued. "General Riley and Principal Everhart are waiting to speak to you."

"Where's the comms terminal?" Finn asked, tossing another brick.

"It's in the prosecutor barracks, in what used to be the Chief Prosecutor's office," Trip explained. "We've set up our command post there, since it has all the facilities we needed."

Finn laughed, weakly. The prosecutor barracks had been his home for the nine weeks of intense training he'd undergone while being transformed from a reclamation yard worker to a professional killer. There was some irony in the fact that the place had now became the new base of operations for the resistance.

"Some of the children are bunked in the barracks too,"

Trip continued. "The others, we're finding space for in condos and apartment blocks that the golds have vacated."

"Vacated willingly?" Elara asked, raising an eyebrow.

"No," Trip said with a satisfied smile. "But we still have plenty of room in Metalhaven, so I say let those fancy fuckers slum it for a while."

"Okay, let's go," Finn said. He was reluctant to leave the rescue effort, but the crews hadn't found anyone for hours, at least not anyone alive.

"Scraps and I will remain, if that is okay?" Chiefy said, while continuing to dig. Scraps was sitting on the larger robot's shoulder, using his scanner to probe the wreckage. "I still have two-hours and fifteen minutes before I need to recharge."

Finn nodded. Once again, he admired the robot's positivity. "Okay, Chiefy, if that's what you want."

Finn scrambled down the steep pile of rubble, using his armor to help navigate the treacherous terrain without adding too many more cuts and bruises to his body. Elara followed, managing the descent with her usual grace, and soon they were back on flat ground. Trip opened the rear door of the ground car for them, as if he and Elara were dignitaries, then jumped into the passenger seat beside Xia. The engine was turned on and Xia engaged the gearbox, but before the car could pull away, there was a shout of elation from inside the search area.

"Wait," Finn said, touching Xia's shoulder to make sure she didn't drive away.

"They've found someone, I think," Elara said. She threw open the door and stood on the car's side-sill. "It's Chiefy."

Finn also climbed outside then watched as a crew from

another rescue team raced across the rubble toward Chiefy, who was holding a child in his arms. It was boy, seven or eight years old, and he wasn't moving. Medical teams rushed to the scene and an ambulance car, requisitioned from the Authority hospital, raced toward them, lights and sirens blazing.

Come on, be alive... Finn said to himself. *Please, be alive...* His gut churned

The medical team got to work, and for a moment, Finn's view was obscured. The wait was unbearable, then Finn heard coughing and spluttering, followed by cheers and cries of joy and relief. The medical team drew back and Chiefy picked up the boy, now very much alive, and carried him to the ambulance, skipping and dancing across the rubble at a speed that no human being could match. The robot carefully placed the boy onto the stretcher, then the doors were shut, and the ambulance raced away.

Chiefy was suddenly surrounded by members of the rescue team, who patted his metal back and slapped his chest, as he nodded and smiled and accepted their praise with grace. Finn managed to catch the robot's eye, and he saluted. He didn't know why that gesture in particular felt right, but it did. Chiefy nodded his head in reply, then returned to the wreckage to continue his search. Faith restored, at least in part, Finn slid back inside the ground car and closed the door.

"Okay," Finn said, suddenly feeling warm, despite the freezing temperature. "Now we can go."

26

A SPARK OF HOPE

The prosecutor barracks looked no different to when Finn had last seen it, and as he counted the number of days, he was shocked to realize how little time had actually passed since he had last walked its halls. On route to Chief Prosecutor Voss' old office, he stopped by his own room, which had been cleared and cleaned with robotic precision since his departure. It was now home to a group of children, who had rapidly converted it into their own personal den. The sound of laughter and playing was utterly alien to his ears and, he suspected, it was a new experience for the children too. There were no governor robots to keep them in line and tell them to shut up, and do their work.

Zoe was amongst the group of eight children, all of similar age – twelve or thirteen – that occupied the room. Her overalls had been cleaned, and it looked like she and other children had also availed themselves of the shower and bathroom facilities, but Finn could still see Briggs' tin star on her collar.

"Everyone okay in here?" Finn said.

Suddenly, the children stopped playing and formed up into a square, as if on parade, their faces stern.

"Hey, sorry, I didn't mean to interrupt," Finn said, softly. "And you don't have to do this anymore," he added, making a sort of box gesture with his hand in an attempt to represent their formation. "In this room, you can do whatever the hell you like."

A smile appeared on Zoe's face. "Anything?"

"Anything," Finn said, also smiling.

"Even bouncing on the bed?" Zoe asked, somewhat timidly.

"Especially bouncing on the bed," Finn replied.

The girl's restrained smile became a broad grin, then she broke formation, charged into Finn's old bedroom and launched herself onto the super king-sized mattress. Giggling, the others followed her lead and soon the room was filled with deafening laughter.

"You're a good man, Finn," Elara said, kissing him on the cheek. As usual, he hadn't noticed her sneak up behind him. "Come on, let them play."

Finn nodded but loitered for a second or two longer to soak up the sound of joy, letting it fill him like a tonic, before reluctantly leaving Zoe and her friends so he could attend to a more somber duty.

Trip, Xia and Briggs were already waiting for them inside Voss' office, which was as palatial as the office suite in the gene bank, in Metalhaven's yard four. Briggs looked stronger and it was clear that medics had attended to his breaks and sprains.

"We've got them on hold," Trip said, nodding to Xia who seated herself at the desk, in front of Voss' old computer. "This room has holo emitters, so they'll appear just over there," the man added, pointing toward a lounge area, replete with a full-sized bar, which, Finn noted, Trip had already put to good use.

The holo emitters energized, then Pen and General Riley appeared as spectral images, in startling high definition. Pen smiled briefly, but it was evident that she was also in a somber mood. General Riley, as ever, looked stoical.

"Mr. Briggs has already filled us in on the broad-brush details," Pen began. She stepped forward and tried to take Finn's hands, though of course this was impossible. "I'm sorry, Finn, but you should know that this wasn't your fault."

"I know," Finn said, though he didn't believe it. "But let's skip ahead to what comes next. If Briggs has told you everything, then you know we don't have much time."

Pen was intuitive enough to know that Finn wasn't interested in being consoled, and she was also cognizant that they were working to a very tight deadline. Since Reznikov had given his ultimatum, twelve of the forty-eight hours had already elapsed, leaving them only thirty-six to surrender, or face the consequences, whatever they might be.

"My only real question is why forty-eight hours," Pen said, getting straight to the nub of things. "Why not just demand that you surrender then and there?"

"We've had time to consider that too," Finn said. He nodded to Xia, and she worked on the computer console, adding an aerial view of Spacehaven into the room as a second holo image. "We managed to get some recon footage of Spacehaven, before the drones were shot down," Finn continued, walking up to the image. "As you can see, every single launchpad in the sector has been prepared, and all the

Nimbus rockets are being moved into position and fueled. That's fifty rockets in total."

"They're evacuating…" Pen said, at once understanding the significance of the intelligence.

"Forty-eight hours is the timescale they needed to make these preparations," Elara added. "It's how long Ivan needs to load and fuel the rockets, and launch within the narrow window of calm weather that we're experiencing."

"But what are they loading into the rockets?" Riley grunted.

Finn shrugged. "We don't know for sure, but from the data we've gathered, it's everything from precious and rare metals, processors and robot parts, to chemicals and genetically-pure infants."

"*Babies?*" Pen said, her face twisting in horror.

"Yes," Finn said. There was no easier way to say it.

"But why ask for our surrender, if they're leaving anyway?" Pen added. "Why does Reznikov care what happens to us after he's taken what he wants, leaving Zavetgrad with table scraps?"

"Because he's going to launch a nuclear strike and wipe out Zavetgrad anyway," Riley said, his voice filling the room with a weighty resonance.

The general had seen it first. Perhaps, Riley had known the moment he'd seen the rockets being moved to their platforms.

"The surrender is just a diversion to keep us preoccupied," Riley continued. "Once the evacuation is complete, Reznikov will nuke the city and wipe his hands of Zavetgrad."

Riley's proclamation caused a stillness to fall upon the

room, as if a doctor had just given them all the same terminal diagnosis.

"A nuclear strike?" Pen said, gasping the words. "Are you certain?"

"Yes, ma'am," Riley answered, flatly. "When I was Head Prefect of Stonehaven, we were given a project to build a storage facility outside the border fence, which was highly irregular, until I learned the purpose of the facility. It was to store nuclear warheads recovered from intercontinental ballistic missiles left over after the war. I never knew what happened to those warheads, but it's a good bet they're now on Nimbus."

Pen seemed aghast. "He would really destroy Zavetgrad, the city his ancestors built from nothing?"

Riley nodded again. There was no doubt in the old soldier's mind.

"I never personally spoke to Reznikov, but of course, my regent did," Riley explained. "They were of the same mind. Zavetgrad is a means to an end, nothing more. The future of humanity is Nimbus. Nothing else matters to Reznikov. Once he has everything he needs to be self-sustaining, he will wipe this city from the face of the earth, cleansing the planet of the last remnants of the old world."

Again, a stillness fell over the room. No-one questioned Riley's assessment – the man was not given to hyperbole, and no-one knew the Authority better than he did.

"What about Haven?" Finn asked, remembering that Zavetgrad was not the only pocket of civilization that remained on Earth.

"Haven is a nuclear bunker, so the chances are that we will withstand an orbital bombardment," Riley replied, though his answer turned out not to be the silver lining Finn had thought. "We will survive, but not indefinitely. The radiation will trap us here for centuries. Eventually, despite our resources and self-sufficiency, things will break that cannot be replaced or repaired. And, as our filters degrade, radiation will seep inside the silo, slowly at first, but enough over time to poison this refuge. It won't happen immediately, like Zavetgrad, but Haven will die nonetheless, and when we're gone, there will be no humans left alive on Earth. This planet will be a graveyard."

Chromes from Metalhaven were a tough, hardy bunch, but Riley's cataclysmic evaluation of their future prospects was enough to knock the wind out of all their sails. Trip was too doom-struck to even drink. Finn, however, wasn't beaten. They'd come too far and sacrificed too much to simply roll over and die.

"Then we have to be on one of those rockets," Finn said, shocking everyone, even Elara, with his sudden declaration. "The only way to stop Reznikov is from Nimbus."

Finn could have said more, but it wasn't necessary. Everyone knew that he'd spoken truth, and despite the enormity of the task, their minds immediately turned to the question of how.

"It would have to be done without them knowing, or Ivan would shoot down or disable the rockets we infiltrated," Riley said, seizing any opportunity to keep fighting. "That means a small team. Two or three at the most."

Finn nodded. "I agree."

"And to achieve that we'll need a diversion," Pen added, getting on-board with the plan, since it was their only option.

"Perhaps we could pretend to surrender. It would buy us time, and throw them off guard."

"No," Elara said. Her refusal was unambiguous and absolute. "We're not surrendering, no matter what. I'd choose to be vaporized in a nuclear fire before I'd bend the knee to Volkov or anyone else."

"Don't you think that's a little extreme?" Pen asked, tentatively.

"Elara is right, we don't surrender, even as a misdirection," Finn cut in, standing shoulder to shoulder with his partner. "If you want to know why, it's because fuck them, that's why."

Pen recoiled slightly, but again her perceptiveness meant that she knew not to argue. The Hero and Iron Bitch of Metalhaven had spoken, and that was that.

"How about a ruse of a different kind," Briggs said. Finn could see a renewed spark in the man's eyes. "We put Maxim Volkov and Gabriel Montgomery on trial. We put on a show, just like those bastards used to do, and we make sure that Ivan Volkov is watching."

Finn smiled. He liked the way Briggs was thinking.

"With any luck, Ivan will attempt a rescue," Finn said, finishing his co-rebel's thoughts. "And while they're distracted, diverting their resources, we launch a massive attack on Spacehaven, giving Elara and me the chance to sneak on board one of the rockets."

There was a contemplative silence, but while Riley seemed convinced, Pen was less certain.

"But didn't Ivan Volkov throw his father to the wolves?" Pen asked. "He basically told you that you could execute him, as if Ivan didn't care one jot about his father."

"That was when Reznikov was watching, but as soon as the president signed off, Ivan demanded that we set his father free." Finn nodded to Riley. "The General was right. The Volkovs may be poisoned souls, but they're still human, and Ivan still has love for his father. We can use that."

They were reaching a consensus, and the faith Finn had lost after the bombing of the workhouse was starting to return. On top of Chiefy's improbable rescue of a child, a spark of hope ignited inside him. *Perhaps, we can still do this... Maybe, I can still make it right...*

"To pull this off, we'll need your forces," Elara said, her intense green eyes locked onto the ghostly image of General Riley. "It doesn't matter if you're ready or not. Now is the time."

Riley chewed the inside of his mouth and the man's dark eyes narrowed, then the general finally released a long, low, disgruntled growl.

"Very well," Riley said. "It will be messy, but I can do it. I will personally lead a force to attack the fence at Seahaven, then make a run across the coastal sector to Metalhaven, then to the Authority sector, where the airspace is ours." Riley paused and sucked in a pensive breath of air. "We will lose many soldiers in the attack, maybe as much as fifty per cent or more of our skycars. But Elara is correct. We no longer have a choice."

Pen nodded and it was settled. They had a plan, and as impossible as it sounded, they had beat the odds before, and Finn had to believe they could do it again. He'd never wanted to be a leader, but he was one, whether he liked it or not. And, come what may, he would lead the attack on Nimbus and stop Gideon Alexander Reznikov, no matter what it took, even if it meant giving his own life in the process.

"I know we're all scared, and we've already lost so much..." Finn paused and the pain of those loses cut at his insides like he'd swallowed glass, "...but if we don't do this, we lose everything. No matter what happens, and how many workers and soldiers die, Elara and I have to be on one of those rockets when they launch. Only from Nimbus can we stop Reznikov."

Riley nodded. "I agree." The general then deferred to Pen. She was the principal, and ultimately, it was her unhappy duty to give the command.

"I also agree," Pen said, standing tall. "God help us, but the mission is approved."

The images of the principal and general flickered to nothing and Finn found himself staring into Elara's eyes, but within them he saw courage, not fear. They were of one mind. Reznikov believed that he could bomb and murder children with impunity from his orbital palace, but he was wrong. Together, Finn and Elara had beaten the regents, and taken control of the Authority. With Haven's help, and with steadfast determination, they would take Spacehaven too. All of the barriers that Reznikov had erected to keep himself safe, they had torn down, one by one.

"Nimbus will fall and Reznikov will die," Finn said. "Then, finally, Zavetgrad will be free."

The end (to be concluded).

CONCLUDE THE STORY

Conclude the story in book #5 of the Metal and Blood series, Revenge of Metalhaven. Available from Amazon in Kindle, paperback and audiobook formats, and in Kindle Unlimited.

ALSO BY G J OGDEN

Sa'Nerra Universe

Omega Taskforce

Descendants of War

Scavenger Universe

Star Scavengers

Star Guardians

Standalone series

The Aternien Wars *(Kindle Storyteller Award Winner)*

The Contingency War

Darkspace Renegade

The Planetsider Trilogy

G J Ogden's newsletter: Click here to sign-up

ABOUT THE AUTHOR

At school, I was asked to write down the jobs I wanted to do as a "grown up". Number one was astronaut and number two was a PC games journalist. I only managed to achieve one of those goals (I'll let you guess which), but these two very different career options still neatly sum up my lifelong interests in science, space, and the unknown.

School also steered me in the direction of a science-focused education over literature and writing, which influenced my decision to study physics at Manchester University. What this degree taught me is that I didn't like studying physics and instead enjoyed writing, which is why you're reading this book! The lesson? School can't tell you who you are.

When not writing, I enjoy spending time with my family, playing Warhammer 40K, and indulging in as much Sci-Fi as possible.